Throb

ADDICTED TO YOU
BOOK THREE

LYDIA MICHAELS

THROB
Addicted to You 3
Lydia Michaels
Contemporary Romance
Copyright © 2023 Lydia Michaels
Cover Design by Lydia Michaels
Developmental Editor Trudy L. Kozak

Dedication

For Pam Godwin—my book bestie and dark souled girl crush.

Listen to the Addicted to You Playlist!
Click Here to Listen!

One

December

DECEMBER LAY in a tangle of sleeping limbs, her thoughts wandering as she stared through the curtains of the guest room window. The third floor bedroom wasn't a place she usually slept, but the view, so distinctly picturesque, soothed her. Bare branches winding from the old sycamore tree were starting to bud with new growth, new beginnings of life. The limbs stretched wide across a blue sky painted with fleece white clouds as her sense of contentment grew. Watching life from above, secure and warm, the outside world didn't intrude.

It was finally spring, the cold winter having passed, and life had resumed where, only months ago, all seemed lost. Staring at the sprouting branches of the large tree, her mind leapt from one random thought to the next.

Summer was coming, and her body twitched with the memory of such heat, a sultry flash of time that always revived her from the chill of winter. Lazy days followed by long, languid nights...

She smiled, her lips lifting in a rueful smirk. Both Austin and Cord's arms rested heavily across her abdomen, a strange yet familiar weight. Her visit to Cord's yesterday, landed the three of them here, something she would never have guessed in a million years. She'd pinch herself to see if she was dreaming, but her body was still recovering from what started in the den and continued in the third floor bedroom. This was real.

Growing up without roots, craving stability while her parents scoffed at tradition had driven her in the direction of everything ordinary, but her life —at the moment—seemed *far* from ordinary. Here she was, pleasantly derailed from her search for normalcy, taking comfort—and pleasure—in the arms of two men.

Her mother's musings crept into her thoughts, not as outlandish as they once were, considering her current situation and absolute sense of contentment.

Who has seen the wind? Who cares, December Skye? Don't chase the wind, child. It will never be as warm as actual touch. Give your love to something that can return your affection, and love with every ounce of your soul.

Her mother usually imparted such words of

wisdom after one of her *special* teas. December loathed such talks, prayed to know what a normal mother was like, the sort that buttoned up a rain coat on stormy days, or had the common sense to own an umbrella, but that wasn't Rona.

But for the first time in December's twenty-seven years, she wondered if her mother was right. Rona was happy, blissfully so, because Ember's mother never apologized for loving others, deeply or otherwise. She simply let her heart lead.

Ember's heart had led her here—to Austin and Cord—far outside the bounds of traditional love. But she was happy. Could everything she'd been fighting be the answer she needed? Although her situation was outside of anything she'd ever expected, the disquiet in her was gone, replaced by a subtle and comforting sense of contentment.

The past year had been long and excruciating at times. But yesterday, as she and her husband breached the boundaries of traditional marriage and shared their love with Cord, she'd been more her mother's daughter than ever before. And today she was experiencing a level of joy she hadn't known could exist.

Pulling her gaze from the window, she regarded the arms twisted around her. Both were corded with sinew and already sporting a light tan beneath the fine sprinkling of hair. Two sets of hands, so similar in size and shape, scarred and calloused. Masculine. Yet belonging to two different men.

Breathing deeply, she let the sense of satisfaction soak in, replenish her heart and wash away any lingering sorrow. She loved them both, a torture she hadn't been able to navigate on her own, until her amazing husband had come back to her and reclaimed control.

It was how Austin had always been, so self-assured and absolute. When he'd lost his way, she'd feared they would drown together.

Cord's love had pulled them back from the edge of despair, together and then apart, but without Austin, her anchor, they all seemed lost. And what a great toll their despair had taken on Cord, who they both loved to unexplored degrees.

She was still trying to figure out how to label her feelings, let alone categorize Cord. This past year had introduced her to emotions she'd never imagined.

The three of them were starting a new chapter, one none of them had predicted. This was not the traditional life she'd chased. It wasn't traditional in any sense of the word. Yet...it was right. It was them. Her and her boys, together as one.

Her body stretched languidly between them, cocooned in their overwhelming strength. Was it possible to wake up with a sex hangover? She hadn't heard of one before, but when she cataloged certain delicious aches in her body and the burgeoning need for the hair of the dog—

She grimaced. That old adage about drinking seemed so wrong, a tired philosophy that had landed her marriage in a nightmare. She didn't want to think about that today. Not on such a beautiful morning.

Her lips twitched back into a satisfied smile. How had she gotten so lucky? The two men she loved and admired the most in the entire world were both hers. They had much to discuss, so many future decisions to make. Last night changed *everything.*

Oh, there would be bumps in the road and likely, detours, but she hadn't missed the unspoken, emotional exchange between Austin and Cord. Her husband, a hard man defined by all things masculine, was opening up in ways she'd never expected. After such a long battle with addiction, she worried he'd never be the same. She'd been right, but this new Austin was more than she ever envisioned.

Last night, when she watched him confront Cord, admit the truth and extent of his feelings, something came to life inside of her. It was as if all the orphaned pieces of her heart had finally found a home, one big enough to hold all the love shared between three deeply affectionate hearts. Not to mention the intense chemistry. They could only build on this thing between them honestly, encouraging each other each and every day, and she was determined to see that happen.

Austin shifted in his sleep, and she rolled onto her side to study his ruggedly handsome features. Slim hips swathed in a sheet, the rest of the covers clumped around his ankles, one bony foot poking out like a little kid's. Her heart swelled and her belly clenched.

His light brown lashes twitched, appearing almost blond in the morning light. Giving into the temptation, even knowing she'd likely wake him, she reached out and traced a fingertip down the length of his assertive nose made slightly crooked by mischief and courage.

She drifted her soft touch across the curve of his sensuous mouth. A few tendrils of hair trailed over his forehead. His disheveled appearance was a youthful betrayal of the impressive man he was when awake.

She kissed those impossibly long lashes she'd coveted forever, the heat of his skin warming her lips. With a flutter of lashes, whiskey brown eyes, dotted with flecks of warm caramel, stared back at her. As he smiled, the skin above his cheeks creased, conveying the warmth of his gaze, something that never ceased to amaze her.

"Morning, baby." He regarded her with love—and lust—as his body rolled closer.

This is how it's supposed to be, how it always was before...

She shoved the unpleasant thought of the past away with a determined push. Those horrid memories were unwelcome on a morning as lovely as this and she wanted to keep them at bay.

Burying the last fourteen months deep in the recesses of her mind, she leaned forward to press a kiss on his lips. New day. New outlook.

"Morning, my love. My sweet husband."

He smiled against her murmuring lips and wrapped her up tight. "Husband. That's the most incredible...title. Triggers my possessive streak."

Like he had any other side. The man defined possessive—or so she thought. His open-mindedness of late was a game changer.

Rather than reexamine recent events too closely,

she nestled closer, his solid erection nudging her belly. "Mmm...you're *awake* this morning," she teased.

He rolled her to her back, his bulk effectively pinning her to the mattress as he levered over her, battling for space beside a slumbering Cord.

December reveled in the sweet sensation of capitulating to his desires, finding nothing more erotic than satisfying a man as large and in charge as her husband. Her thighs parted under his wordless command of her body.

"You're wet." His tone was ripe with satisfaction as his cock slipped against her sensitive folds.

"Careful you don't knock Cord onto the floor."

Her husband's gaze shifted to their bed companion and held for a short moment, his expression unreadable. When his attention returned to her, he smiled. "We won't hurt him."

Though his words were indifferent, there was deep affection in his tone. And he scooted their bodies closer to the center of the mattress, leaving lots of room.

She arched her hips, her lashes lowering as her body blossomed in his hold. "Please, Austin."

He smirked, then nipped at her throat. "Begging becomes you."

She wasn't above begging. Not for this. Not for Austin.

A frisson of something darker curdled her mood as she fought another memory of begging, begging for his attention, longing for the partnership that had slipped away. The stench of stale beer somehow wove an olfactory memory between them.

No.

She dismissed the traitorous thought and concentrated on the exquisite brush of his lips against the slope of her breasts. That was then and this was now. Her husband was back, her partner, and his attention was completely focused on her.

He nuzzled and sucked at random curves, leaving her no opportunity to predict his ministrations as he effectively set her senses on fire.

"Austin. Don't tease."

"You're not rushing me."

When he spoke in that dominant tone, his words muffled by her nipple pressed against his full lips, she resigned herself to waiting, to anticipating. This was one of those generous moments meant to be all about her, so best she lie back and surrender to her talented husband.

Abandoning her swollen breast, he clasped the other in a strong hand, trapping the tender tip between callused fingertips. She moaned as a tiny shard of pain lit off an arrow of sensation directly to her core—right where his clever mouth was approaching.

Dragging his tongue over her soft belly, he dipped into her navel before lancing the tip ever so slightly between her naked folds. Her thighs relaxed, as his warm breath washed over her sex.

"You smell like Cord." He inhaled deeply again. "Different than when I make love to you."

A fresh trickle of arousal slipped from her. "Does that bother you?"

His perusal paused for the briefest moment as he tilted his head, the soft hairs behind his ears tickling her quivering thighs. "Makes me want to fuck you...*hard*."

These intimate forays reaffirmed so much that had been taken from them over the past year, and they would have plenty of time to talk later. Together.

Opening for him, her channel pulsing, she was even more aroused by the memory of the night before. That moment between her boys...that kiss. She closed her eyes against the erotic images of Austin and Cord together, so strong yet tender, so vulnerable yet indomitable.

"He tastes different on your skin, too," he murmured, stretching her folds as his tongue pressed deep.

"We'll have to try a blind taste test," she dared, voice breathless.

Austin stilled his ministrations, but only for a moment. His determined efforts renewed and her clit pulsed in desperation. If Cord awoke...

She wanted him to join them, but they had no protocol in place yet. Was an invitation required?

Her thoughts jumbled as Austin drove her higher with teasing forays into her opening, exploring all her crevices while avoiding her sweet spot. Her eyes screwed shut as she tried not to reach for her orgasm, accepting Austin would get her there, yet it hovered so close, just out of reach. Surrendering control to him made the end result all the sweeter, so she accepted the pleasure he gave.

The energy of the room shifted, announcing another strong presence. Tipping her head to the side, she peeked through her lashes and caught Cord's waking smile.

He rolled to his hip, facing them, his features soft as he watched them with a sleepy smirk. She noted his jutting cock, but her gaze drew back to his heated stare. The possessive way he studied her sent a shiver of excitement down her spine.

Glancing to her husband, she watched his gaze move from hers to Cord's. There was a split second when time stood still and then her husband's fingers slid deep, going at her twice as hard and drawing a gasp from her lips.

Cord watched Austin pleasure her, his gaze predatory. Top of the food chain.

Her need was making her fanciful. Cord's hand dropped, nudging away the rumpled bedding and wrapping around his cock. Realizing his focus was on Austin as much as her drove her arousal up another notch.

He steadily observed her naked, sprawled form beneath Austin's determined sensual ministrations, his gaze transfixed on the long, graceful line of her husband's strong back. Cord's jaw twitched and she desperately wanted to know what he was thinking.

"You're a fucking waterfall, Ember." Austin growled appreciatively, at last turning his attention to her throbbing knot of nerves silently begging to be touched.

With a sharp gasp, her entire being concentrated—*right fucking there*—and she tumbled along on the rush of her climax, her heels unyielding against the bed as she quivered and shook. Her eyes closed, but she retained the image of Cord's work-roughened hand, all blunt nails and defined veins, stroking over the thick erection she greedily coveted.

Austin caressed her gently, easing her return from intense pleasure by dropping a tender kiss on her mound. Her gaze lifted. Determination etched Cord's features, but a hint of vulnerability lingered in his eyes, dimming the heat.

Ember put everything she was capable of communicating into her stare. *Do it. Don't hesitate. We both love you and want you. Trust this.*

Cord blinked, his inner debate transparent and so full of what she truly believed was denial. He hesitated, his brow pinched tight as he seemed to weigh every possible consequence, before giving in to the temptation and lifting his hand.

Her heart fluttered, then thumped wildly in her chest as she saw the flash of pure dominance in Cord's eyes as he reached for her husband. She'd never met such a Jekyll and Hyde, so easy-going by day and such intense virility by night. Well, hopefully not only at night.

Cord's strong fingers sifted through Austin's hair, a sensuous theft of authority. When he yanked her husband's head back and took his mouth, Ember gasped with excitement. Shivers shot through her body as liquid heat pooled at her sex.

Tongues dueled as Austin's hand rose to grip Cord by the back of the neck. Their soul-destroying kiss went on and on, a visible test of dominance.

She drew in great draughts of air, her head full as she tried to catalog the intense emotion overwhelming her. More than lust...

Releasing Austin's mouth, Cord growled, "Morning."

Austin's face was flushed, his eyes dazed, as he stared at his friend. Swollen lips twitched into a cocky grin. "Had to steal a taste of her, didn't you?"

She tried to swallow back her laughter, not wanting to detract from the moment, but it burbled up and filled the room. It was a joyous sound, and more than enough to steal their attention.

Her mouth twisted, but it was impossible to contain her smile. "That was picture perfect."

"Trouble maker." Cord tweaked her nipple and leaned in to kiss her. "Morning to you, too, sweetheart."

Her palm caught his cheek as her shoulders lowered to the pillows, the marked contrast between the way he tenderly kissed her and the way he kissed Austin abundantly clear.

She sighed as her body softened under the touch of his sweet lips. "Good morning." Running her fingers down his forearm, appreciating the muscle straining there, she grinned.

He caught her hand and directed it to his cock, wrapping her fingers tight around the thick length. The love in his steel-blue eyes swallowed her gaze and she slowly stroked. There was no noticeable uncertainty, and any concerns she had about the awkwardness of the morning were soothed.

"Fuck, Ember," Cord murmured as she stroked and her thumb grazed the crown, sliding through a pearl of moisture.

Her heart trembled with implication as her fantasies came to life. This was what she wanted, exactly where she wanted to be. His lashes lowered and his head tipped back on a deep, satisfied sigh, and her gaze sought Austin's.

Noting the uncertainty on his face as he watched her hand moving over Cord, she whispered his name. "Austin."

His attention lifted from her caressing fingers to her face. Though Cord might have knocked her husband off his mark with that kiss, she would always defer to his authority. She needed him at her back, guiding her through whatever they were building here.

Responding to her plea, he shifted to lie beside her. His lips pressed to her shoulder as he watched her pleasure Cord.

Voice pitched sensually low, he whispered, "Do you like touching him?"

Cord's eyes opened, his focus on her response.

Her fingers paused for a beat before picking up the pace. *Honesty.* "Yes."

Austin guided her other hand, filling her empty palm with his rigid length. Heat flared in Cord's eyes, and there was no denying his desire as he stared intently at her husband's cock. His objections from last night seemed a thing of the past.

Stroking with languid pulls, she reveled in the erotic picture the three of them painted, her touch split down the middle while they each focused on the other. Freaking hot.

When Cord reached out and folded his fingers around hers holding her husband's cock, she willingly seceded, while Austin visibly tensed for a split second and swallowed audibly, his Adam's apple bobbing.

"You're not always the frontrunner," Cord said.

"What the fuck does that mean?" A curious mix of sexual need and worry creased her husband's brow.

Cord chuckled. "I'm the one in charge this morning."

"Yeah?" Austin gave scant warning, a mere drop of his shoulder signaling his intent before lunging across the bed at his friend.

Ember let go of Cord, scrambling against the headboard. She grabbed a pillow and tucked her legs out of the way. Her mouth gaped at the vision of two muscled, bare-assed, handsome men, as they fell into what she hoped was a playful wrestling match.

Grunts and obscenities filled the air, along with the scent of sweat and testosterone. Austin usually won past play-altercations, but this time she was putting her money on Cord. Determination laced every fine inch of him.

They rolled, wrapped together, until Cord had Austin's slightly larger body pinned beneath him. Their gazes clashed in unspoken challenge and Ember held her breath, unsure if she'd misread their mutual understanding of the situation.

Cord leaned his head forward, trying to trap Austin's mouth, but Austin rolled and overtook him, pinning Cord to the mattress, and dropping his weight down.

"You know I've always been stronger," her husband growled, as Cord seemed to surrender rather than struggle.

"Goddamn it, Austin. Watch your knee!"

"Wouldn't want to put you out of commission," Austin quipped, blanketing him with his body and shifting his legs into a safer position.

With a mighty heave, Cord's biceps flexed. The veins in his neck stood out as he threw Austin off of him. They rolled to the floor with a mighty thump and she winced.

Cord gained the advantage, pinning her husband. His forearm landed across Austin's throat, his weight lying heavily on his bulky frame as they caught their breath, chest to chest.

Austin froze, staring up at his friend. Both were breathing heavily, and she suspected it wasn't merely from the scuffle.

"You give?" Cord panted.

After a brief, thwarted effort to escape, Austin barked, "I fucking give."

Cord eased off him in one smooth motion and levered to his feet. She drank in his naked body, her gaze lingering on his ass. Offering a hand, Cord pulled her husband up, only to wrap his other hand around the nape of Austin's neck and direct him to his knees.

Austin's jaw locked and his shoulders bunched as he knelt. Time stood still as the air seethed, spiked with testosterone.

"You still sure this is what you want?" Cord growled.

Austin's nostrils flared as twin darts of red bloomed on his cheeks. "You don't intimidate me, Cord."

"You sure?"

"Positive," her husband growled through gritted teeth.

Ember stared unblinking as Austin balanced on his knees before his best friend, not an ounce of subservience in the position. Despite their competitive nature, there was acceptance in the set of Austin's shoulders and a hint of dark anticipation evident as his thick erection jerked.

Cord's big hand, usually so rough and demanding, loosened to stroke gently over her husband's head, smoothing his tousled locks. Austin's shoulders lowered, the knots of muscle loosening under his skin as he calmed beneath the tender caress. Her vision blurred as he leaned into Cord's touch.

"Then *I* take the lead." Cord's voice was quiet, almost a murmur, yet it rang true. "Not saying I won't give in to you at times, but I take the lead. You have so much of her, at least give me this with you."

Ember shivered with uncertainty, only slightly distracted by Cord's qualification. Until they had crossed the bounds of monogamy, Austin had all of her. He strove to give her what she wanted and needed, but with his usual, unconditional authority she wasn't sure he'd surrender an inch, not even to someone he trusted as much as Cord.

Dominance came effortlessly to both of them, possibly more naturally to Cord. While he seemed to accept that she'd always defer to her husband, perhaps Cord needed this line in the sand with Austin now.

She held her breath, waiting anxiously for

Austin's response, those lines blurring more and more with every passing second.

With a shuddering sigh, Austin inclined his head a small degree.

She sensed Cord's visceral awareness of her in the room. But this moment was theirs and she wouldn't intrude.

"You ever sucked a cock, big guy?" Cord asked, the words coming out low and oddly flawless for such an unparalleled question.

The fragility of the moment shattered as shock registered on her husband's face. "What? No. Fuck, Cord. You gotta know that. We grew up together."

"How far are we gonna take this? Is it a game or are we being real? Because I don't have the patience for any more games, Austin."

Her husband dropped his stare and focused on Cord's erection, thick and heavy. Ember noted the way his own cock twitched, as if in excited response. Her pussy was throbbing, wet and needy, and she worked one hand behind her back to deflect the temptation to touch herself.

Dragging his tongue over his bottom lip, Austin edged forward another degree, and then his dark gaze landed on her, his black pupils swallowing his irises. The unfamiliarity of that look pierced her arousal, seeking deep enough to penetrate her soul.

He was asking, but she couldn't decide this for him. If he could share her with Cord, she could surely share him—if that was what he wanted.

Her chin dipped, a slight communication that she wouldn't object, and the tension in his shoulders eased.

His attention returned to Cord. "I never—"

"Me neither." Cord's voice was low and thick with emotion. "It's just you, Austin. No other. I swear."

"And Ember."

"Of course, and Ember," Cord echoed.

Austin drew in a deep breath and let it out in a jagged exhalation. "Okay."

Cord's hand slipped from the back of Austin's neck and fell to his side. She recognized the move for what it was, a transfer of control. The choice was left to Austin.

He swallowed, the tight shift of his throat an audible click in the silent room. His body edged forward and he hesitated, as if considering his approach. A split second later, his lips and her eyes went wide as he enveloped the corona of Cord's cock.

In concert, three distinct sounds combined, Cord's groan, Austin's moan, and her whimper. Austin cast a wild-eyed look her way at the same time Cord slanted a sideways glance at her.

"I love you," she mouthed to her husband, encouraging him. Her voice seemed smothered by too much emotion to actually speak.

Austin's lashes lowered and Cord's attention focused as he took him deep.

She knew how to pleasure Austin orally—he'd taught her exactly how he liked it. She'd always enjoyed doing it, loved to drive him insane with her honed skills, but maybe she'd been doing it wrong all along.

Her husband went after Cord with single-minded focus. One hand settled on his friend's hip, fingers biting into the muscles of his ass. The other cupped his testicles, working the tender flesh as he took Cord's cock deep. Nothing tentative about his effort. Maybe one man knew what another wanted.

Austin's shoulders bunched and he jerked back. She remembered that too, the first initiation and novel experience of having something so big lodged in her throat.

Much like her husband had done with her, Cord's voice remained gentle, if strained, his words encouraging. "It feels so fucking good. Don't stop."

Austin closed his lips over Cord again, this time taking him deeper.

"Fuck. That's it. You got it." Cord dropped his head back, nearly moaning the words. His legs visibly trembled and his ass clenched, as he urged Austin on.

Intrigued by Austin's technique, she watched his throat work, his face tight with strain, and his cheeks taut around his friend's cock. Cord's fingers threaded deeper into her husband's hair as his hips jutted forward.

Austin worked Cord with determined focus, his length emerging from his mouth on the upstroke, glistening with saliva and precum. Ember's belly clenched as her clit throbbed.

She desperately wanted to touch herself. The more she watched the harder her heart beat, an echoing pulse thrumming through her veins. Her fingers itched to feather down her body, but she held back, not wanting to detract from this incredible moment.

"Gonna come."

Her need spiraled as Cord's hips pumped, his deep, gritty warning spiking another pinch of excitement between her legs.

Austin's cheeks hollowed and his eyes leaked, his shoulders bunching until Cord's fist tightened in Austin's hair, tugging him away. "It's okay."

Dragging his swollen lips back, her husband gasped for air as Cord took over, his cock jerking in his grip as he came, pearly semen coating his abdomen and dripping over his sheltering hand.

Ember gasped through an erotic shiver, thrown into release by the intense vision unfolding before her.

Cord dropped to mirror Austin's crouch, his other hand drifting over her husband's shoulder. Heavy breaths worked his chest in cadence with Austin's, the only sounds in the room.

"Jesus, Austin. You sure that was your first time?" The wry observation was at odds with Cord's hoarse tone. "I damn near came down your throat."

Austin arched a brow, the back of his hand swiping at his mouth. "You afraid you can't compete?"

His belly glistened and she understood he'd also ejaculated at some point while servicing Cord. Holy shit. What had been unleashed here?

Everything you hoped for...

A puff of laughter slipped from Cord's lips, his features suspended in disbelief. Then something shifted and he looked away. His gaze, so full of bluster a second ago, jerked to the ceiling and concern immediately gripped Ember.

"Cord?" She moved to go to him but he held up a hand, halting her attempt.

Austin caught her concern and frowned, leaning toward his friend. "Hey... You okay?"

His head lowered, shaking slowly from side to side, dark curls hiding his eyes. "Fuck," he muttered, clearly distraught by the surge of emotion they were all experiencing.

She slipped to the floor and reached to rest a hand on his shoulder.

He flinched, then laughed, the sound disparaging and misplaced. "I don't fucking cry. I don't know what's happening."

"I think we're all emotional right now," she whispered.

Austin nodded. "It's a lot to take in."

Cord cleared his throat and quickly stood, his usual demeanor shifting back into place like battered armor as he paced a safe distance away. "I'm good."

She eased toward the door as the silence stretched. Her boys needed a moment. "I'll go put breakfast together. Give you two some time." She collected her robe, drawing it over her body.

"Come here." Cord's tone demanded compliance and she stilled.

Catching the bemused smile on Austin's face, she moved to Cord, who rose to his feet. His hands gripped the lapels of her robe, the swathed fabric tightening as he pulled her close.

"You two have a head start on me," he murmured. "You've thought about the three of us being together for a while, so I'm gonna have to catch up. But know this, Ember. We're *all* in this together if we're in it at all. Nobody gets left out. And I'm *all in.*"

She couldn't agree more. Smiling into his blue eyes, she cupped the stubble along his hard jaw. "Thank you."

Austin approached her back, towering over her and kissing the side of her neck. His body pressed close as she was sandwiched between the two men.

"To be fair," he said, "I don't think any of us imagined *this*. I might have thought about you and Ember, but I never pictured..."

Cord's mouth sketched a smile his lips couldn't seem to hold. Something flashed in his eyes, and then his expression shuttered, blanking into a neutral mask, as if he was hiding something.

He cleared his throat, loosening his hold on her robe. "There's a learning curve to figure out."

"Definitely," her husband agreed, patting her ass with a hint of ownership. "How about some coffee, baby?"

She pivoted and searched his face, seeing nothing but love and affection reflected in his eyes. He smelled of sex and Cord, and despite what had been a major milestone in his sexual journey, he appeared okay with this unexpected turn of events.

She'd poke at their feelings later, after the dust settled. For now, she decided to take their words to heart.

"Get cleaned up, you two." She squeezed their

hands, marking the similarity in size and strength. "We have a lot to talk about over breakfast."

"We'll be talking forever," Cord moaned, reverting in a heartbeat to the irreverent male she knew and loved as much as the commanding individual she'd had the pleasure to meet in the bedroom.

"Twenty minutes." She hustled to the door.

Coffee was an immediate necessity, but her biggest priority was convincing Cord to stay longer than one meal. Nothing worried her more than the fear that he might leave and have a change of heart the minute he walked out the door.

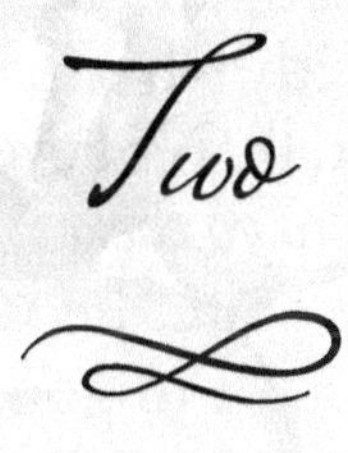

Two

Austin

EMBER DISAPPEARED down the hall and Austin had no idea where to look, bombarded by the strange sense that he was being watched. Too closely.

Despite his earlier comment about this...whatever it was, he didn't need a moment with Cord. He wasn't sure he wanted a moment to think about what just transpired. "I'm gonna shower."

Disoriented by waking in the guest room, he scanned for any of his belongings. Right. Not his room.

"You okay?" Cord asked just as he made it to the door.

There was no doubt in his mind that December would analyze what happened from every fucking angle and want to discuss it at great length, and that was fine, women needed that. They needed to dissect everything to death and he wanted to make sure she was still okay with what happened. But men... Men didn't need to talk. Not even when they—

Nope. Not ready to go there.

Avoiding Cord's stare, he used the most casual tone he could muster, "I'm good. Just need to rinse off."

"No doubt." Cord's dry response sent heat rushing up this throat as he glanced at his belly.

Fuck. He wasn't bothered by what they'd done until December left the room. Taking her out of the equation shed a blinding fucking light on the fact that he was wearing his and Cord's come.

At a loss for words, he gave a quick shake of his head and hustled down the hall, belatedly realizing his departure might have looked like flight. He'd have to correct that impression as soon as he cleaned up and had a few minutes to himself. Once in his own bathroom, he started the shower and set a towel on the sink.

His body stiffened at the sharp rap on the door. Not Ember. When she knocked it was with that self-effacing style she had, the one that helped her slip into a person's heart. And, he was procrastinating.

"Yeah?"

"Not talking to you through a door."

He cut the water and manned up, yanking open the door.

Cord set a hand on the jamb, leaning his weight against it. Just two naked friends hanging out. "We cool?"

He'd just come, yet his cock wasn't getting the message. It thickened along his thigh and he willed his arousal back. "Yeah. We're cool."

"Then why won't you look at me?"

Jesus. In a few minutes they'd be sitting down having breakfast, going over Ember's plans for the day and drowning in awkward aftermath. Could he not get a few minutes to himself?

"I'm looking at you. I just have nothing to fucking say, Cord."

Cord intruded on his space, edging him back toward the shower. "I need to know that you're cool with this, Austin."

His mind whirled, wanting to evade any discussion about what just transpired. "I told you. I'm cool."

"Austin."

He glared at his friend. "What, man? We only have a few minutes. I don't want to keep her waiting."

"We have plenty of time."

"Jesus, Cord, we're *fine*. Now, can I get a fucking shower?"

Their eyes locked for a few uncomfortable seconds when Austin wanted nothing more than to look away.

Cord's lips twitched as he muttered, "Is this how it's gonna be? Some sort of show for her, but awkward as shit when it's just the two of us?"

He rolled his eyes. "*You're* making it awkward. I told you I'm fine." Cord's hand reached for him and he took a quick step back. "What are you doing?"

With a cold huff of laughter, his friend shook

his head. "You're so full of shit. I'll get my stuff and get out of your way. Enjoy your breakfast."

Jarred, Austin shadowed him into the master bedroom. "What are you talking about? You can't leave."

Cord's smile was in complete contrast to the hostility radiating from him in waves. He shook his head and snarled, "I can do whatever the fuck I want. *This...*" He waved a finger between the two of them. "I'm not fucking doing *this.*"

"Doing *what?* What the hell are you talking about?"

"Come on, Austin! I see what you're doing. This is bullshit. You had my dick in your mouth ten minutes ago. Ember leaves and there's suddenly miles of distance between us."

Cord's honorable side, the one that insisted on speaking the truth, confronting it head-on, shattered Austin's pretense. Heat rushed to his cheeks and his nostrils flared as the unvarnished truth smacked him in the face.

"First of all, lower your fucking voice. Second, stop with the hard ass act. And third, you leave and she'll be upset, so pull yourself together."

The deep lines of Cord's face softened, as they always did whenever he played the Ember card. Austin hated using her to manipulate his friend, but they all needed to get a grip.

Deep breaths lifted Cord's broad chest and Austin's stare involuntarily dropped lower and jerked away.

"Nothing's fine, Austin. You never stop to think about the consequences. I'm not waiting around for the fallout this time. And you're *running*, whether you admit it or not. Telling me Ember's gonna be upset isn't going to get you out of facing what happened, because you and I both know she won't let you dance around the issues this time." He rolled his eyes. "I'll see you once you man up."

As he turned to leave, Austin caught his arm. "Wait." The bitterness and regret coloring Cord's words thumped in his gut—hard.

"For what?" Cord shook his head and scoffed. "This was a mistake. I didn't think things could get more fucked up, but I guess I was wrong."

Austin needed time to get his thoughts in order, but that clearly wasn't an option. He had plenty to say but no clue how to put it. "Cord, I know this is crazy, but I still don't believe we made a mistake."

"Then be upfront and honest with me." His friend's shoulders bunched with tension as his voice dropped low. "I don't get you, man. How do you shut it off like that?"

"I'm not...shutting anything off. I just..." He hated his uncertain tone. "What do you want me to say?"

As his grip loosened, Cord pulled away and sat on the edge of the bed. His shoulders slumped and his head drooped forward so his curls hid his eyes. "Was it all about her, *only* for her?"

Austin stilled, accepting the truth rattling through his brain like a runaway train, but the words refused to travel out of his mouth. What he'd experienced in the last twenty-four hours, it wasn't anything he'd expected. It was beyond lust, though the hunger was there. Not just for his wife, but for his friend.

"I..." He struggled to communicate. "Cord... we're all doing the best we can."

Silence enveloped them as his flesh chilled. They should clean up, head down for breakfast. Ember would be waiting on them. He fought the urge to go to Cord, so much pain and distrust banked in his steel-blue eyes.

He thought he was finished hurting the people he loved, he made that resolution months ago, yet here he was doing it again. These fucking feelings, so unfamiliar and jarring, he couldn't seem to process them all at once.

Cord sighed, his anger ebbing into what seemed reluctant acceptance. "I know."

"Does that mean you'll stay for breakfast?"

Eventually Cord would have to leave. They'd all have to get back to their ordinary lives. He was both looking forward to that reprieve and dreading it. *Still processing...*

"I'll stay."

Relief shouldn't damn near knock his legs out from under him. "Good."

Cord shoved up from the bed and faced him. "Is it out of your system?"

"Is *what* out of my system?"

"Whatever you felt last night—and this morning."

His mind halted at the fork in the road. Go right and everything went away, no therapy needed, no repeat performance. Turn left and... This time his mouth cooperated and the truth emerged. "No, it's not out of my system."

Cord drew back, surprise and something else written on his face. "Really?"

He dropped his gaze, unable to match Cord's steady stare.

Although he commanded his household and ran several crews on the job, he couldn't seem to out-master Cord when it came to *this*. This new dynamic between them he'd yet to name.

It wasn't a simple step down from the top either. Every time he deferred to Cord it scraped and bruised, though maybe not as much as he might have thought. Sort of like a new pair of boots, uncomfortable at first, but with the promise of more support later.

Though he was still processing, he could at least confess he wasn't giving up. "Really."

His heart jogged into a gallop as Cord stepped closer, the soft press of his rough fingers on Austin's chin made him flinch.

"Easy..."

Austin breathed through his nose as Cord leaned closer. How was he so natural about this? He held his breath as warm lips traced the stubble of his jaw. And damn his dick for firming up the second he breathed Cord in.

The heat of his friend's body warmed him, his mind cataloguing every nuance. The wiry feel of another man's chest hair. The sheer breadth and height of him. His earthy scent, so unlike Ember's. His pure masculinity was suddenly alluring, when a day ago it was merely admirable.

Fuck.

His neck stiffened as Cord's hand fit around his nape.

"It's okay," Cord whispered, leaning closer.

At the first brush of his lips, Austin panicked and made to jerk away but Cord's steady gaze and strong grip calmed his instinct to flee. The heated press of his firm kiss slipped past his guard and Austin's eyes drifted shut.

A dark, throbbing need took hold as he wrestled to deny how right it felt to taste another man. Not just any man. Cord.

"It's okay to kiss me back," Cord whispered, sealing his lips over his once more.

It wasn't like kissing Ember, or any woman for that matter. There was a sturdiness to Cord, something unbreakable, something solid. Dark need sprang its leash as he mirrored Cord's hold, catching thick curls between his fingers.

He dove in, his tongue thrusting and parrying. Heat flared as they crowded one another. Blood boiled through his veins, flooding straight to his heavy dick. The urge to fuck overwhelmed him.

Breaking the kiss, he panted. *Fucking?* His mind did *not* just go there.

Cord drew his full, lower lip between his teeth and smirked, blue eyes dark with raw lust and speculation.

Austin nearly dropped his gaze in response to that heavy stare, disturbed by his awareness of his friend as someone he wanted to—

He couldn't swallow, his mouth suddenly parched. "We should get to the kitchen," he rasped.

"Sure. I should rinse off too." Cord lowered his hand, his touch drifting away. "Meet you down there."

His attention drawn by Cord's effortless—naked—saunter, Austin's brain slowed as all the blood rushed south. Whatever *this* was, it was far from out of his system. His cock twitched, as if concurring, and he nodded. Returning to the bathroom, he set the tap to cold.

Despite the frigid temperature of the water, Austin's body didn't calm. As he shivered into his clothing his mind fell into turmoil. He was dealing with what happened, proud of his insistence that the three of them confront their true feelings, but something still needed to be done about his unfamiliar position in the mix.

As much as Cord—and Ember—expected him to discuss his feelings, he was still searching for the right words to describe everything he was experiencing. It wasn't running away from the situation so much as it was pacing himself so he could take it all in.

As he entered the hall he paused, hearing the pipes rattle in the walls from the other shower. Good. He needed a few more minutes to find his bearings before seeing Cord again.

Taking the steps at a natural pace he entered the kitchen and smiled at the familiar sight of Ember wrapped in her summer robe, placing the final touches on a table set for a king. *Kings.*

"Hey, beautiful."

Her brown eyes lifted under full lashes and she matched his smile. "Hey."

His dick pulsed, lingering need surging into fresh desire. Though there was something disarmingly appealing in the recent shifts of his authority, when it came to December, he needed his position secure.

"You doing okay?"

She placed freshly folded linen napkins beside the plates, her fingers trembling the slightest degree. "I think I'm a little better than okay."

This was his wife, happy in her domain, proud to be the source of all the love and nurturing filling their home. Regardless of what happened or might happen again, he wouldn't let their dynamic go. He needed to make sure—no matter what—his wife still saw him as a virile, capable man after what he'd done that morning. He didn't want her to worry Cord's presence might change their favored roles as husband and wife.

Sniffing the air, he figured breakfast wasn't far from being done, and as Ember turned to the counter to retrieve the silverware, he caught her hips.

She stilled, tensing then relaxing into his strength as he pressed his body behind hers. "Wife."

She glanced over her shoulder, a playful smile teasing her lips as she registered his intention. "Breakfast will be ready in—"

"Now, December. I need you right now."

She nodded slightly, comprehending his need and meeting his request. "Yes."

He made short work of unbuckling his belt and flipping up the back of her robe. His hand rode along the center of her back, levering her upper body over the counter as he lined up the tip of his throbbing cock with her slick opening. She was always ready for him, responding to the assertion of his intimate authority as much as he needed to affirm it.

There was no preamble as he thrust deep and her moan escaped on a quivering breath. He thrust again, hard and commanding, claiming her and affirming his position in their marriage.

Exposing the back of her shoulder, he pressed a kiss into her skin. "I love you, baby."

Her palms flattened on the granite countertops, fingers splayed. "I love you too."

His hips pumped as his soul sought balance, the return of their spontaneity long overdue, yet as familiar as riding a bike. He yanked her robe lower, and reached for her breast.

"Tell me you like it when I take you like this. Tell me it's what you need."

Her panted moans grew louder as he took her harder. "*Yes*. I love when it's like this. So...so unrefined."

He thrust deep and held, teasing her nipple with a rewarding pinch. "No matter what, this part of us won't change, Ember."

"Never." She swiveled her hips, stealing a bit of pleasure for herself, a movement as familiar to him as his own techniques. "I never want it to change, Austin. I need this."

Relieved and assured in his role, he gave a few more thrusts and locked his fists in the bunched fabric of her robe as he came inside of her on a long groan.

He bowed his head to her shoulder and caught his breath, his lips pressing into her delicate skin. "I think my soul would die without you, my other half."

She shifted as their bodies disconnected, turning to face him. Her fingers gently cupped his jaw as she stared into his eyes, a contented smile pulling at her lush lips.

"And you're the other half of my soul. But we grow, Austin. We're both growing."

He loved her so much. Once again, he lacked the words to accurately describe his feelings. "Em—"

The sound of movement upstairs cut off his confession.

Stepping apart, they righted their clothing and Ember reached for a handful of tissues. Their eyes met, this moment only for them, yet there seemed a prickling awareness of approaching change. Excited anticipation pounded in his heart as he braced for whatever came next.

Three

December

EMBER PLACED the breakfast casserole on the table just as Cord entered the kitchen. The sight of his damp curls, stubble, and another one of his signature flannel shirts over well-worn jeans warmed her heart. The air thickened with tension, but not the sort that had her shying away. Their glances caught, simmering with promise.

"Smells incredible," he announced, and she blinked, back in the moment.

He shifted toward the table where Austin was already ensconced, studying the food. Cord tugged out a chair for her and she settled into it with an appreciative smile.

Savoring the satisfying ache in her body, she

reached for Cord's plate. "It's an old recipe. Blueberry French toast."

She traded his plate for Austin's and then added a spoonful to her own. The boys dug in—*her* boys. She hid a satisfied smirk.

Cord hummed with appreciation. "Jesus, how you guys aren't fat I have no idea. This is delicious, kiddo."

She preened under his praise. "It beats the hell out of tomato soup."

He laughed and Austin paused, giving them each a questioning look.

Cord took a sip of coffee and cleared his throat. "I, uh, was living off soup a while back."

Austin's brow lifted. "Why?"

It was no secret Cord made enough money to live well and afford a substantial diet, but their little exchange reeked of something her husband hadn't been privy to, something from a time when Austin was unreachable and she'd been trying to find solid ground.

Cord shrugged. "Bachelor."

As they ate, silence lingered, and she fumbled for a way to lighten the moment. She didn't want the quiet to consume their morning, afraid too much thinking might somehow tarnish their newfound ease.

"So what are we doing today?"

Finished with his breakfast, Austin shoved back his plate and stood to refill his coffee. "I had something in mind. Maybe Cord could join us. You got plans today, buddy?"

Her gaze shifted to Cord, who appeared a touch

surprised by her husband's invitation. "Free as a bird. What'd you have in mind?"

Austin returned to the table. "Well, being that I'm back to work, I figured it's time I treat my wife to a little luxury. Let's go car shopping."

Ember stilled, her mind jerking out of La La Land and sprinting into the mathematical corner of household finances. "Are we ready for that?"

Austin had always spearheaded big household investments, but she'd maintained their monthly budget, so he usually discussed such decisions before committing to anything. True, he'd been back with the union for a month, but a car was a huge investment.

"I don't like leaving you home alone without a dependable car. We might have to finagle some financing, but with proof of a steady income I think we can handle it."

She hid her uncertainty. Was their income steady? Stable enough? What if Austin got laid off again? Shouldn't they firm up their savings first, build it back to the nest egg it once was?

His large hand settled over hers and gave a gentle squeeze. "Hey. We're just looking. Let's see if we find anything and run some numbers. I won't make any rash decisions. I know we're still building back what was broken."

"I think it's a great idea," Cord chimed in.

Ember paused, struck dumb by his input, finding it both welcomed yet misplaced. "You do?"

"Yeah. Your Jeep's pretty much on the scrap heap. Austin's right. You need a car while he's at work and we shouldn't have to worry that you might break down again."

A strange sense of having two husbands washed over her. Again, it was welcomed yet misplaced. Was this how it would be, two highhanded men deciding for her? For their home? She was getting ahead of herself and oddly uncertain if the idea was more appealing or troublesome. Time would tell—*if* this was how things would be.

Cord had his own home. They hadn't even discussed him possibly moving in. But at the same time, her heart clung to the prospect.

She loved that Austin had always been such a firm man, so capable when it came to guiding them in the right direction. That's how it had always been until...

Rather than traipse down the unsavory parts of memory lane, she decided this was a good test. Transitioning back into the natural order of things seemed a healthy return to the dynamic they knew and loved—plus, Cord was somehow fitting in. Austin had included him, whether consciously or not.

They needed to talk, however, a serious discussion she'd envisioned before she got too far ahead of herself. Though sometimes actions spoke louder than words. They'd spend some time visiting car lots, but at some point today they were sitting down and addressing her concerns.

"Okay. Let's go car shopping."

While she cleaned up from breakfast, the men went out to evaluate her old Jeep. Their voices carried through the screened windows and she smiled each time she heard them laugh. Her heart pinched with the familiarity, old wounds slowly healing with the hope that rough edges would soon be smooth.

Once she had the kitchen back to rights, she went upstairs to take a quick shower. As she was fussing with her hair, Austin yelled for her from downstairs.

"Ember, you about ready?"

She smirked, a newfound appreciation for having a husband present enough to hassle her to hurry up and spend the day with him. "Five minutes."

"Shake a leg, woman, you're already beautiful enough."

"You hush!" She giggled and rushed through the last of her preparations.

The boys were pacing as she descended the stairs. "Some women take hours to get ready. You should be glad I can manage in under thirty minutes."

Two appraising gazes—one blue, the other golden brown—scanned her body and heat warmed her cheeks.

She grabbed her purse. "Well, are we ready?"

Cord shook his head and smiled. "Mouthy little thing."

"You have no idea," Austin agreed, dark promise lurking in his assessing gaze.

Now, not at all certain she wanted to look at vehicles, December put a little swing in her step as she exited through the door her husband held for her, rewarded with a firm swat on her butt.

Being that dealerships were closed in Pennsylvania on Sundays due to state law, they had an hour trek to New York. Austin backed his truck out of the drive as Cord clipped her seatbelt. Sandwiched between the men in the front seat, she soaked up their heat while the cool air from the vents lifted the ends of her hair.

If she concentrated on their proximity, her financial worries eased a little, but the stress was there. Maybe they'd just browse and take a few test drives.

The conversation volleyed easily around mundane topics—guy things. Austin told Cord about the deck he intended to build out back and she suspected it wasn't the first time Cord was hearing about it.

"I can get you the treated wood, but I think you're wrong on the brand," Cord argued.

"Harley says it's the best. He did his deck years ago and it still looks new."

Every time Austin mentioned the name of his sponsor she tingled with pride yet suffered a pinch of envy. It was good he'd found someone he could relate to, someone who had also overcome addiction and knew the struggles up close and personal. But there was also a salty part of her that envied the other prominent figure in her husband's life and wished she could share in that relationship. But Austin had never introduced them.

Cord rolled his eyes. "Well, if Harley says it's the best..."

Was that jealousy? She shot him a glance, seeing a certain amount of strain on his face.

"I mean, what would I know? I just own a hardware store and sell the stuff."

"Don't be like that," Austin said, his attention focused on the road. "I'm just saying, I know it holds up."

So, he'd been to Harley's? She squashed another bite of envy and made a mental note to suggest Austin invite his sponsor for dinner.

Before her boys got into some sort of pissing match, she chimed in. "We're building a deck?"

Austin glanced at her and smiled. "Wouldn't you like that? It would be great for picnics and, in the cooler months, we could put a chiminea on it."

Her mind flashed with images of past picnics they'd hosted, every guest wearing a smile and toting a bottle of beer. She suddenly mourned the loss of entertaining in their life, even as she shied from the idea.

"I wasn't sure if we'd still have parties like that."

Her husband frowned and tension tightened her shoulders.

"What do you mean? We always have a Labor Day picnic. It's my only chance to play with explosives."

Cord's body felt stiff at her side and a glance at his profile confirmed his similar reservations. He was unusually silent, considering summer picnics were the only time she allowed fireworks on their property and both he and Austin were pyromaniacs at heart.

She wasn't sure this was the time for such a conversation. Strange, that they hadn't discussed situations where alcohol might make its way back into their home, possibly right in front of Austin's face.

Since Cord still wasn't commenting, she said, "I just assumed..."

Austin's expression eased. "Because of people drinking?"

"Yes."

He drew in a long breath and let it out slowly. "Well, I don't want any of it left behind in the house, but if people bring their own and take it with them, I'll survive a few hours. I don't want to lose our traditions."

She had yet to even sip a glass of wine since returning home, terrified that one touch to her lips might somehow drown her husband's progress. "I'll think about it."

His hands tightened on the wheel.

While Austin maintained his role as head of the household, he never made her feel like her opinion was in any way less than his.

"Fair enough," he agreed.

Cord's bulk tangibly relaxed beside her, and she surreptitiously squeezed his hand before quickly releasing it. They were on the same page where Austin's addiction was concerned, and intuitively they also knew better than to give her husband any reason to feel like they were ganging up on him.

When they reached the dealership she was overwhelmed by the selection. They hadn't been car shopping since buying Austin's truck after their wedding. Her Jeep had been a hand-me-down purchase that came into their marriage with her.

"Look at these prices," she fretted. "Maybe we should ask someone about buying pre-owned."

Neither man paid her suggestion any heed.

"These are nice," Cord said, pointing out a large SUV. "She should absolutely get four-wheel drive."

"Definitely," Austin agreed. "What do you think of these, Em?"

She assessed the SUV, marking all the expensive additions such as the sunroof, leather seats, and aluminum rims. "I don't think I need anything that fancy."

Both men rolled their eyes and moved on. They spoke about various safety options and, as the sun rose higher in the sky, tiny beads of sweat gathered under her clothes. It wasn't long before a salesman found them and hovered like a pesky housefly.

The novelty wore off the longer they browsed. Stress about finances crowded her every thought and soon she was fighting the urge to burst into tears and demand they go home. Austin and Cord seemed to have no sense of her inner turmoil.

"You wanna give this one a spin, Ember?"

Her thoughts scattered as she looked at her husband. "What?"

The salesman held open the door to a bright blue model with luxurious, black, leather interior. As much as she loved the make of her old SUV, the new models were out of their price range. Why drive something they'd never afford? She shook her head, overwhelmed.

"Give us a minute," Austin muttered to the dealer as he moved closer to her. "What's wrong?"

"They're really expensive, Austin."

"But you love your Jeep."

"I just don't think a new one's in our budget."

His jaw twitched, but he didn't argue about the

expense. "A new car's going to cost, baby. We'll have payments. I want you to love whatever we get."

"I *will* love it. I just don't need something that fancy."

She sensed his urge to insist that she deserved the best of the best, but thankfully Cord stepped in and pointed to a lower priced SUV. "That model's nice. The lines are similar to the one she already has. That's about ten grand less. Maybe show her that."

Grateful for his sensibility, she smiled. "I do love the look of my old SUV."

Austin stilled, and it felt like a pivotal moment. Maybe Cord shouldn't have added his two cents.

He and Cord locked gazes and communicated in that familiar, silent way. She held her breath.

"Okay." Seeming satisfied with her compromise, Austin asked the dealer to show them the other model.

She'd be lying to herself if she didn't admit falling in love with the SUV on the spot. The pearl red was rugged yet feminine. The car handled like a familiar friend and she dared to dream that they could somehow manage the payments.

Once they were sitting at a mahogany desk discussing numbers her anxiety returned. The salesman ran a few reports and returned with the disappointed look she'd been dreading. By the regret that flashed in the dealer's eyes, she knew they couldn't swing it.

"I'm sorry, but with these minor dings in your credit, I can't work the approval."

Her heart sank, not for the loss of a lavish gift,

but for her husband's sensitive pride, which was just punctured in broad daylight.

"It's okay, Austin. We'll try again in a few months." Or a year. They'd been late on so many payments who knew how long it would take to rebuild their credit?

His lips firmed as he struggled to accept the reality of their financial situation. "What about a six year loan?"

Watching him negotiate only hurt more. They shouldn't have come here. She should have suggested a different way to spend their Sunday, suspecting this would be the ultimate outcome.

"It's not the length of the loan or your collateral, it's the score. I'm sorry—"

"Run mine," Cord interrupted.

"Cord!" She gaped at him, not at all comfortable with his suggestion and certain her husband would reject the offer on the spot. She didn't want an argument, especially not here. "No."

"Why not? My credit's good. You need a dependable car. I know you guys are good for it."

Her breath reached only the shallowest crevices of her lungs. So many arguments about the loans she'd accepted from Cord when they were in financial crisis came hurtling back to the forefront of her mind.

How could he suggest such a thing, knowing Austin was the way he was? *Why* would he even suggest stepping in?

The dealer raised a questioning brow at Austin and she wanted to race back to their truck and get as far away from this place as possible. "If you have a co-signer that changes things."

Austin eased back in his chair and folded his hands over his chest, his eyes hidden by his lashes as he considered the offer. Her heart thundered as she waited for him to blow, knowing it wouldn't be pretty.

"Run it."

Startled by his consent, she stared after the salesmen as he headed to the back office. Was he biding time for them to tuck-tail and escape in private or was he seriously considering taking Cord up on his offer?

Exhaling slowly, he glanced at her, his expression blank. "I want you in a safe car. That's what matters."

Her vision blurred as she tried to equate his reasoning with the illogical man he'd been only months ago. Here he was, doing what he'd always done, putting her needs and safety before his pride. It wasn't appropriate to break down and sob on the show room floor of a car dealership, so she blinked back the onset of tears and swallowed tightly, her gratitude for his open-mindedness choking her.

There were no words to accurately summarize his concession, no possible way of describing how monumental his acceptance of Cord's help was, how it showed he'd changed. Her husband *was* coming back to her. Little by little, she recognized more familiar parts of his compassionate soul.

The dealer returned before she had a chance to fully find composure.

"That'll do it. If Mr. Bay's willing to co-sign I

see no reason why you can't drive her off the lot today."

She held her breath. Now was the time for Austin or Cord to object. Her husband glanced at their friend, the one who pulled them out of so many holes before. "You sure you're good with this?"

Cord inclined his head. "Do it. I wanna see her in something safe as much as you do."

She didn't need a car. They had the truck and her Jeep was good enough to get her around town, though the key sometimes got stuck in the ignition and the battery died occasionally with no plausible reason. But they could have waited. They could have continued to save money and made nice with their creditors and eventually built back their credit.

But that wasn't what was happening here. Her husband, the most prideful man she knew, was putting his pride aside to invest in something bigger. He was opening himself up, showing he could accept help, and emphasizing how much he trusted Cord.

"Start the paperwork," Austin said and both the salesman and Cord grinned. He turned back to her the moment they were alone again. "You wanna drive home?"

Thank God the salesman was preoccupied, because her restraint finally slipped. She dashed away a tear and laughed. "I've missed you."

His gaze held hers, comprehension in his eyes. He knew exactly what she meant. *This* was the man she'd married and this was a big sign of his return.

He took her hand and squeezed. "I'm not going

anywhere, baby. I told you I'd fix everything. This is just one little part that needed fixing."

She shut her eyes and smiled. Releasing a sharp breath, contentment bloomed inside of her chest. She glanced at Cord, smiling at him as well. She truly loved them both, Austin for his determination and Cord for his generous soul.

"I love you both."

Her husband beamed, his smile burning away any lingering doubts.

Cord's expression briefly faltered but recovered, eyes warming as he threw her a playful wink.

She excused herself to find a restroom and a mirror and hopefully pull herself together while they finished the paperwork.

There was one brief, awkward moment when they went out to the lot, hesitating beside Austin's truck—her new Jeep gleaming in the sunshine.

Cord reached for the keys dangling from Austin's hand. "Drive home with your wife. I'll try not to abuse this piece of shit too badly."

Austin laughed, a sound so natural and carefree she wished she could bottle it. "Don't disrespect a man's truck."

With a mock punch to her husband's shoulder, Cord yanked open the driver's door with a flourish and climbed in. "See you at home."

Four

Austin

AUSTIN WAS PLEASED with the way the new car handled on the drive home. It suited Ember and she looked good driving it. He was thrilled with the fact that his wife was finally in a dependable vehicle, and it removed a great deal of worry from his shoulders.

"I'm so excited," she kept repeating.

Each time she voiced her pleasure it filled him with more satisfaction than the last. She'd never had a new vehicle—neither had he, as his truck was pre-owned, but she came first.

"You look good in it. Hot."

"I'll let you borrow it—if you're good."

The camaraderie was a balm to his senses, and

he basked in the lighthearted banter. "I've been good."

She risked a glance before turning her attention back to the road. "You have. You're a good man, Austin. The best. I love you." She sobered, her tone turning serious.

Shit. He loved hearing that, but knew it wasn't one hundred percent true. He sensed a discussion bearing down on them, and he wasn't ready.

He and Cord had done the man thing, buying a new vehicle, talking horsepower and transmissions, fuel savings, while she'd kept an eye on the budget and the color of the car.

Maybe they could put off the analytical discussion until he knew what it was he had to say. "I love you too."

"Cord needs to hear that as well."

From him? Did she mean, from him?

He loved Cord. He was the brother he'd never had, his best friend. So yeah, he loved him. But guys didn't go around saying that sort of thing. "He knows."

"We have to sit down and talk, all three of us, Austin."

She signaled and passed a slow moving car and he approved her technique, the one he'd taught her—

"Austin?"

"I heard you, baby. We'll talk. We'll get to it." They had many things yet to discuss. But a whole lifetime to do it.

Never put off until tomorrow what you can do today.

He shoved that old adage out of his head. One day at a time, that was what he'd learned from Harley and that was the way he was approaching life from now on.

"Okay," she said, appearing satisfied. "But don't forget we need to include Cord in that talk."

She wasn't going to give it a rest. He'd blown Cord off that morning, the thought of talking about feelings and *stuff* still slightly unbearable.

Despite his promise to have *the talk*, his wife went on. "We have to consider our future."

Our future? Did she mean theirs or everyone's?

His throat tightened with awareness and he sought self-control. He wanted his best friend in his life—*their* life—sure, he did. It was just going to take some doing to figure out what that looked like.

Cord pulled up behind them at the house, making a show of revving the engine before he shut off the old truck. Austin loved his Ford and he'd kept it in good repair. He hid a smile, letting his friend think he'd gotten to him, but deep down Austin knew he'd treat his truck much like he'd treat his own. Perhaps that sort of shared respect went beyond possessions.

Cord was a one of a kind friend, and there was a shared relief in the way he cared about things like Ember's safety as much as Austin. Though he lacked the words to thank him for his help today, his gratitude was there and he believed Cord sensed it. Sometimes men didn't have to talk to convey their feelings. His wife couldn't really get that.

When they climbed out of the vehicles, Ember

was giddy with joy. She inspected every hidden compartment of the new car and climbed over the seats *oohing* and *ahhing* at all the modern features.

"Look at this! It's a little net so our grocery bags don't go rolling all over the place!"

He laughed—the things that impressed her.

"She loves it," Cord commented, wearing a goofy grin as he came to stand by his side.

They watched her clamber into the backseat and lean over the center console. Great view.

"I, uh..." Austin cleared his throat, his wife's words leaving more of an imprint than he'd expected. "Thank you, for what you did back there."

"Thanks for not making a big deal out of it," Cord murmured, his attention following Ember. "It's worth it to see her this happy."

It was. He couldn't recall a time in the past year she'd been so animated or excited. He had a lot of atoning to do, but being able to do this for her was a good start. That he couldn't do it on his own should have grated, but instead he accepted his friend's help and it didn't sting as much as it could have.

Smiling to himself he murmured, "She looks great when she's happy. It's how she should always be."

Rough knuckles brushed his, sending a jolt of awareness though his belly. "And you. You should be happy too."

He glanced at Cord, the last couple days putting him in a new, somewhat jarring, light. But he liked what he saw. "I am. Happy, I mean."

Cord studied him before giving a slight nod.

"Good." Stepping closer to the car, he rested a hand on the lifted tailgate. "I'm gonna take off, kiddo."

"What?" Ember squirmed out of the side door, a look of disappointment on her face. "Why?"

Cord shrugged. "Work tomorrow. Laundry to do. It's been a long weekend."

She blinked up at Cord, objection and disappointment clear on her face, and Austin debated asking him to stay, but wondered if their friend needed time to himself. Maybe they could all use some time to themselves.

Austin met them both in the middle. "Will you come by tomorrow night after work?"

"Yes, for dinner," Ember invited with a nod of agreement.

"Sure. I can do that."

That seemed to appease her. Knowing they'd likely want to exchange a more involved kind of goodbye, and unsure if he was ready to openly start that sort of ritual, Austin excused himself.

"I'm gonna go put on coffee. I'll see you tomorrow, man."

Cord's hand lifted before falling back to his side. "See ya."

He took the porch steps and watched through the foyer window as Cord tucked a short strand of hair behind Ember's ear. She smiled and laughed at something he said. Then Cord leaned in and kissed her.

That's your wife. He waited for the anger that didn't come.

Cord's hands glided possessively over her hips, pulling her smaller body into the shelter of his much larger one. He held her with a show of ownership, but Austin wasn't threatened. He was secure in his connection with his wife, believing her heart was big enough for both him and his friend.

The relief of accepting that astonishing reality brought about a sense of security he'd been lacking. Should he ever fail her again, Cord would be there —just as he'd been there before, as dependable as rain. It had been a difficult decision to let his friend in, to give Ember what she needed, but seeing them together assured him he'd done the right thing.

Loving both of them had ripped her heart in two. His consent had been borne of a desperate need to spare her further misery, but now... He closed his eyes in mute appreciation of all these recent changes.

He blinked just as Cord gently set Ember away from him and walked slowly to his truck. After watching him climb in and drive away, Ember returned to inspecting her new Jeep and Austin went about making a fresh pot of coffee. As it brewed, his belly rumbled. And just like clockwork, December came inside, anticipating his need, right there to meet it.

"I'm going to make a chicken Caesar salad for dinner. That should only take a few minutes. You're probably getting hungry."

"That sounds great. I have my meeting in an hour, so something fast is probably best."

She dusted up the crumbs of coffee grounds he'd accidently left on the counter and threw him a smile over her shoulder. Such simple gestures could be staggering when he'd gone so many months without them.

"Today was awesome, Austin. I can't believe I have a new car. I've never had a *brand new* car before. I mean, I know the truck was new-*ish*, but that was yours. This is mine."

"Come here," he rasped, needing to touch her.

Her lips softened and curved upwards as she abandoned the crumbs and moved into his arms.

"Do you know how incredible you are?" He teased the tip of her nose with his. "You should've had a new car years ago. If I'd known how happy it would make you I would've filled the driveway."

"It's more than the car, Mr. Garret, and you know it. Today was significant."

Every day with her was significant, but he understood what she meant. He'd watched her eyes shimmer when he accepted Cord's help with the loan.

Touching his lips to hers, he savored the moment she lifted to her toes and pressed into him, her body subtly requesting more. His responded, but they were short on time.

"Make dinner, baby. I want to enjoy a meal with you before I have to go."

"Later?" she asked, her gaze soft and full of temptation.

"Later." That was a promise.

Their dinner conversation flowed over easy topics like household tasks and current issues in the news. December kissed him lingeringly as he left, and he drove to the meeting with a sense of wellbeing, knowing what awaited him on his return.

His attendance at AA was a necessary part of his day, not because it was mandatory—it wasn't—but because it had become an important part of the routine he'd come to value. Missing the night before had been an anomaly—one he didn't regret—but it felt good to get back to his newfound norm.

Settling into his usual chair—funny how people staked their claim, even here—he surreptitiously surveyed the room. Nobody stared or deliberately made anyone else uncomfortable, except maybe with the exception of Harley that first night Austin had attended a meeting.

There were three newcomers that joined a couple of weeks ago. Their signs of discomfort were less apparent tonight, as they'd been absorbed into the group.

Initially, he'd resisted everything AA stood for. He'd been terrified, and thought he was above such help. He wasn't proud of himself, labeling the members losers without taking the time to actually meet them, but that had been a bad time for him. He hated everything and everyone—himself most of all.

The new members hid their discomfort well, but afterward he went out of his way to give each one a brief, encouraging nod. Nothing intrusive, but enough to show solidarity. One of them, a pretty young woman, blinked back tears before firming her mouth and looking away. He remembered how tough it was, especially in the beginning. Even now, no one ever knew who would be back the next night.

He joined Harley for a quick cup of coffee after the meeting, but didn't divulge any new details about his private life. Sometimes their relationship crossed into the personal, but other times it was a simple comfort they both enjoyed without expectation.

"You're looking good, Austin."

"Thanks, I'm feeling good." It was true. The momentous events of the past couple of days had enhanced his well-being despite his occasional soul searching.

"Well, whatever's working, work it." His sponsor grinned widely. They sat in a comfortable silence for a while, sipping coffee.

"A few new members," Austin commented.

Harley's face tightened and his mouth set in a thin line for an instant before relaxing into his usual resting expression. "Not enough sponsors at the moment. It's a bit of a worry."

Austin hadn't thought about that. He was so grateful Harley had reached out when he needed someone to guide him, without suffocating him. He had a great mentor and, selfishly, he didn't want to share.

Part of him feared the sponsor pinch might interfere with *their* time, which he greatly depended on. "So, what happens?"

"Some of the more recovered members will step up. It's time they did."

But not Austin. No way was he ready. He was still *recovering*. Far from *recovered*. He gave a relieved nod, and then, as he realized he might be a Harley in the future, his shoulders straightened and his chest expanded with a desire to fill such a meaningful position in a stranger's life. The other man quirked a brow.

With a self-conscious laugh, Austin said, "Maybe I can be there for somebody. In the future."

"A fine goal, Austin."

"I've got enough on my plate right now, but down the line…" He could clearly see that time, which motivated him all the more and made him believe achieving such a goal was possible. Not only that, he liked the idea of helping others. In the meantime, he'd be as welcoming and supportive as possible—in preparation for that future goal.

When he got home the house was mostly dark, but the hall lights were left on and there seemed a sense of balance where Ember's presence lingered. Little things, like the coffee pot set for dawn and his work boots brought from the coat closet to the front door, ready for him to step into them come morning, filled their home with love.

He took the stairs slowly and entered their bedroom quietly, not surprised to find her already asleep. It had been a long weekend, one full of many revelations.

After using the bathroom, he removed his watch and placed his clothes in the hamper. She stirred as he slipped into bed and pulled her close.

"How was your meeting?" Her sleepy murmur accompanied the scent of warm female.

"Good."

She nestled closer. "You met up with Harley. I smell fresh coffee on you."

"Just for a cup. I wanted to get home."

"Mmm. I'm glad you're home." Her hand

brushed over the front of his stomach, teasing close to his cock, and his blood heated.

Tipping up her chin, he found her mouth and made love to her full lips, slowly coaxing her body beneath his. She was his sanctuary, his welcome home after the longest of days. This connection they shared at the close of most nights seemed the best affirmation that they were healthy and whole.

As he filled her, her languid body stretched, her eyes shimmering in the shadows as she stared up at him, and he savored their joining. How could he have forfeited such an incredible gift?

"I love when your body surrenders to mine," he whispered, before taking her mouth again.

There was no haste in the way he touched her. These moments were theirs, sacred and timeless. As her knees clung to his hips, he shivered at the amount of gratification she offered while he provided the same.

Her moans shifted into low, keening cries as their bodies heated, melding into an intricate twist of limbs under the solid thrum of their beating hearts. As he closed in on his climax, he reached between them and gently caressed her, making sure they finished together. With one final thrust he let go and she came apart in his arms, quivering gently as he held her close.

She sighed as they rested together, bodies still entwined, their pulse slowing to a manageable rhythm. And suddenly his thoughts jolted to Cord.

It had to be significant that he'd think about his best friend at this particular intimate moment. Rather than resist, he let his mind wander.

Was Cord at home trying to sleep, thinking about what they'd shared? Thinking of just Ember? Was he wondering what the future held? Was he alone?

The thought of Cord with anyone else stabbed at something in the very heart of him. Ember was right. Eventually, they had to talk.

"Are you thinking about him?" she whispered.

"Cord?"

"Mm-hmm."

His gaze traveled over the shadows on the wall. "For a moment. Mostly thinking of you."

Her fingers teased softly through his hair as they rested. "Are you thinking about this morning?"

His mind flashed to those erotic moments of having Cord deep in his— "I wasn't thinking of that."

She shifted to lean on her elbow so she could see his face. "Can we talk about it?"

Here it was, that analytical moment he'd known would come. At least they weren't discussing feelings again. No doubt that conversation was far from over. And then there was the "big talk" they all needed to have, but Cord wasn't here. So he could handle this. Unless this was worse. "Sure."

"Did you...like it?"

Fuck. Maybe this *was* worse.

Be truthful. You made an oath. You owe her that.

He considered her question and his stomach clenched with intense desire, an unfamiliar yearning unraveling inside of him. "Yes."

Lightning didn't strike and her dimple showed in a strip of moonlight as she smiled. "I did too.

Watching you two together, it's... I don't think I've ever seen anything so...intensely moving. It's like it was right, like it shouldn't have taken so long to happen."

He didn't know if he'd go that far. It definitely felt new to him. He dug deep and spoke more of the truth. "I'd do it again."

"Really?" She shifted closer, her smile flashing in the moonlight. "We...we could do it together."

Suck off Cord? Together? The thought stirred something dark and wanting inside of him. His hand slid to his stirring cock without thought, gripping tightly. "He'd love that."

"Cord loves *you*."

He paused, caught by the strange emphasis he sensed in her words. "We've been friends forever—"

"No, Austin. I think it's more than that—for both of you."

"Maybe." Everything was still new. They could experiment with the physical side, but...love? *That* kind of love? "I'm still processing."

She dragged her fingernails slowly over his abs and he caught her hand, directing it to his cock. She took up stroking him and whispered, "It's so different when you're with him. I'm used to you being the authoritative one."

His ego twitched. "I still am."

"With me. But when you're with him something changes."

He stretched his back and legs, placing his body at a better angle for her. "Does me changing bother you?"

"No. It seems...right. You being that way with

him changes nothing about the way you are with me."

"Cord's a control freak."

She snorted, interrupting his thoughts. "My, Mr. Kettle, you sure are black."

He laughed, but his assessment of his friend was spot on. Regardless of that aw shucks, goofy act Cord pulled at times, Austin knew the other side of him, the one that micromanaged the important things in life, like the store. They were both control freaks, but Cord seemed to really need control when it came to—

Any label he considered for the three of them stirred up emotions he didn't want to acknowledge. Maybe he wasn't ready to label it yet.

He pinched her nipple. "I thought we were discussing blow jobs."

She giggled. "We were."

"All this talk..." He thrust the covers back, the rustling sound a signal in the dark.

She slithered down his body and put her mouth to work. His fingers trailed through her hair, softer than Cord's thick curls and he again wondered why she'd cut it, if she intended to grow it back.

His toes curled as she took him deeper at a leisurely pace. "Fuck, Ember. You're so fucking good at that."

"You taste like me." Her breath cooled his wet flesh before the heat of her mouth returned.

He wondered if Cord would ever do this to him. Wanted to push the issue and make him try it. The things he found himself open to were a bit shocking and hard to admit.

His cock throbbed and he believed it was because of his wife's talented mouth, but his wandering thoughts were arousing the fuck out of him. Visions of working his cock deep into Cord's mouth... Tugging those thick curls... Holding him steady...

Fuck. His blood was on fire. How far would they go? How much could Cord take? How much could *he* take? His mind thrust him into a heated frenzy and a cold sweat.

Baby steps.

Ember's fingers worked lower, caressing his sac as her mouth rode up and down his cock. Lifting his knees, he made more room. The knot of his ass throbbed and he tried to ignore the strange desire crawling through his veins.

Her touch skimmed his taint and he sucked in a sharp breath as a needy sensation took hold. "Lower." The word escaped on a breathy exhalation.

Her ministrations paused as she lifted her mouth.

He shut his eyes, unable to face her. Even under the veil of shadows, he hadn't meant to say that.

Her hand released his sac and feathered downward. "Here?"

Breathing hard, he couldn't muster a response.

"Austin?"

"Never mind. Just do what you were doing."

Her lips returned, but he'd distracted her and it became obvious. She once again sucked him deep and massaged gently, and now he second-guessed the stability of their once unshakable foundation. So much had transpired and maybe they were moving too fast. Was he asking too much?

He hissed in a breath as her finger trailed between his ass cheeks and everything quieted. Doubt, shame, and worry rushed at him, but all those things were somehow overshadowed by his immense desire to be pushed a little further over the line.

She nudged, applying the slightest pressure to the tight ring of muscles and he grunted. He swallowed repetitively and braced for the unknown, uncertain if he'd freak or love it.

Her mouth dragged slowly over his cock and released him. All his focus zeroed in on where her finger teased. His heart pounded faster as he waited, suspended in a state of desire and denial.

She licked up his dick and pressed her finger against his flesh, now wet with saliva. The tight knot gave way and welcomed her intrusion by the slightest degree as air rushed from his lungs and returned in rapid pants.

"Is this okay?" she asked softly.

His eyes remained screwed shut as he gave a hard nod, regardless if she could see the gesture or not. "Do it."

Her breath beat softly at the underside of his cock, as the pressure expanded and his body struggled to welcome the intrusion of her little finger. Jesus. How did people do this? It felt...tight. Extremely tight, but in a good way. Thinking of anything bigger than Ember's finger in there had him breaking out in a sweat.

"Should I move it?"

He wasn't sure. This was brand fucking new to him and far from his radar. "Yeah. Slowly though."

"Maybe this'll help." She returned her mouth to his cock, sucking slowly as her finger gently pulled back and eased deeper. Fuck. She was really in there. He could feel her knuckle pressing against his taut skin with every slow advance.

His sac tightened as her finger sank a nudge further and his body tensed, sensing something new happening.

"*Fuck.*" Whatever she was doing felt incredible. "Don't stop."

His fists tightened in the blankets as that devious digit massaged deeper and his body involuntarily locked, pleasure tunneling through his veins with enough force to make him see stars. "*Jesus Christ.*"

Trigger pulled, a blanket of sweat broke across his skin as his mind flashed with a blinding light. His jaw opened on a silent groan as everything he thought he knew shifted into something indescribable. The deeper she pressed the more he wanted, but it seemed too much to take in at once.

His body jerked, every muscle responding to her touch, locking in a euphoric zap of pleasure knifing through his veins. Come rushed from his balls and up his shaft. He tried to warn her, but words escaped him. All he could do was experience the intense pleasure.

Fuck. He couldn't catch his breath.

"Was that okay?" Ember whispered.

The sense of being exposed should have left him feeling vulnerable. He was helpless, spent, and too fucking comfortable to move an inch. No walls. No masks. Just him and his beautiful Ember. Trust.

His hand reached for hers and squeezed as he searched for his bearings. "That...was fucking incredible."

Taking a minute, he slowly opened his eyes and found her kneeling between his sprawled legs. She was his wife and he'd been her first, so this was clearly a new experience for both of them.

Though he loved taking on the role of dominant lover, he was pretty much a basic, white bread guy. Anal play was a whole new spectrum for them and one he hadn't expected to *ever* be on the receiving end of.

Her posture seemed shy and a touch unsure. Maybe he'd asked too much of her. "Are *you* okay?"

Her narrow shoulders lifted in a dainty shrug, silhouetted in the dark. "I'm fine."

He laughed, thinking it a never ending surprise what an amazing wife he had. Pulling her to his side, he kissed her, the lingering taste of his release still on her tongue. His body was wrung out and sapped of strength, but he dug deep for the energy to hold her in his arms as his mind searched for words.

"You are—by far—the sexiest woman to walk the face of the earth."

"I doubt that."

He caught her chin, tapping a finger on her cheek. "December. You are."

She smiled and despite the shadowed darkness he sensed her blushing. "Thank you."

When she slipped from the bed and made her way to the bathroom, he keenly felt a loss. He considered following her, but doubted his legs would hold him.

Climbing back beneath the covers, she eased close.

He cradled her against his shoulder and kissed her temple. "Let's get some sleep."

"I can't wait to drive my new car to the market."

He laced his fingers with hers and squeezed. Whatever made her happy. "Goodnight, baby. I love you."

Five

Cord

CORD QUIETLY ENTERED the house and breathed in the scent of home cooked food. Following his nose, he walked to the kitchen and paused to savor the view.

December.

Her trim waist was wrapped in a floral apron he'd bet his left nut she sewed herself. She leaned over the counter, one bare foot lifted to rest on her calf. The sole wore a dark tinge—typical Ember, never wearing shoes. As she moved to steal a taste from the ladle, he admired her sexy legs.

She slid the lid back on the saucepan, turned, and started. "Cord! I didn't hear you come in." Her voice was filled with happiness.

God, she was gorgeous. Moments like this took

every ounce of his willpower not to take her in his arms and ravish her, claim her. *Fuck* her.

"Where's Austin?"

A shallow dimple formed in her cheek. "He just called. They're keeping him late. He said we should go ahead and eat without him."

"Oh." Working late. Right. That sometimes happened. "How long do you think he'll be?"

She gathered a stack of plates and returned one to the cabinet. "Not sure. Can you get me the white pitcher from the top shelf?"

As she carried the plates to the dining room table he grabbed the pitcher, unsure how the night would unfold without Austin there. They hadn't really outlined any ground rules regarding just the two of them. Alone. Together.

Ember returned with a stack of linen napkins and used the kitchen table to fold them. The white fabric obeyed the insistent movement of her dainty hands and he wished he could be on the receiving end of her touch.

"How was your day?"

Playing house. Yeah, he could get on board with that. "It was good. How about yours?"

She shrugged, casting him a sweet look over her shoulder. "Good. Normal." She laughed. "There's something to be appreciated about an ordinary day, especially after so many unordinary ones, don't you think?"

Was this ordinary? Yesterday morning the three of them woke up in the same bed. He certainly didn't recall any episodes of *Leave it to Beaver* where June and Ward started their days with a friend's naked body between them. But she was right. Ordinary felt good.

He approached as she folded the last napkin, such attention to detail. Dragging his knuckle from her neck to her shoulder, he eased closer as she shivered.

"Ordinary is definitely nice from time to time."

Clutching the napkins to her chest, she turned and peered up at him. Those dark eyes of hers would get him in trouble every time.

Being that he hadn't yet kissed her, he leaned in slow, a sort of *hi honey, it's good to be home ritual* he never felt compelled to share with anyone other than Ember. The second his lips brushed hers he drew in a long breath. Heaven.

"Hi."

"Hi," she echoed, voice a touch breathless. "I'm going to set the table. Can I get you anything?"

Such a nurturer. "I'm good." He followed her to the dining room, admiring the practiced way she dressed the table. Such a perfectionist when it came to keeping her home. "Hey, did you get to show off your car today?"

"I did." She beamed. "I even got to take Eloise for a ride."

"Eloise?"

"She's my friend at the craft store, the one who hooked me up with the quilting gig."

Quilting gig? His mind scrambled and he vaguely recalled her saying something about teaching a class at the craft store during dinner at his parents' the other night. "Oh, right. When do you start teaching?"

"Next week. It's only a four week course, but I'm really excited."

He loved when she displayed passion for her hobbies. Always adored the way she'd show off some new item gracing their home whenever he stopped by, so proud that she'd made it from nothing.

"I think you'll be a hit."

"Thank you, Cord." Her hand brushed over his stomach as she passed him to return to the kitchen. He followed, hard on her heels. Hard, period.

"So…what are you making?"

"Italian wedding soup. I have a loaf of home-made bread in the oven."

He could smell something delicious baking. He glanced around the room, searching for anything to do. Being that it wasn't his house and Ember kept everything in perfect order, he gave up and focused hard on not fidgeting. "Ember?"

She paused from mixing tea in the pitcher he'd set out for her. "Hmm?"

"Is this weird for you?"

"This?"

"Us. Me being here without Austin."

"Well, Austin will be home eventually and you've been here before."

"You know what I mean."

Her gaze lowered and she moved to a chair. "No. It's not weird. I've been looking forward to seeing you all day. Is it weird for you?" Her fingers twisted in her apron as he pulled a chair away from the table, sitting across from her.

He caught her hand, rubbing it gently so she'd stop fidgeting. "A little."

Her lashes lifted as she looked at him with concern. "Why?"

"Well, I'm holding your hand for one, and you know I'm not holding it as a friend."

"I know."

"And yesterday…"

"We talked about it, Austin and I. It really *is* okay, Cord. He's okay."

"But are you?"

She smiled and nodded. "I haven't been this okay in a long time. I like what's happening."

"Me too—I think."

"Is there…something you wanted to talk about?"

He pulled her hand. "Sit with me."

She lifted and edged closer. He gave her arm a gentle tug and she lowered to his lap. A perfect fit.

"I love you, kiddo. I just want you to know that nothing will ever change that. If this is what you truly want, I'm all in, but if you change your mind, I'll be okay with that too." He told himself he meant it, though knew he'd never come back from another rejection.

She tipped her head so their foreheads were touching and gave him a charming smile. "I'm not going to change my mind."

His thumb traced the arch of her cheekbone. "Just know that nothing will make me stop loving you."

Her lashes lowered as she nestled her cheek against his fingers. "Feels good…"

The scent of her hair and skin crept into him. His hand traveled down her neck and her body became more pliant with each caress. She was so fucking sexy, everything he wanted and never dreamed he could have.

"You like when a man's in control, don't you?"

"I like when you and Austin are in control."

Good answer. His body thickened as he dragged his touch lower, pulling the thin strap of her dress over the slope of her shoulder. "I like being in control."

He lowered her other strap and her breathing picked up pace. Adjusting her shoulders, he settled her on the center of his lap, her legs dangling along opposite sides of the chair. Looking in her eyes, he lowered the front of her dress, exposing her pretty breasts. Her nipples tightened, but he didn't touch them.

Resting his hands on her hips, he held her tight against him, letting her feel what she did to him. "Do you know how much you turn me on?"

She quietly laughed, her dark eyes glowing. "I'm getting an impression."

He guided her hips into a slow rhythm and she caught on quickly, riding him slowly through his jeans. It was a mediocre comfort for his throbbing need, but still a relief.

"I miss you at the store. Sometimes I go to the front, expecting to see you there, but you're not."

"I miss being there."

"You could come back."

"Cord."

His eyes closed. His dick was ready to explode. "Ember..." Fuck. He hadn't meant to get this close without Austin there, wasn't sure of the rules. "I wanna fuck you so bad right now."

She stilled and he opened his eyes. She didn't look offended or even remotely put off by his utterance. "We need a condom."

Was that a yes?

Call him a Boy Scout or dangerously optimistic, but he'd never been so grateful for the foresight he'd had that morning. Reaching in his pocket, he removed his wallet and pulled a condom from the center compartment.

Tossing the wallet on the table, he pressed the condom into her hand. "Put it on me. Just like this."

She hesitated a second then took the little foil. Scooting back, she unbuckled his belt and slowly lowered his zipper.

His heart raced as he considered what they were about to do and he tried to shake the sense that they were breaking a rule. As she lined the latex over the top of his throbbing cock, he caught her hand.

"Wait."

She glanced at him in question and he debated if the pain of blue balls was worth nobility. Fuck him and his damn guilty conscience. "I don't feel right doing this behind Austin's back."

She frowned. "We're not. I told you we talked."

"About *this*? How could you know this would happen?"

"I mean, we discussed the possibility of us being alone together."

The sharp sense of being left out of an important conversation that concerned him, stung. "What did he say?"

"Cord..."

"I'm serious, Ember. I need to know. You two can't make decisions about *us* if I'm not a part of it."

Understanding his position, she nodded. "I'm sorry. From now on we'll include you. He said we could. He said... *this* is fine, so long as we don't do anything new."

"Explain new." It wasn't like she was a virgin.

"Like...stuff I've never done."

Again, it wasn't like she was a virgin. "Such as?"

Her gaze shifted away and she blushed. "Stuff. Things I've never tried."

Dizzy with curiosity, he chuckled and turned her face back to him. "*Such as?*"

Her mouth pursed and she tipped her head, glancing over her shoulders. "Things back there..."

"Anal?"

Her flush darkened as her gaze flared.

"You and Austin never... Holy shit. I just assumed you'd done everything. I mean, you guys have been together forever."

"We never felt the need. It's not like that part of our relationship was deficient before he stopped..."

Shit. He hadn't meant to remind her of the time her marriage was in the gutter. "I know. Austin never had any complaints. I guess I just expected you guys to dot all the I's and cross every T."

"Well, we never got around to dashing the A's."

He laughed. "We'll have to remedy that."

"Not without Austin."

"No, that's not what I meant. He'd be there. I

want him there." *He can have your virgin ass while I take his.*

His body flinched at the direction of his thoughts and he returned her hands to his cock. "Put the condom on me."

The latex slid over his dick, and he shivered at the gentle touch of her fingers. Lifting her, he paused. "Panties."

She nodded and stepped back. Raising her dress, she shimmied the lace down her legs. She held it in her dainty hands and his nostrils flared. With a smirk, he tucked the panties in his shirt pocket.

"Dress too. But leave the apron."

She laughed and awkwardly worked the dress down her hips, leaving the floral apron.

"You make that?" His voice sounded gravelly to his own ears, as he strove to ignore his aching dick.

"Last summer."

"I knew it. Turn around for me."

Her blush traveled upward from the tips of her engorged nipples to her slender throat as she did a slow twirl. Beautiful. Every man's fantasy.

He caught her hips and dragged her to his lap, her backside warming his stomach. His hand cupped her breast, massaging with a possessive hold as his lips pressed into her shoulder.

"You have no fucking idea how much you turn me on."

She moaned as he dragged a finger down her spine to the seam of her ass. "I definitely want to be there for this."

Her breath hitched as he held her, feeling the

warmth of her pussy so close to his cock. "I'm a little nervous about that," she whispered.

"Why?"

He was honestly curious. He liked fucking ass—a lot. The women he'd been with liked it too, or he wouldn't have pushed for it. And he knew how to make it right for the inexperienced ones.

She shrugged. "What if it hurts?"

"There's such a thing as good hurt. We'd be gentle." *We...* "And no one's rushing you. You don't have to do anything you don't want to do, sweetheart. Understand?"

"Yes."

"Good." He lowered her unerringly onto his cock, slipping past her wet folds and into her heat. They both sighed as he penetrated her to the hilt.

"Jesus." He greedily pulled her to his chest, closing his mouth over her neck where her pulse beat rapidly. Lifting his ass, he rolled his hips and plucked at her nipples. "You feel that?"

"Yes," she breathed.

"Who's inside of you, Ember?"

"You are, Cord." She gasped.

"Damn right." He thrust deep, impaling her with each upstroke.

She let him hold her captive, controlling how deep and hard he fucked her, and it was possibly the sexiest experience of his life. His ass scooted to the edge of the chair as he worked his cock in and out, ever harder.

Her cries echoed through the kitchen, mingling with the slapping of flesh. Her beautiful body twisted with pleasure as the walls of her channel tightened to coax his release. He pounded into her, groaning through an approaching orgasm that made his vision blur, and somehow dropped a hand to find her clit.

"Come for me, Ember." He rubbed the tiny knot of nerves to shove her over the edge, eliciting a choked, ecstatic cry.

He wanted her skin-to-skin, desperate to feel everything, but would take whatever she could offer. Cradling her close, they caught their breath. Lust sated, he suffered the overwhelming deluge of emotion and his damn inarticulate struggle to express his feelings for her.

"I love you, Ember."

Tilting her head, her gaze found his and she smiled, nestling into his arms. "I love you too, Cord. So much it sometimes scares me."

He knew exactly what she meant. "Me too."

Helping her to her feet, he admired the picture she made—flushed cheeks, round breasts with tightly puckered nipples, and tousled sex hair. In disarray, the feathery tendrils framed her face beautifully.

Domestic and homey, he grinned at how incongruous the apron was in contrast with his sexy Ember. He debated suggesting she finish preparing the meal wearing only that floral scrap of fabric, but knew that wasn't very practical. She truly was a domestic goddess, born to be worshipped.

"What are you smiling at?" She brushed a wisp of hair from above her eye.

"You. How freaking hot you are."

He loved when she blushed. Running a fingertip between her breasts, he swallowed his regret as she reached for her dress. She stripped off the apron, ducking her head and giving him her back as she slipped her clothes back on.

He dealt with the condom and tucked his cock away before wrapping his arms around her. Helping her adjust the straps of her dress, he nuzzled her temple.

"Do you have my panties?"

"That depends."

"On what?"

"On what you have to trade."

She slapped at his hands and made a futile attempt to grab her underwear from his pocket as a throat cleared.

December pivoted, eyes wide, and squealed, "Austin!"

She sidestepped Cord, and rushed to her husband, who scooped her up in a bone-crushing hug. "That's some welcome."

Cord brushed a hand over his head. There was no mistaking the love between the pair, the pure affection, and he smiled with strange satisfaction. The lack of jealousy surprised him, maybe because she said she loved him too. And showed him with her graceful surrender.

He reminded himself this would take time. They all had some adjusting to do. "Hey, Austin."

His friend kissed his wife one last time and set her back on her feet. "Hey, Cord. Sorry I'm late. Did you guys eat yet?"

"No, but we managed to pass the time." He arched a brow, but inside he was holding his breath.

Austin and Ember might have discussed him, with Austin giving his consent, but he was still walking shaky ground.

"It looks like it." Austin's stare narrowed on the lacy panties protruding from his pocket.

December giggled and Austin gave his shoulder a playful shove. Cord's relief was so pronounced his knees shook.

"Sit down," she said. "Austin, wash up. Dinner's about ready."

Breaking bread took on a whole new meaning. He and Austin tore into the flaky, fragrant loaf and loaded the slices with butter, while Ember ladled deep bowls of the soup.

As he reached to set a piece of bread on her plate, Austin placed one on the opposite side. Their gazes met, and lingered. Warmth unfurled in his belly and he nearly sighed with contentment.

"Job's a bitch," Austin commented, breaking eye contact and leaving Cord to fill Ember's plate.

"Yeah?"

"Nobody wants to work up to standard."

He was having the same issues in the store. Ember had been, by far, his best employee, just ahead of Austin. He had to constantly check up on his latest hires. One guy couldn't even grasp the concept of stacking shelves.

Nodding, he took another swallow of soup. "It's the same all over."

"I don't mind working late. Someone on the crew has to step up. But these guys couldn't possibly work slower."

"There's something to be said to being a self-employed crew of one," Ember added, dipping her bread into her bowl.

Cord glanced around the spotless dining room, knowing the rest of the house was equally well kept. His place hadn't seen a woman's touch or any kind of attention since she'd cleaned it months ago. Back when Austin had fallen under the spell of alcohol and Cord had willingly taken Ember in.

He dismissed that jaunt down memory lane, too many missteps to count. They'd all begun to atone in one way or another, and he refused to think they might backslide to that bitter place.

Ember hopped up to clear the table, and he and Austin moved like a pair of well-trained horses to give her a hand. Again, his comfort level rose as he hip checked his friend to beat him to the kitchen.

"Dick." Austin juggled a bowl and the pitcher.

"I'll make coffee." December busied herself at the counter.

Austin swooped in to drop a kiss on her head, awkwardly depositing the dishes beside the coffee maker.

Batting him away with the brewing basket, she pursed her lips. "Thank you. If you bring in the rest of the stuff from the table, I'll get the mugs. I've got some banana bread sliced already. Then we can talk."

Both he and Austin paused. The great dinner he'd consumed suddenly sat heavily in his gut, and to judge by his friend's hesitant expression, he was feeling about the same. But with one look at Ember, they both silently agreed to keep their reservations quiet. Though he wasn't sure he and his friend harbored the exact same worries.

Sitting back at the dining room table, Cord fiddled with a spoon. "You guys talk a lot."

"We do." Austin didn't sound particularly thrilled. "I thought I talked before...before, well, you know. But AA is huge on talking, and Harley figures communication is right up there with sliced bread."

Harley. Of course.

He ignored that bite of jealousy, because the guy probably had it right. Austin, being that he was the most practiced, could take the lead in the conversation and talk his ass off tonight. Cord would nod and grunt at opportune times to get through—for Ember. *Game face.*

Ember bustled in bearing a platter of banana bread, and a saucer of sliced cheese, three empty mugs dangling from her fingers. Buying time, Cord went to get the coffee and built some points by grabbing that flavored creamer she preferred out of the fridge.

The moment he poured the last cup of coffee, she started. "We need to talk about where our relationship is going."

Normally, the *r* word made him twitch. This time around it evoked a sense of anticipation, coupled with curiosity. Austin avoided looking in his direction, the prick.

Okay, so he planned to leave it all up to Austin, but seeing as his friend, the practiced talker, was silent, he bit. "Relationship?"

With a pretty flush that made his mind wander,

she said, "Well, we've had a friendship. We *do* have a friendship, but it's...evolved."

Having sex with his friends probably qualified as being evolved, though some might question that. He nodded. Austin's smile looked brittle.

On a deep breath, Ember said, "Austin wants to give me what I need. And I want the same for him—for both of you. I love him for that. I love him, period. And I love you, Cord. I want to keep saying that, because it's true and I never tire of it."

"I love you too, kiddo."

"Love you back, baby."

He and Austin replied simultaneously and she grinned in obvious delight, looking between them. "So, that part's clear."

There was another part? Okay, he knew there was. But he wasn't so certain if Austin realized there was more.

His friend drew in a deep breath and wrapped his hands around his mug, his focus on the coffee. "I told Ember I wouldn't mind...that is... I wanted to be with you again."

Cord's heart leapt and lodged in his throat. He swallowed, but the lump stayed put, and he couldn't form words around it. He blinked and hoped Austin would say something a little more specific. Deeper maybe.

Deeper? Was this a fucking romance novel? He ducked his head and kneaded the base of his neck, rasping, "Same here."

"You looked right together." Her sweet, quiet observation somehow echoed in the room and Austin flinched.

Cord manned up, damned if he'd play the prude at this point. "It felt right—to me at least."

No harm in admitting that. They didn't need to know he'd harbored forbidden thoughts about his best friend for half his life. And there was no need to divulge things if they were all *evolving* together. Austin was likely still trying to get his head around the idea of *more*.

"I'm still processing," Austin muttered, confirming Cord's suspicions.

Tiny lines pinched tight around Ember's mouth, and then she blew out a breath, distracting Cord. He sensed her sudden stress, but didn't understand the root of it. They were talking, just as she'd requested.

Her smile appeared painted on as she caught his gaze. Cord gave her a supportive nod, hoping she wasn't stressed by something he'd said. God, he sucked at communicating. Seemed like Austin wasn't quite up to this communication thing either, regardless of his earlier claims.

Cord battled with his own frustration and egged her on. "What else, Ember? We're listening."

Despite Austin's silence, Cord was certain he was paying close attention.

"I want us to be together. There's a name for what we have, although I'm not sure if it applies, exactly."

"*Ménage a trois*," Austin helpfully supplied.

"Yes. But I'd like something a little more committed. Maybe even the sort of relationship where we all... live together."

He hadn't expected that. The idea of coming

home to her every single night after work, waking up with her—them—every single morning, having her extend the nurturing nature she showed Austin to him—

He caught himself, sensing Austin's tension. Yet his mind took him deep enough into the fantasy that there was no denying how badly he wanted it to become his reality.

But what about *his* house? He wasn't sure they were ready for all that—mostly because, if they fucked this up, backtracking would be a bitch.

Rather than chance hearing Austin's rejection of the idea, he spoke first. "Ember, sweetheart, that's moving pretty quick."

"Oh. I...I thought..." She glanced away. "I guess I'm getting ahead of myself. Reading into things." Her voice was thick with banked emotion and he automatically reached out, foiled by Austin's quicker reaction to soothe her. The way Austin's fingers curled around hers, wedding bands side by side where their fingers touched, brought about the wretched sense of being the third wheel again.

Cord folded his hands on the table, staring at his bare fingers as a jolt of isolation tried to eat him alive.

She swallowed and whispered, "I'm sorry if I'm wrong, but we need to talk about the future, figure out how this is going to work on a day-to-day basis. Don't we? I mean, we're together, aren't we?"

Austin wrapped an arm around her shoulders, leaning over her protectively. "Shh, baby. Don't upset yourself. We *are* talking. It's going to take some time for us to find balance and we don't want anyone to feel rushed."

Cord's sentiments exactly—sort of. He pleaded with her with his eyes, wincing as he spotted tears clinging to her dark lashes. Then something shifted in her expression, the vulnerability clouded by what appeared to be some serious irritation and he instinctively leaned back.

Dropping her hand heavily on the table, the muffled sound ricocheted like a gunshot on his frazzled nerves. Okay, she *was* pissed.

"Why can't you just say it, Austin?"

Say what? Cord had somehow missed an important part of the conversation, or maybe this had to do with their last talk, the one where he hadn't been included. He stared at their faces, desperately searching for a clue.

"Ember." Austin scooped her onto his lap, despite her protests.

The way he handled her, so practiced and prepared, left Cord a bit breathless and unsure of his own abilities. Austin calmed her, running a hand down her back before smoothing her hair.

"Please, Austin," she murmured. "We all have to be a little brave when it comes to being honest with each other and ourselves."

Cord couldn't agree more, but whatever she was asking wasn't about him. It appeared Austin was holding something back and December wanted him to literally put it on the table.

It was then he understood she'd never be a barrier between them, but rather, a covered bridge that not only led him to Austin, but also created a place of refuge for all their battered hearts.

An internal struggle played across Austin's face, but in the end, he could deny his wife nothing. In a voice as rough as sandpaper, resonating with honesty, his friend said, "I'm not doing this only for Ember anymore, Cord. I'm...I'm also doing it for me—for all of us."

Cord stopped breathing. Was that his way of saying he was attracted to him? Sure, they'd done stuff, but... To think his attraction was reciprocated by even the slightest degree...

He'd take that paltry offering and believe there was more behind it. Austin was far from a shallow guy, and with time, they'd dig deeper. For now, that little confession was more than he'd ever expected.

Cord cleared his throat, but something remained lodged in his windpipe. "I'm good with all of it, too. So far."

He hated to add the qualifier, but his friend had instigated this threesome, probably without thinking past a one-off. Cause and effect. Consequences. Austin didn't know the love Cord harbored. Maybe *he* had to be the voice of reason despite expecting equal honesty from Austin. His friend would eventually open up—once he *processed*.

"Are you staying with us tonight?" Ember asked, point blank.

He wanted to, and didn't want to see the disappointment that denying her would cause. Torn, he mentally ran through reasons to stay or go, like a bad eighties song.

As much as he wanted to rush to the end, a logical part of him warned they should take it slow. Process—for lack of a better word. Maybe he'd left the stove on.

"It's late," Austin said. "You could stay if you want. The guest room's yours."

He nearly laughed. Guest room, as in just a *guest*? How very convenient for them.

Despite Ember's desires, her husband was still patently conflicted. Maybe they both were. Getting pissed was only going to cloud the issue.

Voice of reason.

"I've got an early delivery tomorrow. Best I head home so I'm not getting up at the crack of dawn and rushing around."

Austin's disappointment surprised Cord as it mirrored Ember's, their brows furrowing and their mouth setting in flat lines. Maybe it was wishful thinking on his part, or perhaps Austin was irritated Cord wasn't fully accommodating Ember. But actions spoke a whole lot louder than words and he needed to be more than a guest if they were really in this together—the three of them.

Austin wasn't the only one with pride, and while Cord could respect the man wanted to see Ember happy, he wasn't some token to be tucked away on the third floor. He'd rather keep separate territory as they moved forward than feel like an afterthought, a convenience. Fuck that.

If Austin wanted him there, he better damn well figure out how to show it and actually meet him in the fucking middle.

He stood and deliberately walked over to the

pair. They visibly tracked him and he didn't bother to shutter his gaze.

Bending, he took Ember's mouth, stealing her breath in a short, intense kiss. As he raised his head, he snatched a handful of Austin's hair to secure him in place, knowing his friend would never struggle with such a precious burden on his lap.

Relishing the firm lips beneath his, he ravished Austin's mouth, tasting the dark flavor of coffee, glorying in what he decided would be his. He didn't let up until he felt Austin's resistance give way to eagerness.

Satisfied, he released him and they all took a moment to breathe.

His days of settling for less than half were over. "I'll take a rain check."

Six

December

EMBER RACED out of the house and started the car, only to run back inside and grab her sewing bag. Why today, when she actually had an appointment with Eloise to go over her lesson plans for the quilting class, did she have to be so scattered? It was as if all the excitement from the past few days was catching up to her all at once.

Tossing her bag in the backseat, she threw the car in reverse, and then her cell rang. *Damn.* Her hand fished through her purse.

"Hello?"

"Why do you sound out of breath?" her husband greeted.

"I'm running late for a meeting with Eloise. It's just been one of those mornings."

His low chuckle was a soft rumble, soothing even from many miles away. "Well, take a breath and slow down. I thought your meeting wasn't for another half hour anyway."

Yes, and when something was important to her she had the tendency to be compulsively early. "Did you need something?"

Not that she meant to blow him off, but her husband had strict rules about using the phone while driving so she was idling at the edge of their driveway waiting for him to state the purpose of his call.

"You brushing me off?" His tone was teasing.

She sighed. "No, but I'm late—"

"Ember." The way he said her name, affectionately and accepting of her many idiosyncrasies, calmed her down enough to appreciate his thoughtfulness.

She let out a breath. Sometimes little tasks could overshadow what really mattered in life—like sharing a simple hello with a spouse. "Sorry. You're right. I'm rushing when I don't have to."

"I just called to wish you luck at your meeting and say hello."

And didn't that just throw everything into perspective? Her body relaxed and she smiled, no longer counting the passing seconds. "Hi."

"That's better. You know you got this, baby. They're the ones who asked you to teach, not the other way around. Enjoy it."

She appreciated his confidence and it bolstered hers. "Thank you."

"I also wanted to let you know not to make big plans for dinner. I'm probably working late again."

"Oh." She tried not to sound too disappointed. Overtime was great and, after such a long stint of no work at all, they could use the money. Plus, they now had a car payment to think about. "Okay."

"Depending on the time I clock out, I might have to go right to my meeting. Can you leave a plate out for me?"

She silently pouted. It was good to see him actively attending AA, but at the same time, it really put a pinch on their quality time during the week—or maybe it was the quantity time she was missing.

"Sure. But try to make it home before then. You need to eat."

Would he be meeting Harley after, carving out time for his friend before he even saw his wife? She stopped herself. She wasn't being fair. Harley was his sponsor. Their association came second to his marriage, but lately, their time together had the tendency to come before her.

She shook her head, again finding her thinking unfair. "I'll leave a plate in the microwave for you."

"Thanks, baby. I love you."

"Love you back."

"And good luck today. You got this."

When she reached the craft store she searched for Eloise and spotted her in the back, white hair pulled into a no-nonsense ponytail and wearing a green employee apron. After finishing up with a customer, Eloise went over Ember's lessons with her and reviewed the list of supplies she required the store to provide.

"This looks great. We already have six women signed up. One of them recognized your name."

Ember's head tilted. "Really? Who?"

"Um," Eloise reviewed the roster. "Gloria Winchester."

Ember grinned. "Oh, I know who she is. Her husband just remodeled her sewing room." She recalled her short time working at Bay's Hardware when she'd helped the older man select some finishing touches for the room. "She makes good pies."

"Well, she was thrilled to hear you were teaching. She might even bring some friends."

"Wonderful! I can't wait. And hopefully she brings a few pies, too," Ember joked.

She was nervous she might somehow let her students down, but everyone else seemed confident she was the woman for the job and that helped.

Leaving, she noticed a missed call from Cord and her belly fluttered with excitement. Rather than call him back, she decided to swing by the hardware store.

The lot was fairly empty this time of day, and she hoped he'd have a few minutes for her. As she stepped into the store she noted some new employees, Cord's college help home for the summer.

"Can I help you?" a man in his early twenties asked, dropping his task to come to her aide.

"I'm looking for Cord."

"Oh. He's probably in lumber. I could page him."

"That's okay. I know the way."

As she worked her way through the aisles, another employee stopped her, this one rather insistent on helping.

"Really, you don't have to escort me," she said, as he moved in close and slowed her down.

"It's no problem. So, are you from around here?"

"Yes." Somehow she doubted Cord had taught this sort of attentiveness in customer relations.

"Do you go to school?"

"No." Where was Cord? "I think I can make it on my own from here."

"My name's Leon, if you—"

"Ember?"

She smiled, happy—and a bit relieved—to see him. Cord's gaze drifted to her left and settled on Leon.

He scowled at the persistent employee. "Didn't I tell you to organize the grass seed display?"

"I was, but then I saw this pretty lady wandering around and offered my help."

Ember glanced away, rolling her eyes, trying to hide a smile.

"Get back to work," Cord all but barked. As Leon scuttled away, Cord's voice gentled. "I didn't know you were stopping by."

Her smile grew. "Neither did I. If this is a bad time—"

"Not at all." He glanced over his shoulder, no one in the aisle but the two of them. Leaning forward, he brushed a kiss on her lips. "I like when you visit."

"You called me, so I figured... I was nearby. What did you need?"

He rubbed the back of his neck and inspected the rafters. "I, uh, just wanted to hear your voice—say hello."

Twice in one day—and from her two favorite people. "Well, now you get to see me too. Have you had lunch yet?"

He glanced at his watch and frowned. "Damn. No time today. We're getting another shipment and I gotta make room before it gets here."

Another second occurrence. "Cord, you have to eat."

He smirked, and subtly hooked a finger around hers. "You worrying about me?"

"Always. Someone has to."

His smile widened as his blue eyes focused on hers. "Sweet December." He sighed. "I wish I could get away, but I can't. If I'm not here when the delivery arrives everything winds up stocked wrong."

"Will you be by for dinner tonight?"

"Am I invited?"

"Cord, you're always invited." She risked a tiny pout. "This is why we need to keep *talking*. One short discussion over coffee isn't going to be enough. We have a lot of ground to cover."

He held up his hands in mock surrender. "Relax, kiddo. We'll talk again. I know the discussion's far from over. I just like to check—for my own reassurance." He glanced at the shelves he'd been organizing. "So long as we get this inventory sorted out and put away, I should be there."

Should? She had a sudden image of herself having dinner alone, and it already tasted cold and unappealing. But she wasn't going to whine.

"Well, try to make it."

"Will do. I gotta get back to work." He again looked over his shoulder. Seeing they were still alone, he leaned in and kissed her, this time lingering and stealing a taste of her mouth. As he pulled away she found herself backed against the metal shelves.

"Damn," he rasped. "Now I *really* wish I had time to eat."

The darkening of his eyes enhanced the double entendre, and a shiver of arousal tickled up her spine. She gave his chest a playful shove, but he didn't budge. "Get back to work, Mr. Bay."

He nuzzled her throat, his warm lips finding her pulse as he murmured, "I wish I had a few minutes to fuck you. I'd take you right in the back—"

"Cord..." The edge of the rack pressing into her flesh reminded her they were in public.

He groaned and eased away. "It would take more than a few minutes anyway."

"I'll see you tonight for dinner," she managed to say, despite the inclination to tempt him right into that back room.

"I'll do my best." Grasping her shoulders, he turned her in the direction of the exit, giving her a smack on the butt as he nudged her to go.

She jumped. "Hey!"

He tugged her back, leaned into her, and murmured against her temple. "That's for the pout. I'll do my best to be there."

She left the store feeling exhilarated, and managed the rest of her errands efficiently. But her buoyant spirits crashed and burned when both

Austin *and* Cord called to confirm they would, in fact, be missing dinner.

She set a plate aside for Austin and took her dinner to the couch, mentally chastising herself for being so needy. She'd find a movie to watch and treat herself to a little girl time.

Her phone rang and she shoved her plate onto the coffee table, racing back to the kitchen, hoping it was one of her boys making an early escape from work. She caught it on the last ring.

"Hello?"

There was a long pause. "December?"

"Yes. Who's this?"

"Rob Garret."

Her shoulders lowered with the weight of something greater than disappointment. Austin's father only called when he wanted something. "Hi, Rob."

They hadn't spoken in such a long time. The man was so self-absorbed, so distant, she had never felt any familiarity. Hopefully, she could make this quick.

"Uh, Austin's at work."

"He's not picking up my calls."

"Oh. Okay."

All their conversations were awkward, this one no exception. Austin was obviously avoiding his father for good reason, though he hadn't shared his reasoning with her. It would've been nice to be warned his dad had resurfaced.

"Did you need to get a message to him?"

"I'm in your neck of the woods this weekend. Thought I'd stop by."

"Oh, I see." She cast about for an excuse that wouldn't be totally rude or make things worse.

"Just the one night. Got a guy who owes me money, and figured it's time to collect. He's getting married so he'll be sure to have the cash."

Wait, overnight? She panicked. "Um, we're kind of under construction here."

"I'm fine with the couch."

"Well—"

"You're acting like I'm not welcome in my son's house, missy. That boy of mine let you think you wear the pants over there?"

Austin and Cord tended to be highhanded males, but neither of them *ever* made her feel as small as this man could. She bit her tongue, because arguing with Rob Garret was pretty much as useless as arguing with a drunk. Even when he was sober, he had a nasty, over-critical disposition she found repellent. Besides, she'd rather take the brunt of his jabs to keep him from moving on to belittling Austin.

Keeping her voice deceptively calm, she asked, "When did you say you were coming?"

Rob gave her the date and she scribbled it on the notepad on the counter, underlining it absently, over and over. "Okay, I'll let Austin know. He can reach you at this number?"

"Yes."

"We'll see you then."

"Sure thing," he said, as if he were doing *them* some sort of favor.

The call ended and she set the phone down as the screen went black, worry gripping her belly. Rob drank. A lot. He'd had no time for his son once Austin's mother passed, and had turned to drinking, much like Austin turned to it when he lost his job.

Wiping a hand over her brow, she shook her head. It wasn't the same thing. Except it was. Her husband had abandoned her just as his father abandoned him.

It's not the same.

Gripping her throat, she swallowed against the lump building there and grimaced when it pained. Seeing Rob could set Austin off again. Their life was going good. Austin was sober. She swayed in place as if the rug were being tugged from a far corner, someone trying to pull it out from under her.

No. She wouldn't let that happen. They would face Rob's intrusion head on and not let this little bump throw them off their path. She just needed to figure out how to approach this, how to tell Austin. If Rob had been calling him and he'd been avoiding his calls, he likely suspected something was coming.

When she returned to her dinner her appetite was gone. Whatever was on the television didn't register, her mind tied up with foreboding about the upcoming visit.

Her fingers clenched over her damp palms as visions of previous visits flashed through her mind. Despite Rob's critical standpoints, there was one sure way of quelling his commentary. Alcohol.

No matter their differences, Austin and his father always found some sort of common ground once they drank enough to tolerate each other. But no amount of booze would ever wash away the animosity between them. Maybe Rob was so miserable because Austin reminded Rob of his wife, or maybe because the life Austin had was the life Rob never could sustain. It was anyone's guess.

She didn't care to psychoanalyze their damaged relationship. She focused on navigating this specific visit, knowing it would be hard on her and even harder on her husband, who never fared well when facing his father sober.

She should have told Rob no, been firm when speaking to him. It was Austin's right to refuse his dad, but not necessarily hers.

She desperately wanted to figure out a way to prevent him from coming, but that was impossible. Men like Rob cared only for themselves and not about the imposition they put on others.

Sighing, she glanced at the clock. Austin's meeting had already started and he wouldn't be home for at least two hours. She went back for her phone, her fingers dialing without a second thought.

"Hey, sexy. I was just thinking about you," Cord answered. "Sorry I missed dinner."

She wasn't in the state of mind for playful banter. "Rob's coming for a visit."

"Rob?"

"Austin's dad."

There was a long pause. "Fuck."

"I tried to talk him out of it, but you know how he is."

"Christ. Does Austin know?"

"I don't think so—at least not yet. Rob's been

trying to reach him. Austin hasn't been answering his calls." And her husband hadn't shared those attempts with her, either. Or with Cord, apparently.

"That's probably smart of him not to answer. Damn. This is going to stress the hell out of him."

"I know. Cord, every time he comes around, Austin drinks for days afterwards."

"Well… Shit. I can't say I blame him, kiddo, but things are different now."

Despite his optimism, there was more than a thread of concern in his tone. She pressed her face to her palm and groaned. "I hate this. Why does he have to visit now, of all times? You know how he gets. Austin's doing so good with everything. I don't want his father to set him back."

He sighed into the phone. "He's been handling everything else really well. Maybe he's better prepared for this than ever before. AA's helping him face a shitload of things from his past and he's sacrificed a lot to get here, kiddo. He's not going to give all of that up just because his dad pisses him off."

"That man belittles everything Austin does. Nothing's good enough for him and he hasn't accomplished half of what his son has."

"I know, sweetheart. He's a dick. But Austin's strong. He'll figure it out. We gotta stay positive."

"I'm afraid to even tell him. Just the thought of Rob showing up is stressful."

"You want me to break it to him?"

She actually considered it, but knew that was wrong. "No. I appreciate the offer, but I'll see him first. I don't want to keep it from him."

"Yeah. Best to give him as much heads-up as possible."

She sighed, fearing an overnight visit could turn into something more. Part of her wished she could camp out at Cord's while Rob was in town, but she couldn't leave Austin to deal with his presence alone.

Another thought occurred. "We'll have to be discreet when he's here."

"Hey, don't you worry about that. I know exactly the sort of small-minded prick Rob is. It's a shame, because I don't remember him being this bad when Mrs. Garret was alive. Either that, or he hid it really fucking well."

"Will you be here when he visits? I think having you close would help."

"Yeah. I can do that if it's what you both want."

"Thank you. Knowing you'll be close by makes him a little less intimidating."

"Hey, don't let him intimidate you. Men like him thrive on that crap. Just let whatever dumb shit that comes out of his mouth roll off your back."

That was easier said than done when the man made her feel like a subservient waste of space only there to freshen his beer. "He can't bring alcohol into the house. I won't have it."

Cord hummed, sounding like he might disagree. "Better talk to Austin about that. It might be easier for him to be around the stuff than to have his father know he's going to AA. I could see Rob picking at that wound and it's far from healed."

"Maybe you're right." She had so much to discuss with Austin and he wasn't going to be home for hours. "I wish he wasn't meeting Harley tonight."

"Well, that's his thing. If you don't talk to him tonight, cut out time for the conversation soon. If he gets home late, save it for tomorrow, but no later. He's going to need a few days to mentally prepare."

She stilled as she heard a car door open and close. "Where are you?"

He chuckled. "Digging the hidden key out of your flowers. It's buggy as shit out here. Wanna do me a favor and unlock the door?"

Excitement prickled through her body as she smiled and raced to the foyer, still clutching the phone to her ear. Her worry about Austin's father diminished significantly now she had Cord there to discuss her concerns in person. She twisted the deadbolt and pulled the door open.

Cord smiled. "Hey, beautiful." His voice echoed in the phone.

"Hey."

Their phones lowered as he crossed the threshold and kissed her soundly, the door swinging shut with a noteworthy snick.

The outside world barred, the two of them alone, she already felt the impact of his strength lending itself to her.

"So how about dinner?" he asked as he lowered her onto her feet. He smelled of summer and hard work.

"I have a sandwich all ready for you." She led him to the living room and handed him her plate.

"Were you going to eat this?"

"I'm not hungry."

"Ember."

"Eat it, Cord. Otherwise it'll go to waste."

He hesitated, but took a bite then groaned. "Even your sandwiches taste better than mine."

He settled onto the couch and she curled into his side, glad for the physical support when her emotions were so rattled. As he took the last bite, he placed the plate on the table and eased back, wrapping his arm around her shoulders.

"What were you watching?"

"Nothing. I just put it on for background noise."

He tipped his chin and eyed her. "Hey. No more stressing. We'll figure everything out." His lips pressed to her hair.

It was strange how right it felt to be in his arms, how natural, as if he'd been by her side for years. There was nothing sexual about the way he held her, yet his hold was completely possessive. She edged closer and rested her head on his chest.

"You're a good pillow."

"Glad to be of service." He stretched and reached for the remote. "We're not watching this."

As he flipped through the channels, her tension eased and she closed her eyes. "This is nice, having you here like this."

He sighed, resting his cheek on her head. "It is nice."

He put on some hunting show and her mind settled. His heart thumped steadily, hypnotically, and she dozed off. Groggy, her mind stirred, sensing movement and she realized she was being carried up the stairs—but not by Cord.

"Austin?" His familiar bulk was easily recognized, and the way he held her was different from Cord's hold, but possessive all the same.

"Shh...go back to sleep, baby."

She yawned into this shoulder. "Where's Cord?"

"He just left."

"What time is it?"

"Almost midnight."

She frowned. His meeting was usually over at nine. "Are you just getting home?"

"Yeah. We had a few others join us at the diner and wound up talking. Lost track of time."

He deposited her in their bed and stripped her with easy familiarity. She obliged, lifting her arms to facilitate the removal of her shirt and hitched up her bottom so he could tug off her jeans and underwear. Sliding off her bra, she added it to the pile of garments in his arms.

Drawing the covers up to her chest, he said, "I'm gonna shower. I'm still in my work clothes."

Though she was tired and only half aware, nothing blunted the envy she felt that he'd spent the entire night with his friends from AA. Usually they made love after his meetings, and talked, but it was too late for that now. The contentment she'd experienced while cuddled with Cord ebbed away.

The shower kicked on and she frowned at the light shining under the bathroom door. She would wait before telling him about his dad's impending visit. Better to talk about it when she was wide-awake and he didn't have a full day of work ahead.

Worrying about his father would only keep him up and it was already after midnight.

Settling into the pillows, she decided to ask Cord to be there when she broke the news. It was amazing how much easier that made the dreaded task of telling Austin about his dad seem.

Seven

December

MORNING ARRIVED, and with it a mad rush to get Austin out the door on time for work. Her worry about Austin's father kept waking her and then they'd both overslept. After getting his promise to be home on time for dinner tonight, Ember put extra effort into making a nice supper, Austin's favorite—roasted potatoes, turkey and the special stuffing he loved.

Once he had a full stomach, and Cord there for support, she'd tell Austin about his father's plan to visit. The menu would surely make the news more palatable.

As she moved the sides into the oven to keep warm, she visited the bedroom to freshen up. The front door opened as soon as she applied a little blush to her cheeks, which seemed paler than usual.

"Ember?"

She went to the top of the stairs, catching Austin still removing his boots. "Hi."

He smiled up at her. "Dinner smells good. I'm starved."

Trying to maintain a natural level of calm, she greeted him with a kiss and carried his boots to the coat closet. "Busy day?"

"Long day."

"Well, dinner should be ready as soon as Cord gets here."

"Hey." He caught her wrist as she moved to enter the kitchen. "How was *your* day?"

Her gaze had a hard time meeting his. "My day was fine."

The corner of his mouth pulled into a half smirk. "When's Cord getting here?"

"Probably in a few—" She stilled and they both laughed as gravel crunched in the driveway. "That's probably him now."

"Good. Let's eat." He brushed a kiss on her lips before releasing her arm, and she went to check on the food in the oven.

Cord came in and kept to the outskirts of the kitchen, probably taking a moment to process that he was welcome. He slowly walked to her, dropping a kiss on her mouth much like her husband had done.

"Hey, beautiful."

Small gestures like that soothed her heart, reminding her she had so much to be grateful for. "Hi."

He leaned his weight onto the counter and eyed her husband. "Austin."

"Hey, man."

Cord scooted out of her way and settled in at the kitchen table. "Good day?"

"The usual. You?"

Cord nodded. "Busy."

"Busy's always good." Their conversation circled the way hers and Austin's did, nice, natural, and at home with one another.

"One of you want to slice the turkey?"

"I'll do it," Cord offered and she handed him the knife as she carried the sides out to the dining room table.

"Roasted potatoes and turkey... Is it my birthday?" Austin asked as he followed her to the other room and eyed the serving dishes.

"I just thought it would be nice to treat you. You've been working so much lately."

He sent her a sweet smile that told her he appreciated her thoughtfulness. Cord carried the main course to the table. "Dinner's served."

As she plated, she caught Cord watching her, his expression giving away that a long conversation was on the menu. She flashed him a look, hoping he understood she wanted to get through a peaceful meal first.

"Why's everyone so quiet?" Austin asked, taking the first bite.

She fumbled for a response. "Just thinking about my quilting class."

"How's that going?" Cord asked.

"Well, it hasn't officially started yet, but we're getting close. I'm excited. Mrs. Winchester's going to be one of my students."

"You had her husband eating out of your hand when you worked in the store."

Austin's head snapped up and he studied both of them before he smiled. "I bet you're having a hard time filling her shoes, eh, Cord?"

"I wouldn't say that," she protested. The bite of potatoes stuck in her throat as she fretted over the need to tell him about his father's call.

"She was the best. A natural," Cord insisted. He pointed his knife in Austin's direction, and slanted her a telling look. "She's great at anything she attempts."

The air crackled with innuendo and her cheeks heated, inducing even more guilt for wasting time when she had something so important to tell her husband. Austin and Cord exchanged smoldering glances and she hated that she had to spoil the playful atmosphere.

After clearing the table she brought out coffee. Austin didn't know, but she'd started mixing the dark roast with half decaf, thinking no one should have that much caffeine. He didn't seem to notice and she figured his coffee habit was more about ritual than anything else.

Cord sent her a speaking glance and she hesitated, her brain struggling to find the best words to deliver bad news.

"Coffee's good, Em."

Better to just come out with it. "I spoke to your father yesterday."

Austin stilled. He slowly placed his mug on the table and folded his hands. "He call your cell?"

"I wouldn't have answered if I'd known it was him." *Why didn't you tell me he was trying to get ahold of you?*

Austin's shoulders twitched with a silent, humorless laugh. "What'd he have to say, aside from his usual bitching?"

"He's, um, coming for a visit. Next Saturday."

Her husband's mouth firmed into a flat line as he turned to glare out the window.

"It's just an overnight visit I think."

Silence stretched and Cord was the first to break it. "You okay, man?"

Austin shook his head. "Fucking figures."

They all knew this visit would be a stressful nightmare, but no matter how poorly her father-in-law treated her, Austin would always take the brunt of his criticism.

"I tried to get him to go to a hotel."

"That must have gone over well."

"I got a *missy* out of it and a stern reminder that this was *your* house." She tried to laugh to ease the sting.

Her husband's scowl darkened. "He shouldn't speak to you like that. This is *our* fucking house. He's lucky he's even allowed through the front door."

She flinched at his tone, but quickly recovered, knowing he wasn't angry with her. "I lied and told him we were doing renovations. Is it possible to make it look like we are?"

Austin scoffed. "Let him see the house the way it is. Maybe he'll get the hint we don't want him here."

"Hey, he's still your dad, Austin," Cord reminded gently. "We all have stress when it comes to parents."

"Forgive me if I don't think your mom's reminders that you wash the dirt out from under your nails is exactly on par with my dad's steady fucking barrage of put downs. Excuse me." He stood and stalked from the room.

The screen door slammed a moment later.

"Well, that went about as good as I expected," Cord commented.

"I should go talk to him." She massaged her temples.

He tossed his napkin on the table. "Let me." As he rose to leave he paused and came to her side and pressed his lips into her hair. "We'll get him through it. It's only a day, kiddo."

"I know. But that man... I hate him, hate the things he says to Austin."

"Me too, sweetheart. Me too."

She flattened her arms over her chest and sighed. "Try to talk to him. I'm going to clean up the kitchen and go work in the garden for a bit before the sun goes down. My mind needs a break."

"I got it covered. Go to your garden. I'll take care of the dishes."

That made her laugh. "Yeah, right."

He smiled. "I know. I almost couldn't say it with a straight face."

It wasn't that Cord couldn't do dishes, but she'd seen his kitchen. The man had science projects growing in his sink because he let things sit so long. "Go."

He hesitated. "Tell me you love me."

Rising from her seat, she kissed his chin. "To a fault. Now go talk to him."

Eight

Cord

CORD WALKED onto the front porch and found Austin standing on the top step, his back stiff. "Hey."

"Hey," he replied, without turning. "Sorry about the crack I made about your mom. I was angry."

"No harm." He stepped beside him, mimicking his posture. "I know your dad's a pain in the ass. I shouldn't have tried to push you to acknowledge him."

"Is Ember upset?"

"She's worried about you. So am I."

He shook his head and let out a long breath. "I don't want him here, in this house."

"I think that's a universal sentiment."

Austin scoffed. "I can already hear him coming down on me about every little fucking thing. *That molding needs touching up. When you gonna get a new truck? You'd think you'd have better furniture by now...*" His head bowed, posture already defeated. "He's relentless."

"You can't take it personally, Austin. He's a miserable man. He's like that with everyone."

"Not like he is with me. And what fucking business does he have speaking to my wife that way?" His jaw noticeably clenched. "I want to throttle him when he uses that tone with her. I don't even have to hear it to know exactly how he spoke to her. I've heard it enough. It's demeaning and she doesn't deserve it."

"So tell him that."

"I have. He treats her like she's somehow beneath me, beneath him. What a joke. It's infuriating the way he sees her. And I know his words fucking bother her even if she's too kind to do more than smile back."

"I know. It's his loss he never took the time to get to know Ember. If he did, he'd see how wrong he is about her."

"He just sees her as this... It's like he thinks she's Rona. Ember's *nothing* like her mother."

Cord didn't comment because although he'd met Ember's parents once, he didn't really know them. But he'd heard enough to draw a decent conclusion. They weren't bad people, just different. Hippies. Drifters. Pot heads.

"I should go talk to her. She's probably freaking out."

"She's okay. She's out back in the garden. If anything, she's worried about how you'll handle the visit."

"I'll be fine. It is what it is."

As much as Cord wanted to believe that, he couldn't. Austin's track record with his father was a volatile timeline of explosive arguments fueled by alcohol.

Cord might have tried to sound optimistic for Ember's sake, but truth to be told, he was fucking worried. "Whatever happens, you know we're here for you. We'll work through it. We're in this together, Austin."

His friend shook his head and turned toward the door. "I can't think about that right now."

Cord frowned, following him inside the house. "What does that mean?"

Austin reached to where his keys hung, and Cord didn't like the sketchy look in his eyes. "It means one thing at a fucking time."

"Hey, don't take this out on me. I'm trying to help you."

"Then back off! I need everyone to just back the fuck off for a second so I can think."

Catching him by the front of his shirt, Cord yanked him close, hopefully rattling him enough to jerk him out of whatever mindset he was entering. "Don't do this, man. He's not even here yet and he's already getting in your head. Fuck him. You hear me? He's nobody. I will not let you backtrack because of that asshole."

"Get off." Austin shoved at his fist, but Cord didn't budge.

They faced off, breathing hard as they scowled at each other. "You want her to see you like this?" Cord growled. "She's who you should be worried about, what *she* thinks, not your fucking dad."

"You think I don't know that?"

"Then stop letting him get to you. His opinion's worth shit. Your private life is none of his business, you hear me?"

Austin nodded, a short, sharp inclination of his head that conveyed his agitation. His golden brown eyes reflected his tension.

As his body relaxed by degrees, Cord leaned his head against Austin's. Saturday couldn't come soon enough.

His friend sighed. "I have to get going."

Cord's shoulders knotted as he considered the time. His meeting wasn't for another hour, so why the fuck was he in such a rush to leave?

Playing it cool, he whispered, "You got time."

Austin twisted out of his grip, this time earning himself some distance. His fingers once again curled around his keys and his features took on that worried, desperate look. No denying he was up to something.

Cord tried to hide his worry. "This what you want? To run?"

"Fuck, Cord. *Enough!*"

Grabbing him by the shoulder, Cord abruptly shoved Austin's back against the wall, a picture frame rattling against the sheetrock. He got in his face and growled, "We. Don't. Run."

"I'm not *running*. I'm pissed off!"

"Then hit something. You want to blow off steam? I'm right here."

His friend shoved his chest hard, but Cord held his footing. Austin's nostrils flared as he glared all his frustration at Cord. "Back. Off."

"Make me."

Fire flashed in Austin's eyes as he audibly drew in a draught of air. His muscular frame coiled, but Cord was ready for him. The moment he lunged, Cord shoved back, slamming his mouth over Austin's, tasting his rage, sampling his despair.

"Show me how tough you are," Cord demanded, before forcing his tongue into Austin's mouth.

Hand clutching the back of Cord's head, pulling hard at his hair, Austin took over the kiss. The amount of fury unleashed under the veil of passion was more than he'd been prepared for, but Cord was determined to take whatever his friend needed to dish out.

Austin surged forward, practically pile driving him into the adjacent wall. More picture frames rattled and shifted with the impact of their bodies.

Austin's hard body ground against his, demanding, almost punishing, as he deepened the kiss. As good as it was, Cord couldn't lose the upper hand—not when it came to this.

He jerked open his belt and caught Austin's wrist, shoving his hand into his pants. Grip closing over his cock, Austin squeezed hard.

Cord grunted, "That a boy."

"Shut the fuck up," Austin growled, shoving his

tongue back into his mouth as he roughly stroked Cord's engorged flesh with firm tugs.

Cord broke the kiss and threw his head back against the wall, panting. "Fuck."

Austin's body shifted, followed by the clank of metal and the rasp of a zipper. He grabbed Cord's hand and shoved it on his own cock. "You too."

Cord pulled back, but then gave in. Hot, smooth skin filled his palm as his fingers circled Austin's thickness. Breath stuttered into his lungs as he tried to process the continuing novelty of touching Austin this way.

He shuddered, a fantasy come true, and fought the sudden need to come.

"Do it," Austin growled against his lips.

Cord shook off his shock and worked his hand in rough pulls, marking the swelling veins and flared tip beneath his touch, etching the feel of Austin into his brain.

"That's it."

As he increased his efforts, passing his thumb over the slit to smear the moisture gathered there, Austin moaned and Cord's hips hitched of their own accord. Their cocks touched and they both froze.

Cord looked into Austin's eyes, all aggression leaving his body in a whoosh.

He loved him.

He'd loved him for so long and keeping that secret had been the burden of his life. Then he'd gone and fallen for his wife, too. His heart was so full his chest ached, so much love to share.

Jesus, he could barely breathe with so many

emotions so close to the surface. Lifting his other hand, he cupped Austin's hard jaw. Faint stubble abraded the heel of his palm as he stared into his friend's familiar eyes.

He no longer cared if Austin had the balls to say it. Cord was done keeping secrets. "I love you, Austin."

His friend's gaze shifted away and he released Cord's dick, sending a sharp and painful hit to his heart, which felt completely unprotected at the moment.

He should walk away, say *fuck you*, and go find Ember to ease his pain, but something held him there. This was about *them* and he'd be damned if he let Austin fall into another pit of denial.

That's what love was—pushing for truth and honesty even when it hurt. Something they were all learning. So much of what he did was for the man he loved.

Tightening his grip on his cock, Cord slid his other hand to the side of Austin's neck, his thumb pressing into the hollow of his throat, tipping his head back. He forced Austin to hold eye contact.

"This is where we are. *No one* is going to take this away from us unless you let them." He drew his hand along Austin's swelling cock in a slow, long stroke. "The only people who can call quits on us is Ember, me, or *you*. Is that what you want?"

Austin's breath huffed between them as his chest pumped.

"Is it?" Cord gripped Austin's dick a little harder.

"No," he gritted. "No."

Relief—and joy—suffused Cord's entire body. "Good." He jerked him, hard and rapidly, squeezing and working the sensitive underside of his cock.

Austin grunted, his knees buckling as his weight leaned heavily into Cord. "Fuck. *Fuck.*"

"We'll get to that. "

As though his promise unleashed his need, Austin swallowed back an unmistakable groan of pleasure. Shoulders jerking, his breath beat a ragged tattoo against Cord's neck as wet heat coated his hand, Austin's cock pulsing in his grip. He wrapped his arm around his best friend, holding him tight with unspoken love and comfort.

Lips pressing against the stubble on his throat, Cord whispered. "You're a good man, Austin. You don't need him to acknowledge that for it to be true."

Austin buried his face deeper in Cord's shoulder, letting out a jagged breath, as Cord's strong arms held them immobile. They stood together for an eternity before slowly easing apart. Silently, once they each had their emotions under control, they adjusted their clothing.

Hopefully, he'd gotten through Austin's thick skull and proved he wasn't giving up on this without a fight. Nor would he let his friend give up on himself.

Nine

Austin

AUSTIN'S FINGERS twitched with the continual urge to reach for something that wasn't there as he sat on the porch swing and watched the edge of the road. Ember was inside, already putting forth too much effort for the unappreciative asshole's stay, and he hated the thought of her lifting even a finger to make his father feel welcome.

The screen door opened and she peeked her head out. "I picked up some fresh cherries from the market today. Want some?"

"No, I'm good."

She nodded, obviously sensing his mood, and slipped back inside.

"Ember?"

"Yeah?" She peeked out again.

"I'd love some cherries."

Her smile reached her eyes as she disappeared into the house, returning a moment later with a bowl of ripe, red berries. They actually helped—gave him something to occupy his hands.

His eyes narrowed as he returned his focus to the road. When he saw a car with a mismatched fender barreling closer, he knew it was his father.

He placed the bowl of half-eaten cherries on the swing and spit a pit over the rail as he stood. "Let's get this over with," he mumbled, braced for anything.

As the car rumbled up the drive, Ember stepped onto the porch. She stood beside him, her fingers wringing in her apron. Austin reached for her hand so they'd both overcome the urge to fidget.

The engine shut off and his father painstakingly unfolded his frame from the vehicle. Though the haircut was the same, the faded khakis and equally faded shirt familiar, age had crept up and left him jarringly changed.

Deep lines cut between his nose and the corners of his mouth and his skin looked leathery in the fading sunlight. Grey had overtaken the brown of his hair, and white stubble dotted his jaw where the razor had missed.

His arms folded over each other, resting on the roof of the car as he made an open inspection of their house. His disparaging sigh was easily heard. "Looks about the same."

"Dad."

His gaze finally settled on the two of them.

"Austin." He glanced at December and her hand tightened around his. "December."

He slammed the car door and ambled around to pop the trunk, but didn't reach inside. Making a slow trek up the porch steps he raised a brow. "Bags aren't gonna carry themselves."

December stepped aside and threw him an uncomfortable glance. His father walked through the front door as if he owned the place.

"I'll get the bags," Austin mumbled. The old man's arthritis aside, he never did for himself if Austin was around.

As she pulled open the screen, Ember asked, "Can I get you anything, Rob? Some sweet tea or some coffee?"

"I'll take a beer."

Austin's shoulders tensed and he shook his head, hefting the bags out of the car. "So it begins," he mumbled, looking forward to the moment he could put the bags back in the trunk.

Dumping the luggage in the foyer, he met Ember's stare and read her panic. His father was already making himself at home on the couch.

"What channels do you got here?" He glanced over his shoulder. "Missy, I thought I sent you for a beer."

"We don't have any beer, Rob." She brushed at the front of her apron and shifted awkwardly.

Austin grit his teeth. "How about some coffee, Dad?"

"How about you run to the store and grab your old Dad a six-pack? You knew you had company coming. Shouldn't the little wife have made preparations?"

Ember scoffed and turned on her heel, fleeing to the kitchen. Cabinets slammed and Austin silently counted to ten. "Have a little respect. You're in *my* house after all."

His father turned and lifted a brow as if his request was some sort of a challenge. Austin already decided not to pussyfoot around him this weekend.

"If you can't speak to my wife with respect then you're gonna have to stay somewhere else."

His father laughed, an ugly sound, devoid of humor. "She tell you to say that?"

He took a step forward and halted, unsure if he lost his temper he'd ever be able to retrieve it. "You've been warned." Pivoting, he went to check on Ember.

She was stacking plates and cups in an already organized cupboard while coffee percolated.

"You okay?"

"Oh, fine," she answered, tone ripe with sarcasm. The counter was covered with the canisters she used for baking.

"You're still cooking?" He wished she'd relax a little so he could calm his own nerves.

"I'm making a pie, Austin. That way I can keep my hands busy and not strangle your father."

As she picked through a bushel of apples, plucking off each stem, he stepped behind her and wrapped his arms around her, pressing his lips to the top of her head.

"I love you. He'll be gone tomorrow, hopefully sooner than later. Bake as many pies as you need."

Her head tipped to his shoulder and she sighed. "He's infuriating."

"I know."

"I mean, the way he just expects everyone to wait on him."

Well, of course. He was Rob Garret. Sometimes Austin really missed his mother. December would have liked her. And his mom would have loved Ember.

"The countdown's on, baby. Let me go see how he's making out. I'm sure he's already got a list of things he wants to bring to my attention."

"Austin..."

He paused at the door.

Her face pinched and he knew this was one of those moments where if his wife used swearwords she'd be letting them fly. "Don't give him an inch."

He chuckled, his resolve firming. "I won't."

When he returned to the den he checked his phone. Cord had already texted him twice asking how it was going. He tucked his phone away.

"Did you find something to watch?"

"What kind of money are you paying for this cable? You have a shitty selection of channels."

Because things are still a little tight. "We aren't big television watchers."

"What the hell else is there to do around here?" He tossed the remote aside.

"Shouldn't you be getting dressed for that wedding?" If the old man got going, maybe he'd stay out late, sleep in, and be on his way.

His father frowned. "These are good pants."

He refused to argue, though there was plenty to

say about the wrinkled slacks. "What time's your friend's wedding start?"

His father shrugged. "Dunno. I'll make it there eventually."

Austin appraised his clothes again. "Dad, were you even invited to this wedding?"

"Garry's owed me money for over a decade. That's my invitation."

Unbelievable. "So you're gonna crash the wedding? Ruin it?"

"I'll just take my money and leave. Once I'm paid there'll be no cause for a scene."

Appalled, he scoffed. "It's the guy's *wedding day*."

His father shrugged. "Seen one, you've seen them all. Besides, it's his second wedding."

"You're shameless."

"What the hell do I have to be ashamed of? Garry should be ashamed, skipping out on a debt the way he did. We used to be friends."

Funny, this was the first time Austin was hearing of the guy.

Something clattered in the kitchen followed by a muffled cry. Austin jumped to his feet. His father grumbled something, but he was already halfway to his wife.

"Ember?" Some sort of smeary, yellowish shit was all over the counter. She cradled her hand to her chest, her face pinched with pain as Austin crossed the kitchen in two strides. "Shit, what happened?"

"I wasn't paying attention."

"Let me see."

Supporting her arm, she slowly showed him. "It's not bad."

"Jesus, did you burn yourself?" A distinct red mark marred her skin.

"A little. I was setting the filling to simmer and an apple started to roll off the counter. I must have knocked the pot over trying to save the apple."

"Here, run it under cold water and I'll get some vinegar." As he turned the faucet to a soft flow, he caught his dad standing in the doorway of the kitchen.

"You burn yourself, missy?"

"Not now, Dad." He found the jug of white vinegar in the pantry and returned to the sink.

"What the hell are you doing with that?" his dad barked. "That'll burn the shit out of her."

"No, it won't. I know what I'm doing. Hold your arm over the sink."

"I'm tellin' you. Get ready to scream, missy."

Ember pulled her arm back and he grit his teeth. He didn't need his father terrifying her. It was obvious the burn was already hurting and they needed to get something on it. He knew there was a painkiller in vinegar as well as antiseptic.

Keeping his voice low, he asked, "Who are you going to believe, baby, me or him? I won't hurt you. Trust me."

She slowly nodded and extended her arm, the dark splotch of raw skin already a angry shade of pink. "I trust you."

He doused her arm and she noticeably relaxed as the vinegar eased the burn. "Better?"

"Yes. Thank you."

Her shoulders trembled as she let out a jagged breath and he kissed her forehead. "I'll put some on a cloth for you. Go sit down."

As she sat, his father drifted closer and inspected her arm. A decent person would be sympathetic.

"This your first time in a kitchen, missy?" He chuckled. "Better get her into some cooking classes, Austin."

Austin slammed the drawer. "Get out. She's hurt and doesn't need your comments or crappy jokes. Five minutes and I've already reached my limit. Go find your money and bug someone else."

His father raised a brow. "Temperamental as a woman. I tell you, you didn't inherit that from me."

Austin shot him a look that said his rescinded welcome wasn't up for negotiation and thankfully the man left.

"Pain in my fucking ass," he grumbled as he crouched in front of Ember with a vinegar-drenched rag. "How's it feel now?" He gently pressed the saturated cloth against her arm and looked into her eyes, surprised to see her grinning. "What?"

Her smile overshadowed the pinched expression masking her pain. "I'm proud of you."

He rolled his eyes. "Don't be proud of me. How's your arm? Still hurt?"

Her fingers closed over his and squeezed. "I know he'll be back, but I'm glad you stood up to him. He's a tyrant."

"Not in our house. Not anymore." He'd had enough and he'd come too far to let one shitty part of his past take him backward.

Cord's words played in his head. *You're a good man, Austin. You don't need him to acknowledge that for it to be true.*

Ember wrapped her arm in the cloth and made to stand. "I'm going to cover the dough up, put it in the fridge for later."

"You sit. I'll do it."

He covered the pie plate with plastic wrap and found a place for it in the fridge, then tackled the mess on the counter. After a few minutes, she joined him, and they cleaned up side by side, working in comfortable silence.

"Dinner will be ready soon," she said. "We should have asked Cord."

"Do you want a hand?"

"I'll take your company, but I think I can manage. The vinegar took the sting away. What about Cord?"

"I know he said he'd be here if we need him, but I can handle my dad." It was important to him that she trusted that.

She smiled widely, the corners of her eyes creasing. "I know you can."

Austin fished his cell out of his pocket. His thumb moving rapidly over the keyboard, as he texted Cord that everything was under control.

Surprisingly, Cord proved to be a man of few words—the right words.

Good. I know you can
handle him.

. . .

The brevity of that response, his friend's faith, felt like a warm, loving hand laid flat on his chest.

"You tell him things are okay?"

"Yup. Let's have a quiet meal before my meeting, just the two of us. And I'll skip the coffee tonight."

His mind wasn't on the meeting. The thought that his old man might get home before AA ended worried the shit out of him. This was one night he should have skipped his meeting altogether. Except it was also the sort of night he really needed to go.

Happy to keep his wife company, they forgot about their unwelcome houseguest and chatted while she prepared dinner. Afterward, he did the dishes and she dried, but soon enough she prompted him to head off to his meeting. He was still reluctant to leave her in the house alone when his dad could suddenly reappear, but she also seemed to think this was one meeting he couldn't miss.

As he kissed her goodbye, he told her to call Cord if she needed anything while he was gone, a gentle reminder that she didn't have to put up with his father alone, should he return. The meeting was a little over an hour and not quite the reaffirmation Austin was hoping for, but it never really was. He took more away from his talks with Harley at the diner, but tonight of all nights he couldn't swing the extra time.

When he declined Harley's invitation for coffee, he noted his sponsor's raised brow. It was no secret to Harley that Austin's father was in town.

He gripped Austin's arm as he made for the church door, slowing him down. "How are things going?" Harley asked, scrutinizing him with a sharp look.

"Good." Austin spoke the expected response, although it was foreign in this setting. He didn't have to hide. "Actually, our *company* arrived this afternoon and I don't want to leave Ember to deal with it. Him."

Harley patted his shoulder. "Then head on out. I'll see you tomorrow. And Austin?"

Austin looked back to find Harley's stare again assessing and a hint of worry around his mouth. "Yeah?"

"You have my number."

Jesus, did he look that bad? He patted his wallet. "I do."

"Good."

He left the meeting, drawing additional comfort from Harley's reminder that he could call at any time. Pulling into the driveway, he pretended his hands weren't shaking from the relief brought on by the sight of only Ember's Jeep parked there.

Ember greeted him at the door and he immediately relaxed, pulling her close and kissing away the lines of worry between her brows. He wasn't going to let his father influence this moment. "Let's watch a movie."

As they expected, his father did eventually return. He stumbled in around midnight waking both him and Ember on the couch where they'd passed out cuddled together.

"He's drunk," Ember hissed.

Austin stood, the stench of whiskey wafting off his father from several feet away. "Go upstairs, Ember."

She hesitated and he sensed she didn't want to leave him alone with Rob, but he wasn't going to expose her to this.

"*Now!*" he barked, not wanting her to see what unfolded.

She eyed his father as she kept to the perimeter of the room and then hurried up the steps. His father, though swaying, watched her with an appreciative leer only a pervert could master.

"Hate to see her go, but love to watch her leave. At least you got it right in the looks department."

Austin's labored breath came at a measured pace. "What the hell is wrong with you?"

His father squinted at him and scoffed. "You're one to talk." He stumbled into the den and collapsed on the couch, stretching out and groaning.

Austin stared at him for a long moment, thinking back to a time when his father seemed like a giant in his eyes. Now he was just a miserable, washed up nobody. Ember was right. He was a tyrant.

"This is the last time you come here without an invitation."

His dad waved away his words. "Go see to your wife."

"I mean it," he growled. "You come in here, barking orders, expecting to be waited on hand and foot. You demean my wife just by looking at her. That's it. I want you gone first thing in the morning."

"Ingrate."

Austin stilled, one foot in the hall, and spun on his heel. "*I'm* an ingrate? *What the hell have you ever given me?* I've worked for everything I own! This house is mine. The couch you're sleeping on is mine. I've never asked you for a single thing! Not even the home you sold without ever giving me a chance to buy it or at least collect my things."

"Oh, boo hoo. Austin wants his mommy's house back."

His fists clenched so tight his knuckles popped. "*She* should have lived. It should've been you in her place." He shook his head, disgusted. "You're not even living. You're just scheming one day to the next, blaming everyone else for your problems."

His father twisted, angling up on one arm, his face ruddy and flushed. "You think you know what problems are, boy? You don't have a fucking clue!"

He had more than a clue. It wasn't about being better or having it easier, it was about having the integrity to try, the fucking dignity to want to be a better person for those you loved. He'd learned that lesson in the hardest way possible and wasn't about to unlearn it.

Nor was he about to waste his breath trying to enlighten some small-minded asshole linked to him only by DNA. "First thing in the morning, you're gone."

He hit the light and went upstairs. There were plenty of wrongs he had to right, but his father wasn't his mistake. He was simply toxic, and like a cancer, it felt good to cut him out of his life once and for all.

Ten

Austin

DESPITE HIS SATISFACTION about setting some long overdue ground rules with his father, Austin couldn't sleep. Ember had been tucked up tightly beneath the covers when he entered their room, her little body chilled when he'd stripped and climbed in beside her.

"Is everything okay?" she whispered.

"It's fine. Try to get some sleep, baby."

"Your dad—"

"Will be gone in the morning." He kissed her temple and pulled her close.

It soothed him that she actually drifted off, feeling safe enough in his embrace to let go of her worry. But his eyes remained open, his brain playing over destructive memories of the past and trying to see far enough into the future to know he'd made the right decision in cutting his only living parent off.

By dawn, his mind rested somewhere on the edge of sleep and his body was more tense than the night before.

"Morning." Ember shifted up on an elbow and peered down at him, worry darkening her eyes and creasing her brow.

He winced, thinking of how she'd asked if things were all right the night before. Was *he* all right? Even now he wasn't sure. "Morning, baby."

"Your father's leaving?"

"First thing," he reminded. "Or at least as soon as he sleeps off his hangover."

She sank into the covers but didn't cuddle close. She seemed distant since he'd snapped at her to go upstairs.

"I'm sorry for being so...firm last night," he apologized.

"You kind of scared me. Not you, but the way you spoke. I didn't want you to fight with him."

"I wasn't going to expose you to him for one more second."

He didn't need her to have his back. Of course she would, but he needed to prove—for his own peace of mind—that he could protect her from a tyrant in their home, even when that tyrant was sometimes him.

He hadn't wanted Cord over for the same reason. These were *his* demons. His battles to fight.

"Okay." Her voice held uncertainty.

Rolling to his side, he tugged her into his arms

and stroked her back, until he sensed her relaxing. He hadn't chased her out of the living room last night to hurt her. It was the opposite, his promise to always protect her.

But he did wonder if she'd forgiven him for his abrupt order. He rarely raised his voice like that since he'd stopped drinking.

"You're the most important thing in my world, Ember. I'm not letting anyone or anything mess that up. Ever." That included him, but he didn't think that needed saying. "Rob won't be coming back unless invited."

She sighed, and turned her body to face him. "You didn't have to take him on by yourself, Austin. I'm your wife, your partner—in all things."

But he did. She should understand that. He forced a smile. "I'm gonna head down and see him out. Why don't you take a bath? I know this sort of tension in the house is tough on you. Then we'll have breakfast. Or we could go out."

"Sure." She sat up, holding the covers to her breasts.

If it wasn't for the unwelcome guest downstairs, Austin might have spent the morning an entirely different way. With a grimace, he climbed out of the bed and searched for his jeans.

Ember watched him, dark eyes solemn. He buckled his belt, leaving his shirt to hang loose outside his pants, then dropped one knee on the mattress.

"C'mere."

She leaned toward him and he tucked two fingers under her chin. "I love you, December."

She returned his kiss and the roiling in his gut eased considerably.

Making no attempt to soften his footsteps, he went downstairs. Bracing to fight with a parent was like going into battle but forsaking all armor. Should he ever consider therapy, he'd need someone with a big ass couch.

His father was sprawled on his back, mouth open, snoring loudly. Austin winced at the familiar stale stench of booze in their home.

Not wanting to touch him, he kicked the side of the sofa. "Hey."

With a snort, Rob shifted a little. Austin kicked the leg of the couch again. "Get up."

"What?" Blurry-eyed and frowning, his father hoisted himself upward and scowled.

"Time for you to go."

"I'll go when I'm ready," his father grumbled.

"You're ready now." He grabbed his father's bags, stuffing some clothing hanging outside the zipper back into the depths of his suitcase. "I'll put these in your car."

Rob mumbled obscenities under his breath, but reached for his shoes, as Austin toed into his boots resting in the foyer. On second thought, he remained inside. No way was his father getting out of his sight while Ember was in the house.

"You're a fine son." Sarcasm dripped like poison.

"And you're father of the year." It took an effort not to roll his eyes, their schoolyard trash talk so fucking stupid. He wasn't going there.

Keys jingled as Rob studied him. "You're really kicking me out of your house."

"There's been no kicking—yet."

"I raised you better."

He bit his tongue. *Not going there.*

Every second the man wasted in the powder room grated on Austin's fraying nerves. At his gesture, his father preceded him through the front door to his vehicle, stomping every step of the way, small clouds of dust rising from the gravel.

Austin tossed the bags in the backseat. They faced off, nothing but bad blood between them, and tension crackled in the air.

"Drive safe," Austin finally said, and turned back to the house.

"Like you care."

Austin ignored the urge to have the last word, knowing some bad habits were better broken by simply walking away.

The car door slammed and those passing seconds before the engine kicked on amounted to one of the longest moments of his life. Tires spinning, Rob tore off down the drive and from the porch Austin watched him go, strangely numb and detached.

Disappointment prickled, but he didn't think hard enough to examine it, just a quick consideration for circumstances making it impossible to love people who couldn't love themselves. It was a new side of the fence to stand on, one he wasn't sure he liked, so he chalked it up to stern decision making and no regrets.

Good riddance to bad rubbish. When the old

car turned the corner, moving out of sight, he went back inside.

Gathering up the linens, so Ember didn't have to deal with them, he hauled them to the laundry closet and stuffed them in the washer. An empty sensation hollowed his belly and gouged his chest. His head pounded, which was strange because it had been a while since he'd had a headache of any sort. Probably just the tension.

He needed coffee and breakfast. He licked his lips and shook his head, stalking into the kitchen at a quick clip. His jaw ached as he realized he'd been grinding his teeth and he attempted, once more, to relax. Setting the coffee maker to brew, he tried to ignore his shaking hands.

"Austin?" Ember walked quietly into the kitchen, making him start. Why the fuck was he so jumpy?

"Yeah, baby?"

"I heard your dad leave. Are you okay?"

"I'll be fine. Let's not waste any more time thinking about him." If he could get his own thoughts to chill that would be helpful.

She nodded, but hesitated as if searching for a distraction. Her face lit up as she said, "Seeing as it's Sunday, maybe I could put together a picnic and the three of us could take a drive later?"

She probably wanted to see Cord. *He* wanted to see Cord, except he didn't.

His temples throbbed. Thinking about his friend, his heart ached, right smack in the middle of his chest, in that emptiness, like he was starving or something. He should eat.

"He might be busy."

"Austin." She moved to him, her hand out-stretched and stared up into his face. Her fingers stroked his forearm. "We need to get past that nastiness with Rob. Like you said. But if it helps to talk about it we can. You don't have to put on a brave face for us."

And she had to involve Cord. Of course she did. Wait, he wasn't upset with her so why the fuck did her comment irritate him?

His thoughts were giving him whiplash. His friend was a good guy. *And so are you.*

He shook his head, uncertain if he trusted that inner voice at the moment. What if he chased his dad off too soon?

Fuck. He tried to shake off any recurring thoughts of his father, but they kept creeping in like unexpected pokes in his back. Maybe they should have talked once he was sober. Austin could have told him how much AA was helping him and—

A mental door slammed shut as his father's voice disparaged all ideas regarding those sorts of "cult programs".

"Austin?"

His wife still looked at him, concern tightening her brow and he was pretty sure he'd just missed whatever she'd last said. An itchy tingle skated over his skin, his clothes weighing on him like heavy wool in summer. Why the hell was the coffee taking so long?

Glancing at Ember he sensed her urge to talk, to analyze, and he didn't want to rehash the things he'd said to his dad, didn't want to own up to the fact that he'd basically just turned himself into an orphan.

Was a shitty parent better than no parent at all? Why couldn't his dad just be normal? *Fuck!*

No regrets. The steady drip of the coffee pot echoed like a church bell beside his ear. They needed to open a window. It was stuffy as fuck in here. How long would she wait to make breakfast? And why wasn't she in the bath?

Goddamn it, was the fucking coffee maker broken? He could have gone to the diner and been back with a to-go cup by now.

"I have something to take care of," he blurted. Brushing past, he paused midway to the door, and returned to drop a kiss on her head.

She blinked. "You're leaving?" The confusion clouding her eyes clawed at his mind.

"I'll be right back." He wasn't even sure where he was going, but he had to get the fuck out of that kitchen and get some air. Before she could object, he grabbed his keys off the hook and was out the door.

Yep, he was a prince, all right. But nothing, not even Ember, seemed capable of interfering with his one-track mind. *Escape.*

As his truck barreled down the road, his mind took him on a different ride, one that highlighted every fucked up moment of his past and suddenly he was steering toward his childhood home. But as he passed the dated house, his foot lifting from the accelerator and his gaze combing the property for any sense of recognition, he only found futile hope.

The house wore different siding and unfamiliar

cars filled in the driveway. There was nothing there for him.

Every sign of his mother was gone. The flowers she'd planted replaced with shrubs. The curtains she'd made traded in for mini-blinds. A pair of dirt bikes sat out back where his swing set used to be. His home was gone—and his family...

Ember's your family.

That inner voice had him punching the gas. Here he was, running away from her, and searching for what? As he drove, he replayed the night before in his mind.

Had he really chased her upstairs to protect her or was it more about protecting himself? With a stifled groan, he clenched the wheel, accepting he didn't want her to see the similarities he and his father shared.

He didn't want her to know his fear that he might someday turn into the man who barely raised him. Another tyrant to rip the happiness from their home. He needed her to keep positive—*hopeful*—that he could overcome everything he was up against.

Yet he'd left her there, knowing exactly what he might do, and knowing any sort of backslide would devastate her. Maybe she would call Cord. He hoped she would, because Cord had a way of pulling him back from the edge when he was close, but maybe he didn't need that right now. Maybe.

Not ready to return home, afraid he might see his wife's small figure watching from the porch much like he'd watched his father come and go—

that's where you stand when you watch losers leave—
he kept driving.

What seemed like only seconds later, he parked the truck—dead center, front row of the lot—facing the liquor store.

He wasn't hiding, wasn't skulking around. His hands white knuckled the wheel as he watched the lighted sign. *Open. Open. Open.* It flickered in rhythm with the pounding of his heart and the tunneling need throbbing in his gut.

Ember. Cord. His father. *His mom.* His mind detoured, searching desperately to recall the way his mother smelled. Nothing. The people closest to him blurred into images that seemed to stare back at him with disapproval. The weight...the fucking pressure, it was back, and ungodly.

"Fuck!"

Peeling his fingers from the steering wheel, he cracked his knuckles and licked his lips. What if he let them down, Cord and Ember? If he went home now, this feeling might stay and he needed to get his head straight before he went back there and said or did something unforgivable. He needed to show them he wasn't going to be like his fucking father.

Or...save them all some time and demonstrate how there was no outsmarting a gene pool as fucked as his. No. He couldn't think like that. They weren't the same. He was his own man.

He'd just get out of the truck. Take a short walk, prove he had the strength to keep walking. He was *not* his father. He was better, stronger. Wasn't he?

The door creaked open and he swiveled to set a

boot on the pavement. The contact sent a shock of awareness clear up to his hip, and he stilled.

What the fuck was he doing?

A vision of Ember's face swam across the forefront of his mind, immediately followed by Cord's. He couldn't do this to them, but more importantly, he couldn't do this to himself.

He had to be more than a failure to them. This was a place he could never visit again. Ever. The idea that he might someday build up a tolerance to alcohol was fucking asinine. There was nothing *temporary* about his circumstances and he needed to get that through his thick fucking skull.

People with diabetes didn't hang around Dairy Queen's and he had no business lingering outside of a liquor store. Addiction could only be blamed for so much. Sometimes his problems were just a lack of common fucking sense.

Climbing back into the truck, a cool sweat pasted his shirt to his skin. He slammed the door and breathed slowly. Maybe he should call Harley.

Swallowing hard, he forced his hands to grip the wheel, holding himself in place.

His world.

This was his life.

No one else's.

His.

He had a choice in what sort of life he led and he did not want to go backward. He was happy. His misery was behind him and if it snuck around again he'd deal with it. Period. Coming here wasn't fucking dealing. It was the first step in quitting and he refused to be a fucking quitter. But what if the urge to give up followed him all the way home?

His molars locked and jagged breaths worked through his nose as his lips pressed tight. His palm slammed repetitively against the wheel. *Fuck this fucking unending argument no one could win for him!*

He was smarter than this, past this bullshit. No. He wasn't giving the fuck up.

Cranking over the engine, he sped home as if he were outrunning his demons. His heart rate kicked up a hundred notches when he spied Cord's familiar truck in the drive.

Ember would always have one of them, if things ever slipped out of control. Perhaps they all needed backup from time to time.

He shouldn't think like that. Cord wasn't insurance. *Austin* owed it to his wife to be the man she married. Owed it to Cord. And he owed it to himself.

Cord stepped out onto the porch as Austin climbed from the truck, greeting him before he even had a chance to walk in the house and blot the sweat off his neck. His friend studied him intently, staring deep into his eyes.

"You okay?"

"Perfect." Maybe not perfect, but he was better, now that he was home with them. There was no doubt in his mind this was where he needed to be, eyes on the future. Fuck the past.

"How's my wife?" His voice rang with such sincerity, Cord blinked.

She would always be his first concern. She always had been, regardless of how anyone else saw his past.

Cord lifted a shoulder. "She's putting on a brave front. Go for a little drive?"

"Something like that. I'm here now. Present, and definitely accounted for."

"Good."

He wanted to check on Ember, apologize for checking out this morning and explain that this wasn't about her, but Cord wasn't moving and his hesitation kept Austin in place. "Out with it, Cord."

"She's calm now, but I got a pretty frantic call before I raced over here. You're lucky she's tough. If tears had been involved I'd be kicking your ass right now."

His wife certainly was tough. No one could take that away from her. "It was a rough morning."

"She told me what happened with your dad, said you told him not to come back."

Although he wasn't one to dissect his feelings, something in Cord's eyes pulled the words from his chest. "He can't come back. Not if I want to keep on the path I'm following."

Cord nodded. "I think that's smart."

It was smart. So why the hell was he wasting his morning beating himself up over the decision? "Still my dad though."

"I know. We can't choose our family."

Did he know the demons would also be there forever? And if so, why didn't he look as terrified as Austin felt? He assessed his friend's scrutinizing eyes. Yeah, he knew. Yet he appeared pretty damn confident Austin could outmatch any enemy, or at least he was hiding his fear well.

Cord wasn't pushing, but Austin couldn't stop his confession. "I drove to the liquor store."

"Okay." His friend nodded, a wealth of understanding in the slight movement. "I have faith in you, Austin. We both do. You know *this* is where you belong, not at some bar or drinking and trying to work through your pain alone. We won't break if you lean on us."

Austin laughed at how simple Cord made it sound when ten minutes ago he was ready to check himself back into the psych ward. "Thanks for... coming here. For believing in me."

"She didn't call me to go get you, Austin. She called so I could help her pass the time."

It wasn't that they were one hundred percent confident that he'd make the right decision, but they at least gave him the space to figure out what he needed on his own. Cord was right. He needed to be home.

Never in his life had he been so grateful he'd chosen to power through, because hearing they both had faith in his ability to make the right choice made his decision to return home abso-fucking-lutely the right one.

He eyed his friend. Cord was no dummy. He knew Austin's gratitude carried the weight of a thousand words, words Austin was still struggling to say. "Thanks, man."

Slowly, the knot in his gut, the trembling of his hands, eased and he could breathe again. No one was waiting around expecting him to fail. They believed in him, trusted him, affirming that belief in himself.

He drew in a deep breath and let it out slowly, as a renewed sense of balance filled him. "Where is she?"

"Inside. She said something about wanting to talk again, and she's being pushy about it."

Fuck. No doubt her pushy mood was his fault, a reaction to his abandonment that morning and her worry over what transpired between him and his father. But the sting was wearing off and he was slowly accepting his life would always be a little better without Rob Garret present.

He'd explain that to her and hopefully she'd let it go. No need to dwell on trash that was already at the curb.

"So let's talk. I got nothing to hide and I want to get back on track." Just like she'd said that morning, get past the nastiness with Rob. Forward.

Cord edged toward the front door, but hesitated. "She can get a little growly, our girl."

He sounded a bit disgruntled and Austin hid a smile. Ember was usually the sunny, optimistic, sweetheart, but when pushed, she could give as good as she got.

"I'll talk to her. I know how she gets when she's worried. Don't take it personally."

"I wasn't taking it personally."

They locked gazes, Austin having to tip his head back a little to look in Cord's blue eyes. He was no longer overcome with the need to claim the higher ground. Rather, there seemed a sort of rightness in watching each other's backs. Maybe it never was a competition, just a matter of making them both fit comfortably in the big picture.

He gripped the door and pulled it open, but glanced over his shoulder at Cord once more before entering. "She wanted a picnic. I vote for a naked one. But first let me feel her out."

He wouldn't make light of her concerns or feelings, but he also didn't want her dwelling on this morning's events. It was a little bump in the road, but not one that sent them careening into the past. He merely took a little detour down memory lane to remind him which way would lead him home—the direction he wanted to go.

Entering the house he called for his wife, "Em?"

"There's whipped cream in the fridge," Cord murmured and Austin chuckled.

"Let's see if I'm in the doghouse first."

Eleven

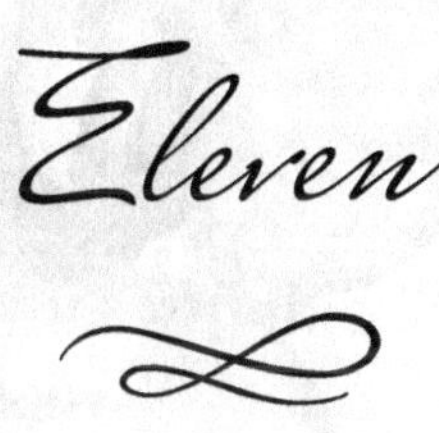

Austin

AUSTIN MOVED into the dining room and caught his wife's attention, hating the concerned look on her face. Ember paused in polishing the sideboard, giving him a composed, polite smile. "Hey."

Fuck that.

He stalked to her, loving the way her eyes widened as he narrowed the distance. "I'm sorry," was the only warning he gave before pulling her into his arms and hugging her hard.

The tension in her posture eased and she sank into him on a sigh. "You just left. You didn't tell me where you were going or when you would be back—"

"My head was up my ass, baby. I didn't know where I was going."

She drew back and peered up at his face, her gaze questioning. "Where *did* you go?"

He'd answer for his misdeeds, but he didn't think almost screwing up was the same as actually screwing up and he didn't want to feel bad when in the end he'd done right. "I took a drive to think some things through, but everything's fine. I'm home. I'm safe. I didn't fuck up. My only regret is that I worried you."

"And Cord."

"And Cord." He shot his friend another apologetic look, but they'd talked outside and that was enough for them. Returning his attention to Ember, he asked, "Forgive me?"

"Are you really okay?" It was what he loved most about her, her concern was always for others first.

"I'm fine. This morning was rough, but I got through it. No short cuts."

"Was it because you threw your dad out?"

"It had to do with him, but nothing I do is *because* of him. I'm responsible for me."

"He's still your father, Austin. If you change your mind—"

He kissed her, not wanting her to finish the sentence. When he pulled away, he grinned. "I know, baby. But he needed to go. Maybe down the line I'll invite him back, but right now it's best if we keep a safe distance from the Rob Garrets of the world."

She blinked up at him, a slow smile forming on her full lips. "You're nothing like him, Austin."

His heart jerked in his chest, her words tying up

a thousand loose ends and obliterating frightening thoughts. Once again, he struggled to express all he felt, but he'd never forget how understanding his wife was, in moments like this and in so many other moments they shared. She always seemed to know exactly what to say.

He nuzzled her throat and hugged her again. "You still got that hankering for a picnic?"

"Yes. We missed breakfast."

Not what he was thinking, exactly, but he was glad to hear she hadn't had a change of heart. "Cord, go ahead and get the whipped cream out of the fridge."

"On it."

"Whipped cream?"

She shrieked as Austin dipped and got a shoulder into her belly, straightening up with her flailing against his back as her feet left the ground. The polishing cloth fluttered to his feet and he kicked it aside.

"Austin! What are you doing?"

"Hush." He smacked her ass, a satisfying whack on her curved flesh and she laughed as he took the stairs at a steady stride.

"Austin!" She grasped the fabric of his shirt in both hands, tugging it from his jeans, even as she relaxed in his hold. "This is *not* what I meant when I suggested a picnic."

"Trust me, you'll like this better." Hesitating at the doorway of their bedroom, he wavered then picked up the pace and made his way to the third floor guest room. He wasn't sure if they were ready to turn their room into a communal space.

December had remade the bed and tidied up the room. He dumped her on the bed, caging her with his arms and body as she settled, a mischievous smirk on her lips. "Are we ever going to eat today?"

"Oh, I plan on eating as soon as Cord gets up here."

"Guys?" Cord called.

"Guest room!" Austin yelled and the resounding sound of heavy footfalls echoed through the house. Looking down at his wife, he rested some of his weight on her, pinning her in place. "Love you, baby."

Utter acceptance reflected in her eyes as she smiled. "Love you back."

Kissing her soundly, pouring out the depth of his feelings, he stole her breath. Sensing Cord's presence, his body shivered with anticipation.

As he eased back, Ember sighed, her eyes glazed with passion. Cord's palm cradled the bowl of whipped cream and they exchanged a look they'd shared since childhood, one that said they were about to do something bad and didn't give a damn about the consequences because the rewards would surely outweigh the crime. Damn if it didn't feel good to be getting into mischief with his partner in crime again.

With an evil smirk, his friend set the sweet treat on the nightstand and Austin stripped off his shirt, as Cord did the same. Ember watched his every move, scanning his chest, her stare settling on his lower body as he freed his hardening cock. A sexy little smile curved her sweet mouth, and he reached to deal with her dress, his masculine fingers fumbling with the dainty buttons.

Cord brushed his clumsy hands out of the way. "You're taking too long."

He peeled apart the fabric, revealing tightly beaded nipples tipping her round breasts, and Austin traced a finger around first one, then the other. She shivered and pushed against his touch. He leaned to nuzzle her belly, tracing his tongue to the waistband of her panties.

"Up, baby."

She lifted her hips off the mattress and Austin slid the underwear down her legs, revealing her glistening folds. He breathed in the scent of her arousal and lowered his lips to press against her thigh, struggling to gain control and draw out their pleasure.

Rolling to one side to make room for Cord, he dragged his stare away from Ember's naked body to appreciate the heavy cock springing between his best friend's legs. Torn, tempted by need for his amazing lovers, he turned back to his wife, gently grasping her calves to tug her forward.

Cord reached to cup Ember's breast in a possessive hold, his sun darkened skin a stark contrast against her pale flesh. She hummed her excitement and Austin's cock twitched.

"Those sweet little buds look like ripe berries, huh?"

Cord chuckled and grabbed the whipped cream. "I like where your mind's going." He anointed her nipples with hefty dollops of the creamy mixture and she shivered.

Austin caught her wrists, drawing them over her

head and pressing them into the bedding. "Keep them here, baby."

She surrendered beautifully, holding still.

"Three, two, one…" They dipped their heads simultaneously and suckled.

Quiet little moans accompanied the sounds their mouths made as his hair brushed against Cord's. The heat from Cord's body sent a shiver from Austin's shoulder down to his cock.

The tasty treat consumed, Austin grabbed the cream and scooted lower, applying it lavishly to her folds. "Want a taste?"

"Absolutely."

Cord scooted lower, his dark head dipping between Ember's thighs and her eyes widened, clear evidence she was enjoying their little game.

"Feel good, baby?"

Her body arched into Cord's ministrations as carnal moans escaped her lips and her gaze softened under full lashes. "So good," she whimpered.

Austin's attention strayed to the bunched muscles of his friend's back, his stare traveling down his spine to the curve of his ass. Big hands slid beneath his wife's buttocks, as Cord lifted her closer to his mouth and Ember moaned in response to the teasing of Cord's lips and tongue.

Watching his best friend devour his wife's pussy, Austin suffered an unexpected sense of satisfaction. He liked seeing Cord pleasure her, drew his own carnal gratification from the act, even from the sidelines.

"Make her come," he urged, and Ember arched

and rocked into Cord's touch, her breasts glistening with traces of whipped cream.

Fuck. It was so goddamn sexy watching the two of them. Erotic. He'd never been much for voyeurism, but Ember was so damn gorgeous like this. He'd never had the opportunity to actually take in the whole picture, as he was usually the man on the giving end.

But with Cord, he saw everything. Saw the way her jaw trembled. The delicate twitch of her eyelashes. When she bit down on her plump lower lip his cock throbbed steadily.

Cord's fingers caught her nipple, and Austin was surprised at the intense way his friend pinched down on the tender flesh. He liked it, and by Ember's panted response she liked it too.

"Oh, my God," she gasped. "Yes!"

Cord released her nipple, the ruched areola dark, and the tip sharp. Ember's hands curled into fists, but stayed above her head. Austin stared, unblinking, as his friend fucked his fingers into her, fast and wet, his mouth performing ceaselessly as she cried out and came.

Cord lifted his head, curls tousled and his lips glossy. He locked his gaze with Austin's before pressing a kiss on Ember's belly.

Unable to sit on the sidelines any longer, Austin growled and shoved his friend out from between her legs and onto his back. "Lie flat."

Cord flopped beside Ember, his contemplative gaze full of anticipation, as Austin scooped a portion of the cream onto Cord's erect cock.

"Jesus Christ, Austin. It's fucking cold!"

His wife rolled her head, blinking, and then gave him a mischievous grin. She was the sexiest partner in crime a man could ask for, so he scooted over, making room.

Leaning forward, she swiped her tongue across the flared tip of Cord's cock. His head jerked off the pillows, his eyes opening wide before he smirked. "Both of you?"

Austin glanced at his wife and a soft smile played on her full lips

"You remembered," she breathed.

He'd never forget the tempting image she'd painted of them both pleasuring Cord, his memory still hanging onto the night they shared such carnal thoughts in their bed. His gaze held hers as he dipped and tasted the length of Cord's shaft, encouraged by his guttural groan.

Austin applied himself to licking and sucking off every bit of whipped cream, pulling back to allow Ember an opportunity, then dueling with her tongue as they drove Cord wild.

"Goddamn. You have no idea how incredible that feels."

Austin took him deeper and Cord yanked hard on his hair. It was enough of a reminder—besides the cock crammed down his throat—that Cord wasn't a submissive partner. Cord's hands were everywhere, fingers running through his and Ember's hair, stroking over his chest, cupping Ember's breasts.

Austin's eyes teared up as he fought the choking sensation, but Ember was right there to relieve him.

Her mouth replaced his, her cheeks hollowing around Cord's fat cock, and Austin couldn't resist guiding her motions with a gentle hand in her hair. "Deeper, baby. Show me how you take him all the way."

Unblinking, he watched as she swallowed him down to the root, Cord's lengthy moan washing over him like a physical caress. Austin kept guiding her as she laved and sucked, driving their friend to ecstasy.

Cord's body writhed and his muscles twitched, every inch of sinew stretching like an embossed work of art. Ember pulled back and Austin eagerly took her place, sucking his cock with enthusiastic pulls of his mouth, his hand slipping lower to cup Cord's balls. Submissive partner or not, he reveled in the pleasure he meted out to his friend.

Cord's cock swelled and throbbed against his tongue, his salty flavor intensifying over the remaining traces of sugar, and Austin pulled back.

"Fuck. Fuck," Cord choked the words, his hands cupping his pulsing cock as jets of come pumped free to coat his belly.

Wiping his mouth with the back of his hand, Austin could barely believe they'd done that to him —together. Ember set her hand on Cord's chest, quickly dashing away the mess with a few tissues before snuggling in beside him, his arm immediately wrapping around her as he caught his breath. The sight of their entwined bodies created bone deep satisfaction within Austin. His own dick throbbed above his aching balls, and he lowered his hand to soothe it.

Cord's unfocused gaze sharpened, a predatory look tinting those blue eyes. "Get over here."

Austin shifted closer, and Cord curled up to meet him, taking his mouth in a dominant kiss. Another ache eased, as Austin gave over to Cord's possession.

As he allowed his friend to ease him to the bed, resting a good amount of weight on his lower body, Austin waited for panic to set in. He wasn't one to be dominated, yet here he was, giving Cord the reins.

Cord's touch was demanding, yet slow and patient, giving Austin plenty of time to object. No panic, and no need to object. Being touched like this, held by such strong, capable, and possessive hands...settled him. Made him feel safe, and an unfamiliar sense of peace slipped over him. Was this how Ember felt when *he* took charge?

"I love your mouth," Cord murmured against his lips, his fingers capturing Austin's jaw as he angled his face to deepen the kiss.

The heat and weight of Cord's body dragged over him, pressing him into the mattress as their bodies fit against each other. Strong legs covered in hair, narrow hips and engorged cocks rubbing with enough friction to set his blood afire. Austin groaned into Cord's mouth, wanting more and unsure how to express such stark desire in the face of everything he thought he knew about himself.

"You feel that?" Cord rasped, biting down on his lip and grinding his cock alongside Austin's. "That's because of you. I'm hard again because of you."

His hands fisted the bedding, and his heart thundered in his chest. His breath jerked as a drizzle of pre-come slicked their contact. "Goddamn, Cord."

"It's gonna get so much better, Austin. Just wait."

Cord's tongue stole into his mouth, delivering a promise of more. Something fractured deep in his chest to allow a flood of warmth as he came to understand this was so much more than superficial lust.

This man, his best friend, the guy he'd grown up with and trusted despite their recent rocky road, loved him—beyond friendship. And Austin dared to accept he loved him back, just as much.

Ember pressed against his side, her lush curves such a marked contrast to Cord's hard frame. He shuddered with the intensity of the moment and fell deeper into Cord's kiss.

Pulling away, his friend's big hand caressed the nape of his neck. "Ember, our boy here seems to be in need," Cord said, easing to his side.

Though he loved when his wife pleasured him, the slight disappointment that Cord wouldn't be handling matters himself spoke volumes.

She scooted between them and trailed her fingers down his chest, catching his cock in the palm of her hand.

Tiny nuzzles and licks drifted over Austin's abdomen, his eyes reflexively shutting as she engulfed his cock in the heat of her mouth.

"Will you look at that..." Cord murmured and Austin watched through his lashes, his wife's head bobbing over his cock as Cord's fingers sifted through her hair.

Cord caught his stare and smiled, positioning himself behind Ember and stroking her back. Eyes on Austin, he pressed a kiss on one of her buttocks.

"Condom?" Cord asked.

Her mouth slid off Austin's cock and he wanted to whimper. She looked at him for a long moment. "I'm okay with no condom if both of you are."

He knew his friend was clean and Ember was on birth control. This relationship was evolving, as she'd said. Definitely evolving. He gave her nothing but reassurance, schooling his features to reflect his acceptance that this was her call, and nodded.

She glanced at Cord over her shoulder. "No condom."

Cord's expression morphed into shock and something else, something intense, like awe. The warmth in his chest heated some more, his friend clearly aware of the gift that was Ember.

As she dipped her head again and sucked him into her mouth, he watched as Cord reached between her thighs. Ember sighed around his dick and Austin lifted his hips in response.

Fingers wet with her arousal, Cord stretched forward and offered him a taste. After a moment of hesitation Austin drew the offering between his lips, his gaze locked with Cord's as his dick pulsed in his wife's mouth. Fuck him, but he sucked Cord's fingers like a second cock and loved it.

"She's ready," Cord rasped, pulling back his fingers.

He grasped his cock and slipped his other hand

under Ember's belly to support her, just as Austin would have done. Austin felt the moment Cord slid home, surging deep into his wife. Her throat opened on a gasp, taking Austin deep. Eyes rolling back, he fought not to come.

Cord gave a firm thrust, possession and domination written large across his handsome features, evident in the lines of his body. He pushed her, yet with that modicum of tenderness Austin knew evoked the love they both felt for Ember.

"So fucking hot. Tight," Cord muttered, his features strained with painful ecstasy.

It was so much to take in, so packed with emotion and sensation, Austin's release barreled up his shaft. "Baby…" he warned, but she didn't ease up. "Baby, I'm gonna come."

She sucked harder and his back arched. His release rushed down her throat, and her lips tightened, milking every last drop. The faint graze of her teeth over his sensitive skin drew a second burst of his seed.

His vision grayed, and his strength gave out, leaving him sprawling backward while Cord fucked her over his prone body. He managed to lift a hand to smooth her hair as she rested her cheek on his chest, her mouth opening on a soundless cry.

Cord growled her name a moment later and sagged over her back, head drooping as he gasped for air.

Austin soaked in the sensation of his beloved wife's silken form sprawled boneless over his own, and his best friend's hand resting heavily on his shoulder as they all panted for breath. If this was dying, it was one hell of a way to go.

Twelve

December

EMBER SMILED DOWN at the large conference table as she brushed her clammy palms over the front of her dress. Her students should be arriving shortly and everything looked perfect. Drawing in a steadying breath, she straightened one of the templates.

"Knock, knock."

Ember's head lifted and she smiled. "Mrs. Winchester! How are you?"

"Oh, I'm quite lovely, dear." She patted a vintage sewing box. "Ready to learn."

Ember waved a hand toward the table. "You're the first to arrive, so take whatever seat you like."

"How organized you have everything." The older woman settled into the seat at the end of the table and slipped on a pair of cat-eye glasses, inspecting the fabric Ember had laid out. "Just lovely."

Ember beamed and shook away the terrible thought that this might be her only student if no one else showed. "How's Mr. Winchester?"

"Crotchety as usual, but he's good for opening jars, so I keep him around."

She smirked. Mr. Winchester could be a bugger, but he had a soft side.

Another woman arrived, this one Ember had yet to meet. She made a polite introduction and welcomed her to the table and soon several others followed.

All of the women fawned over the setup and as they waited for the last few to arrive, Ember placed a tray of oatmeal cookies on the table.

"A true stitch and bitch," Mrs. Winchester cackled. "Did you make these, December?"

"I did."

Several women sighed their approval. "A right and proper homemaker. I think you might have been born in the wrong decade. That's okay. You take pride in all those wonderful touches. Too many forget the true meaning of homemade."

Not December. She savored every bit of tender love and care she could squeeze from her fingers, finding balance in all those thoughtful touches. Her boys appreciated her efforts, too. She fought a blush and a trip down memory lane.

Yesterday had been another fabulous day. Worth the distraction from the talk they were going to have...

"Enjoy them." She smiled at the class. "I have a whole other tray." She glanced at the clock. "I guess we should get started." She was happy to see at least ten of the expected dozen registrants had showed up.

"*I'm coming!* I'm coming! Don't start without me!"

Ember stilled as she recognized the familiar voice. A second later, Cord's mother flounced into the room, catching her breath as she leaned against the doorjamb in a lemon yellow pantsuit.

"Sorry, I'm late."

Ember blinked, startled by her appearance. "N—Norma Jean."

"Hello, sweetie. So sorry I kept you waiting. I couldn't decide what to wear and the parking and... Well, you get the idea." She plopped into a chair and dropped her oversized pocketbook on the floor. "Look at all this. Ooh! Cookies. I had a light dinner."

Ember blinked, her whole equilibrium thrown by Norma Jean's presence. "Um... If we're ready to begin..." She shuffled to the head of the table.

The women looked at her expectantly, but all she could think about was Cord—Norma Jean's son—whom she'd been naked with. Just yesterday. Her face heated as she reached for the stack of cut fabric in front of her, unable to lift her gaze.

"This session is going to focus on cutting, which sounds like a simple task, but when it comes to quilting, accuracy is everything." Why was she whispering?

She cleared her throat, trying to recall the

opening speech she'd planned. "Quilting is more than a craft." Her voice shrank, growing quieter with every word. "It's a part of our heritage. Dating back to…"

Norma Jean leaned in. "You okay, honey? You look a little pale. Here. Eat a cookie."

What was wrong with her? She was prepared. She'd had everything ready and these women were depending on her.

Finding a cookie in her hand she placed it on a napkin and brushed the crumbs off her fingers. She could do this.

It was Cord's mom. That's all. No reason to feel ashamed or guilty or whatever she felt at the moment. Just Cord's mom. The woman who'd been more like family than—

This was so not the time for that.

Lifting her shoulders she drew in a deep breath and faced the class. "Sorry. A little stage fright. This is my first time teaching."

The women sympathized and offered patient encouragement. So long as she didn't look directly at Norma Jean she was fine.

"You'll see I've laid out a selection of various fabrics. These are fat quarters, this sort of stripping is called a jelly roll, and bulks are commonly referred to as yardage…"

The longer she talked, reading each woman's—except for Norma Jean's—receptive expression, the bolder her lecture became.

"If you'll open up your supply kits you'll find a collection of quilting necessities I personally selected. This is your rotary cutter. Please be careful, as it's very sharp."

She walked the women through their supplies, naming each item and explaining its purpose.

"Now, if you'll take a fat quarter of fabric, whatever catches your eye, we'll get started. Place it on your cutting mat and grab a ruler. It might be easier to stand for this part. However you're most comfortable."

As she guided the class through various methods of cutting some students found it a simple task, while others struggled. Unfortunately, patchwork was not a natural talent of Cord's mom's.

"Ember, honey, am I doing this right?"

December circled the table and tried to sound encouraging. "That looks fi—" She frowned at the disaster. "Norma Jean," she laughed. "What have you done?"

"I've never been much for tidy cuts. I'm more of a chopper."

Ember tried for a smile and swept away the massacre of swatches. "Let's start with a new piece. Here, watch me."

As she showed Cord's mother how to line up the ruler, the other woman hummed with understanding. "Just straight through, like this."

"I'll be lucky if I sew a cocktail napkin by the end of this class. I don't have much patience for such things, but when you told me about it, I was so excited I figured, why not?"

Ah, that infamous dinner at Norma Jean's house. It seemed like a lifetime ago and she experienced a stab of remorse that she hadn't reciprocated or been in contact with the older woman since. But thinking of how everything changed after that meal, she couldn't find any honest regret.

"Now, you give it a try." She carefully passed Norma Jean the rotary cutter.

She made one slice then appeared to lose interest, holding the cutter hostage as she folded her hands and faced Ember. "I hear Cord's been spending a lot of time at your house lately."

Her chin trembled and she grit her teeth to hide her nerves. "He has."

"That's nice. And Austin's back to work?"

Ember frowned. It felt like Norma Jean was fishing. "Yes."

"He and Cord are getting along better? Back to normal?"

Normal? Her face heated again. "I should check on the other women."

Norma Jean glanced at the table, where the self-sufficient students were happily cutting away. "I sure hope his being there isn't causing a problem for you two."

Her brow creased and the air seemed to thicken. "No. Of course not. Cord's always welcome in our home."

Norma Jean's smile was discerning and Ember's neck and shoulders heated. She longed for the class to be over, or for someone else to need her help. Any life raft would do.

"Sometimes my son can be a bit presumptuous. I wouldn't want him to...take advantage."

She could no longer maintain her fake smile.

Voice quiet and level, she murmured, "What are you insinuating, Norma Jean?"

"Nothing. I just know things have been...a little rough this past year and I want you to know—"

"This is not the place," she whispered, face numb. "Excuse me. I have to check on the others."

Walking away, she didn't dare glance back at that side of the table. She managed to keep her distance from Norma Jean for the last hour of class.

Ember bid her students goodbye and offered some parting advice for the week, asserting that she looked forward to seeing their progress at the next class. As the room cleared, she swept the scraps into the bin and moved the leftover cookies from the tray back into her Tupperware, certain her boys would appreciate the leftovers.

"I owe you an apology."

Ember's back stiffened. Taking a deep breath, she closed the container and turned to face Cord's mother. "It's fine, Norma Jean."

"No, it's not. That was me being my usual pushy self. *You don't know when to quit,* Reed would say. I'm sorry. I shouldn't have pried."

She didn't want this tension between them. Cord's mother was someone she loved very much. Part of their awkwardness was Ember's fault. She didn't know how much Cord had told his mother, but the way she was acting...she clearly knew *something.*

"Last year was rough, but we're all moving on."

Norma Jean smiled and nodded. "It's not easy being married to men like ours. I'm glad to see

Austin's back to work and acting more himself again."

"Me too and thank you. I know your concern's out of love."

"We would love to have you two over again for Sunday dinner. Cord's always making excuses. He seems harder to pin down now, more than ever."

She suddenly felt guilty for monopolizing all of Cord's free time. "We would love that. Just let me know when and we'll be there."

Her smile grew, appearing more sincere. "You're such a good girl, Ember. Sometimes I wish…"

"What?"

She waved a hand. "Never mind. I'm blathering. Let me know if this Sunday works and we'll make it happen. If anything, your presence will guarantee my son's."

That might be true, but it painted Ember in a terrible light. "I think this Sunday will be fine. I'll check with Austin and call you tomorrow."

"Okay, sweetie." She patted her bag. "Now, how much trouble do we get in for not doing our homework?"

Ember rolled her eyes. "Why sign up for a quilting class if you have no interest in the work?"

"I needed to get away from Reed. His retirement doesn't always suit my sanity."

Ember laughed, feeling as though things had returned closer to normal between them. "I'll call you tomorrow."

Once she had the room tidied, she packed up and drove home. Cord's truck was still at the house and she was glad, because they were going to have words. She opened the front door and tossed her bag by the hall closet.

"Hey, how was your first class?" Austin asked, greeting her in the hall.

"It was good. Where's Cord?"

Her husband frowned. "He's out back cutting wood for the deck. He set up night shift out there. The floodlights are brighter than the sun. I was about to head to my meeting, but I'm glad I got to see you before I left."

She briefly tilted her cheek to accept his kiss, her eyes zeroing in on the back door like a heat seeking missile. "Me too. Have a good meeting."

She marched to the back of the house, practically kicking open the door. "Cordovan Charles Bay!"

A power saw blared and silenced as she glared at him. His sweaty muscles gleamed in all their glory as he lifted a strip of deck wood off the table saw, clad in only his jeans and a tool belt. But she was in no mood for distractions.

He lifted his protective glasses and grinned. "Hey, kiddo. How was class?"

"Don't you *kiddo* me! Why haven't you been over to see your mother?"

His expression turned defensive and a touch confused. "I saw her yesterday."

"You—What?"

"December, she's at the store almost every day."

"But... Why haven't you been to her house?" He wasn't getting off that easily.

He shrugged and glanced at the work he was doing to their house. "I've been here."

"Cord, she misses you. She said you've been blowing her off."

"No, I haven't. And when did you talk to my mother?"

"She's *taking* my class."

"Oh, shit," Austin muttered behind her. She'd thought he left.

She turned and glared at him, all men being in her sights at the moment. "I thought you had your meeting."

"I do, but I wanted to make sure you didn't kill Cord. Everything cool?"

"Yeah," she grumbled then turned and pointed an accusing finger at Cord. "Call your mother! And we're going there for Sunday dinner this week."

She marched back into the house and Austin chuckled. "I'll be back in a couple hours. Love you. Don't be too hard on him. We all have family drama."

She sighed. "I know. Love you back. Try not to be too late tonight."

A few minutes after Austin left, the bright lights shining through the windows from the backyard shut off. Cord crept into the kitchen and lingered silently by the door.

"Are you really mad at me?"

She tossed the sponge in the sink and folded her arms over her chest, as she leaned her hip against the counter and faced him. He'd tugged his shirt back on but hadn't buttoned it so she resolutely kept her eyes up, refusing to be distracted by any glimpses of sculpted muscle.

Her earlier frustration was about her own insecurities, coupled with her fear Norma Jean might find out what they'd been up to and hate her for it. She harbored unspoken worries about the outside world trespassing into their peaceful home. Everything was still so new and fragile. She honestly wasn't that mad at Cord, especially since learning that he saw his mother *yesterday*.

Inside their house, the three of them were so *together*. She wasn't ready to share that with the outside world just yet. "She knows something Cord. About us."

The flush rushing up his neck was confirmation enough.

"Oh, my God. *What did you tell her?*"

"I'm not going to talk about this if you keep yelling."

"Cord, I have to face her." The palms of her hands covered her eyes as she groaned. "You have to tell me what she knows. I was completely blindsided tonight when I saw her and she started asking questions I didn't know how to answer."

"Sit down." He pulled out a seat and lowered in the one across from it.

She frowned at the chairs. "Why? How bad is it?"

"It's not great."

It couldn't be good if Cord was volunteering to have a sit-down conversation. Usually he was the one springing for the whipped cream and any other distraction every time she suggested they talk.

She sighed and dropped into the seat. "Talk."

His posture wilted in the chair as he let out a long breath. "Okay, first, you have to remember I was hurting. You guys were back together and it was like I didn't exist anymore. I was in a lot of pain."

Her brow pinched and a good amount of her irritation fled. "Cord..."

He held up a hand. "Let me just...get this out. After you left the house, my mom asked me what was going on. It's not like I was going to tell her everything, but she asked—point blank—if..."

"If?"

"If we had an affair." He winced.

Her heart sank. Their relationship was so complicated she couldn't possibly expect outsiders to understand.

Okay. This was bound to happen. Eventually. She didn't want them living a closeted life, but she would have liked to open the conversation on her own terms. When they were solid and secure. They were getting there, but any new relationship was delicate.

"What did you say?"

"I told her the truth. I told her yes."

Her eyes closed, the return of shame a still familiar memory that felt fresh and barely gone. "She must think I'm a horrible person."

"No, sweetheart. She thinks you were going through something difficult and I was there for you."

"But your parents love Austin so much."

"They love you, too."

Her head hung as she tried to figure out how she

could possibly face his mother on Sunday. "You should have told us she knew."

"We've hardly had the chance to deal with this on our own terms, let alone allow other people in. Between work, us, Austin's dad, and everything else, it didn't seem a priority. I didn't expect her to corner you or whatever she did."

"She didn't corner me. Not really. I was uncomfortable and when she asked how things were I got defensive."

"I'm sorry you had to handle that on your own."

She sighed. "Me too. Life's easier when you guys are there, beside me."

He grinned. "Do you forgive me?"

"Yes. But you need to make time for your mom, Cord. She misses you and feels put off. Of all our relationships with our parents, yours is the most normal. Don't take that for granted."

"Consider me disciplined. I'll call her on my way to work tomorrow."

"Good. And we need to tell Austin she knows about last winter. We're going to have to figure out how to handle this together."

"We'll figure it out before Sunday dinner." The kitchen grew quiet. "Other than that, your class went well?"

Relieved that she wouldn't be facing Norma Jean alone the next time she saw her, she allowed herself a hint of joy and smiled. "My class was awesome. Other than the awkward moments when I felt like some sort of...adulterer."

"Don't call yourself that." His tone was serious.

"Sorry." But until they straightened out the impression his mother might have of her that was how she felt. "My class was great. Really. I can't wait to see what they make."

"We should celebrate."

She pursed her lips and rolled her eyes. "You wish. I'm tired and emotionally drained."

He scoffed. "Tease."

"How am I a tease? I didn't do anything." Shoving out of the seat she stood and shut off the kitchen light. "Are you sleeping here?"

He followed her through the hall as she shut down the house. She took that as a yes, being that he stayed in her shadow but didn't comment.

Glancing over her shoulder, she laughed. "You're not getting any. I don't reward bad behavior."

He silently followed her up the stairs. When she reached her bedroom door, she laughed again. He looked like a puppy left out in the rain.

"Goodnight, Cord."

He brushed a kiss over her lips. "Goodnight, Ember. Sweet dreams."

She entered her room and kicked off her shoes. Pulling her dress off, she tossed it toward the hamper and—

The door flew open and strong arms banded around her waist, lifting her off her feet and tossing her onto the bed. "Cord!"

"You didn't actually think I was gonna let you get away with that?"

He tickled her sides and she squirmed onto her

belly, crawling in a failed attempt to escape. "No! You're bad!"

He yanked her back, and pulled her panties halfway down. Sharp teeth bit into her butt and she yipped.

"You like me bad." He got her underwear down to her knees and she scooted to the other side of the bed—naked. He raised a brow and groaned. "Aw, your ass is mine."

"No!" She held out a hand and he froze. She tried not to laugh, which was almost impossible.

He stood, not advancing, but shouldering off his shirt. "You can't get rid of me. And there's no way you're going to bed upset with me."

"I'm not upset. I'm just not in the mood."

He arched a brow. "I'll get you in the mood."

"I don't *want* to be in the mood."

"Good. I love a challenge."

"Cord."

"Ember," he mimicked.

"You can't just come in here and demand sex."

He pursed his lips, clearly biting back a laugh. "Let me see you. Show me you're not aroused and I'll leave."

"I'm not aroused."

"Ember."

There was no way she was showing him anything. Besides, she was soaking wet. What was it about playing rough that turned her on? "Go away."

He sighed. "Fine."

She blinked, surprised he'd give up so easily. He rounded the bed and she drew in a breath to call him back when he suddenly spun and captured her ankle, yanking her across the bed.

"Cord! You're such a faker!"

"Hush."

He pinned her legs, forcing them open as he weighed her down with his forearms and settled his knees on the floor. She briefly struggled, until that first swipe of his tongue slid through her folds. Her body fell back on a sigh. Sweet, sweet surrender.

"You're fucking drenched," he murmured, pressing his lips against her clit as his fingers opened her.

He fed a long finger deep and she arched and moaned.

"That's it…" he coaxed, teasing her with his tongue as his fingers stretched and penetrated her. "God, I love it here, between your sexy fucking legs, holding you like this, pleasuring you. It's my happy place."

She giggled.

He pressed deep and she moaned as her body jerked in response. "You're the tease."

"Say that after I make you come a few times."

Cord always followed through on his promises. Angling his touch deeper, he pumped his fingers fast, striking a nerve and cutting off any further protest. She couldn't comprehend how anyone could do it so quickly, but a few seconds later she was sobbing through an explosive release.

"That's one. How many equal a few? I always forget. Is it three? Four?"

Collapsed on the bed, she panted. Was he actually suggesting she do math after that?

His tongue teased her clit and she nearly jackknifed off the bed—too sensitive from her last release. His heavy hand levered her body back down to the mattress.

"Stay put."

His lips closed around her sensitive bud as he sucked, this time skirting her sex and teasing with his fingers. He caught her hips and hoisted her closer, shifting her legs over his broad shoulders.

"I want you here. Like this," he murmured against her folds.

Pressing a palm over her lower abdomen, he wedged his tongue deep as his thumb rolled her clit. Her back arched as she pressed into him, moaning—begging—for that second promised orgasm.

His thumb circled faster and she gasped, her lungs turning shallow as her body coiled tighter. Finally, he gave her one last needed push and she shattered. Her legs slipped off his shoulders as she weakly shut her eyes and caught her breath.

"You're not done."

"Can't." She waved him away, but he only chuckled.

Her body flipped over as he rolled her to her stomach. Rather than part her thighs, he straddled her knees, keeping her legs together.

"Mmm," he growled, massaging the cheeks of her ass with both hands. "This is gonna be nice and tight."

He worked his hands beneath her legs, hitching up her hips but keeping her thighs closed. The blunt head of his cock nudged at her sex and she sighed.

With her thighs together it made for a really snug entrance.

"Stay with me, sweetheart."

He shoved forward and she let out a gasp as he filled her to the hilt.

"That's it. Tell me you're not in the mood now."

She smirked. He was such an arrogant jerk, but she loved him.

Her fingers knotted in the blankets as he thrust forward, pressing her belly into the mattress. His hips pistoned in a rapid rhythm and he gave her little time to prepare as the next wave of pleasure hit.

Hard thrusts smacked his pelvis against her ass as he drove deeper. Every masculine sound that came from him added to the eroticism. His absolute possession of her, the way he held her, took from her, dominated her, was a recipe for her wildest dreams. And when the wave of building ecstasy finally broke, she took him with her.

His cock twitched, buried inside of her, as his body jerked and he grunted through an almost violent release. Shivering in the aftershocks of her own orgasm, she was too numb to care about his added weight as his body blanketed hers.

"Fuck, sweetheart... You okay?" His lips seemed imbedded in her shoulders.

"Mmm-hmm," she slurred, lacking the strength to raise her face from the pillows.

He chuckled, pressed a kiss to the center of her back, and rolled beside her.

She turned her head and gave him a tired smile,

his arrogance plain. Too bad she was a sucker for that exact type.

He nestled into her side. Their fingers laced and she came to terms with not putting much thought into the outside world's opinions.

This was exactly where she wanted to be and no one was going to take that away from her—or from any of them, her insecurities be damned.

Thirteen

Cord

CORD HEARD footsteps before his mind completely registered where he was—Austin's bed. With December's naked body warm at his side. Shit. He'd fallen asleep. The bedroom door opened at the same time as his eyes.

Austin stilled, taking in the erotic picture they likely made, but said nothing.

"Sorry," he whispered so as not to wake Ember. "I fell asleep holding her."

His friend raised a brow and gently placed his cell phone on the nightstand. "I'm assuming you survived her wrath."

Cord gave a cocky tip of his head and then frowned. "What time is it?" He gently slid his body out from under Ember's and replaced it with a pillow. She murmured and clutched it to her chest.

"Late. We got to talking."

Cord nodded. Austin and Harley had an awful lot to say—every night.

He found his pants and slipped them on as Austin worked his off. He moved to the bed and lifted a hand as if to touch December. "Don't wake her."

His friend's head turned, and Cord bit his lip. Maybe it wasn't his place to say, but Austin dropped his hand. "How was she after I left?"

"Upset." He should wait until she was awake for them to discuss everything his mom knew. Guilt pinched, as he considered Ember wouldn't be the only one stressing over his mother's knowledge. "I think she's good now, but we'll talk about it tomorrow."

Austin nodded. "You staying?"

"I was gonna."

Something shifted in Austin's eyes. "You wanna…"

Cord's body immediately responded to the open-ended question and he raised a brow. "You?"

Austin shrugged. "You're probably tired."

He almost laughed, still taken aback by how surreal this side of their relationship was. "I napped."

Austin glanced over his shoulder at Ember. "She's beat. We should probably—"

"Come with me."

They stared at each other in a silent debate and then Austin followed him into the hall. Cord crowded his back before he even had the bedroom door closed, his hand pressing and rubbing over Austin's cock.

"This what you want?" Their breath labored as he gripped him through his briefs, leaning heavily into his back to show he wasn't the only one aroused. "Say it, Austin. Tell me you want it and it's yours."

Austin's forehead pressed into the door as his shoulders bunched, his hands gripping the molding. "That's what I want."

Cord smiled against his skin and scraped his teeth over his shoulder, biting gently. "Me too. Come up to my room so we don't wake her."

They took the stairs to the third floor, avoiding eye contact. The moment they were inside the guest room, Cord stripped off his pants, chuckling at Austin's wide-eyed attention.

The next moment, he was backing him to the bed, his hand wedging in the front of Austin's briefs and tugging greedily. He followed him down to the mattress and caught his lips in a demanding kiss.

Austin lay stiffly below him, surrendering to his touch, but giving little back. Cord caught his wrist and pressed his hand to his hip. "Touch me."

His friend's grip was bruising as he grabbed at Cord's side, hips thrusting into his stroking fist.

Cord straddled Austin's legs and broke the kiss, sitting back on his legs. "Can you handle all this?" He nudged his cock to brush against Austin's.

Austin's lips parted as he watched where their bodies collided, a thousand emotions washing over his face, too quick for Cord to decipher. "Cord..."

"You know it's gonna happen, Austin. Not tonight. Not without her. But eventually."

"I know." His dick twitched and Cord grinned. There was no faking this, at least not physically.

"What do you say we take the edge off?"

"What do you mean?" Austin's shoulders lifted off the bed and Cord shoved them back down.

"Just relax. Let me...have this."

Tipping his head back, Austin shut his eyes as Cord moved his lips over his chest. Although he'd never appreciated another man's body to the degree he appreciated Austin's, there was something deeply satisfying about dragging his tongue down his chiseled abdomen and shucking his briefs.

Austin's hands fisted in the blankets the closer Cord's mouth came to his cock. Cord dragged out the moment, lifting his heavy flesh to admire the way the thick vein traveled from base to tip, pulsing with Austin's rapid heartbeat.

Mouth watering for this brand new experience, Cord took him deep to the back of his throat and Austin tensed, grunting out a breath. That was a hell of a lot better than the guy playing the victim. He sucked hard, stroking Austin and tugging in all the right places as he got a feel for being on this side of his friend's pleasure.

Austin's ragged breathing echoed around the room. There was no way Cord was letting him off easy. He wanted to give him something worth remembering.

Balls tightening as he neared completion, Cord stroked Austin's taint. The little knot of his ass tightened and his hips jerked at the first tease of his blunt fingertip, but Cord could be a persistent son of a bitch.

Saliva gathered at the base of Austin's cock and Cord greased his finger before pressing in a rhythmic pattern against his puckered flesh. Austin's knees slowly lifted and the tip of his digit penetrated that tight opening.

Pulling back along Austin's dick with a slurp, careful to barely graze the wide head with his teeth, he licked Austin's sac and taint, adding more moisture. He'd never had a finger up his ass, but he knew enough from prepping former girl-friends.

"Little pressure..." He slowly sank all the way in and Austin grunted, but didn't freak. "You done this before?"

Speaking through gritted teeth, Austin man-aged, "With Ember..."

Ah...that was unexpected. He'd assumed they didn't do *any* kind of anal since Ember last men-tioned no one had ever been in her ass. He never expected she might play with Austin's, but the thought made him hot.

"Well, my fingers are a little bigger than hers." He pulled back and wedged deeper, this time with a little more enthusiasm. "Relax. Take some deep breaths."

Austin let out a stuttered breath followed by several labored ones.

"Pretty soon, it's gonna be my cock up there, old friend." He continued to stroke his finger in and out while his other hand worked Austin's dick.

"And pretty soon it'll be my cock ramming up

yours," Austin choked out. "Tit for tat—*old friend.*"

Cord stilled and smiled, silently chuckling. Tit for tat. He could live with that. "That's what you want? To fuck me?" *Dear God, just saying it...* He held his finger steady.

"Want it or not, you stick your dick up my ass, mine's going up yours."

He withdrew his touch and Austin let out a sharp breath. Cord twisted around to lie on his side, keeping Austin's cock within reach. Taking hold of his own dick, he guided it toward Austin's mouth— a little sideways sixty-nine action.

"*Tit for tat.* Suck it good, because I plan on tasting your come."

Austin hesitated only a second before easing forward and taking him deep, his own hard, wet dick tantalizingly close to Cord's mouth. Reaching out, Cord stroked over Austin and swallowed him to the root.

Pleasure knifed through him as Austin's mouth tightened in response, sucking harder, and he thrust his cock deeper, giving no quarter. Splitting his focus, working Austin's pulsing cock against the back of his throat, Cord sucked air through his nose.

Fingers gouged into his ass cheek, pulling him closer with each thrust. He blindly worked a finger back into Austin's ass as the salty taste of come teased his tongue. Sucking hard, he pumped his finger deep.

Strong muscles squeezed around his knuckles and Austin shuddered, his moans filling the room as he lost a bit of his control. Austin gave up pleasuring him, which doubled Cord's focus. Concentrating on all the right places, he sucked hard and Austin let out a guttural moan as his release filled Cord's mouth and slid down his throat.

Cord swallowed every drop, savoring the taste, and gently eased his finger out of Austin's clenching hole.

He shifted to face Austin, smirking as he found him resting slack-jawed and sated. "You gonna leave me hanging?" His balls ached and he grit his teeth, needing to come.

Austin's dark lashes lifted, a thousand unspoken words filling the silence. Cord cupped his jaw and whispered, "Finish me, Austin."

With a sharp nod, his friend lifted to shimmy his body between Cord's knees. There was something extraordinary in the way Austin fit between his thighs. He ran one hand over Cord's begging cock, lightly stroking him. Leaning in, he opened wide and took his cock into the hot, wet depths of his mouth.

The moment Austin's brown eyes locked with his, those thick lashes framing so much vulnerability, Cord was undone. Reaching forward, fingers slightly trembling, his thumb stroked through Austin's hair as he sucked him deep.

Tongue teasing along the length of his shaft, a faint rasp of teeth, but above all, that powerful sucking drew his balls close to his body and he let himself go.

His release came with a blinding burst of ecstasy, filling the warmth of Austin's mouth. His friend's shoulders tensed and bunched, but he didn't pull back.

"Swallow it," Cord whispered. "You can do it. I did."

His cock slid from Austin's lips, his eyes watering as he audibly swallowed. Cord's head swam as he sagged back. Utter satisfaction overtook him.

Silence stretched and he felt Austin shifting away, but shot out an arm to hold him close. "Lay with me a minute?"

Slowly, his friend—his lover—moved back. Shoulder to shoulder, they stared at the ceiling. Cord's fingers curled around Austin's and tightened. Gradually, Austin squeezed back in response.

Fourteen

December

EMBER HUSTLED TO HER JEEP. Her mood of late had been a bit fragile, for no apparent reason. Probably a combination of things, what with their evolving relationship and her men not always seeing the same need to talk. It made her nuts that they seemed happy to let things play out without any discussion, while she preferred to analyze their relationship as they progressed, but maybe that was the difference between men and women.

Cord was mostly living with them, but they never seemed to get around to finalizing their arrangement, whatever that would look like. She sometimes felt they were distracting her with sex and, by the time they finished distracting her, she was always too tired for pillow talk, let alone have a serious conversation.

Women talked. They communicated. Men didn't. They seemed to rely on guesswork and smoke signals, but she was determined her men were going to learn the particular skill. That way, they wouldn't be scrambling when it came to even the little things like arranging a ride home when one of them had a car in the shop.

Backing around, she headed down the drive, pointing her car toward the church. Summer was passing by and while the daylight hours were still long, dusk was closing in.

Spotting the church parking lot, she pulled in and checked her phone for any texts from Austin. If the meeting was over already, chances were he'd be having coffee at the diner down the road.

There was no particular time limit on the meetings—it depended on who all needed to share. Well, she'd track her husband down at the diner if she needed to, and maybe get a glimpse of the elusive Harley.

People spilled out of the building, a few walking away and others climbing into cars. A small group near the doors caught her eye and she carefully maneuvered her Jeep in that direction. She found a closer parking spot, surmising Austin would wait there before heading for coffee.

A large black man lifted a hand and headed toward a dark SUV, its lights flashing in response to a key fob. One by one, the cars cleared out of the lot, but that black SUV lingered.

"Come on, Austin." She didn't like dark parking lots at night.

Had her husband known she'd be picking him up, he would have come right out. But he was expecting Cord. *Men and their sketchy plans...*

The two people remaining by the door were embroiled in conversation, intent on one another. Squinting at the dark entrance, she smiled as she recognized her husband's familiar form exiting the side door. Then she noticed the proximity of the woman beside him, her long blonde hair capturing the pool of light coming from one of the security lamps.

Ember wasn't a jealous person, but this woman seemed to trespass on what she deemed personal space. She lowered the car window to call out to Austin, when the words froze on her lips. The blonde closed the distance and leaned against him, pressing her face into his shoulder, lips close to his neck. Austin's arms lifted, hovered, and then settled around her, *his* mouth close to her ear.

Ember's eyes narrowed as her belly tightened and her breath caught in her throat. That was *her* husband, and the other half of him was sitting in the damn Jeep.

Battling her insecurity, she decided to tap the horn, casual like. The sudden blare made them both jerk—Ember too—and Austin turned to face the vehicle.

Her thoughts banged around against one another, her heart telling her not to be stupid, to wait for him to come to her. In the end, her insecurities won, and she threw open the door.

Her feet hit the asphalt so hard her knees rattled with the impact. She marched her way to where they stood, noting Austin had set the blonde away from him and was moving in her direction.

"Ember? Where's Cord?" he asked as if he hadn't just been holding another woman.

She sidestepped him, not sparing him a glance and marched up to the blonde, thrusting up her chin. "I'm Ember Garret. Austin's *wife*."

"Oh, um, hi. I'm Rebecca." Hot pink stained the woman's cheekbones.

"Rebecca *who*?"

"Baby," Austin's deep voice spoke behind her. "We don't share last names with outsiders."

She spun on her heel to face him. "Oh, right. But you hug one another."

"*Ember*," her husband nearly choked, but she was certain—after what she'd observed—little old Rebecca wasn't overly concerned about boundaries. Was he blind?

"Austin?" A deep voice called, and the tall, black man who had been heading toward the SUV approached.

Her husband drew in a breath, the tension in his face easing. "Harley." His posture relaxed as he stepped beside her. "This is my wife, Ember."

For some reason, the introduction of the mysterious Harley both defused her annoyance and fueled it. She kept Rebecca in her peripheral as she turned and forced a smile for Austin's sponsor.

"I feel as though I know you, Mrs. Garret," the man greeted, voice deep and friendly. Of course their anonymity didn't transfer to her, but that was fine.

She took his outstretched hand, briefly. "Nice to *finally* meet you."

"Austin sings your praises." Something about those dark, assertive eyes told Ember this man didn't miss much.

"How nice." Craning her neck to meet Harley's stare left her feeling as though she was speaking to some sort of authority figure, and embarrassment for her erratic, territorial behavior made her shrink a little.

This was not the first impression she wanted to make on this man, and now she wanted to flee before she said or did something else to give him reason to judge her.

Figuring she'd given Rebecca fair warning, she turned back to her husband. "I'm heading home, Austin. I'll give you a lift unless you'd rather grab coffee with your *friends.*" She definitely needed to get out of there.

Her husband hesitated, and her insecurities came roaring back. She fought her confusing emotions, waiting for him to answer. His head tipped to the side as he scrutinized her, as if trying to figure out *why* she was upset. Did he forget his little pink cheeked companion still standing to his left?

Voice level, he finally said, "I planned to head straight home. Just give me a minute."

Turning on her heel, she stalked back to the Jeep and clambered inside, latching her seatbelt with trembling fingers. Staring out the windshield, she tried to read Harley's lips—or at least his body language—but the man didn't stay long. Rebecca however...

Austin spoke to the blonde for what felt like an interminable length of time, standing tall before her, posture assertive—very different from what she witnessed five minutes ago.

Ember tilted her head to the open window but couldn't make out what was being said. Rebecca clutched her hands in front of her and ducked her head.

Stepping back, Austin watched as Rebecca walked to a little, sporty car. As soon as the other woman was inside and the headlights came on, he strode to the Jeep. Ember's body continued to tremble with uncertainty and a continuous surge of adrenaline pumped through her even after the woman pulled away.

When Austin was buckled in, she threw the car into gear and accelerated out of the lot, wondering if the anonymity of AA would allow him to say anything.

"Rebecca's pretty new," her husband offered. "She's struggling and looking for a sponsor."

Biting back a totally inappropriate remark, something to do with an interesting audition, she concentrated on the road. It was jarring to see her husband hold another woman and maybe it was something innocent, but she didn't care about the details. She only knew she didn't like it. She was being ridiculous, yet she couldn't seem to reel in her emotions.

Her mind flashed over the criticisms of AA meetings, the one where people called them meat markets, and she grit her teeth. That wasn't Austin. Austin valued the program for the actual foundation it lent, he'd said so himself. He wouldn't—

"Ember."

"I'm driving."

The leather of the seat creaked as he shifted his weight, and she knew, without looking, that he was choosing his words so as not to piss her off further.

"Some people at the meetings hug. Rebecca's a hugger. She seems to need physical contact. Harley had just cautioned her and she was embarrassed. She kind of, uh, threw herself at me and fell apart—caught me off guard."

She tightened her grip on the wheel and set her lips in a flat line. "Let's not talk right now." Of course, *now* he wanted to talk.

"She crossed a boundary," he continued. "You honked before I could set her straight."

He didn't sound at all defensive. Nope. Cool, calm, and collected. That was Austin. The *new* and improved Austin who had new, unfamiliar people in his life she knew nothing about.

With his truck in the shop and Cord expected to pick him up, she wondered if he would have even told her about this Rebecca nonsense tonight when he got home. If Cord hadn't ended up working late, she might not even have known the woman existed. Again, the unclear statutes of *anonymous* irritated her.

She needed to calm down—and slow down. Her foot eased slightly off the gas.

It might have been innocent, at least on Austin's part, but she could tell when someone was going after a man. *Her man.* And she didn't like feeling threatened.

"It's fine," she grumbled, wondering if she over-reacted.

No, that woman was hugging him...touching him with far too much intimacy. Although, intimacy wasn't always interchangeable with familiarity.

"I straightened her out, made sure she understood I'm a happily married man."

"Good." It was good. It was *fine.*

This was about her and her stupid insecurities and a hefty dollop of envy—jealousy—to top it off. Austin needed his meetings. He needed Harley. It was wrong for her to measure her own worth against those who were valuable to her husband in other ways. This wasn't a competition.

"Ember, please—"

"It's fine, Austin. Let's not talk about it anymore." She blinked against the tears blurring her vision and pulled into their driveway. She should have trusted him to set the woman straight before involving herself.

It was one thing to struggle with her emotions, but she didn't like the way they were influencing her actions. Yet seeing how close he was with those strangers at that meeting made her feel inadequate in ways they apparently weren't.

Not talking until she calmed down seemed the best choice.

He was hard on her heels when she climbed the porch steps and tried to fit her keys in the lock.

Taking them from her, he opened the door and let her precede him.

She hurried inside, slipping off the sweater she'd thrown on over her dress—a simple, cotton dress—no competition for the navy number Rebecca had worn. She winced at her shallow and judgmental thoughts, feeling ashamed. A nerve had been struck tonight and it was still throbbing, that was all.

"Ember." Austin pried the sweater from her fingers and escorted her to the couch.

She sat, but only because her legs didn't want to hold her up anymore. No matter how hard she fought to be the confident wife she once was, the backlash of the last year was sometimes a bigger demon than she could combat.

She needed to hear his reassurance, needed to prove to herself she was overreacting and his loyalty was to her, but for over ten long months his loyalty was to alcohol and that sense of coming second still haunted her from time to time.

Her head lowered as she tried to process the hurt and fear, tried to make sense of why this bothered her so much. "Is she why you've been so late getting home from your meetings?" *And so eager to get to them?*

He reared back, shock tightening his features, and then his eyes narrowed. "No. I go because I need to. And I stay after for coffee with Harley. You know that."

"Does Rebecca ever go for coffee?"

A hint of guilt flashed across his face and her heart splintered. Lies. Like before.

"She came along once." His gaze was intent on her face. "Along with two other newcomers. Once, Ember. I swear that's it. Harley knew she had issues with boundaries. Said it wasn't appropriate for her to seek out male support and he'd find her a female sponsor, but we're a little short on sponsors at the moment."

"Of course *Harley* knew all that." Cynicism crept into her tone.

"Harley's a good friend. He's done nothing but help me since the day I met him. He saved my life."

His words hit hard and sharp, like a bullet to her heart. It was enough of a shot to make her flinch. "Like *I* couldn't."

She shook her head, the agony of feeling less than everyone else returning with a vengeance. But she wasn't alone when it came to her envy of Harley or the vague sense of inferiority she experienced at every mention of the man.

"And like Cord couldn't," she added.

Gravel crunched and headlights swept across the room. The relief on her husband's face might have been comical if this wasn't a serious subject she needed to address with him. Keeping secrets belonged in the past. Their future would only work if they were one hundred percent open and honest, one hundred percent of the time.

Her ears registered Cord's familiar footfalls climbing up the porch steps. He threw the door wide, walking inside and wearing a smile that didn't fit the energy of the house.

"Oh, good. You're home. Ember picked you up,

then?" When neither of them spoke, he tilted his head. "What's going on?"

Austin didn't hesitate. "One of the AA members kind of pushed herself on me tonight and Ember saw it."

Cord scoffed—almost laughed. "Like you'd encourage another woman."

"Exactly," Austin confirmed. "It was damn awkward and it upset Ember."

The mere idea that another woman might think it was okay to put her hands on a married man—Of course she was upset! She sniffed, blinking rapidly.

Cord came to crouch beside her, taking her hand and stroking it. "Ember, I can guarantee Austin would never cheat on you. That's crazy. Come on, sweetheart. I'm sure it was a simple misunderstanding."

"I know." She forced a smile, her lips trembling. And she did know. It was just that she felt so separate from that part of her husband's life, she didn't know the strangers occupying that corner of his world and it was impossible to trust what she didn't know.

Austin edged closer. "Harley warned me she had a tendency to cling to the wrong people."

And the mention of Harley set her off. That probably made her a bad person, but it was what it was. Yanking her hand from Cord's she glared at her husband.

"I'm sick of hearing about Harley. This is about *us*, Austin. You, me, and Cord. So long as Harley remains separate from *our* life, he can't be the solution *here*. We all don't know him!"

"Baby, calm down—"

"I will not calm down. I'm your wife, and Cord's your best friend, yet you act like Harley's the keeper of all your secrets. Do you have to keep everything separate? From *us*? Aren't we deserving of your trust more than some guy you only met this winter? I might not understand addiction on a first hand level like Harley, but I tried."

Despite her best intentions, moisture welled up and spilled over her lashes as her voice broke. They were both staring at her as though she'd lost her mind. Choking on a sob, she wiped her eyes and cried, "I tried."

She dashed her tears away with shaky fingertips and shook her head. The entire night was turning into a muddled smear of confusion and high emotion. He was doing so well and it was wrong to be upset over those who deserved the credit for his success. But she was his wife and she hadn't been able to help him.

"I'm sorry I'm so upset, but..." Her face tipped down as she confessed, "When you said Harley saved your life, that...that was hard to hear."

The room filled with seething, oppressive silence and she glanced at Austin, but he looked away. Maybe he didn't understand how much his past secrets had scarred her, how every lasting wall between them now felt like a crushing blow to her mending heart. He needed to talk to her!

"I just..." She sniffled and her voice shrank to barely a whisper. "Every little truth you keep to yourself feels like a deception. If we're going to move forward there can't be anymore secrets between us."

Cord shuddered through a long breath and said, "You gotta tell her."

Austin's face whitened, every vestige of color draining away. He swallowed, his Adam's apple making a slow bob along his throat.

Her stomach knotted as her upset gave way to fear. Maybe she'd asked for too much. "Tell me what?"

Austin dragged his hand over his face. "This night's totally fucked," he muttered.

An ice-cold hand gripped her belly and she tensed, bracing for whatever confession he had to make. "You tell me what you're hiding, Austin. Right now."

Cord nodded at her husband—speaking in silence again. Austin straightened his spine, his shoulders squaring, his lips tight, but he looked her in the eyes.

No. Whatever he was about to confess, judging by the look on his face, she wasn't ready to hear it. Fear rose up from her belly and constricted her chest.

"Ember..." He lowered to sit beside her and chafed her hands.

So afraid of whatever was coming, she allowed the contact, her fingers suddenly numb.

"Baby...I..."

He shook his head and every passing second sent another knife of dread stabbing into her heart.

His words tumbled over one another in a breathless rush. "I tried to kill myself. Last winter after you left. Cord stopped me, I spent a few days in a psych ward, and then I met Harley and he helped me talk through a lot of what I was fighting."

Her limbs went numb as her brain worked to process his words, but they weren't registering. "What?" she choked, refusing to believe what he just confessed.

Her life, her marriage, her happiness flashing before her eyes and blowing away... Her ignorance of her husband's actions a backhanded reminder that all she loved could be stolen in a rash moment of desperation.

"When? Why?"

Dropping his gaze, he said, "I was in a bad place. My head was all fucked up. I guess I hit some point beneath rock bottom."

Her brain froze as she grappled to absorb what he described, sloppily piecing together the jagged parts of last year to form a sort of timeline in her head. Her chest tightened and she struggled to form words, syllables climbing up her dry throat like blades of glass.

"Why didn't you—*either of you*—tell me?"

Both of them had called her, left messages after she'd run to her parents. Not once had either hinted that she *needed* to come home. Never had they referenced Austin's attempted suicide. Too. Many. Secrets.

She'd been so consumed with her own pain, her own needs, never once thinking beyond Austin's *need* to get sober. How could she know he'd sunk so low when every phone message spoke of improvement? But Austin's troubles had been far greater than hers, his hurt so profound he'd actually tried to give up his life to make the pain stop.

A horrid suspicion gripped her and her stomach roiled as blame found its source and hit her like a ton of bricks. "It was my letter, wasn't it? Oh, God."

Her insides collapsed as she wheezed out a breath, feeling like the blindest wife on the planet. She'd been so selfish, so consumed by her own misery. She'd failed to recognize how deep his depression went. Another vow broken—*in sickness and in health*. His battle had been harder on him than anyone else. And she was a blind, self-centered fool.

"Ember." Cord took one of her hands from Austin, his grip tightening, as her husband hitched closer. "No one's to blame."

"Baby, I was at rock bottom—beneath the normal crap people think is rock bottom," Austin insisted. "When I realized what I'd done to you—and to Cord—I gave up. Only...he wouldn't let me."

She'd nearly been responsible for her husband's death. Driven him to the very edge with no other option to hold onto. She'd *abandoned* him when he needed her most. What would her life have become had Cord not been there to stop him? His idea of escaping pain could have left her in an eternal state of agony, alone with so much blame.

How could they have kept this from her? She would have raced home, put her own pain aside. This was his *life*—their life. How dare he gamble with that!

Absolute sadness washed through her like a tidal wave, amplifying her guilt, as all the pain of the last twelve months seemed to crash over her at once. Her husband intended to abandon her right back—*permanently* removing the other half of her soul.

How the hell would she have survived that? How would she have collected the pieces of her broken heart without the hope that he'd someday come back, that they'd someday recover?

And Cord, to withhold this from her as well... Her eyes closed as she accepted their shared deceit. All those phone messages and neither of them gave her absolute honesty. She would have come home, toughed it out. But she'd removed herself and they decided it best she stay uninformed and removed until they cleaned up a mess they were *all* responsible for making.

Were they ever planning to tell her? If she hadn't overreacted to Rebecca tonight and expressed her envy of Austin's relationship with Harley, told them how deeply the ongoing secrecy gutted her, would Austin have shared this hidden, enormous detail of his past?

A sense of inadequacy weighed heavily on her shoulders. Cord knew. Harley knew. Maybe his entire AA group knew. But she—*his wife*—didn't know.

The kid gloves and secrets were enough to steal not only her sense of efficacy, but also her purpose. If all of those people could save him, turn his life around, but she couldn't... Why was she even here?

Through sickness and health and you failed him...

Her failures—theirs—coalesced in crushing pain and she had no energy left to reassign the blame.

The depth of their withholding felt like a devastating betrayal, too many degrees of separation.

Somehow, she pried her hands free and got to her feet unimpeded. In a voice she barely recognized, she said, "I need some space. I'm going to bed. Don't follow—*either* of you."

Fifteen

Austin

AUSTIN'S FORK clattered to the plate and he glared at yet another reheated meal. It had been three days, three endless fucking days of holding his breath for his wife to speak to him. But she hadn't said a word.

She'd taken phone calls, visited the library, the craft store, and even the local middle school to drop off baked goods for a fundraiser. She'd talked to everyone in their fucking town but didn't have a word to spare for him or Cord. It was like living with a ghost.

"This is fucking bullshit."

"Austin—"

"Don't Austin me. What the hell is she doing at the library this time of night?"

"My guess would be reading."

He rolled his eyes. "Shut up."

Cord shoved away his plate and folded his arms on the table. "Look, she's upset. We knew she would be, the longer you kept things from her. You're the one who's always on everyone else's ass about keeping it honest."

"You think I don't know that?" He hadn't withheld those details to hurt her. Just the opposite.

"Well, you should have known it sooner. You should have told her the first time you talked—or the first time the three of us sat down to talk."

"I wasn't ready. *She* wasn't ready. Damn it, Cord, we had to rebuild our relationship. And that included figuring out where you fit in." He winced. That hadn't come out right. He wasn't doing anything right.

"Where I fit in?" A muscle ticked in Cord's cheek.

"Yes. We're all new at this, and it hasn't been easy. You know that. But it's been getting better." He got up and paced. "What happened last winter... the pills... I was ashamed, okay? I didn't want her to see me as a lost cause, or...or be pissed with you for not telling her the truth."

"We're both in the shit. Ember loves you—*us*. It's the withholding she's angry about."

Austin brooded and continued to pace, trying to figure out a way to make things right. Cord sipped at his coffee, giving him space.

"Why is she so suspicious of Harley? He hasn't done anything." He frowned when Cord broke eye contact. "What?"

Cord opened his mouth, but hesitated. "Look, it's one thing to be close to your sponsor. I get that. But sometimes it does seem like you have this separate life. I mean, there are plenty of nights that I get here late and you aren't even home yet. She misses you, man. You can't get mad at her for wanting more of your time."

It didn't need stating that his wife had missed him enough for one lifetime. He rubbed his temples. "I miss her too. I just... This is working for me. If I change something shit might get messed up."

"Austin, I've been to Debbie's Diner. They serve beer right at the counter. If you haven't buckled yet, skipping out on coffee here and there isn't going to break you. Maybe just cut back to one cup after a meeting or only meeting for coffee once every few days instead of every night."

But Harley got him. He knew what it was like and Austin enjoyed their conversations. Most nights they didn't even discuss drinking.

"I don't know if I'm ready to do that. Eventually, yeah, but right now I don't like the sound of that."

"Then introduce them."

He frowned. "What do you mean? They've met."

"Right. In front of the church—with a woman who came onto you. Introduce them, Austin, the way Ember likes things done. Have him over for dinner. Let her actually see what's so amazing about this guy."

He squinted at his friend. "You don't like him either."

"I didn't say that. How would I even know? But I wouldn't turn down the chance to meet him. He's an important part of your life. I get that. But... so am I. It sort of sucks being kept out of the other half."

He hadn't realized he'd been keeping them out. If they had Harley over for a visit it might change their dynamic in regard to their sponsor-sponsoree relationship.

"He doesn't know about our...situation." He'd tried hedging, but their circumstances were so extraordinary it wasn't like Harley would up and guess.

"Why does he have to know?"

"Because I want him to." The words came out before Austin actually thought about them.

Cord's brows lifted. "Okay."

Austin waved a hand. "I don't know how to explain it. He might not get it, but I put a lot of faith in his...feedback."

"Hold on. I hope you're not basing anything about us on an outsider's approval." Cord's arms crossed over his chest. "Austin, you gotta accept that not everybody's gonna be jumping for joy when they learn you're sharing your wife and fucking your best friend."

"Not fucking."

His friend's lips quirked into a smirk and he gave him the finger. "Yet. Besides, you know what I mean. Why not just say we sort of live together and leave it at that?"

"Because that's not what this is and I don't want another thing in my life I feel like I have to hide."

"You're not *hiding* it. It's called being discreet. Speaking of which..."

What now? He arched a brow. "What?"

"I need to tell you something. I should have brought it up earlier, but between work and the cars going in for inspection and everything with Ember, it's always something—"

"Spit it out, Cord." His patience was wearing reed thin.

"My mom knows I slept with Ember."

His entire body froze and he wheezed, "Excuse me?"

"She knows we slept together last winter. Not that we are now, but I think she has questions and that's why she wants us over this weekend."

"Well, that's just great. Go ahead and tell her we won't be able to make it because my wife, whom you're fucking, happened to see another woman making a move on me and now she's spending all her free time at the goddamn library!"

"It's not about that, Austin! It's that you didn't tell her—"

Shoving his hand through the air, he silenced him. "Don't." He wished he was a smoker or had something to take the fucking edge off. "I know what it's about," he snapped. "Don't forget to mention the attempted suicide my wife's mad at us for. Far be it for me to try to kill myself. What was I thinking?"

"Where are you going?" Cord yelled as Austin stalked out of the room.

"Away."

He marched out back and glared at the deck

that was far from finished. Two guys in one house and shit was taking longer than ever to build. How did that happen?

Lights flashed over the side of the house and he took the path to the front yard, but Cord beat him there. Standing in the shadow of the shed, Austin watched as Ember climbed out of the Jeep, a new sack of books over her arm.

"Did you get some good stuff?" Cord asked from the porch and she halted, staring up at him beneath a spill of light from the house.

Blanking her expression, she moved up the steps, her head down. "Sure."

How long could she keep up this silent treatment? It was killing him.

Cord caught her arm when she reached for the front door. "Ember, we have to talk. You're the one who's always insisting we communicate. You can't just shut us out like this."

"My husband tried to end his life, Cord. *Because of me*. And no one thought to share it with me. Do you know how much that hurts?"

"As his best friend and the person who was there, I can honestly say, yes, I think I do."

"Well, you don't. It was *my* job to love him in sickness and health and I bailed. I walked away and left him flailing because I was too disappointed in my own inadequacies and the fact that *I* couldn't fix him."

"December, the only person who can fix Austin, is Austin."

"That's bullshit!" she snapped. "*You* saved him. And then Harley came to the rescue! Where was I?

Why wasn't *I* enough, or even a part of all this healing?"

"Ember, you were—you *are*. Let's go inside and talk, sweetheart. We'll sit down, the three of us—"

"I have nothing to say."

Austin's head lowered as the silence from the porch stretched to encompass him. He thought about making his presence known, but seeing how upset she still was, he did the cowardly thing and kept to the shadows of the bushes.

He should be glad for his personal improvements and not one bit sorry for the way he'd made them or who was involved. But it broke his heart that his success somehow *still* made her feel incomplete, like she hadn't been enough. She was what motivated him most of all.

His head jerked up as the simple truth hit him like a bolt of lightning, giving him the courage to face her wrath and help her see the truth.

He stepped out of the shadows, rustling the hedges and nearly scaring his wife and Cord half to death. "Hey."

Ember shrieked and Cord thrust his body in front of her, a protective glare transforming his face to one that would have scared the shit out of anyone. *"Austin?"*

He stepped into the light and they both noticeably relaxed. "It's just me."

"What the hell are you doing in the bushes?" Cord snapped.

"I was coming from out back, but that doesn't matter." He took the steps two at a time and didn't stop until he was cupping his wife's face, intensely relieved when she didn't flinch away.

"You, December. You *matter*. Yes, I was devastated to lose you, lost without you, but deep down you were never truly gone. Cord stopped me, but *you* ultimately saved me.

"You were what kept me breathing and what keeps me moving in the right direction. Every decision I make, my first thought is you, my second thought me. I don't know. Maybe I'm third now, and Cord's even before me, but my point is, it's you, baby. You're the person that saved me more than anyone else in this fucked up world. You're my..." He shook his head, struggling to find the right word. "Sanity."

She shivered beneath his touch, her shimmering eyes wide and washed with pain. "But I wasn't here."

He shook his head and pressed her hand to his chest, directly over his pounding heart. "But you were *here*. Always with me. Losing you left me struggling to make sense of a world I didn't recognize. It was dark and terrifying, but somehow I held onto the love we shared and it got me through. I found my way back home, back to you. That's what kept me going, not what anyone said. Cord removed a hundred dangers from this house, but only my determination to keep my promises to you stopped me from letting the bad back in.

"Once you came home, I didn't want to bring all that darkness back, which is why I didn't tell you, not because I was purposely hiding what happened from you. I was protecting you from all the ugliness

I let into our past. Please believe that. I'd never purposely hurt you. I only want to protect you."

"It's true, kiddo," Cord chimed in. "A day didn't go by that he didn't mention you or plan for your future. Every word out of his mouth spoke of his absolute certainty to repair the promises to you he'd broken. And if you see other girls looking at him—at either of us—you can be damn sure we aren't looking back. It's just you, sweetheart."

Austin smiled, once again relieved to have a partner in Cord. "Just you," he echoed.

Her hand pressed hard against his chest as her lips pursed and she whispered, "Well, Cord too."

Austin chuckled, sensing the recent December frost coming to a thaw. "And Cord." He pressed his lips to her forehead. "Please forgive me. I swear there won't be any more secrets."

"I guess I understand. But I'm still more upset than I want to be. Not about Rebecca. She just set me off because I was feeling...less important than the people in that part of your life. What happened... It happened to all of us, and I'm still healing, too. I can't be in a relationship built on secrets. It has to be honest and open from here on out."

He nodded. "No more secrets." His throat vibrated with passion. He'd give the rest of his day to proving how necessary she was to his survival, his sanity. Loving her, atoning for the ways he'd wronged her. It didn't matter, so long as he had her. "Never feel like you're less important than anyone or anything, December. You're the most important thing in my life."

She nodded, then sniffled. "I guess I needed to hear that."

"No more secrets, Ember. I promise." He crossed his heart before biting off the rest of the childhood rhyme.

"And I'm holding you to that promise, Austin Garret." She threw a look at Cord that *promised* he was equally accountable, not that either of them needed anyone to interpret.

"It's a vow, baby." He hugged her close, beyond grateful to feel her arms tightening around him.

Her shoulders relaxed and for the first time in days he felt able to breathe again. He wanted all of this stress put behind them.

"How about we figure out a date to have Harley over. I'm sure he'd love to meet you when things are less...chaotic."

"Really?" Her whole face lit up and he smiled.

"Yeah, really. It was an oversight for me not to invite him sooner."

"I'd love that! Find out what his favorite dish is and I'll make it. Oh! I should go back to the library and grab a cookbook tomorrow..." Her words drifted away as she bustled into the house, obviously on a mission to design her next dinner party.

He glanced at Cord and frowned. "What the fuck's wrong with your face?"

"Nothing." Cord pinched his nose and turned away. Voice cracking, he muffled, "That was just really nice, everything you said to her. Sweet."

Austin silently laughed. Maybe they were all a little too sensitive lately. He clapped a hand on his friend's shoulder and squeezed. "Well, pull it together there, thunder muffin. We got a long night of makeup sex ahead of us."

As he went to find his wife, it took Cord a minute to follow, but eventually the door swung open. "What the hell did you just call me?"

Austin laughed, dodging out of the hall as Cord took a playful swing at him, sidestepping into the dining room. "Calm down, cuddles. I was just trying to comfort you in your moment of emotional need or whatever the fuck that was back there." Mumbling out of the corner of his mouth, he murmured, "Looked a little like crying."

"I *was not* fucking crying."

"Sure thing, tender heart."

"Damn it, Austin! I wasn't. I'm a fucking *man*. Rugged and flannel covered."

December came into the dining room. "What are you two arguing about?"

"Nothing." Cord sent him a death stare.

Austin smirked. "Cord's feelings."

His wife tried to hide a smile, and the relief he experienced at her change of mood made his knees weak.

"Oh, I know. Cord's very sensitive. I have cookies out." She slipped back into the kitchen and his friend glared at him.

"You're such a dick," Cord hissed, and then yelled, "I'm all man, December! *All man!*"

Austin laughed as Cord stomped into the kitchen, likely to prove his manhood. Austin decided it best to follow.

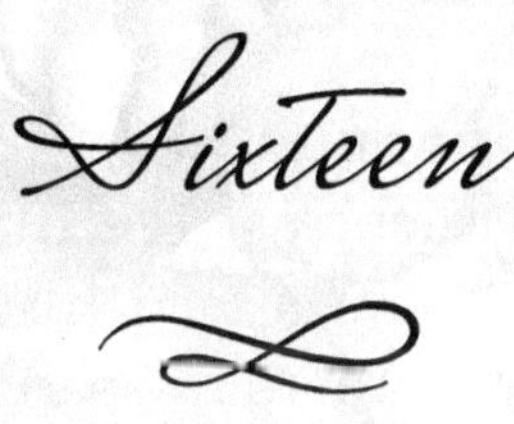

Sixteen

December

EMBER YANKED the dress off her shoulders and tossed it onto the bed with the growing pile of other discarded outfits. She rummaged through her closet as if some miracle dress would suddenly appear.

"Well, isn't that a pretty picture."

She pivoted to find Cord leaning against the jamb of her bedroom door and rolled her eyes. "I have nothing to wear."

He glanced at the mountain of dresses on the bed and raised a brow. "That's more clothes than all the stuff I owned, combined."

Sure. When a guy wore a strict uniform of denim, flannel, and cotton there wasn't really any call for a wardrobe crisis. She rested her hand on her hip just above the waistband of her panties and glared at him. "Did you need something?"

"Austin sent me up to see what was taking you so long."

"Tell him ten minutes."

He chuckled silently. "Ten minutes as in what you said twenty minutes ago? Just pick something, kiddo. We're only going to my parents' house."

But it wasn't just a normal visit to the Bay's— not just a typical Sunday dinner. Norma Jean knew stuff and there was no way of predicting how this dinner would play out.

"Ten minutes."

He rolled his eyes and she went back to rummaging through the closet only to jump when his hands closed around her ribs and pulled her back. Warm lips pressed into her neck, as he whispered, "You have no need to be nervous, December. My parents love you—no matter what. It's just dinner."

Her body sagged into his comforting hold and she sighed. "I know they love me, but I don't know how unconditional that love is. I don't know how to do...*this*."

He turned her to face him and frowned, studying her intently. "Isn't this what you wanted, to put it all out in the open?"

"Yes, but...it's safe here. It's just us. What if your mom's totally disgusted by what we're doing? And what about your dad?"

A deep V formed between his brows. "Ember, we aren't going to have an orgy on top of my mom's dining room table. It's just dinner. If she asks questions, *we* decide what to divulge. It's our personal life, not theirs."

She flinched at his graphic description. "But..."

He reached behind her and removed a sunny, yellow, linen dress with eyelet holes on the hem. "Here. Put this on and stop stressing yourself out. Everything's going to be fine. And I promise, whatever you're wearing won't have an effect on the outcome of the meal. It's just dinner."

She took the dress and pursed her lips. "Fine. I'll be down in ten minutes."

"Five. Austin's on the verge of making a sandwich and he's driving me nuts. We have to get him fed."

She laughed, once again in awe at just how well her boys seemed to have adapted. After her little meltdown this week—totally justified in her mind—she decided they were all in full agreement that forward was the direction to go. And she'd never been happier to see her men take the lead. "Five minutes."

Cord drove her Jeep to his parents and she fidgeted in the backseat. "I hope my cake turned out okay. Your dad likes apple cake, right, Cord?"

The guys shared a telling glance and Austin said, "I'm sure your cake's fine, baby. When has Reed ever not liked something you baked?"

"But he likes apples, right?"

"Yes!" they both answered at once. Of course, how would Austin know if Cord's dad liked apples or not? Her palms slicked with sweat.

When they reached the house Cord parked and came around to open her door. "I'll take that." He lifted the cake out of her hands and she felt like a shield had been stripped away.

Cord led them inside without knocking and Austin took her hand, providing a comforting squeeze.

"Mom? Dad?"

Norma Jean came around the corner wearing a bright smile and a teal pantsuit. Too soon, her husband released her hand to kiss the hostess.

"Norma Jean, good to see you again."

Cord's mother affectionately looked into Austin's eyes and patted his cheek. "You look great, Austin. Younger than the last time I saw you. Reed's in the den. He has something to show you."

With a glance back at Ember, he smiled and headed into the other room to find Cord's father. Cord wasn't so lucky.

"Cord, go get the table leaf out so I can set the table."

It was something Norma Jean always asked of him, but today it seemed a little contrived. The moment she and Cord's mom were alone she took December's hand and pulled her to the table, dropping her voice lower than usual.

"Things are good? You all drove together?"

Ember's heart was already beating too fast. She didn't want to answer these sorts of questions on her own. "Everything's fine, Norma Jean."

"Austin and you are..."

"Mom, I got the leaf," Cord announced, making it back in record time. "Ember, you wanna help me with the table?"

She jumped to help before he finished his question. "Sure."

Once they were alone in the dining room Ember caught Cord up to speed. "She's already asking questions."

He slid the edges of the table against the leaf and snapped them into place. "Just stick with me or Austin."

"I have to help her in the kitchen."

"So I'll help, too."

"But you guys usually hang in the den."

"Ember, you're really overthinking this, sweetheart. You have to calm down."

She let out a long breath. "You're right. I don't know what's wrong with me today. I'm going to freshen up in the bathroom and then I'll meet you in the kitchen."

He smiled and gave her shoulder a little squeeze as she walked out of the dining room. Just as she was closing the bathroom door she heard Norma Jean ask, "Cord, do you think it's appropriate to call your friend's wife, sweetheart?"

Ember dropped her head against the door and sighed.

Once the table was set and Reed emerged from the den with Austin, everything seemed a little less stressful.

"This is really great," her husband commented, examining a motion sensor light Cord's father had given them, before setting it by the door.

"No wires," Reed commented. "You just stick it right to the exterior and the sun charges it. I got them all around the house now. Cord, you should get some."

"I sell them at the store, Dad."

"I mean for your house. And yours aren't like these. These you can only order from the television. I told you Bay's needs an *As Seen on TV* display."

"I really appreciate it," Austin commented, drawing some of the attention away from Cord.

"It was very thoughtful for you to get us one," Ember echoed, as they took their places. Cord pulled out her chair before Austin could, and her husband's lips quirked in a subtle smile before he took the seat directly across from them.

"Mine must have got lost in the mail," Cord mumbled, and Ember pressed a hand to his thigh, comforting him beneath the table.

Once dinner was served the conversation revolved around normal, everyday topics, but Norma Jean seemed quiet, slowly chewing her food, her eyes watchful.

"I hear we have apple cake for dessert," Reed said with a smile. "Love me some apple cake, and yours, I'm bettin', is top notch, December."

"All her desserts are top notch," Cord said, with a bump of his shoulder. "I especially enjoy her—"

"Cord!" Norma Jean's disapproval cut through the air.

Ember's cheeks burned, surmising his mother read too much into the compliment, even if they were just discussing baked goods.

Cord frowned at his mom. "What?"

"That's...not appropriate."

"To compliment her baking?" he asked, his brow furrowed in puzzlement.

Ember glanced at Norma Jean who was staring, tight-lipped, at her son.

"He's right," Austin chimed in. "Her desserts are amazing. Her cookies are the best. You had some the other day, didn't you, Norma Jean? At the quilting class."

Cord was still frowning at his mother. Reed glanced around the table as if wondering what he'd missed. Finally, Norma Jean said, "Yes, they were very good. I'll bring out the cake. Cord, help me with the trash."

"I'll get it after—"

"Now." His mother collected a few dishes from the table and carried them to the kitchen.

Cord sighed. "I'll be right back."

Ember looked at Austin and said, "I'll go help Norma Jean with dessert." She collected a few more plates and headed toward the kitchen.

The sound of Cord and his mom verbally sparring seeped into the hall. "Mom, the trash can's not even half full."

"Why would you make a remark like that, Cord? You know they're still reconciling. I raised you better than that."

"I was going to say *cookies*!"

"I'm not an idiot. I know how to read body language. The nudging and little glances. Sitting next to her in Austin's usual seat. You're going to destroy your friendship with them and cause more problems for their marriage."

"My relationship with Austin and Ember is fine, Mom."

"Well, it won't be if you can't keep your comments to yourself. Why can't you find a nice girl? Maybe join one of those Internet sites for singles and meet someone available?"

The mere thought of Cord looking at an online picture of another woman stoked a burst of jealousy in Ember's belly and she couldn't take any more. Stepping through the kitchen door with an armful of plates, she announced, "He already has a nice girl."

Norma Jean spun on her heel, cake knife in hand, and gaped at her son. "You do? Who?"

He took a moment to look at Ember, giving her that smile that never failed to melt her heart. Stepping to her side, he relieved her of the plates before lacing his fingers with hers. "December."

Norma Jean's face paled as the knife clattered to the floor. "You stop that right now, Cordovan," she hissed. "Her husband's in the next room."

"I know," he said and his mother's focus jerked to December, eyes full of uncertainty.

Ember gave a shaky smile. "Austin knows, Norma Jean."

Cord's mother took a small step backwards. "I... what...how...I don't understand. Still? You said it was just that one time."

Cord stepped toward his mom, collected the knife off the floor and placed it on the counter. "It's not a big deal, Mom, and it's not something we want to make a big thing out of. It's just...the way it is. The three of us."

"The *three* of you?" his mother echoed quietly.

"Yes, the three of us."

Norma Jean shook her head and frowned, her attention turning back to Ember. "You're not just with your husband?"

Ember slowly shook her head. "We're in love, Norma Jean. The three of us. I love my husband, but I also love your son. And Cord loves Austin."

"But..." She glanced at her son, questions written all over her face. "Are you...gay?"

Cord shrugged. "Bisexual, I guess. I don't really care how you label it. It is what it is."

The kitchen door swung open. "Where's that cake?"

They all turned and faced Reed, no one making a peep.

He frowned. "What's going on in here?"

"Nothing," Norma Jean quickly said, collecting the knife from the counter and rinsing it off. "The cake will be out in a minute. Go back to the table."

The door swung open again. "I'm all by myself out there."

"They're hiding something in here," Cord's father told Austin. "Do you guys have cookies?"

"No one has any cookies, Reed. For the love of God, go sit down and wait for your cake!" Norma Jean snapped.

The kitchen plunged into silence and Ember saw the moment Austin registered why Cord's mother was so out of sorts. He approached slowly as she cut through the apple cake with an unsteady hand on the knife. He placed a gentle hand on her shoulder.

Keeping his voice low, he said, "It's okay, Momma Bay. It really is."

"What's okay?" Reed barked, now scowling suspiciously at the rest of them.

Cord's mother set the knife on the counter and flattened her hand firmly over the handle, her shoulders noticeably tensing. "You say that now, but where will my son be a year from now? Two years?"

Austin didn't bat an eye at her concern. "He'll be in a loving relationship the same as he is today."

Norma Jean's shoulders moved with slow, labored breaths that caused her body to tremble slightly. "I need to get something from the garage."

"What about the cake?" Reed asked and his wife shoved a plate into his hands.

"Here. Go eat your dessert." She stormed out of the kitchen.

Reed glanced at his slice and shook his head, mumbling, "I don't know what the hell just happened in here, but I need a fork."

Ember slid open the drawer and passed him the silverware, sending Cord and Austin a worried look. "I'm going to go check on her."

She went to the garage and found Norma Jean standing on a stepstool, rummaging around the shelves—talking to herself. "Where are they? I swear to God, if he threw them out..." She gasped and sighed, producing a crumpled pack of cigarettes from behind a canister.

December frowned. "You smoke?"

Norma Jean flinched with a start, testing her balance on the stool, as she stepped to the floor. "Of course not."

She withdrew a box of matches from the pack and lit a cigarette, her hands shaking until she drew in that first long drag. Ember glanced cautiously around the garage as Cord's mom sighed and relaxed into the wall, her arms folding over each other as she took another inhalation. She smoked like someone who had hidden the habit for years.

Ember pulled over a bucket and gingerly sat on the lid, folding her hands between her knees. "I'm sorry, Norma Jean. I know this was unexpected."

A cloud of gray air passed over her head. "I wouldn't say totally unexpected. Cord told me about the affair after I had, um, picked up on some unspoken signals."

Ember winced. "He'd object to that term. So would Austin."

"Well, I don't know what else to call it."

"Neither do I."

Did it even require a label? Wasn't it enough they loved one another? She hoped Norma Jean would come to see that.

The garage turned quiet, the singeing paper of the cigarette the only sound.

"What about children, December?"

Her head popped up. "I don't know. We haven't gotten that far. I think we all want kids though—eventually."

"And what about *my* grandchildren? There's only one of you, dear, but two of them. Have you decided, I mean, about the father? Fathers?"

Her face heated and she lowered her gaze. "I guess that's a conversation we'll have down the line."

More silence.

Norma Jean snuffed out her cigarette and immediately lit another one, shoving the pack Ember's way. "Do you want one?"

Ember stared at the offering and found her hand reaching for it. "Sure."

Norma Jean struck a match, lighting hers then December's. The first burst of tobacco flavor had her swallowing back a cough. Was this supposed to be relaxing?

Norma Jean sighed. "I should have been prepared for this. I know my son. He's always been close to Austin. Not like other boys. There was something different about the way he cared for Austin. Emily saw it too."

"What do you mean?" Ember rolled the cigarette between her fingers, holding it, but no longer smoking.

"We were close, Austin's mom and I. There was no question our sons would be, too—at least we hoped. But Emily passed away before they were old enough to date and I kept a good eye on her son, treating him like my own. I never understood why Austin was so determined to find a good woman and Cord always seemed...disinterested in settling down—always playing the field, but never looking at anyone seriously."

"I don't think he did that on purpose," December offered.

Norma Jean sighed. "Then you came along and I had to figure out why Cord suddenly looked so heartbroken all the time. I thought it was because he was in love with you, but now I wonder if it was Austin he loved all along."

Ember's head lifted as she blinked at Cord's mom. "You think he loved Austin before this? As more than a best friend?"

She exhaled slowly. "I didn't, but now...it's all making sense. I think my son's been in love with your husband since they were children. He calls it bisexual, but I don't recall him ever looking at other men like that. Just Austin."

Maybe it was the nicotine, but Ember's head was swimming. Cord loved Austin? Of course he loved him *now,* but before her? Was that true? Did Austin know? Why hadn't Cord said, or hinted at, anything?

Her lips parted as so many past interactions played through her mind. Glances, things Cord had said, the way he'd pulled away from them. She'd thought his feelings had initially been about her. But she'd misread the situation if what Norma Jean was saying had any truth to it.

She took a drag of the cigarette and immediately regretted it. She needed to talk to Cord and Austin.

Norma Jean held out the ashtray and December extinguished her half-smoked cigarette beside the other butts. As she stood, she lost her balance.

"Honey, maybe you should sit a minute longer. I shouldn't have given you that smoke."

"I shouldn't have taken it."

"Here, have a sip of soda." Norma Jean popped a can of cola from the cases stacked on the shelf and handed the drink to Ember.

The warm soda helped a little bit, but her

mouth tasted disgusting. "Do you hate me, Norma Jean?"

The other woman tipped her head and sighed. "No, dear, I could never hate you. You and Austin are like family to us. I'm thrown, I'll admit. I have a lot of questions, some I'll probably be happier not knowing the answers to, but I could never hate you."

Relief shook her to the core, making her more lightheaded than ever, and tears pricked her eyes. "I'm so glad to hear you say that," she choked out, "because you're like family to us, too. With Austin not having a mom and his dad being so...terrible... My parents...they're here and there, but nothing like you. You're...consistent."

"I am that." Norma Jean's voice softened, and she patted Ember's hand.

"I mean, if I need something, I know I can count on you. You bring chicken soup when I have a cold and you burn candles instead of incense. You read fiction and vote and you always bring me samples back from the department stores whenever you go shopping. My mom never did any of that. I don't even think she's ever been inside of a mall."

She knew she was blithering, but her heart was so full. Her mind was a cluster of questions and strange revelations. She couldn't leave here until she was certain Norma Jean was okay.

"Well, I've never met your mother, December, but I'm certain she loves you the best she can. There are all sorts of folks in this world, and whether we shop in malls or grow our necessities, we're all just people at the end of the day, trying to make sense of this life." She sighed. "I imagine I'll be trying to make sense of the three of you for some time. But despite the configuration, I know you're still just Cord, Austin, and December, and I also know, no matter what, I'll always love you. All three of you."

A tear worked past her lashes and trickled down her cheek. She needed a hug and hoped Norma Jean did too. Rising from the bucket, she stepped closer and the older woman embraced her with equal fervor. Ember sniffed in the homey scent of her clothing overlaid with the fresh scent of cigarettes.

"Thank you. We love you, too."

With a pat on the back, Norma Jean eased away. "Come on. Let's go eat some of that cake."

Seventeen

Cord

THE MOMENT DECEMBER and his mother returned from the garage Cord sat up, alert. They both looked a little drained, but...good. Ember smiled and he sensed her relief, which loaned itself to him.

"I see you boys had seconds." His mother placed the last two slices of cake on the table for her and Ember, as the men focused on their third helpings.

"We saved you some," his father commented. "Delicious, December. You really outdid yourself."

"Thank you."

"So," his mother said and Cord stiffened. "We have some things to discuss."

"Maybe now is not the—"

"That's enough out of you, Cord. December

and I have talked and we're fine. I'm fine. It's an adjustment, but we're a modern family and we'll adapt. But I won't have this uncertainty weighing on us any longer. If this is going to be out in the open, let's get on with it so we can all adjust."

"What the hell are you talking about, Norma Jean? You get into the cooking sherry again?" his father asked.

"I'm *talking* about the fact that Cord, Austin, and December are all in a relationship together."

Cord held his breath as his father froze, forkful of cake midway to his mouth. "Come again?"

"A relationship," his mother repeated. "A committed—it is monogamous, isn't it?" They all nodded their heads vehemently, and if it wasn't such a serious discussion, he might have laughed at the bobble head effect. "A *committed* relationship. The three of them."

His father's brow creased with three deep-set lines as he glanced at December and quickly looked away. "Austin?"

"Yes, sir."

"Are you aware of this?"

Austin gave a nervous laugh. "Uh, yes."

"And you're okay with this?"

"Yes."

His father let out a huff of cool laughter and flattened his palms on the table. His eyes narrowed and his lips set tight. "Well. Not the man I thought you were."

"Dad—"

"You, be quiet. I don't even know what to say to you. Another man's wife?"

"Reed," his mother intercepted. "I think you need to be a little open minded here. The three of them go back a long time."

"So do Felix and Oscar, but that's as odd as it gets. Cord, how could you do this to them? They're *married*. Does that mean nothing to you?"

"Reed," Ember quietly spoke. "Cord didn't hurt our marriage. He helped it."

His father scoffed "You—"

Cord scowled when December shrank back. "Don't," he snapped, cutting his father off. "Don't you dare judge her for something you can't possibly understand."

"Oh, I understand."

"No, you don't."

"Cord," Austin interrupted in a voice meant to rein in his temper, but it was too late. Cord had to get this out.

"I've done everything you've ever asked of me. I took up working at the store before I even had working papers. You wanted me to take some business classes, I did. When you were ready to retire, I made sure you never had to worry about Bay's, and I never complained."

"You wanted to take over Bay's!"

"I wanted to make you happy!" Cord barked.

"This isn't about the store!" his mother shouted. "Now stop it! We are not going to fight about this!"

Tension stretched across the silent room. Cord lowered his voice. "If you could just try to be a little open minded—"

"About *this*? She's not yours!"

"It's not just her," Austin said, and Cord tried to breathe at a normal pace.

His father loved Austin, looked at him as a son, but without the critical eye of a father. He only saw the good in him and Cord couldn't let Austin destroy that. "Austin, don't."

His friend looked at him and smiled. "All in." His hand settled over Cord's and squeezed, then he looked back at Reed. "I'm as much in love with your son as he's in love with my wife. And vice versa. We want you two to be okay with this, but we aren't basing our happiness on your approval. We love each other. We take care of each other. And we're happy together, no matter how untraditional our relationship is."

His father's face darkened as his lips firmed. "That's not a relationship. It's pornographic. Perverted." His eyes narrowed on Cord. "You've bastardized something sacred, and I don't want it in my house."

"Reed!"

"*Norma Jean, enough!* This is not some soap opera. This is our son's life. How can you be okay with what they're doing?"

"*Because what else am I supposed to be?* Do you want to lose our son? Our only child? I'm convinced this is what he wants. It's what they *all* want and I will not let you decide that it's all or nothing. This is my house, too, my family, and I think you're going to wish you could take back your words once you've had some time to think and cool off."

"*My son is holding hands with a man!*" The glasses and silverware rattled as he jostled the table and stood. "You might be okay with this, Norma Jean, but I'm not!"

Fuming, he charged out of the dining room and a moment later the front door slammed. Cord watched December, waiting for her to lift her head.

"Hey," he murmured.

Her face slowly lifted, her brown eyes swimming behind a wash of unshed tears. He reached for her hand and squeezed. "All in," he whispered and pressed a kiss to her temple. "All in."

Austin came around to their side of the table, pulling their six hands together as he kissed the other side of her brow. "All in, baby."

They helped his mother tidy up the kitchen, and though the silence wore heavily, none of them spoke. Time passed and his dad didn't return. Cord and Austin kept a close eye on Ember, as she visibly tried to hide her upset.

"I'll talk with your father," his mom promised, giving him a hug at the door. She hugged Austin and Ember in turn, then squeezed his hand.

On the drive home, Ember took the passenger seat without protest. Austin sat in the back, his hand resting on her shoulder and Cord's resting on her thigh. She curled her fingers around his fingertips. Once again, nothing was said, though the silence spoke for them, offering mute comfort.

Inside the house, she moved to the kitchen and prepared the coffee machine, setting it up for the next morning. As she went about her usual routine, Cord continued to observe her, too worried to think about his own feelings.

She placed both his and Austin's work boots by

the front door and found them hovering in the den. "I'm going to take a bath and lay down. Are you two coming to bed soon?"

"We'll be up soon," Cord promised, with a quick glance at Austin who nodded.

"I'll walk you up," Austin offered.

Cord met her at the foot of the stairs and brushed a kiss across her lips. "I love you, kiddo."

"I love you, too."

He watched Austin walk her up the steps, his hand resting protectively at the base of her spine. Cord paced, looking for something to do, but found nothing. Ember kept the house so damn tidy there wasn't even something to put away.

He sat on the couch and waited for Austin to return. It seemed the longer he sat in the quiet living room the closer the echoes of their family dinner played in his head. His father's enraged voice ringing in the distance, calling their life perverted and pornographic. The look of disgust in his father's eyes singed into Cord's memory.

"Hey."

He started, not hearing Austin come down the stairs. "Hey," his voice scraped.

Austin breathed a short laugh. "This is one of those moments I wish I could offer you a beer."

"I'm okay."

He came to sit beside him on the couch. "Are you? Because it's okay if you're not, Cord."

He knew his father was an old-fashioned guy with old school values, but he never knew he was... What was the word? Bigoted? Homophobic? "He's never looked at me like that before."

"Me neither. It's not just you he's upset with."

He shook his head, yearning for a diversion. "Is Ember okay?"

"She's concerned about you. Upset, because she feels responsible for making this work smoothly." He shook his head, and laughed with little humor. "She puts too much on her shoulders sometimes."

He hated the idea of her somehow taking the blame for tonight's ugliness. "I'll talk to her when we go up. I'll tell her this is about him not her so she isn't upset."

"She'll be okay, Cord. She's strong, remember?"

He remembered. She was stronger than most realized. "Ah, fuck," he groaned, falling back into the cushions of the couch wishing he could somehow stop hearing his father's words in his head. "This sucks."

Austin scrutinized him, his dark eyes pinched at the corners with a look of concern. "It might take some time, but I think your dad will come around. Your mom handled it pretty well. She'll talk some sense into him."

Maybe Austin hadn't been sitting at the same table. "I don't think people with those sorts of views *come around*, Austin."

"He might have been more thrown by the fact we're all sleeping together. It might not have been the...gay thing."

He looked at his friend, certain that was the first time he'd ever called it what it was. Gay. They were gay. But they also loved Ember. So bisexual was actually more accurate.

Maybe the label doesn't make a difference.

Another secret exposed and another nightmare revealed. Cord was so sick of the hidden parts of their past returning to bite them in the ass. They were all trying to do right, but there were so many reparations to make. Would the future always be one long line of atonement? Then it occurred to him that he might be the one hiding the biggest secret of all.

"Austin, I have to tell you something. You went out on a limb for me today, and there's something you should know, but I'm not sure if it'll make things better or worse." God, he hoped it didn't make things worse.

"Is it about Ember?"

"No. It's about us."

"Okay. You have my attention."

Cord drew in a long breath. "I..." Fuck. Now he wished he had a beer. "Remember when we went to the hops festival?"

"When we met December? Yeah."

"I wanted to talk to you about something that weekend, but I never got the chance. You met Ember the first night we were there and then we were hanging around all those hippies the rest of the weekend."

"What did you want to talk to me about?"

He glanced at his knees, chills racing over his shoulders as if the weight that had been there all these years was about to slide off. "I... I think I might have always been bisexual."

The room seemed uncharacteristically still as he kept his eyes on the floor, his breathing uneven. He gave Austin a moment to let that truth sink in as he processed the anomaly of actually admitting the fact out loud for the first time in his life.

"But...you said I was your first...guy. Was that a lie?"

He typically would have laughed at the possessive note in Austin's voice, but this was serious. "You were my first. My only."

"But you're talking about when we were kids. And you've been with plenty of women, Cord."

"Filling a void. That's all that was, me trying to fill this hole in my heart."

Austin blew out a breath and sat back, his fingers forking through his hair. "You should have said something."

Cord could only look at him from the corner of his eye. "I knew you were straight—recent events excluded."

"Yeah, but that doesn't mean my friends had to be."

He wasn't getting it. Taking a deep breath, Cord let it out slowly and faced him. "Austin, I remember the haircut you had in sixth grade. I hated every girl you dated before December. I played on the same sports teams, whether I liked the game or not. That weekend you met December, I had planned on telling you."

"You should have. It wouldn't have changed our friendship. I'm not a jerk, Cord."

"I know you're not. But I wasn't planning on just telling you I was gay. I wanted to tell you I was in love with you. A Hail Mary hope that it *might* change something."

His friend slowly drew back. His eyes shifted

and Cord worried he hadn't removed a burden as much as transferred it to Austin's shoulders.

Austin's brow tightened as he blinked several times. "You wanted...a relationship with me? Not just...like a brotherly kind of affection."

Cord shook his head. "Definitely more than brotherly love. I never expected you to be something you weren't. I just...wanted to tell you. But then Ember came along, you two were made for each other, and I figured...my feelings didn't matter."

"Your feelings matter, Cord. They'll always matter to me."

He wanted to stop talking and hold that proclamation tight, soak it in, but he saved it for later, because he needed to finish his confession. "You were right, a few months ago, when you said I noticed her first. I did, but mostly because I saw her and knew you well enough to recognize your perfect match. She's...perfect. Perfect for you. More so than any other woman."

Austin's brow creased. "And what about you? You're sure it's not just men?"

Cord immediately read his concern. "I definitely love her too. Don't ever doubt that. There's nothing platonic about the way I want her and care for her. She's...special."

"But there were other women. I saw you with them."

"Scratching an itch. Unfortunately, none of them ever amounted to more than a temporary fix. Nor did they give me what I really needed." No need to go into detail about how much he enjoyed the daring ones who let him have them whatever way he wanted.

"But no other men?"

Cord shook his head. "Just you."

Silence stretched as Austin drew in a long breath and let it out slowly. "I had no idea."

"I should have told you. But you and Ember moved so fast. I didn't want to complicate things. Then over time... I couldn't hate her like the other women you dated, so I tried to like her. Shit, she's gorgeous. And such a good person. There's a real fine line between liking Ember and falling in love with her."

Austin softly huffed out a laugh, his stare glued to the floor. "No shit."

"I think back, and sometimes I swear she called to me. I noticed something special in her the first time I set eyes on her. I saw her. *Really* saw her. Part of me even wanted her, but..."

"I got there first."

He nodded. "It made sense that she be with you. I was so confused and unclear about who I was and what I wanted. Then you two were so happy, so perfect, after a while I seemed unnecessary."

"That's not true and you know it."

"Now, but back then..." He looked away, ashamed that he'd been so jealous and unsettled by his friends' happiness. "I think about how hard this last year was on both of you, how much it beat her up. Fuck, you almost fucking died. But then—because I'm a fucking asshole—I think part of me is glad all of this happened because now I have both of you."

"You're not an asshole." He shifted closer, pressing a hand on Cord's jaw and forcing him to look at him. "Hey. You see this?" He closed his other hand over Cord's. "This is not typical guy-friend behavior. If you *loved* me then—and I believe you did, because I'm not easy to love yet you followed me through hell and back—maybe I've always loved you, too. It just took me a little longer to see what we had here."

Cord's breath rushed out in a jagged exhalation.

Austin's thumb brushed softly over the stubble covering his jaw, tracing along the side of his throat. Cord's heart raced, his pulse pounding beneath his friend's touch.

"Cord, I love you, man. Not because you saved my life, but because loving you is just this unavoidable thing I live with. Ember loves you, too. We're done fighting it. All of us. And if that means I'm gay or bisexual or whatever term fits, I'm fine with it, so long as we all have each other."

Cord chewed his lower lip, letting Austin's words sink in. "I need to believe what we're doing *is it*, Austin. I need that. You have no idea how hard it's been, watching you and Ember, how alone I felt some days. This is everything to me, and I don't want to lose it. I don't want to lose you or her."

His friend smiled, and pressed his forehead to Cord's. "Hey, like I said earlier, I'm all in."

Something tightened in his chest shoving a lump into his throat, choking him.

Damn. He sniffed and cleared his throat. "I love y—you" His voice broke and he blinked. What the fuck was happening to him?

Austin smiled, those whiskey brown eyes glazing. "I love you, too."

Cord nuzzled his nose alongside Austin's, shutting his eyes and exhaling. The burden he'd carried for as long as he could remember, finally off his back.

He breathed in Austin's rich scent, so familiar, so right. His lips coasted over his friend's throat as their fingers entwined.

Slowly, Austin eased him down onto the couch, his hard body stretching over Cord's as he looked in his eyes. As if in concert, they paused and coughed out a laugh, but then the enormity of all that happened sobered them.

Cord cupped a hand on his jaw, angling up to brush his mouth against Austin's. Chills raced up his spine as their lips slowly parted and Austin's tongue pressed into his mouth, not in a battle for supremacy, but a meeting of souls. His back stretched beneath the comforting weight as he stroked a hand down Austin's side.

"I like kissing you like this," Austin murmured, his warm breath teasing his lips. "Slow. Actually appreciating it."

It was the first time Cord truly felt safe in his arms, unthreatened by roles of authority. Equal and not wary of rejection. "I like it too."

Their heads tilted as they took their time, exploring, teasing, measuring certain things they'd been too afraid to face head on before.

"God," Cord gasped, his body heating to a dangerous degree. "I fucking want you."

"Soon." Austin took over the kiss, his calm control now a driving force of passion that left Cord dizzy.

His fingers tugged at his friend's clothes, needing to find skin. "Take this off," he practically begged, pulling at Austin's shirt.

Rising on his knees, he stripped the shirt away to reveal his muscled physique. Fucking sexy.

Cord pressed his palm over his heart, fingers splayed. "You have no idea how long I've wanted to touch you like this. It almost hurts to no longer hold back. Sort of like falling without a parachute."

Austin's mouth quirked in a half-grin. "I'll catch you."

"I know you will."

Despite all of the hurdles they had to jump to get here, Cord never stopped believing Austin was still the strong man he'd always been—stronger from all he'd lost.

His thumb traced over the white tail of a scar marking his chest. "I remember this. We were nine, hopping Mrs. Needleman's fence."

When he'd seen the blood seeping through his friend's shirt that day he'd nearly passed out with fear, but Austin just shrugged and swore it didn't hurt, even though Cord knew it had.

Austin's eyes closed on a long breath as if Cord's touch brought him a level of peace. "How long are we gonna wait, Cord?"

His gaze lifted to Austin's face. "I...I guess until we're ready. All of us."

"When it happens... How will..."

He chuckled. "I don't know. Been a long time since either of us were considered virgins."

"You know my dick's bigger," he teased.

"Shut. Up."

Austin threw him a cocky grin. "It's the truth."

Cord laughed again and rolled his eyes. "It's not the size of the boat..."

Austin cracked up. "Do you think our friends from school ever pictured us like this?"

Cord laughed, but a settling calm washed over him. Like he cared what others thought. He shoved his father's reaction aside. He wouldn't allow it to spoil this moment.

"Do you care what they'd think?"

Austin's smile softened. "I only care about you and December. You guys are my whole world."

And just like that, for the first time in almost twenty years, Cord knew he was exactly where he belonged.

Eighteen

December

THE PIPES GROANED upstairs as December willed the coffee to perk faster. She'd lined up her favorite creamer alongside her biggest cup, the spoon at perfect right angles to the mug.

Her boys would soon be down for breakfast and she needed a shot of caffeine before she could face them—and the day. Despite the love that tethered them together, her brain was tired after sifting through the shocks from yesterday.

Shaking her head to dispel the unpleasant thoughts, she poured herself coffee and doctored it with a lavish hand. A quick stir and the cream swirled through the dark depths to smooth and color the beverage to a beautiful golden brown. Her mind again stirred as her hand stilled.

How could Reed turn on his son the way he had? Cord pretended he wasn't terribly affected, but she knew he was. Funny how his dad hadn't ultimately blamed her but held the men responsible. Though he did look at her with...

"Heavy thoughts?" The man in question sauntered into the kitchen and leaned in for a kiss. Cord's trademark flannel hung open over his chest and his jeans were worn in just right.

She relaxed into his hold and drank in his familiar presence, all damp curls, the fresh fragrance of soap and mint. And she hadn't even showered.

Easing away, she gestured at the coffee. "Pour yourself a cup and I'll start breakfast. Austin's coming down soon?"

A line formed between his brows as he frowned. "Yeah. He's bitching, because apparently I used all the hot water again. Why do I smell smoke in your hair?"

Crap. "Um, I..."

Leaning close, he drew in another deep breath through his nose and pulled back. She blinked up at him as he stared at her.

Say something. Say anything. Any excuse will do... "I, uh..."

His scowl darkened. "Did you *smoke*?"

Her face immediately flushed and Austin barked from the doorway, "She better not have."

Cord bent and sniffed her again. He drew back and continued to frown at her. "Where the hell did you even find cigarettes?" He glanced at Austin. "Are *you* smoking?"

"No! I got enough fucking problems." Austin glared at her. "December?"

She scooted away and bit her lower lip. "I only had a few drags and it made me feel totally gross."

"Where are they?" Cord demanded, holding out a hand.

"I don't have them! They weren't mine."

He appeared ready to argue then his head slowly lifted. "Son of a bitch. My mom's smoking again, isn't she?"

"No."

He scoffed out a laugh. "You little liar. Don't defend her. Wait until I see her."

"Cord, you can't say anything. She'll know I ratted her out."

His glare returned to her. "I don't care. And shame on you for giving into peer pressure."

"I..." She sent a pleading look to her husband, but he only shook his head and folded his arms over his chest.

"Ember. Ember. Ember," Cord said with exaggerated disappointment, eyebrows wagging. "I thought you were a good girl."

Her face scrunched as she narrowed her eyes. "I *am*. I said it made me feel gross."

The side of Cord's mouth kicked up and he tweaked the sharp tip of her nipple pressing against the thin material of her robe. "Nah, you're a bad girl now. We've finally corrupted her, Austin."

"What would the ladies at quilting class say?" her husband teased.

"Not only does she sleep with two men, she smokes!"

For some reason, their levity made her want to cry. How could they act so unaffected by their situation? Especially after the things Reed said last night? She sought emotional refuge in anger.

"You know what? I'm going back to bed. You can fix your own breakfast." As she made to stalk away, Cord grabbed her and pulled her into an unbreakable hug.

His mouth found hers again and he kissed her passionately. Her body relaxed by degrees and softened.

Her resistance gone, he broke the kiss and slapped her ass. Hard. "No. Smoking."

"Ow!" She scowled and rubbed her butt, pouting at Austin.

He raised an eyebrow. No support there. "You're on your own, baby. My wife doesn't smoke." He swooped in and kissed her, stealing her breath.

Turning to the stove, she narrowed her eyes and decided to cook egg white omelets. With spinach.

Cord and Austin bantered behind her, shoving for first dibs on the coffee. She cast a glance over her shoulder and drank in the sight of them. How could she have missed that extra layer of connection? Norma Jean had known them from when they were in diapers, but Ember was their lover and Austin's wife.

Perhaps she'd been too close to it. The way both men always seemed to focus on her made it difficult to see the other half of the puzzle. She felt like a complete idiot, because, looking at them now, their intimate bond was undeniably obvious.

Maybe it was overt on Cord's part, but she believed Austin's feelings were new. There was no denying they shared something intimate, something apart from her.

It was palpable, from the way they teased and mocked one another to the manner in which they had each other's back. Such intimacy, no matter the test. Cord's unwavering support, Austin's unflagging determination, she marveled at the strength each held in their own way.

She automatically separated eggs and whipped them into a froth, before setting the bowl aside and crossing to the fridge. As she sorted through the crisper for the greens, Austin came to hold the door.

"You okay?"

"Hmmm? Sure. I'm fine. Why?"

"Last night was tense."

"More so for Cord."

Cord trailed a finger up her spine, startling her, and peered at her face. "I'm good, sweetheart."

The three of them huddled in front of the fridge, cool air washing over her bare feet. He couldn't be that confident or secure, could he?

"It'll all work out," Austin added with equal confidence.

Unsure where this newfound ease stemmed from, she shut the fridge. "Okay."

They were all at the same table last night, right? Maybe she'd missed something. She'd wait for another time to push a little.

Hopefully, Austin was right and somehow they'd work it out with Reed. Cord loved his father and she didn't want to see him lose that relationship, because it was nothing like the crappy association Austin shared with his dad. Both Austin and Cord needed Reed in their lives. So did she.

"What've you got there?" Austin pointed to the bag of spinach.

"Breakfast." Maybe she'd add the yolks to the omelet, seeing his crestfallen face.

"*Spinach*?" Cord whined.

Austin wrapped an arm around his shoulders. "We should probably think about not smacking her ass anymore."

Cord fixed a pleading stare on her. "Just worried about your health, Mrs. Garret."

"And I'm worried about yours, Mr. Bay."

But she added the yolks and grated in some sharp cheese before folding in the leafy greens. The toast popped and Austin shouldered Cord out of the way to grab it and throw it on a plate. The amount of butter he applied made her wince. Good thing she hadn't cooked bacon.

Sipping her coffee while they ate, she allowed herself to put away outside judgment and enjoy the moment. One couldn't predict the future and she needed to trust in what they had.

"She's thinking again." Cord poked Austin in the shoulder.

Her husband looked at her sharply, his eyes full of worry. She hurried to reassure him. "Happy thoughts."

Austin relaxed and smiled, the lines of strain erasing. "Good. Wanna share?"

"I'm happy with what we have. Our relationship."

She basked in the warmth of their broad smiles and was nearly knocked over by their rush to kiss her, her coffee rocking dangerously in her hands. Austin beat his friend to her lips but Cord placed a smacker on her cheek.

Fake protesting, she told them to finish their healthy breakfasts.

"Good thing I can't taste this green stuff," Cord grumped, returning to his seat.

"It's spinach," Austin told him, a righteous tone to his voice. "Chock full of...some kind of stuff that's good for you."

"Quit sucking up."

"Maybe you should try. You're the one who smacked her ass." Her husband winked at her.

"I'm thinking liver and onions for dinner. You know, lots of iron and protein after a hard day." Both men stilled and stared at her with wide eyes. "Kidding."

The talk turned to the mundane. Austin had a full day ahead and Cord expected a shipload of stock. She decided to purge the guest room and the upstairs closets. Clear the clutter—make more room for Cord.

As she rinsed her mug, she was again surprised by the ease both men shared after such a complicated and upsetting evening. "Did you guys talk last night?" The question fell, almost without thought, past her lips.

Her boys flushed, Austin's blush crawling up his throat and painting his cheeks a ruddy red. Cord ducked his head, likely trying to cover the heat blooming over his entire face.

She laughed. Knowing them, they probably took the edge off by fooling around. "Did you at least exchange a few words?"

"Yes!" Cord nodded for emphasis while Austin smirked.

"We talked, baby."

As they scraped their plates, she conceded that maybe she didn't have to rescue them—or their relationship—every time there was a bump in the road. Everything didn't fall on her, as long as they were open and honest.

The truth in that thought made her feel lighter. Sharing the load with her boys, both capable of sharing it with her, was exactly how she'd hoped their relationship would be.

Nineteen

Austin

AUSTIN TAPPED his fingers on the Formica tabletop, then idly traced along the pattern etched beneath the smooth surface. His cup of coffee cooled in front of him.

"Looks like you're thinking hard."

His mentor's dark gaze was fixed on him, but reflected only gentle interest. Harley had become such an important part of his life, somehow embodying everything Austin thought a father should be.

He barked a nervous laugh. "It's been...a memorable few weeks."

"I noticed."

He stiffened, suddenly feeling exposed, then

forced himself to relax. If anyone should be able to take note of changes, see into him, it was Harley. He'd opened up to this man even more than he had to his own wife—and Cord—when it came to his darkest fears, deepest regrets, and highest hopes. But he was working on moving everyone to the same page.

Harley totally got it. Understood what addiction did to a person, having struggled with it himself. He understood the most important things took time.

"I guess some things are pretty obvious to you." Austin made himself smile. "After that thing with Rebecca, me and Ember talked."

"I'm sure you did." The dry humor helped him settle.

"We worked it out. She's fine with it—knows I didn't provoke the situation. And *I* talked to Rebecca, as you know." He took a gulp of coffee and looked everywhere but at his sponsor. "If Ember didn't forgive me, it would have been the final straw, seeing as my dad's visit pushed me pretty hard."

Harley nodded—and waited. Austin collected his thoughts. He'd been holding onto minor details of his life, minor details that could have derailed his entire world, for over a week. They were toxic and he had to get them out. He needed to unburden himself.

Telling Harley what had almost happened was different than telling Ember or Cord. If Austin fucked up, it might disappoint his sponsor, but his fuck-ups had no direct effect on him.

"I was gonna drink. Got as far as the liquor store —even got out."

More patient waiting, but soon Harley's face softened.

"I didn't do it. I guess that's obvious." Another harsh choke of laughter emerged, and he patted his lips with a napkin to buy himself a minute. "I gained control."

"Probably the most powerful thing, ever."

He weighed Harley's words. It *had* been powerful. Enlightening, too. And a burden, because he'd finally accepted that lurking need would always be there.

"Very powerful. But it's a battle I hope not to fight too often."

"I won't say it gets easier, because for some it doesn't. But it's more manageable when you take that control and live your life in better ways. Choose what you do. Choose what you don't."

About that...

He grimaced at the cold mug and replenished his coffee from the carafe the waitress left. Blessing the relative privacy of their booth and the lack of other patrons at this hour, he said, "My life's pretty good, all things considered. I mean, I know there will be ups and downs. Makes a person appreciate what they've got."

Harley leaned back, stretching one long arm out to rest it on the table. "Glad to hear that, Austin. And now you know it's possible to deal when thrown a curveball."

"It's a good feeling," he admitted. "There's something else, too."

Quirking a brow, Harley asked, "What's that?"

"Ember would like to meet you. Really meet you. She...she sees me having a separate life, one you're part of and she's not."

Forehead wrinkling, his sponsor hesitated. "That's not something that usually happens. I mean, I'd like to meet her, too—outside of a parking lot—but people tend to keep their AA life private."

"It doesn't feel like that will work with us. I mean, it's working for me, but I have to consider my wife, too. I brought alcohol into our lives. AA and all the things that come with it aren't going to just have an effect on me. It's as much a part of her day as it is of mine. But I understand if that crosses a line for you. For my wife's sake, though, I wanted to ask if you'd be willing to sit down with her—both of us." He'd get to Cord once he felt Harley out about Ember.

Harley's expression didn't give much away and Austin waited patiently to see if he'd protest. "A lot of my friends are people I've met through AA, Austin. I'm not hesitating for my own benefit. I'm thinking of you. Are you ready to mingle this part of your life with the one at home?"

That was the only way it could be if he wanted December to understand why he depended so much on the foundation he'd found here, with Harley and the meetings.

"I think I'm ready. Ember and I think full dis-closure is the key to moving on and leaving the past behind. You're...someone I hope to keep in my future."

A wide smile lit up Harley's face. "Damned if I

didn't know you were special, Austin. I'd be pleased to meet Ember if you think it will help. Would she want to join us for coffee, maybe?"

"She'd like for you to join us for dinner—at our house. Next week, if you can make it."

"Well. I gotta say that appeals. Bernice is away visiting her sister, and I'm not the best at cooking for one. You've told me too much about your wife's culinary skills to turn down an offer like that. I'd be happy to join you for dinner."

"Great. Great." Damn it, he sounded like a used car salesman. "Friday work for you?"

"Sure. You planning on a meeting afterward?"

Most definitely. "Yes. So let's make it a little after five."

Harley scribbled the time and date on a napkin and tucked it in his pocket. Austin nearly smiled at the old school method. He entered the information into his phone and sent Ember a text.

Now for the other detail... "Cord will be there, too," he blurted.

One brow raised, Harley asked, "Your friend? The one who owns Bay's Hardware, right?"

Yup, that very one. And the one who surpassed best friend status a while ago.

He nodded. "Cord Bay. We've been friends since preschool if you remember."

"You've worked out your issues with him, then?"

Harley had become his shoulder, the one he could lean on when he feared putting too much pressure on those he loved. Maybe the reason he leaned so hard was because losing someone he just met wouldn't hurt as much as losing Cord or Ember again. But Harley never made him feel judged or wrong for the things he confided, and that gave Austin the courage to keep moving in this new direction.

Harley knew about his darkest dark days, and some of the days Austin never wanted to revisit again. Harley respected those wishes, not even touching on things like his suicide attempt in private conversation. His secrets were safe with Harley. He trusted that. Trusted him.

So why was it so difficult to talk to him about Cord? His mind shifted to Reed. Perhaps the backlash of dinner the other night made more of an impression on him than he realized.

"Hey. You okay?" Harley leaned forward, his features twisted with concern.

Sucking in a breath through his nose, Austin gathered his thoughts. He was sitting with a man he'd opened up to the way a son might seek guidance from a father. He didn't want to see the same sort of rejection in Harley's eyes that he'd caught in Reed's.

But something told him Harley wouldn't hold the same biased views Cord's dad did. Nor would he criticize Austin the way his own father tended to. He had faith and in his heart he knew it wasn't misplaced.

With a sheepish grin, Austin said, "Just thinking you're the kind of man I wished my father had been."

"That's...that's a very generous statement, Austin. Gives me something to live up to."

"Your approval's important to me," he said quietly. "Because it means something and you don't abuse it."

"I get that, I do. But never let another person's approval turn you away from what you know is right. You know your life, your limits, and your strengths better than anyone else."

"You asked about me getting things settled with Cord."

"Right. Not everyone keeps a lifelong friendship. Especially when addiction crops up."

"He hauled me up from the depths." Even now, Austin knew he'd never be able to repay Cord for that debt. "I know I had to take the first step, but Cord was kind of like a platform, you know? And then you stepped in, made yourself available. I needed someone who wasn't judging me, someone I could talk to. I've been damn lucky. Both of you helped me get my life and my wife back. I don't think I'd be breathing right now if not for December's forgiveness. You and Cord helped me earn that."

"I'm glad to have been there for you when you needed an outsider. It's like I said the first day we met, AA is a pay it forward sort of thing. And I believe one day you'll help a stranger the same way I helped you. Your friend sounds like a fine man, too. I look forward to meeting him."

And with someone as astute as Harley, there was no way they could hide anything from him. Not with the way Cord and Ember looked at one another. And the way Austin looked at Ember and Cord.

He moistened his lips. Poured more coffee.

Stacking some of the creamers into a pyramid, Austin cleared his throat. "Cord's pretty much living with us."

There was a flicker of surprise in the other man's eyes. "Okay."

"We—me, Ember, and Cord—we're pretty close."

"You did go through a difficult experience, sounds like."

Time to put it out there. He gathered his courage.

"It's not just that. We're, um, together—the three of us." His quietly spoken words seemed to echo in the diner and he cast a sweeping glance around to see if heads cocked in the direction of their booth.

They were clear. None of the other patrons were looking his way, no stares of shocked disapproval. No one's lips mouthing *threesome*.

Harley studied him for a long moment and Austin braced himself. With a tilt of his head, his sponsor asked, "Everyone okay with the setup?"

"Uh, of course." Austin should have guessed that would be his main concern—cause no harm.

"Then it sounds like you've thought it through and are making it work."

Glad he was sitting down, because his body actually trembled with relief, he tried a shaky smile. "We love each other."

"Even better."

He wouldn't cheapen the moment by asking Harley if he was still okay with dinner on Friday. This felt like their first foray into the somewhat public eye and he needed to know not everyone in their lives was as close-minded as Reed.

Twenty

Austin

THE AIR COMPRESSOR KICKED ON, the echo of its rattling hum reverberating off the trees and siding as Austin plunged a line of nails into the plank of wood. The moment the compressor silenced he picked up their conversation.

"So you think your mom will be in Ember's class tonight?"

Cord moved with him, holding the beams in place as Austin lined up the nail gun. "As far as I know. She came into the store today and said she had to get home because she had unfinished 'quilting homework'—whatever that is."

Eyes focused on the seams, he drove in three more nails. "Any word from your dad?"

"No."

And didn't that little two-letter word say it all? "Give him time."

They stepped back and examined the deck. It was actually coming along nicely. Slow and steady.

"Got all the time in the world," Cord said. "It's his issue to work out, not mine. You planning on painting or staining this?"

Despite Cord's indifferent attitude, Austin knew he was hurting, knew exactly what it was like to strive for a father's approval and not get it. But he also knew his friend, and from his tone he was still banged up about the other night. Austin understood the desire to let certain wounds heal at their own pace, so he let the topic go—for now.

Austin shrugged. "Guess we'll have to put it to a vote. I think Ember wants a natural finish. You?"

Cord faced him. "Uh, natural's nice."

He nodded, his gaze scouring over the seams and inspecting what still needed to be nailed down. "Then natural it is."

He moved the hose of the compressor to the other side and glanced over his shoulder. "Cord?"

"Yeah?" He shook his head as if distracted by thoughts. "Sorry. I was zoned the fuck out."

They worked for another hour, but when the sun started to set and Austin was ready to wrap it up, Cord pulled out the lights.

"You going nightshift again?"

"Yeah. You go ahead to your meeting."

Austin glanced at his watch. "All right. I'll see you tonight."

Cord approached then stopped as if catching himself at the last second. He flushed and laughed.

Austin leaned in and cupped a hand to the back of his neck, stealing a kiss.

"Later."

As he backed out of the driveway his mind wandered. His thoughts seemed lost, somewhere far away as he drummed his fingers on the steering wheel.

He parked outside of the church. Familiar faces walked past and it looked as though Harley was already inside, his SUV dark and tucked in its usual spot.

Austin let out a long breath, knowing he was procrastinating and they had to eventually face the inevitable. He'd do anything for December. That rule should apply in other areas of his life as well, but he was conflicted. He loved Cord, but men were different. Cord might not like what he was considering.

"Fuck."

He threw the truck in reverse and backed out of the parking space, taking Willow Street in the opposite direction of home. He coasted down Roosevelt, not seeing the car he was looking for and knowing exactly where to find the person he needed to talk to.

His breathing was steady, though his heart was beating forcefully in his chest. He hadn't made up his mind if this was a mistake or a good choice, but he kept driving. Like a politician's opinion, his mind wavered every three seconds.

The tinted windows and familiar lights of The Rusty Bucket were unchanged, as were the cars surrounding the lot. There, front and center, was the

Chevrolet he was seeking. Austin's truck slid into a parking space facing the bar like a hand slides into a well-worn glove.

The metal of his keys filled his grip as he shut off the engine and got out, not giving himself the chance to hesitate. His strides were sure, but his heart started to rattle behind his ribs the closer he came to the door.

Swallowing compulsively, he reached out and gripped the metal handle of the bar entrance and yanked it open. The stale scent of cigarette smoke and beer hit him like a sledgehammer and his nose twitched. Familiarity settled over him like a warm blanket.

CCR played from the jukebox and only the regulars filled the stools surrounding the bar, a few stragglers betting over a pool table in the corner. Austin's eyes sought *his* stool on the far right and there, next to his empty seat, was the person he needed to see.

This was his last chance to change his mind. No one seemed to notice him yet. He could turn around, go back to the truck, and slip into the meeting down the road.

His fingers curled into fists at his sides and his knuckles popped. He needed to do this. He *could* do this without his surroundings seducing him.

With long strides, he walked through a cloud of smoke and slid into the vacant stool at the corner. The body next to him turned enough to see his face and then focused on the baseball game playing on the television behind the bar, offering no greeting and filling the air with an unwelcome chill.

"Austin. Where you been?" Tracy, the bartender approached. "Can I get you your usual?"

How easy it would be...

"Hey, Tracy. I'll just take a club soda. Thanks."

She raised a brow, but made no comment. A moment later a glass of carbonated soda slid in front of him. He took a sip, giving his neighbor a moment to assimilate. This was happening, whether either of them was ready for it or not.

"Thought you were done with bars," Reed finally mumbled, not sparing him a glance.

"Done with drinking. But I knew this would be where I'd find you. Who's winning?"

Cord's father sipped a longneck beer, eyes glued to the screen. "Pirates are getting their asses handed to them."

Austin glanced around, noticing details of the establishment that were so dated they had to be a decade old, but he never noticed such things before. Interior design hadn't really been his focus whenever he'd stopped by for a drink—or a dozen.

The Bucket wasn't a place to be bothered by singles or trendy bands. It was a place where the old heads of the town could chill and the alcoholics could drink their fill for a dollar a draft whenever a game was scheduled. He was an alcoholic and Reed was an avid Pirates' fan, so there came their close friendship.

"Oh, come on!" Reed barked at the television, finishing his beer and sliding the bottle forward.

Tracy replaced it with a fresh one and the scent wafted from that little hole in the neck right up into Austin's face.

He leaned back as much as the stool would comfortably allow. "I hooked up that light you gave us. Works great."

Reed nodded. "Good."

"We're building a deck out back, so it's perfect."

He nodded again, no commentary. A commercial played on the TV and he sipped his beer. "What are you doing here, Austin?"

"You know why I'm here."

"And you know we aren't discussing that. Not here."

Though the establishment wasn't one where people came for social hour, he could respect that the man didn't want to have a heart-to-heart about his bisexual son—and his son's *friend*—within earshot of his drinking buddies. He could even honor that, to a point.

"I don't think anyone meant for dinner to end the way it did the other night," Austin said, voice low enough that only Reed would hear.

No comment.

"Do you remember when we were little and you coached our baseball team?"

Reed gave a slow nod, expression blank.

"You were a great coach. We almost won the season junior year. Cord really had some talent. Probably could have gotten a scholarship or something if he'd focused his life in that direction."

"Nothing was stopping him."

Austin's head tipped to the side. That wasn't entirely true.

"He talked about playing for the pros all the time when we were kids."

Yet, once they started working, Cord's dad had already assumed his son would be following in the family footsteps, taking over Bay's eventually. Over the years the talk of his friend doing anything else slowly faded away.

"If you're somehow trying to lay that on me, I'm not having it. Cord could have applied himself to sports if he wanted to. He never mentioned wanting that long-term."

Maybe not to Reed. "I think he wanted your approval more."

The game came back on and several minutes passed in silence. Austin waited him out, giving his last statement time to sink in. When another commercial came on, the older man glanced at him and let out a slow huff.

"You know what kind of man I am, Austin? I'm the sort who likes to watch a baseball game in peace. The kind who enjoys a cold beer on a hot day. I like my shirts and cars made in America. And I don't give a shit about coddling another grown man's feelings or talking about my own."

All true, but Reed had a heart under all that broken-in flannel. Austin was sure of it. "You also love your son and you're man enough to admit it."

"This ain't my son. What he's doing... It ain't Cord."

"You sure about that? He loves you, Reed. You crushed him the other night. I know the kind of son you raised. He's the sort who would do anything for anyone who needed a hand. You want to be mad at someone, be mad at me. I'm the one who slipped. I'm the one who asked him to look after Ember."

"Looked a little too close, if you ask me."

"Do you blame him?"

Okay that was the wrong thing to say. Seeing the unimpressed glance Reed sent him, he switched directions.

"Look, we all get ideas in our heads about how life's supposed to be, but sometimes we're thrown curveballs. We can either swing and hope for the best, or take the bench. Cord wasn't going to just sit out and watch me lose everything. He cares too much."

"I'm not going to even pretend I understand what's going on in that house of yours—"

"And I'll pay you and Norma Jean the same respect. Love's a private thing, Reed. To each his own. But I'll leave you with this…"

He stood, focused his gaze on the players on the screen, but spoke directly to Reed.

"Your son's the same person he was last week, last month, and last year. He's your only son. Your only kid. He's where he wants to be and no one's going to tire of him. So if you're gonna draw a line in the sand, make damn sure you're standin' on the right side of it, because this isn't a phase. It's his life and he's doing something that makes him happy. This is your son applying himself to a dream he's held for a long time, and this is me making sure you're aware of it this time."

Austin slid a five out of his pocket and placed it on the bar. As he turned to leave, he hesitated and rested a hand on Reed's shoulder. The man tensed, but didn't shoulder off his touch.

"You're a good man, Reed, someone who's been

like a father to me, more so than my own dad. I know parents are sometimes disappointed in their children's choices, but sometimes the kids get disappointed too. I think you'll do the right thing. Cord's willing to give it time."

With that, he left the bar. The second his boots hit the pavement he drew in a long breath of night air, glad to be out of that place, and trying hard to erase the stench of alcohol and smoke from his nose.

He drove to the church and cars were still in the lot. He'd catch the end of the meeting then take a rain check on coffee with Harley. Tonight he wanted nothing more than to get home to be with those he loved.

Twenty-One

December

EMBER'S KNEES cracked as she moved along the kitchen floor, scrubbing the kick-board under the cabinets. She hadn't planned on doing the baseboards today, but as she was setting the dining room table a clump of dust caught her eye.

"Em?"

"Don't walk on the floor with your boots! I just mopped."

Cord hovered at the doorway of the kitchen and frowned. "What the hell are you doing?"

"Cleaning."

"Who cleans under the cabinets?"

"Normal people. Go take a shower. Harley's going to be here in an hour." When she didn't hear him move, she glanced over her shoulder. "Why are you just standing there?"

He shrugged. "Hell of a view."

She smirked and rolled her eyes. "Go."

"I don't think he's gonna check under the cabinets. Why don't you join me in the shower?"

She halted her cleaning. It was a tempting offer, but she still had to make the salad. "I can't. Besides, I already showered."

"You're no fun. Let me know when fun December comes back. I like her better than cleaning Ember."

When he left she worked her way to the edge of the kitchen then stood and inspected the room for any other hidden spots of dirt. She wasn't usually this OCD, but after the other night's catastrophic dinner at the Bay's she really wanted tonight's dinner to go well.

Spotting a cobweb strung across her antique canisters high above the pantry, she retrieved her duster and step stool. The front door opened the second she was stretching to swipe away the dust. "Boots!"

Austin's chuckle met her ears. "How did I know you'd be cleaning like a maniac?" He stepped behind her in socked feet and hummed. "You missed a spot."

She scanned the canisters and stretched again, too short to see the surface. Austin's warm lips pressed to her inner thigh and she gasped, nearly losing her balance but his hands caught her hips and steadied her.

She huffed. "Did I really miss a spot?"

He laughed and lifted her off the step stool. "No. I just like looking up your dress."

He took the duster from her and returned it to the broom closet. "Enough. He's not coming with white gloves to do an inspection. It's just dinner with friends, baby."

A pout pulled at her lips, but he was right. She was going a little nuts. After washing her hands, she pulled out the greens for the salad and tilted her cheek when her husband came to kiss her at the sink.

"How was your day?" She rinsed the vegetables and removed any browning leaves.

"Good. Perfect. Yours?"

She raised a brow. Her day had been far from perfect and she'd exhausted herself by noon, getting the house ready for their dinner guest, but she wasn't one to play the martyr. "My day was fine."

"Where's Cord?"

"In the shower. You should get up there too. We only have about forty-five minutes until Harley gets here." Sensing his scrutiny, she turned. "What?"

Her husband sighed. "Nothing. After you're finished with the salad take a break. I know you've been at it all day. You're gonna run out of gas before he gets here."

"I will not—"

"December."

"Fine. I'm just nervous."

Strong hands massaged her shoulders as she tore the lettuce. "There's no need to be nervous. Harley's a good guy and he's looking forward to meeting you."

How would they introduce Cord? *Ours* came to mind, and she nearly smiled at her possessiveness, despite how nervous she felt.

She nodded her agreement and decided maybe sitting still for a few minutes was a good idea.

Cord returned just as she was fluffing the couch cushions. She'd gone to the den to rest, but then—

"I'm told I'm supposed to make sure you're relaxing," Cord said, plopping onto the couch and denting all the cushions.

"I just fluffed those pillows."

He grabbed her arm and yanked her to his side. "Enough, kiddo. House looks great. What's for dinner?"

Outnumbered and exhausted, she sighed and gave up. "Lasagna."

"Yum." He linked his hand with hers, his fingers tracing along her wedding ring. "You nervous?"

God, yes. "A little."

"No need to be." His tone belied his words and she studied him.

Of course Cord was nervous too. People would look sideways at their relationship, and have some unflattering thoughts about her, but even more so when they understood Cord and Austin were also involved.

For a moment she felt defeated, recalling Reed's harsh words for his son. Couldn't he look past his hang-ups and see how happy she and Austin made Cord? How happy he made them?

Her mind returned to Norma Jean's suspicions and December wondered why she was keeping such revelations to herself. Every day they moved further from the shadows of secrecy and it was her turn to take the next step.

"You've loved him forever," she asserted quietly.

His gaze shifted to hers as his shoulders squared. There was no denial in his blue eyes. "Forever."

"I...I thought it was me." And didn't that sound arrogant?

He drew her close in the next heartbeat, squeezing her hand and resting his forehead on hers. "It's you too, kiddo. I love you both. With all my heart. Who knew I'd have room for both of you, but I do."

Snuggling close, she allowed herself to relax as she drank in his comforting scent. "I don't know how much Austin explained to Harley."

Cord chuckled, his broad chest lifting beneath her shoulder. "No idea. But Austin told him I'd be at dinner, so unless he's coming to rain down hellfire and damnation he's probably okay with us. I don't think Austin would blindside the man."

Her husband's footsteps pounded down the steps and the scent of fresh soap intensified in the room. She smiled, because they'd both found the shirts she'd pressed that morning, Cord's a deep blue to bring out his eyes, and Austin's a brown, pinstripe button down.

She decided to ignore her anxiety as best she could and trust that her husband's sponsor was the man Austin believed him to be. "I should probably go freshen up."

"Okay. We'll be down here making a mess," Cord teased and she shot him a threatening scowl.

"Don't you dare. Austin, there's a veggie tray in the fridge. Can you put it on the coffee table?"

"You got it, boss."

She nodded and raced up the stairs. Swapping her dress for a cornflower blue skirt and white fitted T-shirt, she slipped into a pair of sandals and only spent a minute fussing with her hair.

She returned downstairs just as she heard a car pull up. Peeking through the foyer curtains, she watched as a large black SUV parked beside Cord's truck. "He's here."

Facing the den, she stilled. Cord and Austin reclined on the couch, their heads close together, each looking at their phones, but completely at ease with their bodies touching, so similar to the way she and her husband sat. Whatever nerves Cord was experiencing, they seemed soothed by Austin's proximity.

She took a mental snapshot of the picture they made, something to hold onto when she doubted their situation in the face of adversity. This was right. How could anything that looked so perfect be wrong?

"Phones away," she said, hating to break up the moment, but feeling a little more grounded by having them both near.

Austin pushed off the couch and went to the door, opening it wide before his sponsor had a chance to ring the bell. "Welcome to our home, Harley."

Ember drifted to his side and he pulled her close, resting an arm over her shoulder "My wife, December. December, my...friend, Harley Walker."

"It's nice to see you again, Harley."

"And you, Mrs. Garret." The tall man offered a foil wrapped package. "Cornbread. Bernice, my wife, makes the best I've ever tasted. She left me some before her trip and I wanted to share."

"Thank you. And, please, call me December."

Cord hovered by the entryway and Austin waved a hand in his direction. "This is Cord."

"Pleasure," Harley greeted with a hearty handshake.

To her eye, everything appeared normal. The lack of sharing full names with random members of AA didn't seem to apply here. And the fact that Harley and Austin knew each other's spoke volumes about their association. Harley was Austin's AA sponsor, but also his dear friend, and she chose to trust her husband's judgment.

The man was vastly important to Austin and that made him equally important to her and Cord. He was a priceless part of their lives, because he'd been there for Austin in ways they couldn't be. She was coming to terms with that reality and learning to value it and put her sense of inadequacy aside.

Carrying the cornbread to the dining room table, she fetched a plate along the way and set it out. She wasn't sure how cornbread and lasagna mixed, but the sweet aroma of Harley's contribution rivaled that of the garlic loaf she'd made and she wanted to taste both.

She toted a tray of sun tea and glasses to the den. Cord jumped up to relieve her of the burden, setting it down on the corner table with a clatter.

"I have coffee, too, if anyone wants that."

Everyone settled for the tea and she poured four

glasses, focusing on the tinkling ice. Harley had chosen the club chair so she slipped in beside Austin on the couch with Cord slouching beside her.

An awkward silence unfurled and she was extremely conscious of the two big bodies pressing closely against her.

"So…" Cord said, reaching for a sprig of broccoli and swiping it in the veggie dip. "What do you do for a living, Harley?"

Thank God, small talk. Except maybe that information was supposed to be anonymous too. It was a juggling act, trying to respect the anonymity of AA while also trying to get to know someone associated with her husband through the organization. She was more comfortable viewing Harley as a friend of the family and hoped he felt the same.

"Cord owns Bay's hardware, and of course you know what Austin does," she interjected, hoping to ease any awkwardness.

"Bernice ordered our new carpet from Bay's," Harley tipped his head toward Cord. "I work for a medical supply company and my wife was a librarian. She's pretty involved in the church now—where the meetings are held. She teaches Sunday school there."

A Sunday school teacher? *We're all going to hell.*

"Did she work at the big library or the little one?" Ember asked, trying not to get hung up on religion.

"Neither. She actually worked at the elementary school. She loves children."

"So you two met at the church?" Maybe if she

kept him talking about his wife the time would pass and dinner would be ready to serve.

"That's right. Bernice was dropping off supplies for a food drive one night and I offered to help carry boxes. We got to talking and things evolved from there." He smiled, his features softening. "I thought she was some sort of missionary for all the charity work she was doing, bringing donations by every few days. Turns out, she just had the hots for me and was too chicken to say something."

The sweet story put her at ease. "How did you finally find out she liked you?"

"I told her she should organize a singles dinner at the church and she got real quiet. Then I told her maybe if she hosted something like that I'd finally might get to ask her on an actual date instead of lugging boxes of books for her every night. I was gettin' damn tired of carrying boxes."

They all laughed, and she felt compelled to share. "We all met at a festival. I was dancing with friends and these two walked up to me and I forgot what I was doing, because they were *that* distracting. That same day Austin looked me right in the eye and said, 'You're gonna be my wife one day. You'll see.'"

Her husband rubbed her knee. "Story never gets old. I was right, though, wasn't I?"

"You were right." She gave him a smile that told him just how grateful she was that he followed through on his promises.

Cord shifted beside her and she wanted to include him. Without thinking about how it might look, she grasped his fingers and squeezed, setting their combined hands on her lap. Harley's gaze dipped and flowed over them without any visible reaction, but she had to quell the urge to fidget.

Excusing herself, she went to check on the lasagna, hoping her exit from the den didn't look too much like flight. Just as she was pulling the tray out of the oven, cheese bubbling to perfection, Cord stepped into the kitchen.

"So, this is awkward as shit," he said, creeping close to smell the food.

"I think it's going okay. Considering."

His brow tensed. "I don't know. Maybe I should've sat this one out."

"Don't be ridiculous, Cord. We want you here."

"Yeah, but don't you think it all seems a little weird?"

Despite her earlier reservations, she was now more concerned with *his* doubts than her own. She didn't like when he felt out of place in their home.

Stepping close to him, she rose on her tiptoes and brushed a kiss on his jaw. "This is your home, too, Cord."

He stared down at her and she could read the *no it's not* in his eyes.

"We're going to have another talk this weekend, the three of us. We need to address a few things regarding our living situation."

His hands caught her hips, massaging slowly. "You know, you're awfully bossy when it comes to us talking. How do you go back and forth between being little Miss Bossy Pants and little Miss Submissive?"

His hand slid to her backside, pulling her

against him and she let her body mold into his, going pliant in his arms. "I guess it's one of my many natural talents. Don't forget Little Miss Cleaning Ember and Fun December. They're all part of my many personalities."

A deep groan of approval rumbled in his chest as he dropped his mouth to hers, his hand squeezing her ass—

"Oh. Sorry." They broke their kiss as Harley backed into the hall. "Bathroom?"

"Second door on the left," Cord said, still holding her.

Fighting the urge to step away, she smiled at the other man, and he responded with a wide grin of his own. There was no judgment in their guest's gaze, and she sensed relief pour from Cord's big body.

"Go tell Austin dinner's ready," she said once they were alone again.

Cord hustled out of the kitchen and she took a deep breath. Grabbing the oven mitts, she turned back to the stove just as Harley returned from the bathroom.

"Can I help with anything?" he asked. "I'm obviously good at carrying things."

She appreciated the lack of reference to him witnessing the kiss. "I just have to take this to the table and grab the salad."

"You let me take that hot casserole, Mrs. Garret." He put out a hand for the oven mitts.

"It's December," she reminded, relinquishing the mitts. "And thanks."

Efficiently removing the lasagna, he waited for her to pick up the salad and a spatula before following her to the dining room. Austin and Cord milled around the foot of the table as she set out the food.

Austin pulled out her chair, and she nodded her thanks, pausing to enjoy the kiss he dropped on her hair. Harley took the seat Cord indicated.

Harley's relaxed demeanor gave no sign of discomfort even after catching her husband's best friend kissing her—and having his hand on her ass. Beyond relieved, she filled Harley's plate with a big slice of the pasta.

"I'm looking forward to seeing that deck you guys have been working on," Harley commented, taking the plate. "Thank you, December. Looks delicious."

"Why, thank you. It's Cord's mother's recipe."

And just like that the conversation flowed with plain old, ordinary ease. No mention of adultery or signs of uneasiness from anyone at the table. As a matter of fact, Harley was one of the most pleasant people she'd socialized with in a long time. Maybe he'd be comfortable bringing his wife the next time they had him over.

Somewhere around dessert she realized just how long it had been since they'd had dinner guests and how much she missed entertaining. Cord was more reserved than she and Austin, but even he seemed to relax by the time she brought out the coffee.

While Austin and Cord carried the plates and silverware to the kitchen, she faced Harley, an urgent desire to thank him taking hold. "I just want you to know, you mean a lot to my husband. And me. To all of us."

"He means a lot to me, too."

"What you've done for him—"

Harley held up a large hand. "Austin does for Austin. I can't take that away from him."

"But you've been there for him." In ways she couldn't. "You've helped him, Harley. I don't know if any of us would be here right now if not for you. Austin was a different person a year ago." Her voice turned serious. "You helped him find the man he lost, the man he was. I just want you to know I appreciate the friendship you've made with my husband."

He grinned. "I'll accept your appreciation, but not the credit. You like proverbs, December?"

Her head tilted, a little thrown by the question. "Sure."

"There's an old Chinese one that says the best time to plant a tree was twenty years ago. The second best time is now."

She thought about that for a few seconds. Was he telling her to let go of the past and the things she couldn't rewrite?

As she mulled the proverb over in her head, he rose from the table. "I'll just take these last things into the kitchen," he said, and her hands were suddenly empty.

She couldn't help feeling slightly outmaneuvered, her gratitude cut short by some riddle. Did he do that on purpose?

Austin walked into the dining room and paused at the door. "Baby? You okay?"

She looked at him, in his nice dress shirt, his face shaven, eyes crystal clear and his concern solely focused on her. The earth seemed to tilt for a split second and her knees trembled.

Austin does for Austin.

She rushed to him and hugged her arms around his waist, squeezing tight. "I love you, Austin."

His arms closed around her as he chuckled. "I love you back, Em. What's this about?"

She shook her head, certain if she tried to explain everything she was feeling in that moment she'd break down and cry. And they still had company to see out.

Sucking in a breath, she tamped down her emotions and tightened her arms. "It's about me loving you. That's all."

His lips pressed to her hair, and then her cheek. He didn't say anything, because how could anyone sum up something as intangible as their love?

It was everything. It was the dark matter that made the universe, the light that turned the sky blue, the warmth of sunshine on her face and the weight of her heart, carefully protected behind her ribs. No more broken pieces to clean up, no more fears that her world might suddenly collapse and blow away. They were two imperfect souls determined to hold onto each other, no matter what tried to tear them apart.

And she truly believed her husband would tear through any barrier to get to her, because of their incredible connection...he felt it too.

That certainty, that unbreakable resolve, was the foundation of all that they were and she'd been lost without it. But he'd found it. He'd traveled through hell and back and found solid ground again, and here they stood—happy.

Cord and Harley returned, Cord's gaze shooting to her, and then to Austin. He sauntered over to stand by her side as he and Austin shared one of those looks they'd perfected over the years, looks she might not be able to interpret but understood. She basked in their connection as Harley prepared to leave.

Their guest shook hands with the men and gave her fingers an affectionate squeeze. "Night, and thanks again for the delicious meal."

Seeing him out the door, she turned to see her boys regarding her. Austin's eyes glowed with laughter and Cord was clearly relieved, the tension gone from his loose-limbed frame.

"Our first foray into the real world," she teased, shutting the door.

Her boys held out their arms and she drifted into their embrace for a comforting hug. If only Reed could have been as accepting as Harley.

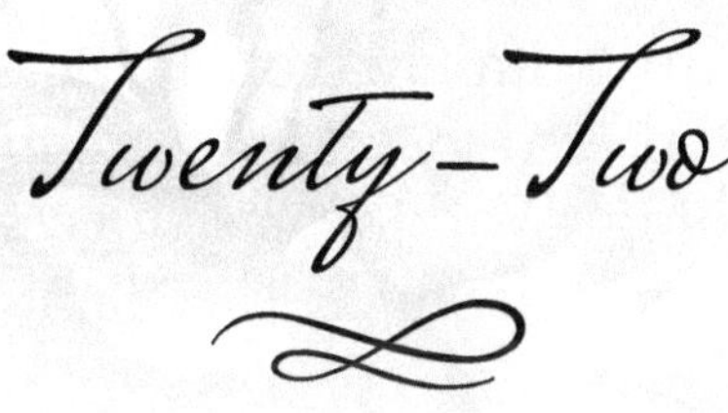

Cord

CORD PACED, checking the time every few seconds. He'd cleaned up after their evening meal, what with Ember running off to teach her quilting class, and Austin still at his meeting. One week left of her classes and she was already talking about signing up to teach another. Maybe he should get a hobby or something, because he was lost without them.

Resolving to fill the time with television, he scrolled through the channels. Lots of chick flicks. A few action series he'd seen before. The porn channel wasn't listed, a good thing because he was primed.

Must be something to do with the great dinner Ember prepared. He was such a sucker for the nurturing bit. She was the whole package. Well, not the whole, but an imperative third. And then there were those heated looks from Austin throughout the meal. Directed at both of them.

Shoving up from the couch, he strode to the window and peered outside, searching for either vehicle. Nothing. Working his fingers through his hair, he tugged, welcoming the slight pinch to his scalp.

Visions of jumping the first one who came through the door filled his head, not helping his circumstances, but his dick twitched in solid agreement. Someone was getting fucked.

A spurt of laughter passed his lips when he considered it would be just his luck for a neighbor to stop by. Or his mother. That thought quelled his libido several degrees, but he was still antsy.

If the deck wasn't finished he'd work on that, but they'd wrapped that project up over the weekend. At this point he was willing to clean something just to have a distraction.

His hand dropped to his pocket and he felt the little bottle he'd stashed there. The Boy Scouts had it right. Be prepared.

When would they get home? Austin better pass on coffee tonight. Cord went back to the couch. No one would know if he watched *Legally Blonde.* He grabbed the remote and settled on the chick flick to pass the time.

The long awaited crunch of tires finally came just as the credits rolled. He clicked off the television and sprinted for the door, watching as Ember swung the Jeep into its parking space.

She had to do a little jump thing to get to the

ground, and he made a mental note to order some running boards. He liked the feel of her ass against his palms when he boosted her inside, but what about when he and Austin weren't around?

His mouth went dry when she spotted him on the porch and gifted him with one of those smiles that said he was the best thing she'd laid eyes on in a few hours.

"Hey, beautiful."

"Hi."

He took the bag she carried and mock-groaned at the weight. "What've you got in here?"

"Quilting stuff. What did you do tonight?"

"Not much." He followed her inside, dropping the bag against the wall and corralling her into the living area.

"Cord!" She stumbled a little, so he picked her up and carried her the rest of the way to the couch.

Dropping down over her, he silenced her protests with his mouth and she immediately softened, submitting to him. When he drew back to give them both a moment to breathe, she blinked up at him. "You're on fire."

He was that. "Thinking about you and Austin all evening."

Running a fingertip along his cheek, she smiled. "Good thoughts?"

"Dirty ones."

Her dark eyes dilated and she shimmied closer, the heat between her legs burning through his jeans as she hooked a leg over his. "Tell me."

"Yeah, tell her."

Cord's gaze jerked over his shoulder. Austin surveyed them from the doorway, his keys dangling from one finger.

"You left the door open," Austin chastised, then smirked. "But I can see why. What do we have here?"

"A sexy little woman." Cord took a moment to check him out, noting the bulge forming in his jeans. "And a hot fucking man."

Without hesitation, Austin strode across the room and knelt beside the couch, his broad shoulder rubbing against Cord's. He took Ember's mouth in a searing kiss Cord vicariously felt all the way to his toes. "Hey, baby."

Turning his head, Austin pressed his lips against Cord's, and his eyes drifted shut at the familiar taste of him.

Austin slowly removed his T-shirt, and Cord watched, mesmerized, as he revealed his chiseled chest. He stole another kiss from Ember, his mouth drifting smoothly from hers to Cord's, driving his need to a boiling point.

"Let's take this upstairs," Austin murmured, lips pressed to the side of his throat as their hands met at Ember's breast. She needed to be out of that dress.

He didn't know if he could climb the fucking stairs, given the state of his cock, but for what he had in mind, the couch likely wasn't big enough. With a grunt, he nodded and helped Ember up.

Austin grabbed his arm, jerking him back for a soul-scrambling kiss.

"I'll just meet you there, then." Ember teased,

prancing to the stairs, loosening her dress along the way.

He and Austin pounded after her, jockeying for position through the hall. Lust, infused with joy, made him lightheaded as he let his friend take the lead up the stairs.

Austin's long strides took the steps two at a time and Cord was right behind him, watching that fine ass flex behind worn denim. He ached for the man, a sensation so deep it drew a muffled groan.

His dick swelled, constricting his pants and slowing him down. But he'd get there. Oh...he'd get there.

"Let's go, old man," Austin teased from the landing, flashing Cord a promising grin and giving him a chance to catch up.

Cord adjusted his jeans and Austin's gaze dropped to his crotch. His brow raised and his grin stretched. Winded by pure anticipation, Cord checked his shoulder at the top of the staircase and mumbled, "And you think your dick's bigger?"

Austin laughed and shoved his way to the bedroom door. Catching up with Ember just inside the room, he spun her into Cord's arms.

Cord's fingers went to the zipper on her dress, loosening it the rest of the way, as he pressed the ridge of his erection against her back. The tiny teeth purred as he tugged the catch down her back and marveled at the gift they'd been given.

"Unwrapping you is like opening a present, sweetheart."

Austin returned to them, now clad only in his briefs, his erection bulging. He helped to draw the fabric from Ember's body and both of them growled at the sight of her in a thong.

"What's this?" Her husband snapped the thin string over her hip.

She jerked at the sting, but didn't complain. "It's a thong."

"I know it's a thong, baby. You've never worn one of these before."

Her flush traveled to her pert tits and Cord's mouth watered. "I think they're sexy."

"I think I want a better look." Austin lifted her off her feet and lowered her to the bed, on her belly, drawing a surprised gasp from her lips as he palmed her exposed buttocks. "*Very* sexy."

"She doesn't need sexy," Cord asserted, although his finger traced the strap bisecting her cheeks.

Austin tapped her plump little ass with the flat of his hand and she wiggled. Cord admired the delicious jiggle.

"You like that, baby?" Austin slapped her a bit harder.

She moaned, relaxing her face against the blankets. "I think I do."

It was a totally different response than when Cord had given her a swat in the kitchen for smoking. "She's pretty in pink," he murmured, bending to kiss the soft curve of her ass and inhale the delightful fragrance of feminine arousal.

Slipping a finger under the thin panel covering her pussy, he grinned. "She's soaked."

Austin's features flared with desire and his hand joined Cord's. He drew his wet digit along her cleft, both their fingers slipping inside of her, and she clenched her sexy ass cheeks.

"I'm feeling adventurous," Austin murmured.

"Got you covered." Cord pried at his pocket, the little bottle in his jeans vying for space alongside his dick. Victorious, he held it up.

Austin's stare shot to the bottle and then to his face, a brow rising as curiosity and need tightened his features.

Popping the top, Austin anointed his fingers, then leaned over Ember, pressing a gentle kiss to her shoulder before whispering, "You okay with this, baby?"

"That depends." Her voice was tentative, but her pussy was telling another story as Cord continued to slide his fingers through her folds.

He worked another digit in alongside the first. His eyes closed as he savored the slick way her body welcomed his touch, so hot and tempting. He pressed a little deeper. "You're so wet, sweetheart."

"Just a little play, baby," Austin crooned, one hand on her hip to ease her into a more comfortable position. "You say if we stop."

Cord's lip quirked. "I think you'll like it. Austin does."

His friend shot him an unimpressed glance as Ember drew in a breath. "And Cord will too, soon enough."

"Touché."

Cord crawled to lie alongside her, leaning in to kiss her while stroking her curves. Not only was his cock throbbing, his ass pulsed with desire. Damn

Austin and his sexy fucking promises. He'd make damn sure he saw this one through, too.

Sighing against Cord's lips, December welcomed his kiss, then tensed. He drew back to read her face. "You okay?"

Austin watched him over her shoulder, trusting him to gauge her comfort level. Cord nodded when she smiled her assent. He ran his tongue along her bottom lip.

"You're gonna feel a little full." He slid his hand back into the front of her panties, stimulating her and helping her relax.

She tightened around his fingers and he teased her sex, angling his touch toward the front of her sheath, careful to distract her from Austin's penetrating finger until it became pleasurable.

"Oh, God. It's— I don't know if—" She jerked and clenched, lashes fluttering, lips parting. "I need something…"

Her eyes pleaded, and Cord circled her clit with his thumb, alternately teasing and pressing the little knot of nerves. "Relax and open to him, sweetheart. We've got you."

He could feel Austin's finger moving into her body, against the thin wall separating them, and the eroticism made him impossibly hard. He stepped up his efforts to send her over, staring into her beautiful face, flushed with arousal.

Her breath came out in little puffs and he kissed her passionately, tasting her softness. Austin crooned reassurance and Ember moaned into Cord's mouth.

She broke the kiss. "I… I'm…" She strained, her

lashes lowering, her full lips parting. Abruptly, she shuddered and climaxed, squeezing hard around Cord's fingers as Austin kissed the back of her neck, quietly murmuring to her.

They worked her orgasm, rolling it into another as she let go, trusting them to hold her safe. Her body trembled between them, arousal slicking his fingers while Austin pleasured her in other ways.

With a long moan and another sweet release, her body sagged into the mattress and her lashes lowered, her face a picture of sated bliss. Cord chuckled. "I think she's had enough for now."

Ember hummed, a crooked smile twisting her lips, as her eyes remained closed.

Austin's face flushed with arousal as he watched her for any signs of distress. "Baby?"

She slowly turned her head in her husband's direction. "It's definitely different. But I liked it—I think."

"That was beautiful," Cord breathed, his fingers glistening with her release. "*You're* beautiful, December."

She blinked and gave a tiny moan as Austin withdrew his fingers. There was a rustle of tissues and then he blanketed her body, banding an arm around her belly.

Cord watched his friend's love for his wife spill over as Austin nuzzled closer, his eyes soft. She cuddled into him, soaking up his touch. Cord's chest swelled, a good ache, as he took in the sight of them. A perfect pair. Yet they'd opened their hearts to him.

Ember stretched languidly, Austin stroking over her damp skin, following the curves of her body.

The intimacy so profound, it infused the quiet with a sense of peace.

"What about you?" she murmured, her eyes barely open as Cord gently teased her folds.

"I have plans," he said and nearly laughed when Austin's gaze shot from his wife's face to his, eyes wide.

Cord worked his jeans and underwear off, wincing at the relief when his cock was finally freed. Austin's gaze dropped between Cord's legs, the whiskey brown of his eyes deepening to a glowing ember.

Ember watched avidly, the orgasmic flush still on her cheeks, her gaze dazed with lust as she rested lazily against the pillows.

Rather than disrupt the pretty picture she made, he stared at Austin, a lifetime of longing making him weak in the knees as he took in his sculpted body and the perfect angles of his face.

Austin's gaze lifted to the bottle Cord held, his eyes flashing with vulnerability. His mouth briefly tightened before softening with trust. Cord gave him a minute to object, the silence stretching, his intentions clear.

"You good with this?"

He wouldn't press, but he knew the decision wasn't easy. He was asking more of Austin than he'd ever given to another. Asking for a shit load of trust.

Austin held his stare and nodded, an abrupt jerk of his head, strain creasing the corners of his eyes.

Relief made Cord's fingers tremble and he tightened them around the bottle of oil, donning his dominant mantle. "Get inside your wife."

Without hesitation, Austin stripped off his briefs, his hands noticeably unsteady, his impressive cock springing against his muscled abdomen. And then he had that silly bit of fabric his wife still sported off in a hot minute, snapping the thin strap easily, ignoring her tsking protests.

"Austin, that was new!"

"I'll buy you another one."

Cord fumbled for a condom, the sexy sight of Austin working his cock inside of Ember distracting him. She raised her knees alongside Austin's trim hips, welcoming her husband home.

Their reciprocated moans were a loving symphony of sound to Cord's ears. His heart surged, his fingers trembling as he sheathed his cock.

Kneeling on the mattress, he centered his focus, reminding himself that a first time could be the last time if not done right. He slowly edged his way closer to them and drew in a deep breath, carefully tucking away the monumental emotions flooding him in that moment.

"Easy. Stay still." He set a hand on the small of Austin's back, reveling in the quiver his touch drew from his friend.

Austin ceded to Cord's authoritative tone and bowed his head to rest his weight on his arms without crushing Ember. *Beautiful.*

"You okay, sweetheart?"

Her gaze locked with Cord's over Austin's shoulders, her hand lovingly soothing her husband as she traced her fingers down his back. "Yes."

Cord's hungry gaze devoured the picture they painted. All those pushups and hard labor would prevent their girl from being crushed, but Cord wanted to keep a bead on everyone.

Drizzling the lubricant over Austin's crack, he coated his fingers before parting his cheeks. He bit back a chuckle when his best friend's fine ass reflexively clenched. Working his touch between his flesh, Cord pressed a finger against Austin's back hole and he tensed.

"Let me in, Austin," Cord all but growled. They hadn't even reached the hard part yet. "It'll be good like before."

A silent moment passed while Cord marked his inner struggle. Austin's surrender heralded a turning point. Gaining entry, Cord zeroed in on his target, working past the tight stricture of muscle. Austin grunted at the first sign of penetration.

This wasn't Cord's first rodeo, although he'd never fucked a man like this before. And never with a third involved. Keeping that in mind, he kept his finger steadily moving. Firm enough that there was no room for cold feet, but gentle enough to ease Austin into pleasurable acceptance. Lord knew his cock was a hell of a lot thicker than his finger and he had some prep to do, because right now his friend was clenching like a virgin bride.

He fed his finger all the way in before pausing, giving Austin another chance to adjust to the intrusion.

Leaning forward, Cord's lips curved as he whispered in his ear. "Who's inside of you, Austin?"

A notable tremble rippled across the muscles in Austin's back as he rested inside of Ember, his breath laboring as he held himself still, face turned against her shoulder, eyes closed. "You are."

"Who?"

"Cord," he panted. "You're in me, Cord."

His eyes closed as he savored the sound of his name rasping from Austin's lips. Withdrawing his finger, he shoved back in with a penetrating shot to all those sensitive nerves and Austin let out a gravelly moan. *Mine.*

Austin might be the first man he'd done this to, but he'd also be his last. Never again would he touch a man so intimately as the one writhing beneath his invasion.

He fit another finger in, widening tight flesh and deliberately delivering little jolts of pleasure to ease his way.

"Fuck, Cord. *Fuck.*"

"Soon," he teased, thrusting his hand in a steady rhythm. "Gotta get you ready first." He added more lube, stretching that snug hole, as Austin continued to moan.

"Right there. I..."

Ember's sweet face peered up from beside her husband's shoulder, alive with need and arousal. Her lips parted and she gasped.

"What do you feel, sweetheart?"

"Him. You. Every time you move, he swells inside of me. It's...incredible."

Cord's dick pulsed, ready to move on. "It's about to get even better."

With his fingers deep in his friend, his own belly coiled with need. Cord carefully withdrew, noting the way Austin's hole pulsed, begging to be filled.

He grit his teeth against the intense need to come and set the head of his cock in place.

A culmination of a thousand unfulfilled fantasies raced through his mind. This was it. What he'd wanted for so long... He hesitated, not in fear, but in a moment of gratitude that nearly broke his soul. Austin would finally be his.

Insane tightness and heat licked over his sensitive flesh and he added more lube, slicking his entrance. "Breathe, Austin."

Shoulders hunching, Austin sucked in a visibly huge breath and Cord leaned forward, pressing inside with slow determination against the drag and tight resistance.

"Fuck."

"Fuck."

Ember's palms swept over her husband's back, her knuckles grazing Cord's belly as he advanced deeper, his mind spinning in every direction as an emotional ecstasy awakened every nerve in his body. His eyes slammed shut against the intense pressure, the constricting squeeze around his dick requiring every ounce of control not to come.

His breath hitched and rattled from his chest in a jagged release as Austin quivered beneath him. A shiver of euphoric gratification swept through him. He was claiming this man, his friend, but Austin had always owned part of his soul. Now he would forever own part of Austin's.

Cord's body folded forward as he nuzzled Austin's nape, dragging his lips and tongue in a loving kiss, trying so hard to convey how much this meant to him. "You okay?"

Austin's breath beat hard beneath him and his voice broke. "Jesus, can you move or something?"

"What he said," Ember added, her breath gasping, her eyes wide and pleading.

He needed to focus. Too many emotions were distracting him and he had to make this good for them. He lifted his weight and stroked, incrementally, short forays in and out, back and forth, his temples pounding with need. Austin moaned long and deep, the muscles of his back trembling with each advance of Cord's cock.

Austin's body opened, the oil slicking the way. As he surrendered, Cord upped his rhythm, the friction and heat insane, as Austin tightened around him.

"Fuck. Fuck. It's..."

Ember keened sweet cries of pleasure, her eyes screwed tightly shut in a picture of absolute beauty and grace.

"Sweetheart?" He tried to ease off, take it slow, but it was too damn good being buried inside the man he loved. "Sweetheart, let me see your eyes."

Her lashes fluttered as dark pupils shimmered with lust. "He's so big, Cord. Austin, you're so... big." She rolled her head on the pillow.

Cord's dick pulsed at her words, shuttling slowly against the place Austin responded to the most. He'd heard hitting that mark could make the receiving man's dick swell. And he thrived on the pleasure he was bringing them both.

How he'd found himself in this place, filling this position of their world...it was everything to him and he never wanted to let them go.

His thrusts becoming choppy, he knew he couldn't hang on. It was more than he'd ever dreamed, because Ember was right there with them. Perfectly three.

Austin's fingers curled into the bedding, his back rolling as his spine lifted and Cord's hips picked up the rhythm. Together, he and Austin found their tempo, moved in perfect measure, tapping out a cadence of pleasure that enveloped all of them. Ember cried out, her hands splaying on the pillows above her head, the picture of submissive elegance.

She called her husband's name as he shuddered his release. Austin echoed her cry but with Cord's name rasping from his lips. A guttural moan tore from his throat and his vision blurred. *Jesus.*

Cord shoved deep, his body convulsing with absolute bliss, his heart overflowing with love as he came... Home.

His thoughts organized in a slow semblance of order and he eased his weight back. Austin's hand clamped over Cord's fist, gripping hard and drawing it against his shoulder, conveying so much of what they lacked the words to say.

Cord stared at his best friend's fingers, feeling the emotion he strove to express. A pinch of envy burned for the band circling Austin's ring finger.

Cord slowly leaned closer and pressed his lips against the wedding ring. "I love you."

"Love you, too," came Austin's muffled response.

Taking care not to jostle them, Cord slowly withdrew, jolts of almost excruciating pleasure sparking as he sagged to one side. He basked in the lingering sense of bliss. Austin let out a groaning sigh and Ember moaned, the sounds of contentment making him smile.

Rolling flat on his back, one arm dropping from the bed to scrape his knuckles across the floor, Cord caught his breath. He dealt with the condom before focusing his gaze on his lovers.

Austin had collapsed, half on and half off his wife. Ember's lashes cast tiny shadows over her rosy cheeks, a sweet smile curving her lips, her hair a sweep of damp tangles. Her fingertips flicked in Cord's direction and he caught them with his own, squeezing tight.

At last, Austin raised his head and looked at him. Unblinking, he stared into Cord's eyes and something deep and powerful flashed between them. Something not requiring words. Cord blinked first and Austin smiled, a knowing, promising grin that made Cord's sated body respond.

He'd relished Austin's submission and would again. His own surrender was a matter of time.

Twenty-Three

December

EMBER SAT BACK on her heels, admiring the freshly planted daisies. Her gardens had never looked so good. Every day Cord brought her home a new flat of perennials to plant, leaving them on the back deck, little surprises for the morning.

Once the deck was finished they'd have a lovely place to entertain, perhaps have Harley over again. She hoped to eventually meet his wife.

Moving inside, she washed up, her mind flitting across various moments from the past few weeks as she worked through her chores. She found herself smiling through the mundane tasks of folding laundry and making the bed.

Same as Cord surprised her with flowers and Austin repaired things around the house, she enjoyed treating them to little extravagances as well. The red velvet cake cooling in the kitchen was one of her husband's favorite desserts and she couldn't wait to surprise him with it that night.

After finishing her chores around the house, she returned to check on the cake, taking extra care to spread the icing with a steady hand, covering the crimson surface evenly. Her phone rang and she swiped it up off the counter, her attention on her task.

"Hello?"

"Mrs. Garret?"

Ember tucked her cell between her tilted head and shoulder, continuing to wield the butter knife through the frosting. "This is Mrs. Garret."

"It's Leon Granger."

Leon? She didn't know any Leon's. Telemarketers were getting all too familiar. "I'm sorry, I'm busy—"

"From Bay's."

Her brow furrowed. *That* Leon? Her guard went up, knowing Cord would not approve of his employee contacting her—and why would he be calling her anyway? She wondered how he even got her number. "Hello, Leon. What can I do for you?"

"It's about Cord."

The butter knife slipped along the side of the cake and tapped the platter casting a spot of red speckled frosting onto the dish. "What about Cord?"

"Um, somebody called his parents, but he said your name and I remembered—"

"What are you talking about?" Her voice

climbed the higher registers, the cake forgotten as she grasped the phone with clammy, frosted fingers.

"There's been an accident."

Her cell phone chimed, signaling a text, and she fumbled with the screen, trying to read the message and focus on Leon at the same time. "What do you mean an accident? What happened?"

Norma Jean's number came up, accompanied by a message, as Leon cleared his throat.

Cord taken to hospital.

Ember's breathing hitched, making it hard to hear, as her surroundings faded to unfamiliar shadows. Hospital? Cord? Her body backed away from the counter, and suddenly she was searching for shoes.

"A shelf collapsed and he was in the aisle. Under it."

"Oh, my God," she gasped, ice shifting through her veins, her fingers shaking as chills raced over her shoulders. "Is he okay?"

Her heart kicked into overdrive. Where was Austin? She needed Austin!

"We dragged the stuff off him, and somebody called emergency services. He was kind of out of it but he said your name and I remembered meeting you, that you worked here. I found your number—"

"When did this happen? What hospital?"

"Not long ago. The ambulance took him and...

and he was still...I mean... They didn't tell us anything."

"I have to go." She ended the call and fumbled with her cell, hitting the icon for Austin.

"Hey, baby." The clatter and rumble of the construction site echoed in the background.

"Cord's in the hospital."

"What?"

"A shelf fell on him!" Her legs wouldn't hold her as she shakily grabbed at the back of a chair for support, her fingers slipping and sticking, like her brain. Her heart pounded and she couldn't get a full breath.

"I'll be there in twenty. Wait for me. Call Norma Jean." The call ended without a goodbye.

Carefully easing her way around the chair, she crumpled onto the seat and dialed Cord's mom. It rang several times before transferring to voicemail. She tried a text, her fingers shaking and clumsy. Then she stared at the screen smudged with frosting, willing a response to come.

Striving for calm, she breathed deeply. Her husband would be here soon and they'd go to Cord. Grabbing a damp cloth, she stared at it for a long moment before scrubbing at her phone and hands, cleaning away the sticky mess. Again, she tapped her phone and the screen lit, but still no reply from Norma Jean.

They were wasting time. Cord needed them. She pictured the various storage and display shelves at Bay's. Surely it wasn't one of the big ones that fell.

A woozy feeling took hold and she considered

calling Austin back, meeting him at the hospital to save time. She should be ready when he arrived.

Staring at her bare feet, she once again registered the need for footwear and made herself stand to work her way to the front closet. Slipping on a pair of sandals, she leaned against the wall, dizzy with worry and trembling with the uncensored images of Cord broken and bloody, without her or Austin there.

A sharp pain pierced her heart. *No.* It couldn't be that bad. He'd be fine. He was strong. He had to be. They needed him.

He needed them.

Breathing unsteadily, she blinked against the strain of tears and looked upward, hoping he could feel her love from several miles away. "We're coming, my love."

She wanted to cry but her tears were locked in a painful knot behind her heart. She needed to get to him. Austin was taking too long. Cord needed one of them there. *Now.*

She stumbled onto the porch, thinking she should find her purse, but intent on getting to the hospital. As she forced her knees to bend and take the stairs, a familiar flash of red skidded around the corner and barreled up the drive. Gravel crunched and spun as Austin slammed to a stop and threw himself out of the driver's seat.

"Ember." His arms banded around her as her trembling body failed to heed her commands.

"I can't reach Norma Jean." She thrust her phone at him, other words falling out in a jumble of confusion, her mind registering that she wasn't making sense.

"Shh." He half-carried her to the passenger side and helped her in, buckling her up with sure hands.

His iron control held his features tight as he steadily situated her. His brow creased and his mouth formed a flat line, absolute determination showing in his eyes and she drew some strength from his unshakable control. Knowing he was here, that he would get them to Cord, loosened the knot in her chest enough for her to breathe.

By the time they were on the road, she'd composed herself—somewhat. Except now tears streamed, unbidden, down her face. But it was okay to cry. Austin was here. He would get them to Cord. It was a broken record that played in her head as the road and buildings flashed by.

She glanced at her husband's wavering image, so brave and focused. That's what Cord needed, strength. Finding a pack of tissues in the glove box, she mopped at her tears and blew her nose.

"Hang on, baby. Almost there."

The closer they came to the hospital its proximity did nothing to ease her apprehension. Each mile should have been a relief, but it packed down her heart with pounds of worry. Her mind couldn't fit into a future without both Austin and Cord. She simply couldn't abide losing either of them.

"Go faster. Please, Austin. We have to get to him."

The thought of Cord lying in some strange bed surrounded by doctors hurt her chest. What if he was scared? Desperate to see them? Her heart ached with the pressure of so many unanswered questions.

The parking lot was full—or so it seemed. With his usual flair, Austin found a spot she wouldn't dare park in, but this was an emergency. She fumbled with the truck door handle, the challenge to her dexterity enough to turn her into a blubbering fool. Her husband was instantly there, opening the door and helping her unlatch the seatbelt, easing her out.

"Can you walk?"

She could walk. She could do anything with this man at her side, and she knew he'd get her to the other man they loved.

Pulling herself together, she sniffed and nodded. "I'm fine."

He slipped an arm around her shoulders, using his other hand to hold hers, and usher her through the parking lot, never taking his support from her.

"You need to breathe," he reminded squeezing her fingers. "Breathe, December."

Following his advice, she inhaled through her nose and exhaled a jagged breath from her mouth. The tight feeling in her chest eased and his warm grip loaned her the strength to make it as far as the entrance.

Austin guided her through the doors with a hand pressed reassuringly to the small of her back. "There's the information and reception desk."

His voice was astoundingly steady, despite his obvious worry. "Cord Bay, Cordovan Bay. He came in a short time ago."

The big welcome sign above the desk proved to

be a misnomer, considering the response they received. The woman sitting primly behind the counter straightened her glasses and tapped the keys on her computer. There was no *welcome* and the information was grudging. "He's here."

"Can we see him?"

"Are you family?"

Austin hesitated. "Sort of."

A thinly plucked brow arching, the receptionist —Marlene, according to her little name tag— pursed her lips. "Immediate family only at this time."

Ember's heart dropped to her toes and she choked on a silent sob. Austin's grip tightened around her and tucked her against him. "We need to see him. He lives with us."

Marlene narrowed her eyes and stared at Ember's left hand clutching her husband's.

Seeing she wasn't going to let them pass, Austin asked, "Can you at least get us an update?"

"I'm sorry, but I can't release any additional information. If you like, you can take a seat there and wait until the doctor approves visitors. I can't offer any more than that." She pointed to a cluster of rigid, unwelcoming chairs surrounding a long coffee table heaped with magazines.

They were more than fucking visitors! Cord was their... Well, he was *theirs*.

Ember looked at her husband, knowing if anyone could fix this, he could. "Austin..."

He squeezed her hand. "Don't worry."

Austin had his phone out, firing off texts as he ushered her toward the chairs. She paced with limited balance and texted Norma Jean again, but continued to get no response.

"Ember, you need to sit." Austin took her hand and pulled her to a row of chairs and she collapsed, numb from the neck down. "It's okay, baby. We'll get to him."

A man entered the ER holding a bloodied rag to his brow and she looked away. "I can't do this, Austin."

"You can. You have to think positive. I am." His strained features and staring eyes belied his statements, but his tone was strong and reassuring.

"I need to go to him."

"*We* need to go." He shifted his chair closer and wrapped an arm around her shoulders. "Someone will tell us something soon."

Her cell pinged and she flinched, silencing the device as the woman from reception scowled and pointed to the sign stating NO CELLULAR PHONES.

"It's Norma Jean," Ember whispered.

"What did she say?" Austin crowded close, and despite his outward calm she felt his body tremble.

Ember blotted her eyes and tried to read the small font on the screen. "She says she can't leave him—" A sob interrupted her words and he wrapped her up in a sheltering hug.

"Shh. Breathe, baby."

Gulping, she squinted at her cell. "She's sending Reed. Oh, God, please..."

"It'll be okay." He rubbed her back, his breath warm against her temple. "Cord's tough."

She let him convince her, despite the painful

truth that her men were in fact breakable. As she forced herself to trust his confidence the stricture around her heart eased.

"Okay," she whispered, making herself say the word.

"Watch for Reed." He held her close, their bodies filling the chairs that faced the doors where patients were taken.

Peering into the depths of the back corridors, her face tightened at the sight of Reed's tall, thin figure hustling their way. She jumped up and rushed toward him, Austin hard on her heels.

"How is he?" Her husband asked what she couldn't force past her numb lips.

Rubbing a hand over his face, Reed said, "They're cautious but figure he'll be o—kay." His voice cracked and Ember hugged him, instantly overcoming the strife between them.

His arms pulled her close and a sob shook his frame, carving a hole in the center of her heart. "I thought he'd been...kill—ed," he choked. "My boy. We got here the same time as the ambulance and he was so...*still*. Bloody—"

His words jerked out as if driven by jabs to the stomach, Reed's worry and love for his son unarguable in that moment. All their differences set aside.

Staying strong for him galvanized Ember's courage. She hugged him harder and Austin stepped close to rest a supportive hand on his shoulder. She felt the moment when Reed gained control and took her cue, easing her hold.

Rubbing the heel of her palm over her eye, she collected herself. "Can we see him?"

"He's been asking for you. Both of you." His Adam's apple worked on a big swallow, and he blinked rapidly. "He's damned lucky to have...the two of you."

As an apology, it was sketchy at best. As a blessing—profound.

"We're lucky to have him, Reed," she murmured.

"C'mon. He's waiting."

Austin pulled her into the refuge of his body and kept her close as they followed Reed. Her husband's determined strides guided them as his work boots slapped the tiles and her sandals faintly mimicked the assertive sound.

It took forever to trek down the sterile hallways. The clinical scent of sterilized air mixing with the energy of concern did nothing to settle her stomach or calm her nerves.

Reed led them to an area draped with long white curtains attached to tracks on the ceiling. She caught a glimpse of people in different positions on hospital beds, semi-hidden by the fabric, and her throat tightened. She could smell the fear and worry.

Reed swept one of the drapes aside and revealed his son, lying flat on his back, his beautiful face bruised and misshapen, curls awry and coated with dust. His expressive eyes were closed and Ember's heart stopped, her body flushing colder than ice, before she heard the reassuring beep of the monitoring machines.

Austin's grip tightened on her arm and she took in the additional details as she controlled her desperate need to throw her arms around Cord. A small whimper escaped as she mentally bargained everything she valued just to see him open his eyes.

Norma Jean sat beside the bed, holding Cord's swollen hand, the back of the other pierced with an IV needle and his index finger pinched with a clothes-pin-like apparatus that led to a big, white machine.

His mother gave her a wan smile, her face streaked with dried tears, her pallor evident. Cord's usually tan face was nearly as white as the pillow and his big body seemed diminished, somehow.

Ember swallowed another sob as she moved to lean over the bed, both hands gingerly clasping Cord's forearm. A single drop of pain fell from her lashes to splash on his wrist.

His eyelids fluttered and slits of blue focused on her face. Releasing a jagged breath she seemed to have held since she got that terrible call a lifetime ago, she forced a smile.

Lowering her head with a sigh of relief, she whispered, "Hey, handsome."

It took obvious effort for him to part his lips, his cheek twitching as he flinched in what seemed a painful effort. "Hey..." His voice was a shred of sound compared to his usual baritone. "... beautiful."

Her eyes briefly closed as she let the slight relief sink in. *He's talking. His eyes are open. A little.*

His gaze shifted and she read his mute plea as he searched the room.

"He's here," she whispered, stepping aside, so he could see her husband.

Cord's lashes lowered, a slow smile curving his lips until the evident pain halted his effort. "Hey, you," he grated.

Austin sniffed, his fingers folding tenderly around Cord's. Ember's jaw clenched as her husband's eyes flushed with pink, shimmering with unshed tears.

Cord's lashes lowered, his face a mask of contentment behind the colorful bruising as he let out a choppy sigh.

"You just rest," she urged. "We're all here. You're going to be fine."

Norma Jean whimpered and Reed moved to rest a hand on her shoulder. "You take this little lady's advice, son. Rest."

Another sigh passed Cord's lips as he relaxed and the monitors slowed their agitated beeping. Ember let herself go, weeping silently. Austin stuck beside her, his face tucked against her neck, the hot scald of his tears gathering on her flesh.

A nurse urged them out, talking about overnight observation and checking vitals, and the four of them stumbled into the wider area near a big white desk.

"He won't want to stay," Norma Jean commented.

"They wouldn't keep him if it wasn't warranted," Reed replied, staring around the emergency unit. "Maybe there's a place close by we can wait."

Ember didn't want to leave the vicinity and threw a desperate look at Austin, who gave her a gentle shake of his head, letting her know he'd figure something out. Right. Good. Because they needed to stay close in case Cord called for them.

Reed had come around, was taking charge when it came to the crisis involving his son, and she had to give him that. Norma Jean was nearly grey with exhaustion, and clearly needed her husband's decisive direction. The apple didn't fall far from the tree.

But Ember wasn't going anywhere. "I'll just... hang out...here." She gestured to a narrow slice of real estate presently unoccupied by medical equipment.

A nurse approached, her efficient but warm demeanor focused on their little group. "Mr. Bay will be moved upstairs shortly."

"Do you know his room number yet?" Norma Jean's voice was barely above a whisper.

Consulting her clipboard, the nurse said, "Room three-twelve. He'll be taken up in the patient's elevator. You'll need to wait in the guest area, please."

Ember didn't want to let Cord out of her sight, his sheet covered legs barely visible past the nurse's diminutive frame. The smells and sounds of the hospital were chipping away at her brave façade and she was standing only because of her husband's unfailing support.

Austin urged her toward the corridor, her feet dragging as she craned her neck to keep an eye on Cord's cubicle.

"We aren't going past here, baby." Austin shoulders squared as they stopped just inside the automated doors.

Resigned, the nurse sighed and turned a blind eye.

Reed disappeared and soon returned with coffee. Ember sipped mechanically, the heat of the beverage fighting the chill that had settled over her entire being. Medical staff floated in and out of her view, the curtains billowing as they did their jobs.

"They're moving him now," Norma Jean murmured and Ember's gaze narrowed on the gurney being pushed past the partition.

Surrounded by men and women in scrubs, she lost sight of Cord and whimpered, swallowing the sound out of respect to the other patients.

"C'mon." Austin hustled her to the elevators. Reed drew Norma Jean along behind them.

As they traveled upward, Austin had calmed enough to ask questions. "What happened?"

Reed let out an agitated breath. "All I know is there was a problem with the stacking of the shelves that held the tile and grout. Cord spotted it when some customers were looking, cleared them out. He was heading to get the forklift when it all came down."

"I took care of that aisle," Austin said quietly, and she straightened.

Ember recognized the guilt in his eyes, knowing it wasn't deserved. She rested a hand on her husband's arm and stared up at him, trying desperately to convey that this was an accident and no one was to blame.

Austin shook his head slowly, his eyes creasing at the corners. "When I worked there... Cord's been complaining about the summer help."

"It was an accident, Austin." The whispered reminder did little to ease the tension in his face.

"The doctor said the tests showed a concussion, but no skull fracture." Norma Jean shuddered, her voice a mere thread of sound, and Reed took her arm. "Broken clavicle, severe bruising of his face and upper body. He'll probably need to see a dentist. And they were concerned about something called an orbital fracture."

"He'll recover, honey." Cord's father brooked no argument. "Those tests were extensive and that doctor knew his stuff."

"I know he will. He'll come home and I'll look after him."

Austin spoke before Ember could verbalize her objection. "We'd like him to come home to us."

"But..." The older woman looked between them, and then at Reed.

Maybe this wasn't the time or place, but Norma Jean moved fast and Ember didn't want her making arrangements when Cord would fight her in the end. She knew her boys, knew where they were most comfortable and there was no way Cord would mend in his childhood bedroom when he belonged in theirs.

"Our house is open to both of you," Ember offered gently. "But I think he'll want to be home."

Not that they'd discussed it, exactly, but their home was Cord's and it was time they admitted that. As soon as he was better, they'd talk about moving him in permanently. Her exhausted mind gave a little chuckle. *Cord will be so happy to know another talk is coming.*

"We'll let Cord decide." Norma Jean's lips trembled and Reed awkwardly patted her hand.

"Norma Jean," Reed said gently. "The kids are grown. You think he won't want to be with his...uh, with Ember and Austin? I know you're his momma, but he's a grown man and you and I both know they're right."

She sighed and looked at Ember. "You're right. I know. It's just—"

"It's just that you're his momma." Ember gave her a compassionate smile. "And you'll bring him soup and treats. Every day."

They trooped down the hall to three-twelve, Ember's pace picking up, hoping he was already inside. He was, though they had to cool their heels outside the room while the medical staff got him settled.

"You go in first. It'll be two visitors at a time." Reed said, leaning against the wall, looking every bit his age. "I know he's gonna be okay, and we'll talk, but later."

Norma Jean locked her gaze on Ember, understanding reflecting in her eyes. It was a significant victory on an otherwise horrific day. Cord needed his father and Reed had discovered he needed his son.

Eventually, the two men would communicate in their own way. His dad being there would ease much of Cord's pain, the kind that didn't show with bruises.

Twenty-Four

Cord

"I'M GETTING UP." Cord threw the covers back and rolled to his side, hiding his wince.

His collarbone screamed, despite the intricate sling protecting it. Fuck, he had bruises on top of bruises. Strange, odd shaped marks were dotted all over his body, shading from purple to a nasty yellow green.

His vision was clear and his headache was mostly gone—until he moved around too much. The signs of healing.

"She'll have a fit." Austin held out a warning hand—pecking away at him like a mother fucking hen. "You were up to the bathroom earlier and you barely made it back. I'm strong, Cord, but you're fucking heavy."

He sagged back on the pillows. "She's not the boss of me."

"Or of me," Austin agreed amiably. "Yet she rules this house and you know it."

"I can't stay in bed forever."

"It's not forever. It's been two days."

"Three."

"Two days at home."

Home.

They'd brought him home, Ember fluttering around like a worried butterfly, Austin doing the heavy lifting, because Cord couldn't even lever from the wheelchair into the fucking Jeep without help. But he was home.

That silly little four-letter word seemed to ease his pain more than any drug ever could. God, his balls were shrinking by the minute, because calling this house his *home* did something to that once vacant organ filling his chest.

And he desperately needed the two of them to get through this nightmare without losing his mind. His head felt detached from the rest of his body, when it wasn't throbbing with vicious pain. Not to mention the accompanying dizziness and nausea taking his freakishly sore frame hostage.

Home. He kept thinking the word, honing in on the bright side of shitty circumstances. Not to his parents' house, although he understood there was almost a duel fought over that. Not to his place, abandoned and dusty. But here. He smiled, closing his eyes to savor the reminder.

"Happy thoughts?"

He eased back into the bed. "I'm home," he said quietly.

The mattress compressed as Austin lowered his weight on the edge, resting a big hand carefully on Cord's hip.

"This *is* your home. Ember's fretting about how to move all your crap here while you're banged up."

Cord silently chuckled. It *was* crap. A bunch of useless shit he'd collected over the years and was too damn lazy to donate to Goodwill. There were some things worth keeping, though.

"She's wondering what you'll do with your house. I told her we'd talk."

They both groaned, simultaneously. "I suppose talking with her isn't so painful."

Austin laughed. "Not when it suits us."

"Cord?" Her musical voice announced her proximity and he couldn't hide his grin.

Despite all her womanly demands, she made him happy. The soft rattle of dishes clinked with her approaching steps as she nudged the bedroom door open.

"I brought breakfast."

"I gotta go. We're getting close to the end of this job." Austin's fingers tightened on his hip and Cord's groaned. He might ache in places he couldn't fathom, but certain parts of him were still in good shape.

Taking care not to put weight on him, Austin leaned low and brushed his lips to Cord's, giving one of his curls a gentle yank. "See you after work."

Watching as Ember offered her lips to her husband and was kissed resoundingly, Cord was hit with another pang of envy, resentment building that he was out of commission and would be for a long ass time according to Ember's standard of health.

Austin released her and she swayed with a dizzy look of longing in her eyes. Damn. *He* wanted to give her that look, too. He should remind them both he wasn't *totally* broken.

Austin's steps sounded on the stairs and then paused. Probably putting on his boots. The door slammed a couple seconds later and he found Ember staring at him.

"Hey, kiddo. Brought my prison rations?"

"I'll have you know this tray contains everything an invalid could desire. Especially one who hasn't yet mastered his nausea."

Crap. It had been Austin who'd helped him up the stairs on day one—and dealt with the end result. And supported him *again* while he got sick in the bathroom on day two. "I'm good today."

"Have your breakfast and I'll play nurse."

"Do you have a cute candy striper outfit?"

She smirked, but made no comment as she carried his tray to the bed.

He wanted a shower. Despite her careful fussing with his hair and diligent use of washcloths, he could feel the residual blood and dirt left from the accident. On the other hand, her tender washing of his entire body was a reasonable trade-off. But three fucking days with no real shower was pushing it— even for him.

"I'm not doing anything sexual, Cordovan Bay, so quit thinking so hard."

At least she hadn't used his middle name. He

mustered a sheepish grin. "Not my nurse fantasy then?"

"Eat."

She adjusted the tray, and he stared at the contents with wilting interest. Apple juice, water, tea and...cream of wheat, also known as wallpaper paste. He needed meat. Eggs. Protein.

"I'm not going to gain my strength back eating this."

"Your mom's coming with your lunch. You'll graduate to better things by then." Ember gave him a warm smile and he decided he'd eat dirt for her.

Scraping the last of the paste—at least she'd flavored it with some syrup—he let her take the tray and set it aside.

Putting a basin on the nightstand, she wrung out a cloth in the steaming water. The faint scent of citrus wafted to his nostrils. "You shouldn't be carrying heavy basins."

"I carry turkeys and pork roasts heavier than this."

"You shouldn't."

"Then you'll have to stay home all the time and help me."

"I could do that."

He held his breath as she carefully peeled the sheet down to mid-chest. With gentle efficient movements, avoiding his collarbone and pulverized shoulder, she washed his neck and upper arms, slipping the cloth under his armpits. It was soothing, but emasculating at the same time.

"I can wash myself, Ember."

"I want to do it for you." Her dark eyes pleaded

as she patted him dry. "You're supposed to minimize movements until at least tomorrow."

With a sigh, he gave in and relaxed—as much as a red-blooded male could relax, especially under the ministrations of the beautiful woman he wanted badly. She washed him to his waist, tracing his abs with dedication. Such a beautiful person.

Covering his chest with the sheet again, she unveiled first one leg, then the other, stroking the cloth with long sweeps to his ankles. She gingerly bent his knees so she could do the other side.

"I'll leave your feet."

"You better." He was ticklish and the first sponge bath had made him jump and laugh, disastrous for his headache and sore chest.

"Can you roll a little? I'll do your back."

He maneuvered onto his side with a grunt as he swallowed the pain and she quickly scrubbed his back, taking a little lateral trip for a pass over his ass. He rolled back before she dried him and narrowed his eyes. Even that hurt—and tortured him in other ways.

"Sorry. You have such a nice tush."

His ass was something he'd never thought much about until Austin. And now Ember seemed entranced.

To cover his instant arousal, he said, "I'm an injured man, sweetheart. But you did say nothing sexual."

Pink flooded her cheeks and her full lips twitched. "I did."

He pointed with his good arm. "You missed a spot."

"I think I'll let you tend to that." She passed him the cloth. "I'll get some fresh water to do your face."

Holding the bunched up washcloth he stared ruefully at his crotch. With his sling he had no easy way of moving the sheet without getting it wet. Water ran in the bathroom as he reflected on his dilemma.

She emerged with the basin held carefully in front of her, bottom lip caught between her teeth as she concentrated on not spilling. He held his breath as his heart swelled. After putting the fresh water down, she met his stare. "What?"

"I love you, Ember."

"I know. And I love you." Her brows lowered as she noticed he'd yet to wash his junk. "You haven't —Oh."

She moved closer to the bed and lifted the sheet and politely glanced away, but he noted her smirk. Awkwardly, he washed himself, wincing at the chill of the cloth, although it served to cool his jets, which looked about ready for lift off. "Done."

She cleaned his face with a fresh washcloth, pausing to press a whisper of a kiss on his nose. "That's the only place that isn't bruised or cut, I think."

"Surprising, seeing as it's definitely a big feature," he teased, wishing he had the balls to remind her his nose wasn't the *only* unharmed part of his body.

Her eyes suddenly filled and he panicked, all sexy thoughts out the window.

"I'm fine, Ember. Don't. Please."

"I'm not." She blinked and turned her face

away. "I know you're fine and I'm not going to think about it."

"Austin thinks about it enough for all of us."

"He was upset," she defended.

"He and my dad finish shoring up all the shelves at the store yet?" He tried to distract her from getting upset.

"Not quite, but close. And your employees have been given a training course in safety. I think Austin might have used a big stick to make his point."

"Comes from new staff and me not supervising enough."

"Well, it won't happen again." She said it as though she could control the future.

"Probably not."

"Never."

"Wanna take a nap?" He patted the bed. "I don't like sleeping alone."

"We've been taking turns sleeping with you, Cord."

He kind of knew that, waking on his own from time to time and being woken to answer questions and take medication. The sight—if a blurry one—of Austin's unshaven face and worried mouth imprinted on his mind, as well as Ember's exhaustion which showed in shades of purple beneath her beautiful eyes.

When she hesitated he asked, "You busy or something?"

She laughed. "No. My day's yours."

"Then you just like making me grovel?"

She smirked. "A little groveling never hurt anyone."

Rolling his eyes, he sighed. "Ember, my beautiful nurse, will you *please* lie down with me and take a nap."

"I can do that." She slipped carefully alongside him and nestled close without putting any undue pressure on any part of his body.

"You know," he grumbled, "I'll eventually get my strength back. When that happens, you better watch out. You're first on my list."

"I look forward to it."

He breathed in the scent of her shampoo and the pure essence of Ember as her fingers settled on his wrist. More tired from the minor exertions of the morning than he liked to admit, he closed his eyes and drifted to sleep, content just to have one of them by his side.

As the days moved on, Cord's strength slowly came back and Ember eased up with her restrictions. It was a glorious thing when he tasted her usual cooking again. It would be even more incredible when he got to taste *her* again.

His truck keys had been missing for well over a week and no one seemed to give a shit that he had obligations at his store. God help him if Leon was making any big decisions. Luckily, his dad had picked up the slack and Austin visited often to lend a hand when he wasn't working his usual shifts for the union. But it was Cord's responsibility and he was growing damn tired of pawning it off on others.

Ember drove him around like he was Miss Fucking Daisy, which was considerate, but did nothing to boost his mood. Multiple check-ups and specialists left him with the same advice. "Give it time."

Time seemed all he had. He'd blown through his usual shows, binged on a few new series, got a little restless and nosed around the house looking for minor things he could fix, earning several lectures from Ember. The day he'd tried to open a jelly jar for her was a real ego booster. At this rate, he could hardly picture himself getting back to his usual strength.

"What are you watching?" Ember asked as she sat down in what Austin lovingly deemed her sewing chair.

Cord actually had to think what the show was called. "Some bullshit about treasure hunting." He'd never admit he needed to know if that trove was really hidden on the fucking island. "What are you working on?"

She rummaged through the tacky bag overflowing with fabric. "A new quilt for our bedroom. I'm adding blue, to match your eyes, and little gold accents to match the brown of Austin's."

He laughed to himself and dove in, head first. "We're gonna need a bigger bed."

With a faint blush, she nodded. "You and Austin should talk about that."

"We will," he promised.

Ember turned her attention back to her search and held up a hank of material. "Here's the blue."

She'd make something beautiful out of nothing, just some thread and cloth. "You're amazing."

She smiled, soft and modest. "So are you."

"No, Ember. You're...special. Priceless."

She gave up trying to thread the needle and dropped her hands to her lap. "Cord, don't make me cry."

"Good God. I take it back."

She snickered, finally got that needle threaded, then casually said, "You're priceless, too."

He sighed, feeling his value as a man dwindling every day he passed sitting on his ass. "I'm going to work tomorrow. I can't stay home anymore."

The contented set of her features faded as she lifted her gaze. "You don't like being home with me?"

"I love it, kiddo, but I have a job to get back to. Man's gotta work."

"You sound like Austin."

"He's a smart guy."

Her lips pursed and she returned her focus to her sewing. "Fine. I'll let you take that up with him as well."

Exactly why he had to get back to his usual routine. The longer he was forced to rest, the more fragile they treated him. He was a man, goddamn it. As much as he loved being near her, watching her, he couldn't sit through another afternoon of Ember's cozy craft corner. "Come here."

Her hand paused. "I'm sewing."

"So take a break."

"Cord." She pulled the thread through another patch, popping a pin in the fabric to hold its place.

He considered letting it go, but he couldn't. His pride remained bruised worse than anything else and he wanted things back to normal. Their normal.

Edging off the couch, he shifted his sling and

shut off the television. She didn't look up from what she was doing until he was standing directly in front of her chair, towering over her. Her eyes blinked up at him questioningly.

"Put down the sewing stuff, Ember."

She held her silence, drawing in a slow breath and then quietly placed the thread aside and the material back in the bag.

"Good girl." *Now what?* He didn't feel like making a trip upstairs. "I want you naked."

The corner of her mouth twitched, but she fought the smile and won. Her fingers slid the strap of her little dress off her shoulder and folded the material at her waist. Fucking beautiful.

"God, I missed seeing your body."

Her nipples tightened into little points and his mouth watered. Glancing around the room, he thought about the best possible way to do this. His fingers fumbled with his belt buckle, but he'd be damned if he'd let her undress him with the clinical proficiency he'd experienced from her over the past two weeks.

Peeling his zipper open, he adjusted his straining cock. "Follow me."

Moving back to the couch, he used his good arm to situate the pillows and gingerly sat down. Ember eyed him with a playful glint and gave a half-smile.

"You know you're not fully heal—"

"Hush. Get your ass over here."

She shuffled closer and waited for direction. He withdrew his dick and stroked slowly, his gaze tracking every telltale sign of arousal she showed, from the tightening of her breasts to the way her breathing accelerated.

"Drop the dress, sweetheart. You're going for a ride."

Her smirk bloomed into a full smile and the dress hit the floor. "Okay, but if I hurt—"

"Shh. Off with the panties."

She rolled her eyes and complied. His entire lower body lit up as her sweet pussy was unveiled. She stepped closer to the couch, her knees brushing his. He eased back, releasing his cock.

"You know what I want."

"Cord…"

"Ember, please. Don't make me beg. I fucking need you and it's been too long—"

"Okay. Okay."

She gingerly straddled his lap, the first brush of her fingers sending a jolt of pleasure through him as he sucked in a deep breath and shut his eyes. "Yes."

She lifted over him, guiding the tip of his cock through her slick folds. He'd be lucky if he made it two minutes inside of her without coming like an untried teen.

"Fuck, sweetheart, don't tease."

A soft gasp left her lips as she lowered her body, taking him slowly into her heat. His heart pounded against his ribs, his good hand landing on her thigh, squeezing tight. She seated herself, taking him to the hilt and their breath quickened.

"I missed this. Us," she murmured, sliding her tight channel up his length. "Is this okay?" She gripped the back of the couch so not to put too much weight on his shoulders.

"Perfect." He was in heaven.

Leaning forward, he captured her nipple in his mouth, resenting his limited range of motion when the slight shift caused him pain. He flopped back into the cushions, already winded, a shard of pain shooting through his neck.

"Fuck!"

Ember flinched and he quickly apologized.

"Sorry. I'm just...frustrated. This sucks."

"Cord, this is nice. It doesn't have to be wild."

"Fuck wild. I'd settle for—" His words cut off the second he caught her expression, noting the way she pulled into herself. "Shit, Ember, you're fine. I'm pissed off at myself."

She nodded, but wouldn't meet his gaze. "I know. Old insecurities and all that..."

"Hey." He brushed a finger under her chin, lifting her face. "I will *never* stop wanting you. I'm fucking miserable because all I do is crave you and Austin and I'm too fucking broken to have you the way I want."

Her mouth curved and she blinked, forgiveness shining in her eyes. "I know what it is to feel broken."

His heart pinched, his arousal flagging at her whispered words, so full of past heartache and telling of the battle scars she kept hidden behind so much beauty. "I know you do, sweetheart, but you're the farthest thing from broken."

"Chipped."

Weren't they all?

He sighed and reached for her. "Come here."

He pulled her close, outmatching her when she protested. "I'll hurt your arm."

"Put your fucking head on my shoulder, Ember. Let me hold you for a second." She gave in and he softly cupped the back of her head. "We're all a little banged up, but we're whole."

She drew in a slow breath and sighed. "You make us whole."

And didn't that just make all his ridiculous aches and pains go away?

Her nose nestled into his throat, her lips teasing as his pulse skipped a beat. His cock swelled and she eased back, glancing between their bodies. "Well, hello, Mr. Bay."

He chuckled and gingerly thrust. Her breath hitched so he rolled his hips again, making do with his physical limitations. Her sex tightened and he groaned.

"Yes. Do that again, sweetheart."

"This?"

"Mmm. More."

"I'm not used to being in the driver's seat with you. I kind of like it."

"Don't get used to it." His fingers slid up to her waist, his grip tightening. "Keep moving."

She lifted, coming back down with a delicious glide and taking him deep. Her rhythm increased and soon they were breathing fast, kissing, and approaching a star-spangled finish.

"Yes. Fuck. Faster, sweetheart."

She rode him harder, gasping, tits bouncing, her face pink with exertion. "Cord..."

"Ember..."

"You feel incredible."

"That's it, sweetheart. Keep going. Almost."

Her head tipped back as her breathy cries grew louder. "Cord!"

"Harder—"

"Hello? Cord? December?"

They stilled and Cord hissed, on the verge of exploding, his balls shriveling to raisins at the sound of his mother's proximity. "*Fuck*."

His mom called again. "Anybody home?"

"Don't come in here, Mom!" His effort at a shout was thwarted by his strangling need.

"*Ohmygod...*" Ember's body clenched as she tried to cover up, huddling against him and groping for her dress. She nearly ripped his dick off as the floor creaked.

"Mom, no!"

"Cord?"

"Mom, *stop!*"

"Oh, Jesus, Mary and Joseph!" His mother gasped, pivoting to face the opposite direction.

He grit his teeth and shut his eyes. "She never fucking listens," he growled.

"I just...brought you some of the last tomatoes from my garden. I'll...I'll put them in the dining room and leave them for December."

"Oh, my God," Ember whimpered, her naked body twisting into his armpit as she curled into a human pretzel.

"Ember..." his mother continued to shout while facing away from them. "They're on the table."

"Thank you, Norma Jean." Ember's voice muffled against his chest.

"I'll leave you two..." There was a pause and though he couldn't see his mom, he also didn't hear the door. "That's probably not good for Cord's—"

"*Mom!*"

"Right. Sorry. I'll just go."

The front door closed and he leaned his head on the back of the couch, not letting out his breath until he heard the gravel crunch and his mom pull away. Ember's body shook and he blinked. If she was crying... No, please no, he couldn't deal with that too.

He peered at her face. "You're *laughing*?"

Twin dimples showed on her bunched cheeks, as she giggled hard enough to strangle the sound. Then it came, a full out belly laugh that shook her little body and was completely contagious. He cracked up and then groaned.

He was never going to come again. Ever. His whole lower half now ached dully and all future erections were hiding in an emotionally traumatized corner of his psyche.

Once they settled, Ember gave him an apologetic bat of her eyes, dabbing at the moisture there. "I'm sorry. We can try again."

He shook his head, certain he'd never forget this moment. "Just sit with me. And don't yell at me when I avoid my mom for the next few days." *Or weeks.*

Twenty-Five

Cord

CORD'S BUM shoulder was finally past relying on the damn harness contraption and he'd graduated to a basic sling. His bruises had faded to nothing—all but the bad one beneath his eye. But even that was barely noticeable. His jaw hadn't ached in days and his face wasn't swollen anymore. He was good to go. And damn fucking happy about it.

Sure, he loved being home with Ember, kind of like a house husband, enjoying all the advantages, now that she'd quit treating him like an invalid and they'd learned to lock the door so random people didn't come bursting in with produce. If his head would quit with the occasional weird spinning and blistering headaches, life would be perfect.

Well, perfect except for Austin. With an exasperated shove, Cord clambered to his feet and frowned at the guy. Something was going on with his friend.

"How's work going?"

"Huh?" Austin dragged his attention away from his phone, as if just noticing Cord had stood and was glowering at him.

"*Work*."

"Oh, good."

"How long's this new contract for?"

His friend blinked, and Cord's heart pinched. He was definitely hiding something, putting that much thought into a simple fucking question.

"Don't really know. A long time, I hope."

"Right." Whatever.

He stomped to the kitchen, wishing Ember was home instead of out on some mysterious errand with his mother. He needed her right the fuck now, needed her to orchestrate a "talk", seeing as Austin was curiously tongue tied of late. Withholding.

He didn't pay Austin any mind as he followed Cord into the kitchen. Two could play at this game.

"What's wrong? You not feeling okay?"

Now he wanted to pay attention? Despite being pissed off, Cord could admit to acting like a total bitch and not wanting to admit his feelings. "I'm good."

"You look good." A thread of something else wove through Austin's tone and it occurred to him that he wasn't the only one who'd been going without.

Well, maybe not totally without. Cord had the pleasure of passing the days with Ember. Their infrequent attempts to make love usually exhausted him before he got off the way he preferred, but it was still nice. They'd learned to improvise. Draw it out. Make it sweeter.

But he was getting better, stronger and stronger every day. And he missed having them together.

Stepping into Austin's space, he worked his fingers into the gaps between the buttons of his shirt. Holding him in place, he leaned in and set his mouth against Austin's lips, nearly groaning at the feel of him.

Lips parting, their tongues dueled for dominance and he pressed the advantage. He nudged the growing bulge behind his jeans along Austin's arousal, swallowing his gasp. Fuck, it had been a long time.

Austin circled his arms around him, holding him close without putting any pressure on his shoulder. This was more like it. His friend's undivided attention eased a bit of Cord's worry that he might be keeping a secret. Maybe he was just being too sensitive lately.

Leisurely exploring, they continued to kiss and Cord savored each swipe and nibble, the faint stubble around Austin's mouth prickling against his own. They drew apart, sucking air, and he leaned his forehead against his, Austin's eyes drifting shut.

"Fuck me, Cord," he breathed raggedly.

"You have no idea how badly I want to."

With a groan, Austin dropped his arms and stepped back. An exasperated huff was shared between them. "I gotta be somewhere."

"What?" Cord's head jerked up, his dick protesting.

"Yeah. I have an appointment."

"It's Saturday. Or is it with Harley?"

"Sure." Austin dipped his head as he adjusted his shirt.

Cord frowned, that suspicious sense coming back two-fold. He'd been running out so much, for more than minor errands and AA meetings, something had to be going on. But every time Cord asked Ember where Austin was, she blew it off, like his absence was totally normal. Yeah, right. Something was going on.

"Ember said she'd be back in time," Austin mumbled, grabbing his keys off the hook on the wall.

"In time for what? I can be left home by myself, for fuck's sake."

Jesus, had they been babysitting him all along? If Austin was so fucking worried maybe he could delay his "appointment", code for *I'm fucking avoiding and hiding something*.

"Of course you can be left home by yourself. But you scared the hell out of us and you're still having dizzy spells. Why take a fucking chance if we don't have to?"

Austin wasn't being aloof now. His eyes were dark with emotion, and his fists were tight at his sides.

But something else was going on. "You feel... distant," Cord muttered, disliking the needy tone in his voice.

Austin approached and cupped a hand around

the back of his neck, pressing his brow to Cord's. "Hey. I'm right here. Everything's cool. Trust me on that. I love you. Ember loves you. This has just been a big...adjustment. We'll find balance soon enough. You need to believe that, Cord. I wouldn't do anything stupid."

His sincere tone deflated Cord's suspicions. Maybe he just had cabin fever. That or blue balls. Maybe both. "I'll be back to normal soon, Austin."

"I know. And then we'll get back to life as usual—a new and improved usual."

The front door opened, and feminine voices signaled the arrival of Ember and his mother *a.k.a. the cock blocker.*

The girls bustled into the kitchen, Ember bearing an enormous box. Austin immediately relieved her of it and set the box on the counter.

She crossed to Cord and went up on her toes for a kiss. "Hey."

"I missed you. Left me home with that guy." He gestured at her husband.

Austin snorted, shoving the box labeled "mixer" back toward the wall.

Ember rested her palm on Cord's chest, right over his heart. "I missed you too. And I don't know what I'm going to do when you go back to work."

With his mother looking on, he nuzzled Ember's hair. He ached to get back to the store, to help his dad, though he knew he couldn't run it by himself. Not yet.

"Few more days and I won't be up in your business every second."

"I'll miss my helper," she countered.

He might be a wounded warrior, but he'd become slightly useful once he could navigate without wanting to puke. The stuff Ember did around the house was phenomenal, and he'd gleaned an even greater appreciation of her skills over the past few weeks. She was an unstoppable force.

"We'll have to talk about hiring additional help in my absence," he teased. "Maybe a cleaning lady or something to pick up the slack."

Laughing, she shouldered him off. "Oh, I think I can handle it. Unless you find me a cleaning *man*."

He managed to swallow his growl, but narrowed his eyes. As if there'd be another man in this house.

He looked to Austin, expecting the same outrage despite Ember's teasing tone, but once again he appeared preoccupied, muttering something to his mother Cord couldn't quite hear. Unbelievable.

Sensing his stare, Austin turned in Cord's direction, something close to guilt flashing in his whiskey brown eyes. "I gotta get moving." He glanced at Cord's mom. "Want a ride?"

"Sure. Save Ember going out again and me spending the entire afternoon here."

"You're always welcome," Ember protested, but she was already following the others to the door.

On one hand, he was relieved he didn't have to avoid looking his mother in the eye for an extended period of time, but on the other... The whole exchange struck him as odd. Where the hell was his mother's car?

Ember walked them to the door and Cord waited in the kitchen. As soon as she returned, he asked, "Did you pick her up this morning?"

"Hmm? Oh. Yeah. We had some errands to run." Without making eye contact, she went to the box on the counter. "I want to try out the new mixer."

Weird and weirder. He shook it off.

Trudging behind her he watched as she yanked at the cardboard. The box resisted her efforts, and he scooted her out of the way, fishing his pocketknife out of his pocket. "Let me."

Slitting along the tape, he opened the flaps. It must have been returned, to be sealed like that. He wasn't impressed with the repackaging job. "This from Bay's?"

"Where else?" Ember raised a brow. "The best hardware store in town."

One handed, he pulled out the stand and the bowl with only a bit of difficulty. He'd been lifting weights to keep his strength up, but this contraption was a lot heavier, and unwieldy. Still, he managed it.

The shining red and chrome finish glared in the simple kitchen, and he glanced at Ember, who was studying it with a critical expression. Her nose wrinkled. "Where's the beaters?"

He felt around and rattled the box, hiding his irritation that one of his employees obviously didn't check the return properly. "Not in here."

"Really?"

"Somebody didn't check it." Another reason he needed to get back to the store. This was inexcusable.

"I'll take it back. I really wanted to use it for tonight's dessert. For dinner. Wanna come with me to exchange it?"

"Absolutely."

Aside from the trips to the doctor, he hadn't been anywhere fun. Moving vehicles still tended to make his head hurt. But he really wanted to find out who wrapped that box without checking first to see if all the pieces were there. There went two hundred bucks out of the store's bottom line.

"Can you carry that?" She fretted as he managed to stow the stand and bowl back inside.

"It's more awkward than anything, Ember. You get the doors."

He hoisted the box in the backseat of the Jeep as Ember clambered in, checking her phone before tucking it away. Austin rode both their asses about distracted driving, and Ember was a good little rule follower. He smiled to himself. Two alpha males calling the shots, and yet their woman coped beautifully.

She backed around smartly and he held his breath, but so far, so good. Relaxing into the seat, he focused on maintaining his equilibrium. He longed for the day when he could ride in a car without vertigo. Sunglasses helped.

"Are you doing okay?" She stopped at an intersection and stared at him.

"I'm good. Really good, actually." A little desperate for some hot and dirty sex, but he figured it best not to share that while she was driving.

"Okay." She accelerated and took a direct route to the store.

Cord noted the seasonal changes as summer was winding down. Fall would be here before they knew it and he mentally considered the inventory at Bay's.

He really needed to get back in the saddle, check to make sure their fall inventory was where it should be.

"When we get there I just want to go over some things. Check to make sure certain orders are done."

"Okay."

He frowned, expecting an argument. This was good. Progress. "I also want to make sure the summer help is packing up as much seasonal stuff as they can so it's not all left to my dad." Lord knew Cord could only lift so much.

"That's a good idea."

A good idea? Why was she being so agreeable when she'd been the most reluctant to let him return to his usual routine? "I'll take it slow."

"I know you will."

Okay, what the fuck was going on? "Em—"

She pulled in front of the store and he blinked, his words cutting off.

The engine ticked over and he stared, thunderstruck. Removing his sunglasses, he squinted at a huge banner was slung from corner to corner of the building above the doors. *Welcome Back, Cord!*

"What is this?" His voice caught in his throat.

Ember's eyes glistened and she reached for his hand. "Just what it says. We all know how hard it's been for you. Waiting."

They got him a banner? This had to be her doing. He was suddenly overwhelmed, his chest pounding and his throat scratchy. "I don't know what to say. Um..." Jesus, he needed to get a grip. "Thank you?"

"You're welcome."

"Does this mean I'm discharged?" he teased, recovering some of his steadiness.

"It means I'm going to really miss having you home during the day, Cord, but this is where you belong. Here."

He laughed. "The mixer?"

"Just a way to get you out of the house. The beaters are in the glove compartment."

He shook his head. "I thought I was gonna have to fire someone for doing a shitty repackaging."

"I know. It was the easiest way to get you to come with me."

He squeezed her fingertips and nodded, his own eyes prickling with an unfamiliar sting. Strange that he'd been so eager to get back to work, but everything suddenly felt different now, like he was giving up a part of her he'd come to know over these past few weeks and love more intimately than he already had.

They made a *thing* out of his return—for him. God, he fucking loved her. "I guess I'd better go in, then."

The moment he stepped onto the pavement the big entry doors slid open and people tumbled out. He saw his mom and his dad, his summer staff, and did a double take when he recognized the tall figure of Austin. "Austin's here?"

Laughing, he shook his head and again lifted his sunglasses. The man was sporting a Bay's apron.

Ember smiled and quietly took his hand as they walked toward the store. The group of Bay's employees formed a roughly shaped U around him, but he could only see one person.

Austin watched him, a slightly wary look in his eyes, as Cord slowly approached. Was this where he'd been disappearing random times throughout the days over the past few weeks? Wearing a stunned grin, Cord stepped close to his friend, his head shaking at the amused sense of being duped.

Clearing his throat, he asked, "You've been working here?"

Austin grinned, that cocky smile holding enough charm to negate his arrogance. "Appears so."

"For how long?" What about his job with the union? The new contract? Austin had always been a union guy.

"Seems like family members at Bay's spend their lives working here. Together. Until their kids take over. I'm a little late, but I'm here."

Cord's lips trembled as comprehension sank in, nearly knocking him on his ass. He knew his employees were watching. His mom. And his dad. Sparing the others a quick look, he noted nothing but happiness and acceptance in their expressions.

Family. Kids. Holy fuck.

He wished he could steal some privacy and throw his arms around Austin and Ember, his family, his partners. But he'd save that for later. For now, he gave an approving nod, hiding his deeper emotions behind laughter. "Can't mess with tradition."

Austin, apparently, didn't give a fuck about who was watching and waited for no one. Stepping closer, he wrapped his arm around Cord's shoulders, squeezing tight, and whispered, "Love you."

Okay. That did it. Cord adjusted his sunglasses

and struggled to get his emotions in check. Clearing his throat, he rasped, "Love you back."

Austin gave him a second, using his body to block the others' view as Cord tightened it up. "You good, man?"

He was better than good. He was fucking great. He cleared his throat again and nodded. "Best you show me around. I expect you've made some changes."

"Starting with that half-ass shelving," Austin retorted, turning to head into the store.

As if reeled in by an invisible thread, they both halted and looked back at Ember who was bouncing on her toes, smiling from ear to ear.

"You coming, kiddo?"

She raced to join them, fitting her petite body between theirs and they crossed the threshold as one. Partners. A family.

Twenty-Six

Austin

"YOU'RE LOOKING GREAT," Austin commented, scrutinizing Cord's clear, unblemished skin marked only with the odd white tracings of a scar where so many cuts and bruises had been.

Cord smirked, rinsing the razor and setting it on the edge of the sink. A faint trail of dampness traced the edge of his hard jaw and Austin longed to follow it with his tongue.

Cord made a muscle, showing off the arm that had been affected by the broken collarbone. "Good as new. If not better."

Austin let his stare track over Cord's chiseled chest and flat belly, then dropped lower. Despite seeing him every day at the store and sharing many moments at home, it seemed like an eternity since he actually got to look his fill. Look his fill... The thought should feel strange, but it felt...so right. Hiding a smile, he stared as his partner's cock twitched against his thigh.

"Like what you see?"

"I do." And he'd missed *him*. Austin dropped his own towel, casually stroking his hardening dick.

Cord's lips quirked as he arched a brow. "What's going on?"

"You used all the hot water again. And flushed while I was showering."

"Pussy." Cord laughed and turned, heading for the bedroom.

Shaking out the fabric, Austin whipped the end of his towel, snapping it against Cord's perfect ass.

"Jesus! Fuck." Whirling around, Cord glared and advanced.

Austin moved, meeting the challenging glint in his eyes, too turned on to let him go. Staring into his baby blues, he watched Cord's pupils dilate, their cocks brushing between them.

Reaching down, he gripped Cord's hardening length and tugged. Cord mirrored his action, grabbing him, and Austin hissed, fighting the urge to give over.

Not this time.

Cord's need for dominance in the bedroom was his trademark, something others might appreciate—as he did—but this time around Austin was in charge.

"Get on the bed."

Cock pulsing in Austin's grip, Cord shuddered. "You feeling hard this morning?"

"The hardest." He squeezed and drifted his thumb over the head of Cord's cock, teasing the notch, watching the other man's face tighten.

Understanding flashed in Cord's eyes as he held his stare. "What about Ember?"

"*Ember!*" Austin yelled, then gave a quiet chuckle. "You didn't think I'd leave her out of this." He yelled again. "Ember! I need you!"

A patter of bare feet sounded on the stairs. "What?" She ran into the bedroom, calling out, skidding to a halt as she took in their stance. "Oh. *Oh.*"

"Breakfast ready?"

"Um, no. I made coffee and put the casserole in the oven, but it'll be at least an hour. There's fruit cut up, though."

He smiled at her anxious face. She fed them with single-minded purpose, worried when they missed a meal. "Baby, it's fine."

"I could eat some fruit," Cord commented and Austin tightened his fist.

A pinch of humor visibly transformed her worry as she shook her head. "Poor Cord."

"Ganging up on me," Cord complained.

"And you love it." He eyed his wife, taking in her tousled hair and tiny frame, all wrapped up in a swath of material she'd sewn into a new robe last week. "Cord's hungry, baby."

Catching his drift, she slid out of the robe and sashayed to the bed. Cord didn't seem in such a rush to get to breakfast anymore, his gaze tracking her, his eyes flaring with lust.

"Dessert first?" she asked, letting the robe drop to the floor.

"Fuck me," Cord grated, his gaze locked on Ember's ass as he pressed into Austin's grip.

"I intend to."

Cord's stare shot to him, and settled there, eyes wide. "What?"

"You heard me."

A long, steady look eased into understanding as Cord's lids drifted lower. His dick pulsed in Austin's hand as he inclined his head. "Right."

Releasing Cord's cock, he waited for his partner to give up his own hold, instead rewarded with a firm tug that set him on his toes. Biting back a curse, Austin gestured toward Ember, sprawled in all her glory in the middle of the mattress, positioned exactly as he wanted her.

Cupping the back of Cord's head, he gave him a nudge. "Have a taste."

Cord let go and pivoted, reaching Ember in two long strides, eagerness apparent in every muscle. He dropped to his knees and adjusted her feet on the edge of the bed. Even from a distance Austin could see her pink folds, flush with arousal.

Cord dove in and she gasped, her neck arching in immediate response. Austin tore his gaze away and yanked open the top drawer of the vanity, pulling out a bottle of lube and a condom, his hand slightly trembling.

Ember's tiny pleas melded into whimpers. Austin paused to watch his partner pleasure his wife and rubbed his chest with delight. Such a connection. A connection between the three of them, and she was the cornerstone.

"Don't get her off."

Her eyes opened wide and pleading. Her full lips parted. "Austin, please."

"No." He softened his tone at her pout. "Not yet."

Cord lifted his head and glared over his shoulder. When he spotted the lube and the condom, his scowl morphed into a pure intrigue. "Need some help with that?"

Now that you mention it...

Wordlessly, Austin handed over the condom and Cord ripped open the foil to extract the ring of latex. Pinching the end, he quirked a brow and Austin stepped closer. Ember angled up on an elbow and watched, her pretty face alight with interest.

Austin caught Cord's wrist, stilling him, and looked into his eyes, moved by how much trust rested between them and how unfathomable this outcome had been a few months ago. His throat clenched around words he couldn't quite get out, so he gently ran a hand through Cord's curls and smiled.

Interpreting everything he longed to say and failed to voice, Cord matched his smile and nodded. "I'm ready for this. Are you?"

Austin nodded. "Yes. Been looking forward to it."

Cord slowly fit the condom over the head of Austin's cock, an experience in and of itself. Austin's anticipation doubled, and he shivered, as

Cord handled him with sexy-as- fuck ease and familiarity.

"There." Cord leaned back, and Austin met his wife's eyes. Her stare smoldered darkly with lust and his belly flipped. There was nothing but eager acceptance and love in her eyes.

Again, he was jolted by a wave of emotion. "I love you, baby."

A smile bloomed across her lips. "Love you back."

Getting a grip on his slipping control, he waved a hand. "As you were."

Cord huffed a laugh and crawled slowly over Ember, his face lowering between her spread thighs. Ember gave a passionate, little yelp, her fingers clenching in the bedding as she arched her back, pressing her pussy against Cord's talented tongue.

Stepping behind him, he tapped his foot along Cord's inner ankle and Cord widened his stance, bracing his knees on the edge of the bed. Austin's cock throbbed within the confines of the condom as his eyes measured the breadth of Cord's back and the curve of his ass. That belonged to him. *He* belonged to him.

Taking up the space between Cord's thighs, he pressed a hand on his shoulder, conveying the same comfort he'd been afforded his first time. Cord had taken such care with him and he hoped to do the same.

Drifting his fingers to Cord's neck, tracing the wild beating of his pulse, he bent to lick over the length of his spine. Skin rippled beneath his tongue and Austin's cock leapt as it brushed Cord's ass.

Ember cried out in pleasure, a counterpoint to his own need, and he moved into action. Opening the lube, he poured it generously over his fingers and Cord's crack, marking the way he tensed. Keeping his movements gentle yet firm, he found Cord's taint and greased his hole, pressing the pad of his finger steadily inward.

Cord's shoulders lurched as he grunted under the slightest penetration. Austin slowed his progress, taking the time to experiment and tease as he let the anticipation build.

"You being good to Ember?" he asked as he worked in the tip of his finger as far as his first knuckle. Cord relaxed against his invasion, his reply muffled by Ember's flesh.

"He's dedicated," his wife slurred, as her hand stroked over Cord's hair.

Adding more lube, he used another finger to spread the muscle of Cord's ass wider. He really wanted to put his cock in there but he wasn't going to rush things and hurt him.

"Make him work for it." His own need made his voice thin and sharp. "Wife."

Arousal colored Ember's tiny moans. The erotic sound of Cord lapping at her folds had Austin's dick aching to get in the game. He sank his fingers deep and Cord tensed.

"Don't forget our girl."

Pumping slowly, scissoring his fingers, Austin's breath labored in anticipation of drilling his partner's slick ass. Cord's shoulders bunched as his head lowered on a groan, but Ember was moaning again, so he hadn't forgotten her.

Reaching between Cord's thighs, he stroked his sac as he wedged his fingers deeper.

"Fuck, Austin…" Cord's head jerked upward to the sound of Ember's protest.

"You can take it."

"I know I can take it. I'm worried I'll come."

His hand found Cord's cock and squeezed the base—*tight*. "Not yet. You either, baby."

His wife let out a frustrated groan and Cord chuckled, angling his face back between her thighs. Both of her hands flew to his hair, fisting his curls and Austin's nostrils flared at the scent of sex filling the air. She was close.

"December."

Her eyes flashed open, dazed with lust as she panted quickly.

"Arms up," he directed and she slowly released her fingers to rest her hands above her head in surrender. "Good girl."

Austin worked his fingers deep as the oil did its part. "You're opening now."

Cord's ass rocked with his pumping hand as his groan muffled against Ember's slick skin. It was the hottest fucking sound and almost enough to make him shoot his load before the main event.

With a third finger, Cord lost his stoicism and moaned, the sound no longer stifled against Ember as he rested his cheek on her thigh and panted. Austin stroked his lover's hip, allowing him to adjust.

"You okay?" he murmured.

Cord lifted his head a bit, his brow tight. "Not so sure about this."

He leaned over him, kissing his shoulder and inhaling his familiar scent. "It's fucking awesome once you get past the first part."

Huffing out a breath, tiny beads of sweat gathering on his brow, Cord muttered, "I have a better appreciation for being on the receiving end."

He drifted a trembling hand up to Ember's breast, cradling the soft flesh. She pressed her hand over his and sighed.

"Get her off, Cord. Make our sweet girl come."

Without hesitation, he turned his face back between Ember's thighs. She squeezed her eyes shut and panted sharp breaths as Cord relentlessly drove her to the edge of ecstasy. Screaming out her orgasm, a flush coloring her chest and throat, every muscle in her limbs trembled under the intensity of her release.

Beautiful.

A sheen of sweat broke over Cord's flesh, and as Austin bore down, his lover's fingers tangled in the sheets. Afraid he might put too much weight on Ember, Austin eased back and said, "Give us some room, baby."

Ember rolled out from under Cord and scooted toward the headboard. Resting in the mess of pillows, she wove her fingers through Cord's curls, her face close to his.

"Love you," she whispered.

"Always, sweetheart."

Austin withdrew his fingers, slicked his cock, and moved in on his target. Go time. With a deep breath, he pressed steadily, the wide head compressing as he gained ground, and pleasure-pain lanced up his spine.

"Jesus." Cord flinched away and Austin took hold of his hips, holding him in place, halting his own progress.

Working his thumbs over the top of Cord's ass, he did his best to soothe him. "Deep breath."

As Cord relaxed, Ember stroking his head and murmuring to him, Austin pushed past the tight ring of muscle.

"Jesus!" But Cord pushed back and Austin slid all the way inside.

His eyes rolled back in his head, as his cock strangled in the volcanic heat. So. Fucking. Tight. So different... "Holy fuck, Cord. You're..." He sucked air and bowed his head. "Fuck."

"Do it. Do *something*."

Gripping his hips and finding his balance, he shuttled his cock in as gentle a rhythm as he could manage, while his need screamed for him to go faster, to take him.

Cord's moans took on hints of pleasure, particularly when Austin swiveled his hips and pulled back. He paid attention, repeating the motion over and over, subduing his own ache to spill.

There was something indescribable about taking Cord like this, owning his pleasure, delivering it. Something potent that amplified all the love he felt for both his partner and his wife. His chest lowered and he pressed his lips to Cord's back, voice just above a whisper, "Being inside of you... It's... God, Cord. I fucking love it."

Cord choked out something incomprehensible. His big body tensed, shuddering, and Austin lost his control. His hips snapped forward, powerful and demanding as he staked his claim. Cord let out a jumbled slur of words, his fingers clenching the bedding as he rocked into Austin's every advance.

"Fuck. Yes. Harder."

The strength of him was Austin's undoing. So unbreakable. So stable. So dependable. He fucking loved him. Emotions stemmed from the depth of his soul, flowing side by side with all that he felt for his wife.

"You're ours," he hissed, shuttling deeper and harder with each thrust.

Ember's fingers entwined with Cord's as his face tightened, the picture of unrefined ecstasy. "Yes," he cried, letting out a long moan. "*Yours.*"

Shoving deep, he held hard to Cord's hips as his orgasm shot up from the base of his spine and hollowed his balls. He groaned Cord's name, the word escaping like a prayer, scraping up his throat to tumble past his lips.

Sagging over his back, he set his teeth in Cord's shoulder and gripped his biceps. Their sweaty skin clung together as their breathing synchronized and slowed.

After an eternity, Austin gathered his strength and levered up on one hand, catching Ember's wide-eyed stare.

"Wow," she mouthed, as she traced her fingers around one of Cord's curls.

Cord rested, eyes closed, lips parted. Still trembling, Austin carefully pulled out. His lover released a guttural groan as his hole tightened before Austin's fascinated stare. "You okay?"

"Never. Better."

Ditto. Swallowing hard, he eased off the bed. "Be right back." He hustled to the bathroom and dealt with the condom, then dampened a hand towel in warm water.

Cord had rolled to his back, his head cradled in Ember's lap, his gaze on Austin as he approached the bed. That soft, sated, blue-eyed stare tracked him as he dropped his weight beside Cord.

"Still good?"

"You were right. It got better." Cord gestured to his belly, glistening with come, a wry grin ticking up the corners of his mouth.

Austin laughed. "Told ya."

He handed Cord the towel and his fingers trailed over his. Austin's chest swelled, a freakily common experience around this man, and he leaned over to kiss him. Cord opened his mouth and Austin tasted his surrender.

When he pulled back, Ember angled closer and he took her mouth next.

"Mmm." She pulled back, her smile soft and full of unspoken satisfaction. "Breakfast?"

"In bed, maybe?" Cord replied, drawing her laughter.

"You're spoiled from being on bed rest. Fine." She slid off the bed and scooped up her robe, wrapping it around her body, depriving them both of the view.

Flopping beside Cord, Austin absently coasted

his fingers over his hip. Cord twitched and pressed closer. "Love you, Austin."

"You too, Cord."

"I'm gonna want to do that again. Not right away. But again."

On a chuckle, Austin said, "I suppose you get the top next time."

"Yup."

"Gonna keep a roster?"

"You better fucking believe it."

He'd never openly admit that Cord's dominance in sexual matters did something unexpected for him, but he definitely treasured today's moment of surrender. It was good to have a little *give* when Cord knew just how to *take*. Austin would take him any way he came, because at this point he wasn't letting him go. Ever.

Twenty-Seven

Austin

"WHERE'S CORD?"

Austin took the bags from his wife and carried them up the porch steps. "He's at the store."

"Again? It's Saturday."

Yes, and their lover hadn't been pleased when Austin asked him for a few hours alone with December. But once Austin explained why he needed the time, Cord happily obliged, predicting that tears would likely be shed at some point today. Austin hoped not too many.

"He's happy to be back. He mentioned cleaning out his place after, possibly crashing there for the night."

She stilled, hauling two more bags out of the Jeep. "He's not coming home?"

"Maybe," Austin amended. "We'll play it by ear."

He held the door, taking another bag off her hands as she walked the rest of the groceries to the counter. "Austin, we can't let him pack up all his stuff alone. We should be there, helping him."

"Then we'll go later. He's at Bay's right now anyway."

She unloaded the dairy stuff into the fridge, her brow tight. "He shouldn't be working. I mean, it's the weekend. This is Reed's day. I know he's back, but he still needs to take things slow. He's not up to his normal pace yet."

He quickly unloaded the dry goods into the pantry, hurrying her along. "It's just one day, Em. He'll be back."

"Well, maybe he just wanted a break, I guess."

He couldn't keep lying to her. She'd worry herself to death. And God help them all if Cord came home with even a hangnail. "Is that all the cold stuff?"

She peeked into the last bag. "I think. Why? Were you looking for something? I got everything on the list."

He took her hand. "Come with me."

"But the groceries—"

"Will be fine." He led her to the back door and drew in a steadying breath, waving her ahead the last few paces. "After you." He held the door.

Ember glanced over her shoulder, her eyes full of suspicion. "Why are we going out back?"

He raised a brow, done with the inquisition. She

stepped through the door and stilled, her eyes wide as she took in all he'd done.

Twinkle lights strung from the siding to the trees, sparkling in the early dusk. Votive candles lined every wooden rail and various corners of the gardens. The table was set for two, a bottle of sparkling water between two champagne flutes and a bowl of fresh raspberries he'd picked from her garden.

"Oh, Austin..." She did a slow three-sixty, her gaze landing on him in the end. "What is this?"

"I did it for you." Despite all his good intentions and planning, he flushed. "It's *all* for you."

"It's..." She shook her head, tears glazing her eyes. "Beautiful."

Taking her hand, he led her to the table. "These are for you, too." He lifted the bouquet from the seat of the patio chair and offered her the blooms.

"Lilies! Oh, they're lovely." She sniffed and smiled. "Why are you doing all this?"

He didn't need a reason to spoil his wife, but it just so happened, today he had one. A big one. "Sit down, baby."

She lowered to the seat, her nose returning to the flowers and her eyes taking in the setting.

"I asked Cord to go into work today for a reason."

Her focus shot back to him. "You did? Why?"

"Because I owed you this moment. I owe you a lot."

She frowned and placed the lilies on the table. "You don't owe me anything, Austin. But I love this. You worked so hard." She gasped. "Is that a gazing ball?"

He took her hands and rubbed them between his. "Ember." Damn. This was harder than he expected. "You know I love you."

"I love you too." Her excitement settled as she focused on him.

"I did this, because I love you. There's no other motive, nothing you have to be afraid of."

"Okay," she said slowly, her eyes appearing on guard.

"I also...did this because I'm ready."

Her head tilted, her hair falling from behind her ears. "Ready?"

"I'm ready to talk."

She laughed. "That's good, Austin, but what are we discussing?"

He licked his lips. "Everything that happened to me. Everything I put us through."

Her shoulders pulled back and her smile fell. "You don't have to—"

"I want to. I thought a long time about what I would say to you when this time finally came, and I wanted to get it right. You asked me to confide in you, and I want to. I'm ready now and I think this is a conversation we need to have, so we can put the past fully behind us and move forward."

Her lips pursed as she blinked and audibly swallowed. "Okay."

"Do you want some water?"

She nodded and he filled the two glasses. When he saw her hand tremble slightly he said, "How about a kiss?"

She leaned in, brushing her lips against his. When they pulled apart she appeared calmer. Lord knew he borrowed from her strength.

"I'm just gonna start."

She nodded.

He blew out a breath, trying to pinpoint where to begin. "When I lost my job...things got bad. For me. For you. Everything just fell apart. I saw it happening, but I couldn't stop it. I wanted to. With every bit of my soul, I wanted to stop what was happening, desperately. But I couldn't."

Her lashes lowered and she silently nodded.

"I want you to know, every time I told you I was done drinking, I meant it. And when I failed, it absolutely killed me, because I knew I'd let you down again. Let us down. My life became a constant game of Russian roulette. There was always a bullet waiting, and a loaded gun at my head. I never knew which time I'd end up living, and suspected, sooner or later, I'd die, but I kept trying. For us."

She sniffed and he folded his hands around hers again.

"I never wanted to leave you, Ember, but I knew I'd die if I ever completely lost you. So I pulled that trigger. Over and over—I couldn't stop trying for you. I needed to get us back to normal, but every attempt came with so much risk. It's the most fucked up feeling in the world, having absolutely no control of an outcome, but I finally realized that was the only truth I could count on. I had *absolutely no control* over what I was doing."

His heart pounded harder as his mind went

back to the scattered mess of memories collectively capturing the last year. It hurt, to recall the moments he'd lost, desperate to escape himself, each failed attempt pushing her further away.

He scooted his chair closer and stared at her wedding ring, loving the way it caught the fading light of the August sky.

"When I admitted my life had become completely unmanageable, I knew I'd come close to pulling that trigger one final time. It had to end, one way or another. I was...terrified. Everything I loved was on the line and I had not one guarantee I could do this. So I put everything I valued into the hands of the one person who'd been by my side longer than anyone else."

"Cord," she whispered.

"Cord." He nodded. "Admitting that what I was up against was bigger than me, it... Well, it was fucking excruciating. I hated admitting it to myself. It was worse admitting it to you."

Her head lifted, her lashes spiked with fresh tears. "Austin, it was bigger than *all* of us. I never expected you to beat it alone."

His lips tightened. "I know you didn't. I know you would have sacrificed yourself and everything you love to save me one day of feeling like that. But I couldn't let you do that. I couldn't take any more than I'd already taken from you. So I made the hardest decision of my life, and passed the reins."

He recalled the end result of that decision, the moment he realized his choice had transformed her unfathomable love into something akin to hate.

He'd read her letter a thousand times, each word imprinted on his soul. His private tears had worn the paper thin.

"I'm so sorry, baby."

"That's over, Austin." She wiped her eyes. "And look where we are. I was angry. Lost. We all were. But we made it through. I can honestly say, I don't think I'd take any of it back now, because I can't imagine my life without you. Maybe this needed to happen so we could get to this point, so *you* could become the man you are today."

She let out a slow breath, the stress of those memories seeming to wear on her like a chilling wind. Noticeably shivering, she looked into his eyes and gave a sad smile, so true and trusting, so full of acceptance and understanding.

"I used to cry at night, wishing my husband would return. But he was never coming back. You're here, but you're so changed. You, the strong man sitting before me, are the man I love. And I love you a million times more than I loved the husband I lost." She smiled, her eyes simmering in the faded light. "And I already loved him more than the sun loves the moon and all the stars."

A warm sensation bloomed in his chest, curling around his heart. His little hippie. "You love me more than any man deserves, December."

"Would you accept anything less?" she teased.

He smiled into her eyes. "No. But never forget, baby, I love you more."

Her expression sobered. "I know."

He leaned in and kissed her. Giving them each

an emotional reprieve, he slid the bowl of berries closer. "Here, taste."

She leaned in, her lips closing over his fingertips in an unarguably sexual way and awakening his body. "Tease."

She giggled. "They're good."

"They're yours. I picked them this morning."

She grinned and sat back in her chair, giving him a strange look. "I'll never forget the day you made me that garden. It's one of my fondest memories."

His too. "Do you have more? Fond memories." He hoped the good far outweighed the bad, but there was a lot missing from his own recollections.

"So many, Austin. You're an incredible husband."

He'd never take such words for granted again, not that he ever had. But those meaningful reminders were the things that made him keep trying.

"You're an incredible wife."

She stole another berry and nibbled it, the juice coloring her fingertips pink. "Will you tell me more?"

"I'll tell you whatever you want to know. I've got nothing left to hide."

As the moon climbed above the trees, candlelight cast amber shadows on the deck. Little flickering flames danced in the votive cups, witness to one of the most intimate conversations of his life.

Austin continued to walk her through his journey, filling in all the blank spots and answering any questions she asked as honestly as he could.

"...That day I walked into Bay's, I wasn't expecting to work. It had been a pivotal moment for me. Major. I'd been so self-involved, so focused on my own self-pity and resentment, I lost sight of what real life felt like. It was the first day I actually felt like I might have a shot at recovering everything I'd forfeited."

"I remember that day. Your voice sounded different when I listened to your message. Strong. It gave me hope."

His lips pressed tight as he prepared to tell her the truth. "Realizing I had something to recover from—I remember thinking that actual word, *recover*—it told me more about myself than I wanted to admit. I'll never forget thinking, if I have to *recover*, then I must be an alcoholic. It was so simple, so disturbingly obvious, and at the same time...it blindsided me. It was all the truth and evidence I needed to make it through the next day, and I've repeated that fact to myself every day since. *I'm an alcoholic*."

The pronouncement fell between them, but not with the damning effect he might have expected had it been any other woman sitting beside him. Her hand closed around his.

"It doesn't change how much I love you, Austin. It's just something we acknowledge—together."

His amazing, beautiful wife. Ever loving, ever accepting.

He told her about how he'd met Harley, this dark angel that drifted out of nowhere and somehow got through to him the way no one else could. He admitted his weak moments, almost stealing the tip from the waitress at the diner and feeling victorious when he'd done the noble thing and walked away.

"Integrity, my memory of it and my desire to own it, got me through a lot of dangerous moments. I think that's where a lot of my resentment for Cord stemmed from. He's always had this impeccable moral compass and there I was, floundering, too damn drunk to even figure out which way was forward."

"Austin, no one's that perfect. Cord has plenty of flaws. We all do."

"I know that—*now*. But back then I was my own worst enemy. If there was a day I felt a little up, my insecurities were right there to beat me back down."

Her fingers tightened, offering a sympathetic squeeze. "All of us have that bully in our head, the one who sees us at our worst and never lets us overlook our ugliest parts. It's enough to make you..."

"Try to kill yourself?"

"I was going to say cut your hair."

He looked at her, seeing the changes that occurred over the past year. "Baby... is that what you did?"

She blinked fast, but not fast enough to stop her tears and his heart broke. "I felt so hideous, so wretched inside...I..."

"Shh." He pulled her to his lap, pressing his lips to her temple. "You will *never* be those things. Ever, December. You. Are. Beautiful. Inside and out. Do you hear me?"

She nodded and wiped her eyes. "So long as you

know the same is true for you." She glanced up at him, resting her brow against his. "You're a beautiful man, Austin Garret. Inside and out." Pressed close, their hearts beating as one.

"So, is this one of your steps?" she asked once they let those words sink in.

"Sort of. I've had a lot of atoning to do, a lot of amends to make. You could say I saved the most important one for last."

Her fingers traced his. "What now?"

What now? Life suddenly seemed limitless.

He shifted and reached in his pocket. "Can I put you down for a second?"

She slid into her chair and he removed the box he'd been holding all day. Dropping to a knee so they were at eye level, he looked into her beautiful eyes.

"December, I know when I met you, I *told* you we'd get married, but now...I figured it was time I asked." He cracked open the box, revealing a stunning diamond band woven with two others, one silver and one gold.

"Will you have me as your husband, love me through sickness and health, and trust me to always put you first, every day of our lives?"

"Austin..." she whispered, her fingers trembling to her lips. "Of course I will. You didn't have to do this. You know I'll always love you. I never thought to stop being your wife. That's all I've ever wanted."

"I want to marry you all over again, baby. Have a little ceremony right here in our backyard with those we love as our witnesses."

"But...what about Cord?"

He reached into his other pocket and withdrew another box. "Did you think I'd forget about our boy?" He pressed the box into her hand and she cracked it open.

"Three bands. Like mine."

Three bands wrapped into one, the ring representative of Ember in a rose gold. "Three of us. Forever."

Her face pinched as she sniffed and a tear fell. "Forever."

She looked at him with such adoration. A glance like that could bring a thousand men to their knees. But she was theirs and theirs alone. "Will you have me?"

She chuckled, the sound a watery impression of her usual laughter. "Yes, I'll have you. I couldn't imagine a life without you."

"Should we call our boy and tell him he can come home?"

Her smile grew and she wiped her eyes. "I don't know. I can't seem to stop crying. You know how he gets when women cry."

"I think he can handle it." He slid her his phone. "Call him."

Her hands shook as she dialed his number. "Cord... I'm fine. He's fine too. No, I'm not crying." She rolled her eyes. "I just sneezed."

Cord's voice carried from the phone, his words too muffled for Austin to make out.

She laughed and shut her eyes. "I called because...we need you to come home. Come home, now, okay? We need you."

She ended the call. "He's on his way."

"That man is wrapped around your finger."

"He is not."

He took the box holding her ring. "Let's put this on."

Her fingers curled into a fist as she pulled her hand to her chest. "What about your ring? You should have the same as Cord."

He slowly grinned. The idea hadn't crossed his mind, but now that she mentioned it, that sounded perfect. "We'll go back to the jeweler that designed them tomorrow."

Satisfied, she held out her hand. He slid the ring over her knuckle, butting it up against the one he'd given her many years ago. "I love you, baby."

Her hand cupped his jaw as she leaned in and kissed him. "I love you back, Mr. Garret."

Cord's truck rattled up the driveway and a second later a door slammed. "Ember? Austin?"

"We're out back," she called.

Cord came through the back door and staggered to a halt. "Whoa. Who did all this?"

"Austin. Isn't it beautiful?"

Cord tipped his head, giving him an impressed look. "It looks incredible." He glanced at Ember and frowned. "You okay?"

Her eyes betrayed her. Although she'd stopped crying, the traces of tears were there. Austin squeezed her hand.

"I'm better than okay. I'm wonderful."

Cord noticeably relaxed, the worried crease in his brow smoothing as his shoulders lowered. "So, you two...talked?"

"Yes," she answered. "And you missed it. But don't worry. You'll catch the next talk."

He rolled his eyes and sighed. "I'm sure."

She glanced at Austin, her fingers closing around the box that contained Cord's ring. He gave her an approving nod and she slipped off the chair, onto her knees beside him.

"What are you guys doing?" Cord stared down at them kneeling before him. The corner of his mouth quirked up. "I like the looks of it."

Ember passed the box behind her back and Austin gripped it tightly. "We have a question for you, Cord."

"Shoot." He shifted from foot to foot, his blue eyes now a little wary.

Cracking open the little case, Austin held it up as Ember asked, "Will you marry us?"

Cord's mouth went slack as he blinked at the band made of three entwined metals. His chest rose and his labored breath filled the silence. His stunned gaze met theirs. "Is this for real?"

Ember nodded and Austin said, "We love you, man. You're a part of us. We don't ever want to let you go."

"The three of us," Ember added. "Forever."

Austin watched as Cord's composure slipped. His lips sealed tight as his brow creased, his lashes flickering hard as a muscle twitched in his cheek. He made an admirable effort, but lost the battle in the end when his chin started to tremble and a lone tear fell.

Cord brushed it away, sniffing and clearing his throat. Shaking his head, he growled, "Fuck."

Austin chuckled. "I think that's his word for yes."

Ember rolled her eyes. "Is that a yes?"

Cord laughed and mumbled. "Is that a yes?" He shook his head again. "Yes, it's a fucking *yes*." He dropped to his knees and pulled them into a back-breaking hug, first kissing December and then Austin. "I fucking love you two, do you know that?"

Austin removed the ring from the box and wedged it onto his finger. "We love you too."

Collapsing in a pile, they lay on the deck, staring up at the night stars, keeping close contact. Austin clutched his wife's hand, his other resting on Cord's chest, marking his steady heartbeat.

Ember held up her hand, admiring her ring and Cord did the same. "We're ordering Austin's tomorrow," she said.

"Good."

It was a perfect moment. A perfect day. A perfect life.

Despite all their trials, they'd made it. Together forever. The three of them.

Cord sighed and Austin smirked. He couldn't leave it alone. "I can't believe you cried."

"Fuck you, Austin."

"Boys! Be nice."

He looked past Ember's head and found Cord watching him, an incredible smile stretched across his face and his eyes full of contentment. *His.* Husband, lover, partner, best friend—the label didn't matter so long as Cord was his.

Okay, theirs. *They* were *his*. And he would be forever theirs.

Austin's gaze shifted back to the starry sky, a sense of peace enveloping him.

"Austin?" Ember stroked his hand.

"Yeah, baby?"

"I'm happy."

"Me too," Cord whispered.

Austin sighed and smiled. "Me three."

Epilogue

December

EMBER STOOD before the window of the third floor bedroom, staring down at the arbor her boys had made, watching the guests filter into the backyard. Broad shoulders filled the end seat of the first row and she smiled, recognizing Reed's stoic posture. He'd come around and accepted his son's decision to be happy, never again voicing an objection after Cord's accident.

Her father, Misha, worked his way through the aisle of white folding chairs and she smiled as he shook Reed's hand. No doubt Cord's father was taking in her father's hemp shirt and matted dreadlocks.

Austin's father would not be attending, as it was a universal decision to leave him and his toxicity out of their future. But a single white rose lay on one of the chairs, representing Emily Garret's beautiful soul. She only wished she could have met Austin's mom.

A soft knock tapped on the door and Ember turned. "Come in."

Her mother, wearing a vibrant sheath, slipped inside and smiled. "December Sky, what a vision you make."

She glanced at her dress, a work of her own creation and one she was particularly proud of. "Thanks, Rona."

"I have something for you."

Ember drew in a breath, hoping it wasn't something as outlandish as the herbs her mom had expected her to wear around her neck at her first wedding. "What is it?"

"Norma Jean told me it's custom for a bride to have something old, something new, something borrowed, and something blue. Come have a seat."

She sat beside Rona on the bed as she unraveled an ivory silk kerchief on her lap.

"These were your grandmother's. She wore them on her ankles. We always knew when she was nearby."

Ember held out her hand as the tinkling jewels slipped into her palm. "They're beautiful." Each little cockle jingled softly from a string of silver. "Should I put them on?"

Rona nodded and helped her latch the anklets. Ember gave her foot a little shake, loving the way the beads chimed. "Thank you."

"There's more." Her mother unveiled a shimmering slice of blue stone. "This is agate crystal. It soothes and heals. It also promotes communication, which I imagine you'll need with two husbands."

Ember laughed, accepting the strung crystal and sliding the leather cord over her head. The pendant dropped between her breasts, her dress cut low enough to reveal its beauty.

"I'll wear it always. Communication's tough with these two."

"And these are from Misha. They can be your something new." She dropped a wax packet of tiny seeds into her palm.

Ember looked at her mother suspiciously. "What are they?"

"Nothing that will attract the police. They're yarrow seeds. Yarrow's the symbol of everlasting love. Plant them with your men and, in late spring, you'll have lovely blooms. They're also good for bee stings."

She laughed. "Am I supposed to keep these with me all day?"

Rona shrugged. "These rules are new to me."

Ember tucked the seeds beside the lamp on the nightstand. "I'll have to thank Misha."

Her mother folded the kerchief, pressing it into Ember's palm. "And this is something you can borrow. I know it's nothing extravagant, but it's all I have left from the dress I wore when your father and I had our ceremony. We didn't have a formal wedding, but I looked beautiful and so do you. So I thought it would be something I let you hold onto for a while. We don't see each other as much as I'd like, but not a day goes by that you aren't on my mind, December."

She pressed the silk between her fingers and drew in a sigh. "Thank you, Rona—Mom. I love all of it."

"I love you."

She blinked, angling her stare toward the woman who raised her, thinking of all the peculiar similarities they shared that Ember had once thought to escape. "You gave me the courage to do this, you know."

Her mother shook her head and tapped a finger on December's chest, right below the pendant. "Your courage is here, baby. I just helped you find it when you were scared. But you always had it. You're tough, my love. Tougher than me, taking on two husbands. What's the sex like?"

"*Mom.*"

Her mother laughed. "What? I'm curious."

Luckily, there was a knock at the door. "Come in!" Ember called, desperate for a diversion from her mother's unfiltered questions.

Norma Jean peeked into the room. "Am I intruding?" The woman always knocked since that day she burst in on her and Cord.

"Not at all. Please come in."

She stepped through the door and gasped. "Oh, December! Look at you!"

Ember stood and Norma Jean gripped her bare shoulders affectionately, admiring her dress.

"I'm going to check on Misha. Do you need anything else?" her mother asked, edging toward the door with a smile.

"We should be down in a few minutes. Could you just check in on Cord and Austin, Mom?"

"Sure." She pulled the door closed and Norma Jean sighed.

"You make a lovely bride, but I already knew that." She winked.

"How's Cord?"

"Happy. Austin too. You have two handsome men waiting for you."

"And Reed..."

"Reed's fine, honey. Don't you worry about him. I came up to ask you something."

Ember raised a brow. "Oh?"

Norma Jean bit her lip and ushered her to the edge of the bed. Her gaze wouldn't meet Ember's. "Being that this is...my son's wedding and you're to be his wife... I was hoping—and you could absolutely say no if this makes you uncomfortable in any way—"

"What is it, Norma Jean?"

"Well, I was thinking it might be nice if...you called me Mom—if you want to, that is. It's completely up to you."

Ember smiled, her shoulders sagging with relief. "Norma Jean, I'm honored."

"Really? I didn't want to sound pushy and I know this isn't a traditional marriage and—"

"Nothing would make me happier than calling you Mom. *Mom.*"

Her face split with a wide grin as she pulled her into her arms and sniffled. "I finally have a daughter. Oh, I'm going to muck up my makeup." She pulled back and dabbed at her eyes, her smile lingering as she patted Ember's hands. "I love you very much, December. So does my son."

"We love him too. And I love you. You've always been like a mother to us. Family."

Norma Jean cupped her cheek and grinned. "Shall we?"

December nodded, checking the room for any last minute items. Her gaze settled on the fancy shoes resting on the carpet. She edged toward the window, noting the radiant foliage coloring the trees.

"Do you have everything, dear?"

Giving the shoes one last look, December turned to the door, her bare feet slipping across the floor, anklets jingling softly as she followed Norma Jean to the stairs.

Cord

Cord fussed with his tie, the foreign feeling of anything around his neck not easily accepted. "Is this knot too big, Rona?"

December's mother had shown up a few minutes ago to check on him. Thank God, because he'd been trying to do something with his hair and she assured him he looked fine and he should chill.

He supposed that was the sort of thing a mother-in-law was good for, though December's mother was a far cry from June Cleaver. Rona looked more like a sister of Ember's, her small frame and pixie-like hair adding to her youthful appearance. But she'd mussed his curls and told him they looked fine and that was good enough for him.

"If it bothers you, take the tie off."

He stilled from fidgeting with the knot. "Really? Is that allowed?"

She shrugged. "Why not? It's your wedding."

He yanked the silk through the collar of his shirt and tossed it on the bed. "Thank God. I'm not a formal guy and that thing was choking me."

Rona grinned. "I think it's better to go as you are."

"Yeah." He nodded. "Me too."

He paced, peeking out the back window, and noting that Harley and his wife had arrived. December's dad was sitting a few seats away from his father, which was probably for the best. "So... Did you guys have a far ride?"

"About eight hours."

"You took a bus?" He couldn't imagine being crammed in a seat amongst strangers for so long.

"Yes."

She had little shoes on her feet, the sort that looked lived in and were maybe nice a lifetime ago. "December's happy you made it."

"Are you nervous around me, Cord?"

"Uh, no." *A little.* He never had in-laws before.

She smiled. "Good. After today we'll be family. I'd like us to be close."

He wasn't sure if he should say something, maybe call her Mom. Come to think of it, even Ember didn't always call her that. "I love your daughter very much, Rona."

"And Austin," she added.

He nodded, once again astonished by her open-mindedness. "And Austin."

"Do you know what I like about you, Cord?"

"What?"

"I like that you're a true friend to them. You know, your name means honest advisor. I think you're a very honest man and you helped Austin and December through some defining moments."

This was weird. This woman was definitely weird. "I just...like to take care of them."

A heavy hand knocked at the bedroom door and he rushed to open it, finding Austin on the other side. "Thank fuck," he murmured, letting him in.

"Are you about ready—uh, hey, Rona. I didn't know you were up here."

"Austin." She rose, her gaze greeting her son-in-law with familiar affection. "You look so nice and neat. I have something for you."

Cord stepped aside as she slipped something into Austin's hands, closing his fingers over the tiny item. Cord wondered if she'd give him something, too. Then he panicked, because he had nothing to offer her in return. No one mentioned gifts for the in-laws.

Rona lifted to her toes and whispered in Austin's ear. "It's for fertility—when you're ready."

Austin met Cord's stare over her head and smirked. "Thanks."

His future mother-in-law turned back to Cord and eyed him from head to toe. "I'll bring you something on my next visit. I wanted to meet you first."

In a way, he was relieved. Maybe.

Rona let herself out and he sighed. "She's a strange bird."

Austin chucked the satchel of whatever she'd slipped him into the drawer where they kept the lube. "Rona's harmless." He turned and stilled. "You look great."

"I got rid of the tie."

"Does Ember know?"

His mouth flattened. "No. Do you think she'll be pissed? Damn it." He went to retrieve the noose off the bed and Austin laughed.

"Relax. You look fine. She probably won't even notice."

He eyed Austin and forgot what he was doing, all thoughts scrambling into nothingness. "You're..." He laughed to himself. "You look like a fucking centerfold for GQ."

Austin rolled his eyes. "Knock it off."

"I'm serious. You look incredible."

A flush worked past his collar as he pulled on his cuffs. "Thanks."

Unsure of wedding rules when it came to grooms, he slowly approached and stared into his whiskey brown eyes. "We're getting married."

Austin's lip hooked into a half-grin. "Sounds strange hearing you say it."

Fuck. His best friend was going to be his husband. And Ember, his other best friend, was going to be their wife. He blinked, feeling a little lightheaded.

"You okay, man?"

"Yeah. Just sort of absorbing all of this. It just hit me all of a sudden. This is *it*. Us. Forever."

"Last chance to back out."

Cord shot him a glare. "Not a fucking chance."

How the hell was Austin the calm one today? Cord was usually the calm one. The guy with the jokes. Easy, breezy. Fuck, he needed a drink and this wedding was dryer than the Sahara.

"Hey, take a breath." Austin's hand landed on his shoulder, massaging firmly. "You want some water or something?"

Cord looked into his eyes and calmed, his fingers coming to rest over Austin's. "No. Everything I need is right here—and wherever Ember's hiding. When do we get to see her?"

"At the altar."

He didn't like this enforced time apart, like they were in some sort of holding pen. "What's the holdup?" He'd gone from dizzy to deliriously eager to get this done.

Austin laughed again, his forehead pressing into Cord's. "Relax. She's getting fancy. Someone will let us know when it's time."

He sighed, leaning into him, letting some of his anxiety go. "You're so fucking calm."

"Not my first rodeo. Plus, I'm happy. Got my wife and my best friend for the rest of my life after today. What more could a guy ask for?"

"Nothin'. I don't know why I'm nervous."

"Because this is forever, Cord. We don't quit on each other in this house. Ever."

He shut his eyes and breathed in his familiar scent. "Forever." His lips dragged over Austin's jaw, finding it softer than usual. "Love you, man."

"Love you back." Austin's mouth chased his, stealing a taste with his tongue that soothed him like nothing else could. "Ah, hell. Let's go get our wife."

Cord stepped back and gave the lapels of his suit jacket a tug. "Let's do this."

Austin

Austin led Cord down the steps and they followed the sound of the voices coming from the backyard. They halted at the door, pausing for one last shared look before stepping over the threshold. Determination and a hint of terror warred in Cord's eyes but quickly softened into happiness when he stared back at Austin.

Moving into the yard, Harley's was the first face Austin saw, his wife Bernice sitting by his side. Then he spotted Reed. Norma Jean was likely helping December somewhere in the house. Rona was at her seat beside Misha's empty one.

"Where's Misha?" Cord asked, keeping his voice low.

"He probably went to see Ember before he walks her down the aisle."

Cord nodded and Austin chuckled. He never saw him so nervous. It wasn't a large gathering, but made up of people who accepted them. Many who loved them.

He gripped Cord's forearm as they took their spot at the arbor, leaning in close to whisper in his ear. "Just wait. The moment you set eyes on her all your anxiety will disappear."

"I believe you."

The back door opened and Norma Jean scurried down the aisle to sit beside Cord's dad. Her gaze skittered to her son and then to Austin. He smiled at the woman who had been everything a mother could be to a man over the past decades. Now it would be official. She'd be his mom. He'd finally have a mother again and he couldn't pick anyone better than Momma Bay.

The deck was wrapped with white ribbon and woven with flowers—Ember and Rona's handi-work. The scent of the garden filled his lungs, all the emotions of the past hour settling into con-tentment.

Ember wanted a deck to entertain and they'd built her a beauty. It was incredible, to see what he and Cord had constructed, embellished by his wife's loving little efforts. It was the picture of a happy home, right down to the garden spade stashed by the hose bib. Signs of ordinary life camouflaged by elegant touches everywhere.

After the ceremony they'd eat the various dishes their guests had brought along, wonderful smells that had tempted him and Cord all morning. Then they'd dance, and soon enough the guests would be gone and it would be just the three of them. His husband and his wife.

The back door opened as Misha and Ember stepped onto the deck. His breath lodged some-where behind his heart as he set eyes on the woman he was about to marry—again. He'd marry her every day for the rest of his life if she asked.

Her dress was beautiful, like her. Kind of shim-mery and made up of pieces of material that suited his Ember. Her hair, longer now, flew about her shoulders and shined in the sunlight.

Over the murmurs of the guests, he heard a tinkling jingle and his breath whooshed out on a chuckle when he spotted her bare feet. Intricate anklets he hadn't seen before graced her ankles. Their little hippie. She moved toward the edge of the deck, and he blessed the hours of sanding he and Cord had lavished on the wood.

"No shoes," he whispered to Cord.

"Of course not."

Ember's pert mouth twisted in a smile as her father took her arm and she pointed a remote to the stereo. A familiar beat kicked on and he laughed as Cord leaned close.

"What. A. Vision," his partner said in awe. "Um... Is this Marvin Gaye?"

"Yup." As the duo sang *Ain't No Mountain High Enough* the guests smiled and bobbed their heads.

"That's *our* wife," Austin said, his eyes never leaving her beautiful face.

"Damn right."

They drew in a deep breath and seemed to let it out at the same time. The song was perfect. Nothing would keep them from her.

She took a final step and smiled up at them, her face alight with joy. "Hello my handsome husbands."

"Not yet," Cord said, taking her free arm. Misha offered her other hand to Austin, and he grasped it tightly, the faint tremble in his fingers instantly soothed by her touch.

The three of them faced her father who grinned with open acceptance of the future they had planned for his only daughter. "Are we ready?"

"Yes," the three of them answered at once.

"We're gathered here to mark the union of three souls as they become one, entwined for eternity in this life and the next."

As Misha spoke, Austin glanced at his wife and future husband, certain there had never been a more content sense of rightness inside of him.

They exchanged vows they'd each written themselves. No surprise, Ember's were eloquent and so loving he had to blink hard against the moisture that pricked his eyelids, aware Cord was also fighting to keep his composure.

His best friend choked out a few words about never believing his dreams would come true, promising to never let them fade. Cord shot both him and Ember a heated glance made all the more powerful with the love that brimmed in those familiar blue eyes.

Austin intended to keep his vows traditional, promising to love, honor and cherish the two most important people in his life—and never withhold himself, but when it came his turn to make his vows he found himself speaking from the heart.

"Ember, I will continue to love and honor you, uphold my promises, and always put your happiness first. I know I'm not an easy man, but you make our life easy. You're always there, the cornerstone of everything we are, an endless source of encouragement and acceptance. There isn't anything I wouldn't give you. You've given me everything I need simply by standing by my side."

He turned to Cord, his hand sliding easily into his, an almost exact replica in shape and size. "Cord, you're my rock, an unshakable part of my life I've always been able to lean on. You've shown me what it is to love and accept the things we can't change, taught me how to be courageous through times of fear, and proven how deep unconditional love goes. I love you. We wouldn't be us without you, and I intend to honor our promises today with that same unshakable fortitude you've shown me through the years. I promise to honor what we have, cherish it, and fight for it, because this is us and we're forever."

Cord's mouth pressed tight as Ember dabbed her eyes with a scrap of silk. Misha grinned approvingly at Austin and nodded. He didn't know where the words came from, or how he could even make such a public speech, but he felt them, knew them for the truth they carried.

Trying to lighten the mood and save his friend from embarrassing himself, he leaned close to Cord and said, loud enough for everyone to hear, "That's me expressing my feelings."

As their guests chuckled, Cord pulled himself together, his shoulders lifting and falling on a deep breath. "I got that."

Misha addressed the small crowd. "I think it's perfectly clear how much these three souls love each other and belong together as one. You may now seal the promises made today with a kiss."

Cord shouldered him out of the way claiming *dibs* on December, to another chorus of laughter. As they pulled apart, Austin soaked in the pure happiness reflected in their eyes.

"*Wife*," Cord whispered.

Austin pulled her close and took his time kissing

her, as their guests hooted and hollered. Easing away, he steadied Ember as she found her balance.

"Show off," Cord grumbled.

Austin grabbed him by the lapels and jerked him closer. "Your turn, *husband.*" He planted his lips on Cord's and conveyed all of his love and affection.

Easing back slowly, Cord exhaled heavily. Moving as one, they each took Ember's hands, raising them into the air. He'd never felt more victorious, considering the battle—*battles*—he'd fought. And won. The battle they'd all won. Together.

The guests surged from their seats and cheered. Music kicked on and well wishes and congratulations came from every direction as they were enfolded in many supportive hugs. He lost his hold on his loves during the jostling, but felt them close by, always within reach.

"Let's get Cord to the food," Ember said, as she maneuvered back into his arms.

Holding her close, Austin dropped a kiss on her head. "Only his fear of your wifely wrath kept him from raiding those dishes earlier."

Giggling, she stretched out her hand to Cord who, with a last look at his mother and father, accompanied them to where the food was set out.

"You look absolutely beautiful," Austin whispered, nuzzling his wife's neck as she filled his plate.

"You do." Cord spoke around a mouthful of one of the bread rolls he'd stolen.

"And you both look incredibly handsome. Even without a tie."

Cord choked and pasted on a smile. "Austin and your mom said it was okay."

"Sure, throw me under the bus."

Dimpling, Ember patted his arm. "I'll let it slide, but because this is only the second time I've ever seen you in something other than flannel or denim. Baby steps."

They carried their plates to picnic tables draped in white linen, while all around them people dug into their food. Cord worked on his second helping while Austin offered Ember a bite from his plate, soaking in the beauty of the autumn afternoon. "Are you happy?"

Her eyes found his and she smiled. "It's our second wedding day. Of course I'm happy."

Together they glanced at Cord. Ember's fingers folded around Austin's and squeezed. "I think I'm beyond happy."

"Me too."

Guests mingled, some dancing, and he sensed Ember wanted to join them. "Cord," he called before he went up for thirds. "I think our wife wants to dance."

Austin laughed as terror flashed in his husband's eyes, but he quickly recovered when Ember leaned close and said, "Relax, Cord. Think of it like making love but with your clothes on and while standing up. You can do it."

She tugged them into the crowd and, for once, they allowed her to take the lead. Ember danced like she had the first day they laid eyes on her, over a decade ago. She'd stolen their attention then and held it ever since. Safely.

The day rolled out too quickly and at the same time took too long. As dusk descended and the garden torches were lit, people began to say their farewells and filter out.

Rona and Misha were staying at Cord's old house and his parents offered them a ride home. Harley was the last to go and Austin walked him and his wife to their car.

"Thanks for coming, Harley."

His friend turned and smiled. "I wouldn't have missed it for the world, Austin. I'll see you tomorrow night?"

"I'll be there." He watched him drive away and welcomed the sense of calm that settled over him.

Climbing the porch steps, he let out a satisfied sigh and opened the front door. Cord and Ember were sitting on the stairs waiting for him. His wife's wedding dress spilled over the treads, her elfin beauty reminding him of a fairy with her wispy hair, flushed cheeks and shining eyes.

Cord's shirt was untucked, the collar unbuttoned, and his hair looked like he'd run his hands through it a hundred times. Or maybe Ember had.

It was the perfect picture and he fixed it in his mind's eye, wanting to remember the sight of the two of them for the rest of his life, holding hands as they reached out to him.

His fingers slipped into Ember's tiny hold and then into Cord's larger one as they stood as one. They held his heart and soul in much the same way, with firm, tender love.

"Bed?" he asked.

"Bed," they echoed. And together, they took the next step toward their future.

THE END

Want more MMF *menage* romance from Lydia Michaels?
Read *Breaking Perfect* next!

Are you follow Lydia Michaels?
Stalk her on <u>TikTok</u>, <u>Instagram</u>, <u>Facebook</u>,
<u>Goodreads</u>, and <u>BookBub</u>!
<u>TikTok @LydiaMichaels</u>
<u>Instagram @lydia_michaels_books</u>
<u>Facebook @LydiaMichaels</u>
<u>Goodreads</u>
<u>BookBub</u>

Show Your LOVE
If you enjoyed this book, please <u>leave a review</u>.

A Note from the Author

To the Decembers out there...

You are beautiful and it's not your fault. It's not about you. It never was.

To the Austins...

It's not your fault. Your determination and devotion tell an incredible story of love and courage. Keep going.

To the Cords...

Buy some toilet paper.

And to the Harleys...

Thank you for listening and never judging.

Dear readers,

Let it be said that the characters of this book are fictional. However, their struggles are real and were treated accordingly from beginning to end. If you *know someone struggling with addiction, please, listen to them, be patient with them, and help them find the tools to recover. For only they can win this battle. But it can be won.*

~Lydia

JASPER FALLS

Wake My Heart *

The Best Man

Love Me Nots

Pining For You

My Funny Valentine

Side Squeeze

CALAMITY RAYNE

Calamity Rayne Gets a Life *

Calamity Rayne Back Again

Calamity Rayne Gets Hitched

BONUS: Calamity Rayne Veiled & Railed

Calamity Rayne Over the Moon

Calamity Rayne Knocked Up

THE SURRENDER TRILOGY

Falling In

BreakingOut

Coming Home

Ruthless Billionaires

One Billion Secrets *

Two Billion Enemies

MASTERMIND

Blind

Untied

NEW CASTLE

First Comes Love *

If I Fall

Shattered Vows

ADDICTED TO YOU

Crush *

Bang

Throb

THE ORDER OF VAMPIRES

Original Sin *

Dark Exodus

Prodigal Son

Immortal Bastard

Primal Kill

Blood Moon

STAND ALONES

La Vie en Rose

Simple Man

Sugar

Breaking Perfect

Hurt

Protege

About the Author

To receive Lydia's Newsletter and 7 FREE Books, click HERE !

Free Books Here!

Lydia Michaels is the bestselling and award-winning author of more than forty novels. She writes heart-clenching, unpredictable romance with dark elements and high heat. Her work is character-driven and bursting with broken heroes and badass females. With a sweet spot for overbearing, territorial types, her deeply emotional books are spicy, emotionally satisfying, and guaranteed to leave readers with many book hangovers.

Lydia is the consecutive winner of the *2018 & 2019 Author of the Year Award* from *Happenings Media* and the recipient of the *2014 Best Author Award* from the Courier Times. She has been featured by *USA Today*, *Romantic Times Magazine*, the *Women in Publishing Summit*, and more.

Michaels started her author career in 2007, becoming a recognized presence and advocate within the publishing industry. She is the CEO of LMC Consulting, a certified author coach specializing in character and plot development, and the founder of the *East Coast Author Convention*, the *Behind the Keys Author Retreat*, and www.Lydia-MichaelsBooks.com.

She is happily married to her childhood sweetheart. Her favorite things include cooking Italian cuisine, hosting extravagant dinner parties, sipping espresso martinis, listening to her husband play piano, and escaping to her coastal home on the Jersey Shore. She's an LGBTQ ally, a BLM supporter, a firm believer that the patriarchy must end (women's rights are human rights), and an advocate for pediatric cancer research.

LYDIA

Follow Lydia Michaels on social media!
Facebook | Instagram | TikTok

Thank you for your review!

Reviews help authors so much! If you left a review for this book, I greatly appreciate it!
Thank you,
Lydia

Click here to leave your review!